INVENTED
August

AN IMPERFECT ESCAPE TO CAPRI

A Novel

Dear Rosemary,
Embrace your journey!
All love,
Genie Frisbee

GENIE FRISBEE
&
MELISSA FARNSWORTH

To our mothers

"And there it is: Even though we're standing in the same patch of sun-drenched pavement, we might as well be a hundred thousand miles apart."
— Lauren Oliver, *Delirium*

POMPEII, ITALY

FALL

1979

PROLOGUE

Consider my predicament. If I hadn't stayed on Capri that extra week, I could have walked away with a clear conscience. You have to understand, the Isle of Capri is a temptress, and I had found it impossible to leave after finishing the assignment.

That particular morning, fog clung to the cliff top. It blanketed the terrain with a salty stickiness as it smothered the incessant twittering of birds. The sun slid upward, also subdued. Tripod positioned, camera loaded, I waited on the rock stairway for a slice of light. A burst that would illuminate the granite Sphinx above. From far below came the toll of bells breaking the silence. Six bells announcing the hour. And then a wail. Like a child, hurt. Like a cat. Startled, I dropped my notebook. I watched helplessly as the rings sprung open, releasing the pages. My written observations flew off into the distance like a flock of birds. When I turned back around, I heard someone calling my name. I recoiled with a thud of recognition.

And so, because I was there at dawn, photographing the Sphinx, I'm involved.

Coaxing the frenzied one back to equilibrium. Dodging the flirtatious one. This is stuff a guy might forget over time. Were it not fused with a promise made under duress. And an image.

After that, it was too late. Too late for changing my mind. And so a promise of silence plagues me. And worse, I'm tormented by the answer to a question, a question I pray I'll never be asked, again.

LOS ANGELES, CALIFORNIA

Five Months Earlier

SPRING

1979

AN INVITATION

1. QUINTON

Quinton knew what to expect. Lily would be draping muslin on a dress-maker dummy, looking decidedly serious. An appearance exaggerated by the arch of her eyebrows thrust above deep-set eyes. And her dark hair cut into an asymmetrical bob. Add to that her habit of wearing starched white shirts. Quinton knew better than to misjudge Lily White. He understood her intensity. She was driven. As was he.

Quinton smiled as he parked in the underground lot, imagining Lily's reaction to the news he was bringing. *Her hazel eyes will sparkle, she'll act a little giddy.*

And then Quinton frowned. He was counting on Dirk, Lily's husband, to be out. Playing golf. But it was a breezy Los Angeles morning with a prediction of showers. When Quinton arrived at the glass doors of Antonio Caldo, on the sixth floor of a high-rise in the fashion district, Dirk was plainly in sight. Giggling with the young receptionist, Darleen. The pair examined a travel magazine, flipping pages and folding corners.

"Oh, Mr. White, sir," she was saying.

"Oh, you clever wacky wabbit," Dirk was replying. Darleen wore pink glass earrings, danglers, and her blonde hair was pulled into a side ponytail. *Unfortunate styling, with those large ears,* Quinton thought.

Quinton felt Dirk's disapproving once-over as he approached the formal reception counter. Quinton wore jeans with a striped sailor jersey and a sports coat. His loafers were polished but looked comfortably worn. He stood at least one head higher than Dirk, who was dapper in golf attire.

"Quinton again, aren't we lucky?" Dirk jerked his thumb toward the showroom and Lily's workroom beyond.

Quinton passed glass-walled offices and menswear displayed on male mannequins. He rapped lightly on the open door of Lily's workroom. She was placing pattern pieces on a swath of taupe gabardine. Several bolts of linen and rayon stood on end awaiting her attention. The back wall held an array of clippings, sketches, and swatches.

Lily looked up. Today her signature white shirt was paired with a black pencil skirt and black patent heels.

"Quinton! Look at these *amazing* neutrals," she said, pointing to the fabric, "oh, and I found a source for the bamboo buttons yesterday."

"Well, kiddo, your *amazing* neutrals and my photography bought us a ticket! *H.I.S.* accepted our proposal. I heard first thing this morning."

Lily beamed. She clapped her hands and spun, a pseudo pirouette. "I knew we could get this!"

"But, they need samples, like *now.*"

"Yikes!" Lily, excited, dashed across the showroom to the reception area. Quinton followed her at a distance.

"Dirk, *H.I.S* wants *us!*"

Dirk scoffed. A throaty dismissal. Darleen flushed, rapped her pink nails on the counter.

Quinton could smell Darleen's perfume wafting. It annoyed him. *Shalimar,* he thought, *jasmine and vanilla.* He liked the scent and that made it all the more annoying. He had just bought it for a girlfriend. *Darleen has expensive taste.*

"Will you rework the numbers for twelve sets of samples *instead of—*" Lily continued.

Dirk interrupted her. "How about you tell *H.I.S.* to forget it *instead of—*"

"But you said—"

"Changed my mind. It's not an option for us."

Quinton flinched as Lily shrank with disappointment. *He just flipped off her light switch. What is this, a power play?* Dirk had been in agreement at the outset. An agreement that Lily should compete for the editorial coverage with Quinton as photographer. In about ten seconds, and without explanation, Dirk had withdrawn his blessing.

Dirk White, CFO of Antonio Caldo, swaggered to his glass-walled office. Toward something more pressing than a discussion of opportunity. Quinton watched Dirk pick up a golf club and putt. The ball entered his putting machine swiftly and was spat out. *Kclunk-shst.*

Lily walked back to Quinton in exasperation.

"Now what?" she asked. After searching Quinton's face, she turned away from him and stared blankly at a row of mannequins.

Quinton spoke calmly, controlling his frustration. "Lily, five years we've been working for this. For some international recognition."

Lily shook her head and covered her face with her hands. No longer playful like an effusive terrier, she was like a swan floating away on dark thoughts. Quinton waited for her to look up. *What are the invisible strings? Clearly she doesn't need Dirk running/ruining her life.* Words didn't come. He remained silent and stared at the penny in his right loafer.

Finally, she looked up. Their eyes met. Would she defy Dirk? Quinton hoped he saw determination in Lily's moist eyes.

"Convincing him will be rough."

"I'll tell Mr. Golf Pro in there, he's in the rough."

Lily shook her head, looking conflicted.

Quinton set the clock ticking with additional information. "The magazine won't wait. We have till five tomorrow to formally accept or decline."

Quinton headed back to his studio deep in thought. *Given Lily and Dirk's relationship, the opportunity will slide away. But Lily has someone else in her camp. Grace. Lily's best friend Grace just might be able to tip the scales.*

2. GRACE

Grace partially pulled aside the curtain of a dressing room in Quinton Keller's photography studio. She extended one lean, bare leg in a teasing kick toward her husband, Marc McCrea, who sat with his nose buried in *Variety*. Completely absorbed with the industry news, he didn't notice.

Disappointed in Marc's lack of reaction, Grace strutted out sexy catwalk style, and did a model turn in front of him. Her long, glossy, chestnut hair swung and bounced just as she'd meant it to do. Marc's eyes lifted from the page and he smiled.

"Sweet, Gracie. You've got million-dollar hair," he commented before returning to his magazine.

Grace was deflated momentarily, then took a breath. "Honey, I was thinking. My parents have Jemima for the night and since you won't be filming…well, maybe we could…you know?"

"Grace, I need another five minutes for setup here. You doing okay?" Quinton called from across the studio.

Grace saw relief in Marc's face at the distraction. "I need to run over to the production office," he said. "Give my assistant a call when you're finished up here."

Grace tipped her mouth up for a kiss, but Marc gave her forehead a quick buzz and her shoulder a gentle pat.

Grace tried again. "Marc, about tonight?" but her words went unanswered. Marc had already turned toward the door.

An intern dashed in Marc's direction. "Mr. McCrea, sir? Could I have a minute of your time? Please?" Marc stopped and discreetly appraised the young man.

Rats! Her husband was accustomed to being sought out by wannabes: extras, actors, heck, even script girls thought he could hire them. He treated them all with respect, never dismissive. He hadn't forgotten how hard it was to get a break in the business.

She looked at Marc's departing back; he still made her heart beat fast. Although forty-nine years old, and eighteen years her senior, he looked as good as ever. He'd been the young director for *Murder Between the Sheets*, a stylish, campy detective series on TV in the sixties. The program starred her parents, Hope and Jimbo Derringer, who'd been instrumental in his landing the job. By age sixteen, Grace thought Marc was the most handsome man she'd ever seen. At age eighteen, despite her parents' weak protests, she married him.

Embarrassed, hoping no one had noticed Marc's lame excuse for a kiss, Grace turned back to Quinton and the waiting set, a display of hair products she was hired to advertise. Having modeled since her preteen years, she was comfortable in the skimpy camisole and tap pants.

"So, where do you want me?"

"First the good news," responded Quinton. "Have you talked to Lily this morning?"

Grace shook her head.

"We got the gig with *H.I.S.* We go in August. The three of us—we're in." Quinton's excitement spilled over.

"What a coup for Antonio Caldo! But are you sure? I haven't heard a word from my agent." Grace was cautiously enthusiastic.

"You'll hear by day's end," Quinton assured her. "But you need to call Lily now."

3. PENN

Penn wasn't so sure at first. She had inherited her mother's Asian features, dark mysterious eyes, and a valentine mouth. Yes, her eyebrows needed tweezing, and feathery pencil strokes wouldn't hurt. But to try bright red lipstick and custom-mixed powder, instead of her usual Mocha Polka and Ivory #1 base?

Grace had been firm. "Just give it a try." Penn did want to impress everyone at George's office party next weekend. So here Grace was spending her Saturday afternoon playing makeup artist, giving Penn a trial run.

Penn adored Grace. Grace was a listener; she paid attention when Penn talked. Unlike Cat, who interrupted. And Grace remembered details, listened for nuance. She was available for a phone call on an evening when both husbands were working. Penn could whine about having to entertain her Mummy. And Grace could let off steam about Hope with her complaints of lumbago. This calmed Penn. (Maybe her life was normal and not as out of control as it felt.)

Penn sat on a barstool, her black hair contained with a pixie band. Grace hovered over her, commenting on the progress. Penn's boys and Grace's Jemima produced a steady hum as they raced toy cars, their faces mask-like with the DayGlo paint Grace had applied to each.

Amazing how Jemima can hold her own, tussling with my boys, Penn thought to herself. She observed that Jemima, though slight, had something of Grace's sturdiness and stoicism about her.

"Eyebrows perfected. Take a look." Grace handed Penn the mirror.

"Don't make me too perfect," Penn whined (but she liked what she saw). The phone interrupted them. Penn answered the kitchen wall phone. It was Marc looking for Grace.

Penn twisted the wired ribbon on her pot of African violets, perfecting a lopsided bow. She couldn't help herself. She didn't intend to eavesdrop on Grace's phone call. But she found herself trying to imagine Marc's half of the conversation. Marc radiated the excitement of show biz. Grace was lucky to have such a dynamic yet genteel husband (compared to George, that was).

George, Dirk, and Marc should have finished a round of golf hours ago. Probably they were rallying around the Nineteenth Hole. Jack Nicklaus, Arnold Palmer, and Pete Rozelle's *Monday Night Football* were sufficient topics to drive many conversations, and arguments.

Sadly, no group BBQ had been planned for today (or George would be home by now). Penn looked forward to hosting those lazy events. On BBQ days George would come home from golf earlier and get a few chores done. He'd play pitch with his sons, Phillip, Charles, and Henry. Aged nine, eight, and seven, they needed their father's attention and discipline (try as she would to control them). Those social afternoons could safely accommodate the guys' beer drinking while including the wives (her five best friends in the whole world) and their brood of children.

Grace hung up the receiver; she wore a new, weary expression. Penn wondered why.

"None of my business, but is Marc headed home? I hope all the guys are. George isn't usually *this* late."

Grace hesitated a moment. "No. He has preparation for Monday's filming. He says he'll be sleeping in his trailer."

Penn felt a twinge of jealousy. A break from George's after-hours pestering would be nice. "Want to stay for dinner?" she asked.

Grace turned away abruptly and sorted through her large makeup case.

"Dieting again?" Penn asked.

"You might call it that," Grace said softly.

When both Grace and Penn were satisfied with the makeover, Penn located her spiral-bound, lined notepad. She wrote a list of all the cosmetics Grace used on her party face. (Why she wanted to look prettier was hard to explain, but she did.)

A song on the radio caught Penn's attention. "It's a song about piña coladas, Grace!" Penn hopped up. She turned the volume a bit louder. "This is so romantic." She and Grace began singing along, dancing side by side. They giggled, looking like the young brides they were when they first met, in the sixties.

"I like this part about escaping with your lover." Penn sang the chorus over and over even though the song had finished.

The dull grind of the garage door opening. A sudden jingling/jangling/rattling of glasses on display over the bar. A clattering of broken glass on tile. Penn gasped, covering her mouth with her fingers. She followed Phillip, Grace, Charles, Henry, and Jemima, who dashed to the kitchen-garage door. Phillip reached the door first and jerked it open.

From the open door, Penn and Grace gasped; the kids stared, mouths open, painted faces aglow.

Penn's voice sounded piercing. "George! Not again."

George, a tall, freckled redhead, sat dazed in the car with the engine running. His Volvo was smashed into three wall-mounted bikes. Exiting the car, drunk and confused, George shrugged, palms up.

"Speed racer, he crash!" Jemima screamed with earsplitting five-year-old enthusiasm.

Charles wailed, "My two-wheeler!"

"Turn off the engine, George," Penn barked. Closing her eyes, Penn visited that private place. That private darkness where her mind galloped ahead, hurdling all the fears flung in her path. She could hang on. Tomorrow was Sunday. Church. With Pastor Barnes preaching, and the comfort of prayers. Penn turned to Grace, her neck tendons rigid.

"Please, don't tell the others, I mean, especially not Deedee."

4. DEEDEE

It was all Deedee could do to sink gracefully into the den sofa, keeping her knees together like a proper Southern lady. The resemblance ended there, however. She balanced a Jack and Coke highball in one hand, eased her high-heeled shoes off with the other, sat back, and sighed loudly. She'd worked eight solid hours standing, bending, measuring, and placating women with all manner of complaints about their brassieres—she was ready for downtime.

Nanette, Deedee's thirteen-year-old, was comfortably plugged into the wall phone in the kitchen. *Lordy, can that girl yak*, Deedee thought to herself. Nanette seemed to have plenty of friends she'd somehow charmed. *Wish she'd ooze some of that honey here at home. Her poutin' and whinin' isn't that far off from my customers at Nordstrom.* Not for the first time, Deedee reflected upon Nanette's sad resemblance to her father, Deedee's first husband, Ryan White. He'd been short-legged and stocky, and a drip from the get-go.

Deedee looked over at her mama, who sat in a La-Z-Boy chair, crocheted afghan over her lap, TV tray full of prescriptions at her side. Mama sipped tea from a dainty china cup and almost seemed content. Almost.

"Deedee, my feets is all swole up," she complained.

"Deedee, baby, where ya been?" Hugh said, bouncing into the room. "I'm starvin'. Let's go for dim sum and saki." Tall, lean, boyish, and five years Deedee's junior, Hugh Stone, husband number two, was impulsive, impetuous, and rather self-centered. *But dang, he sure is cute*, thought Deedee.

"Hugh, you know I can't go anywhere. I've gotta get some dinner on for Mama and Nanette."

The sound of keys flung against the aluminum screen door was quickly followed by Hugh's accusation as he headed out. "You never have time for me. Just that crabby old sow and your snot-nosed teenager!" The door slammed shut.

"Hugh, you can just knock it off! Your tantrums suck!" Deedee hollered.

"Deedee, how many times I gotta tell ya? My feets is all swole up. I needs help an' I needs it now!" Mama's screech rattled the windows.

Nanette had disconnected her ear from the phone; she peeked around the corner,

"Mom, y'all go with Hugh. I can take care of Gran," she offered.

Deedee slipped on her shoes and called out to Hugh, "Hold your britches on, I'm comin' after all." Privately she thought, *I can't believe I'm caterin' to another husband. This is what Amelia would call keeping the peace.*

Deedee checked herself out in the hall stand mirror: Yep, makeup in place and thanks to a blow-dryer, huge brush, and a good spritz of hairspray, her spooley blonde hair was still looking soft and natural. "Not bad at all for thirty-five."

5. AMELIA

"You two are swimming like fish," Amelia laughed at her six-year-old twin boys. "I bet you'll be all over the deep end of the pool this summer." A huge wave of bath water splashed out of the tub, drenching Amelia. She grabbed a towel from the shelf. "Andy, Don! Keep it in the tub, please."

A can of shaving cream hit the tile floor and exploded. Eight-year-old Ken III stood on the toilet with a safety razor in hand and shaving cream smeared all over his chin and cheeks.

"Mommy, lookit me. Just like Daddy."

"Kenny, careful. Give Mommy the razor, easy now." Amelia quietly coaxed her son to surrender the dastardly tool. Once in her grasp, though, Amelia altered her tone. "What in the world are you doing? You could have sliced your head off. Never, never, never touch Daddy's razor!"

Ken III's face crumpled. "Sorry Mommy." Amelia pulled him close and hugged him. *My sensitive one*, she thought. *The twins will tear up the world. I just hope the world doesn't tear up Ken III.*

"Okay, kids. Time to get out of the tub. Who wants ice cream?" Amelia held out towels to the younger boys and called out to eleven-year-old Jennifer, "Jen, can you bring the twins' pj's in, and help me get them all dried off, please?"

Amelia cleaned up the shaving cream and wiped down the bathroom. It was getting late. Ken Jr. should've been home a couple of hours ago. The meatloaf was going to be dry. Again.

Once she'd tucked the troops in bed, Amelia took some time to freshen herself up. A quick brush of her honey-toned, curly hair, a swath of blush across her cheeks, a brush of mascara and creamy pink lipstick. And of course, a splash of Emeraude. Ken Jr. always appreciated it when she fixed up a bit before he got home. He had no idea how exhausted she could be at day's end, and she'd continue to do all she could to keep the mystique in place. Tonight they'd share some wine while Ken Jr. ate dinner and then…well, Amelia knew what would happen then.

The ringing telephone interrupted her little daydream. She dashed over to her bedside princess phone. After a hopeful "Hello?" she listened, then said, "How much later?" She paused. "So I shouldn't wait up?"

Amelia sat on the bed, flooded with disappointment. She tried to count her blessings. She didn't have to work, like Deedee. She didn't have a rigid mother-in-law like Cat. She was thirty-three years old and had everything she'd prayed for as a little girl—from the big house filled with kids to the abundant garden and successful husband. Who she hoped was keeping his promise.

6. CAT

Cat, Catherine San Carlo, had prepared Lily's birthday brunch with a flair not one of them could match. Looking pert in a smocked floral sundress, Cat proudly led her five friends into the dining room. Noni San Carlo snapped a photo of the six young women. And several of the lavish tabletop from different perspectives, at Cat's request. Cat detested having her mother-in-law rule the roost at home. And she especially detested being under Noni's thumb at the family's wine shop. Noni and Pietro so rarely allowed her any creativity. But this morning, Cat had to admit, Noni had been an asset, tending the boys while she applied her skills.

The table was set with china, Pink Roses Chintz, an ornate gold-rimmed pattern, polished flatware, blatantly baroque and water glasses, painted with pink cabbage roses. All this atop a coarse lace cloth that overlaid pink damask. Dominating the table's center, a half watermelon, its edges carefully crenulated, held skewered fruit garnished with maraschino cherries. For each guest, a wedge of bubbling quiche, bacon with cheddar, perfect slices, golden and gooey, crust just flaky enough to be tender and yet hold together for transit from ovenware to china plate.

"You're a natural-born stylist," said Lily with sincere appreciation.

Cat especially valued Lily's compliment. She held Lily above the others, identifying with Lily's artistic talent.

Leo's squeals punctuated the meal. Only Noni San Carlo's crooning could comfort him as he pushed his way through the "terrible twos." Her voice and his whines competed with Pavarotti's arias, irritating Cat, who intended for Jason, Leo, and Noni to nap while the group dined in operatic ambiance.

Grace calmed Cat. "At that age Jemima's screams could have awakened a mummy. Leo's are nothing!"

"We're mothers too," Penn said.

"Sweetie, this is just so lovely," Amelia added.

Deedee's humor kept the friends laughing as they each ate and drank a good deal of wine. But Leo's wails persisted even as Cat presented dessert, Baked Alaska. Unnoticed, Jason continued to entertain himself, fascinated by a *National Geographic*.

After Lily opened her gifts, each guest expressed an urgency to leave. *To leave in search of quiet before heading home*, Cat thought a bit sadly.

In defense of Leo, Cat begged them to stay a little longer. From the kitchen she brought her portable tape player.

"You need to understand Leo. I haven't wanted to share this before, but now..." She scrolled the tape forward, watching numbers ascend. Audible was the squeak of a female voice blurring at high speed. "Here," Cat said, stopping and restarting the tape.

A woman's speech began midsentence: "—carrying the spirit of an Italian Renaissance master, my dear Catherine. Da Vinci, perhaps Bernini... Certain things remain a mystery, but the anima cannot be denied."

Cat backed the tape up and the resonant voice repeated, "—Renaissance master, my dear Catherine. Da Vinci, perhaps Bernini...Certain things remain a mystery, but the anima cannot be denied."

"I felt it, you know, in the womb. The most amazing sensation." Cat glowed, rubbing her belly. "Leo's a Renaissance artist, Daulphine is certain! *You* heard her. Leo is simply an ultrasensitive soul."

Lily spoke in her *famous author's voice*. "Look at you, like a caryatid encircled by ivy and morning glory vine." Lily raised her glass of champagne, "To your good fortune."

Grace snorted a little, but just a little, and restrained herself in short order. Amelia and Penn nudged each other.

"So who's this here Dolphin?" Deedee blurted.

"*Daulphine*, Deedee, not dolphin," Grace retorted. "*Daulphine* is Cat's psychic."

In retrospect Cat wondered what Lily had been on the verge of sharing. Just after the opening of gifts, Lily had pulled a folder from her patent leather briefcase/purse. But the others hadn't noticed, so intent upon leaving, and Lily had put the folder away. *What had Lily been about to say?*

7. LILY

Oblivious to her husband, Lily sketched at the ironing board, struck by an idea for a pocket detail. Dirk, late for golf that Saturday, began fuming.

"My shorts still aren't ironed?" He swiped at a stack of sketches on the ironing board, and they flew across the room.

Lily recoiled at his outburst. She looked sidelong at her mate, not wanting to catch his eye. *How he's changed*, she thought.

He had changed, since their graduation day at Parson's in New York. The day she had accepted his wedding proposal. Since the days when they collaborated, she utilizing his textile designs, he complimenting her ingenuity. Now, thirteen years later, he'd graduated from complimenting to criticizing. *Who is this pompous hobgoblin?* His jaw had grown square, his belly had gone soft. He was parading like a dictator in jockey shorts and argyle socks. Somehow she had failed to make him happy; that much seemed obvious.

"Looks like you're off in a daydream. About that trip? If you remember, I never gave my full consent." Dirk's scowl disappeared briefly as he pulled a knit golf shirt over his head. It was cream, piped with gray, soft Peruvian cotton, a recent gift from Lily.

"I'm sorry about the shorts," Lily said gently, "but as to the trip," she hesitated, "you did agree, last month." She opened his bureau, found crisp gray linen shorts, and handed them to him. Dirk pulled on the shorts, zipped them up, and admired himself in the mirror.

Lily buttoned a white, tailored shirt skirt-style over her turquoise bikini, grateful that at age thirty-five she still had a decent body. Then, in almost a whisper, she began again. "Listen, the magazine has already begun making arrangements, assignments, reservations too. We did agree, remember? And I've started on the extra samples—"

He whirled around. "Then I'll say it louder. No trip." He returned his gaze to the mirror and admired his profile. "Don't cross me on this one," he warned.

Lily's eyes darkened with anger. Dirk's face softened. He turned to Lily; he lifted her chin. Then, in a compassionate tone, he offered some advice. "That's the problem with you, Lily, always walking on a rainbow without the sense God gave the common, the common...you silly goose. Be a good girl."

It was true. Dirk, the failed textile designer, self-appointed CFO of Antonio Caldo, had vocalized his pessimism when Quinton first announced Lily's opportunity. But, Dirk *had* relented late that same afternoon when Lily had taken an uncharacteristically firm stand, Grace by her side. Now, two weeks and four days later, Dirk was negative once again.

"I hope you have something special planned for dinner, sweetheart. You do forget about me on your girlie-girlie beach days."

Lily grimaced, caught unprepared.

"And as to your other harebrained idea, we're *not* buying Callie a wetsuit. We don't want to encourage the surfer chick thing. I found her a set of junior clubs at the Pro Shop, bag and all."

Dirk combed his dark wavy hair, replaced his comb in its proper tray, and finished dressing. Lily clenched her fists, fighting tears, determined not to cry in front of him.

A car pulled into the drive. Lily heard slamming doors and the eager voices of three boys.

"Auntie Penn," Callie was saying, "can Charles and I swim now, now, pretty please?"

"You ask your dad," Penn answered a bit nervously.

Lily headed downstairs behind the man she had promised to love and honor until death parted their ways.

Looking concerned, Penn nodded. "If it's okay, we'll choose a spot and set up."

Lily headed indoors to see Dirk off while Penn directed the trek to the beach. She loaded the striped umbrella on Phillip's shoulder. She piled beach towels in Henry's outstretched arms. She hoisted the well-stocked cooler herself, amused as Charles and Callie raced ahead with boogie boards and challenges.

Somewhat later, seagulls emerged from clouds and circled above the seashore. Lily, toting a straw beach bag, a small cooler, and a jug of iced tea, walked toward the ocean. Just ahead, a dozen children busied themselves with Tonka trucks and shovels and pails. Nearby, five mothers, ages ranging from thirty to thirty-five, lounged on a brightly colored spread under an umbrella. She could see them engaged in animated conversation, unself-conscious in their bikinis.

They're probably fussing about me, Lily thought. *I'll bet Penn told them I'd been crying.* Lily's friends jumped up and circled around her as she neared the enclave. She appreciated their concern, but not their distaste for Dirk. He could be a funny, sweet guy in private moments.

"I know you've been talking about me," she reassured them. "I'm fine, just fine."

Once settled again, Deedee, looking especially buxom, passed around Cheetos. "Lily girl, you gotta stand up to him. Dirk's just like his brother Ryan. Hard-hearted as a lump of coal. Which was why I divorced him, if anyone's askin'."

Squinting her green eyes, Cat made a pronouncement. "Dirk isn't as bad as Pietro." She began rubbing a baby oil-iodine mixture over her Rubenesque body while looking around expectantly. She took a gulp of Diet Rite Cola and choked a little.

Cat's comparison annoyed Lily, but she kept a calm demeanor.

Amelia patted Cat's back. "You okay, sweetie? Guess I'm glad to stay home with the kids. Although, it was fun working. Or should I say, uh, flirting at work with Ken Jr., before we were married." She fluffed her hair and repositioned her sunglasses.

Penn, seated at the group's edge, anxiously scanned the children's activity. Just now they cooperated—the girls dragging enormous leafy seaweed from the tide, the boys carting it in trucks to the sand castle, the ceremony of popping the amber bulbs, the squealing. Relaxing a little, Penn offered Lily some red licorice. Seeing that the package was almost empty, she pulled out her purse-size ring-bound notebook and made an entry. She looked into Lily's face with a kind smile.

"Lily, Pastor Barnes would call you long-suffering."

Grace spoke up. "In Lily's case, it's no virtue." She pulled a Tupperware container of celery from her cooler and passed it around. Model lean, she wore a wide-brimmed hat to protect her fair skin. Her dark hair was pulled back in a ponytail, accentuating her violet eyes.

Lily was glad to have the focus shifted by Leo's squeal. He didn't like sharing his Tonkas or his Matchbox collection with Amelia's Ken III. All the wives turned at the disturbance.

Lily took pity on Leo squatting there—with trademark frown and squint—beside the infamous lineup of yellow, slightly rusted dump truck, bulldozer, grader, steam shovel, garbage truck, auto carrier, and a bucket full of die-cast metal cars. Distraction was needed.

"Callie, do you want to swim now?" Lily asked. Enthusiasm followed. Penn's boys grabbed their boogie boards, as did Callie and Amelia's Ken III. They struggled through the breaking surf and soon were floating easily on the smooth swells beyond.

Penn, lifeguard whistle around her neck, hands on hips, paced at the water's edge. "Careful, Henry! Charles, watch out! Phillip, not so far. Callie, stay where I can see you!"

Lily walked beside Penn, gently kicking through the warm sand. "No riptide today, Penn," she comforted, "they're okay."

Amelia stood apart, hovering and alert. Amelia was armed with towels and sunscreen. *Such a mother*, Lily thought. Lest any child get chilled or sunburned on her watch. And look at her, after four babies! Amelia was picture perfect in a black two-piece suit, a broad-brimmed hat and sexy sunglasses. As was Deedee, who sunned her back and read a juicy story in *True Confessions.*

Cat sat in the shade and rocked Leo; it was his naptime. Jason joined Grace and Jennifer with the younger set. They dug for sand crabs, exclaiming over each slippery gray find.

A bit later, all the children lay wrapped in their towels, munching the triangular, crust-trimmed PB&Js Cat had prepared. The mothers regrouped to regain a few precious minutes of adult time.

Amelia anchored paper napkins with a jar of pickled ginger. "Hey, let's eat too, we're starving! Penn and I made spring rolls. All the vegetables and herbs are from my garden."

Grace rose to her knees. "Amelia, food can wait! Even yours! Lily has news and you won't believe how she's including us!"

Lily felt sick. Grace didn't know about Dirk's ultimatum. But she reached into her straw bag and withdrew a folder. She set a stack of photos on the blanket; Grace passed them around. "The Isle of Capri," she said. "C'mon Lily, tell them."

Hesitant, almost sorrowfully, Lily began, "*H.I.S.* magazine wanted to feature my Mediterranean Collection in their January '80 issue. Eight full pages of photos to be taken here, on Capri."

"What do you mean, *wanted to*?" Grace looked hard at Lily and saw indecision. "No, Lily, you're making it happen!" Grace was forceful.

"Now I'm not sure it's a good idea."

"Is it Dirk, *again*? The one who flopped at textile design, the one who's riding your coattails? He's jealous as hell."

"Honey, don't let Dirk squash this. I remember when you got that huge bonus and started Antonio Caldo. Look how far you've come." Amelia's voice was soothing. "You'll get famous on Capri!"

Lily sat up straighter, a smile teasing at the corners of her mouth.

Penn gave Grace a jab in the ribs. They burst into song simultaneously. "'*Twas on the Isle of Capri that she found him…*'"

Lily laughed, excitement kindled. "Quinton won the photography contract! Edwin, the photo editor, is hiring local Italian men to wear my fashions…and *Grace* has been signed as the only female model."

"Imagine! Grace's alabaster glamour set against Eye-talian bronze!" Deedee was genuinely awed.

Cat lit a cigarette, caught up in thought. She took a drag, released the smoke, and watched it drift away. "Yeah. This must be the change Daulphine sees. I'm going as your stylist, Lily!"

Distracted by seagulls squawking overhead, Penn blew her lifeguard whistle. More than once. Successful in commanding the children's attention, she hollered, "Stop feeding those birds, you know what happens when you break the rules!"

Cat pressed on. "Right, Lily?"

Lily looked heavenward and grimaced. "Cat, hiring the stylist isn't up to me."

Cat took another drag on her cigarette and stared off into space. Lily could not read her expression.

Lily stepped over the awkwardness. She spread out more photographs, various views of an ochre villa in a garden setting.

"Villa Bianco. A family-owned property; it comes fully equipped and staffed. We'll be staying here during the shoot, and I was thinking. Well, maybe you four could join Grace and me afterward for a little vacation. If I go—"

Deedee cut in. "Oh, you lil June bug, Dirk never lets up. A few weeks away from him will have you smilin' like Mr. Jack Daniels."

"Time away from *any* husband is a guaranteed attitude adjustment." Cat patted Lily's hand.

"All that time. Just the six of us. No kids. No husbands." Penn shivered with excitement, almost losing her black swim top. With girlish modesty she quickly repositioned it to cover her small breasts.

"We'll come back new women," Amelia sighed.

Excited, Cat leaped up and twirled, arms outstretched, cigarette in hand. A coughing fit overtook her. She sat down, hard, breathless. "Just us girls. How could we keep our sanity without one another?"

"Remember that play, *Enchanted April?*" Grace referred to one they'd seen together at the community theatre.

Deedee piped up. "Sure, that was where all those unsatisfied women rented that deserted Eye-talian villa."

"*Secluded,*" Grace corrected, "and by act three, with all that quiet and isolation, they find new energy for their lives back home."

"Yeah, but one gal ruined it by invitin' the menfolk to join 'em." Deedee scowled.

"Yes, and that's when they all fell in love again," Lily said. Her friends had energized her. She pulled out a green sheet of paper and displayed it. "The budget. Look. Split six ways we could swing it!"

The wives exchanged glances charged with a heady mix of exhilaration and apprehension. Penn smiled broadly, eyes and mouth open wide as she defied the dainty features of her Asian-American genes. Amelia asked the question they were all thinking. "Can we? Without our husbands?"

"Lily, tell it like a story," Cat begged.

Using her *famous author's voice,* Lily spoke: "And so, six wives conspire to abandon their husbands for a week of solitude and renewal. An Enchanted August!"

Locating the Polaroid camera from the depths of her beach bag, Lily called out, "Callie, come take a picture of us!"

8. PENN

The kitchen window to the patio was open. Penn worked at the sink shucking corn. She could smell the carnations in the window box. And eavesdrop on the husbands outside (without being obvious). Their banter about the day's round of golf was both boastful and demeaning, with much razzing about lost bets. Penn marveled as she listened; guys could say the meanest things to each other without harming their friendship.

As golf talk dwindled, Dirk's tone became newly serious. "I've got a little bomb I'm gonna drop here," he said. He leaned against the picnic table watching George grill hotdogs. "You poor bastards better stick together on this."

"Go ahead and hit me!" George said, sparring with his longtime golf buddy.

Hugh began air boxing, bouncing around a pretend boxing ring. "Pow, pow, uppercut!"

Dirk ignored Hugh. "Lily's been offered a photo op for our company—translation boondoggle! If you suckers cave"—he looked around at each of them—"we'll all be babysitting for a week. Or more. Including Labor Day, because Lily's inviting your women to join her. In Italy."

"Dirk, hold on!" Marc's voice had a director's authority. "Grace said you gave Lily the green light. She and Lily invited the gals yesterday."

This caught four husbands' attention. It was the first they had heard of any trip their wives were scheming.

Penn craned her neck to see George's reaction, but he still faced the grill. Oh, dear God, how she dreaded a scene. Stepping away from the window, Penn motioned to her co-conspirators. Deedee dropped the celery she was smothering with Cheez Whiz. Amelia nicked her finger on the vegetable peeler. Cat handed Leo another cracker and tiptoed in behind

Penn. Lily blanched, and Grace pulled her forward. Six nervous wives at the sink, each quiet as a queen on a chessboard. Each wore a sundress under her apron, showing off tan arms and small waists while looking demure. Lily had made the wardrobe suggestion, hoping that a united visual would help their cause.

The plan was to present the trip today, all together. It would require a tricky combination of skills, to be docile yet resilient. Penn had baked George's favorite dessert, German chocolate cake, with extra coconut. Yes, the plan had been to present the trip after dessert, after beer and sangria had been consumed. When the fellas were most likely to be feeling jovial. And perhaps amorous.

Was Dirk's announcement a checkmate? Penn's stomach tightened. Just then, she realized how very much she was counting on a getaway.

"Don't underestimate the marketing power of a fashion magazine," Marc said, facing Dirk. "Gracie is thrilled at the prospect." Addressing the others, he said, "And I don't mind if she stays on the extra week…you know, so your girls can join her and Lily on Capri."

Pietro tugged his mustache, squinting his brown sad eyes. "If Cat's going to Italy, it will be with me. Till then, my wife b-b-belongs at home."

Penn watched with fear as George pulled off the floral hot mitts and sputtered, "Labor Day weekend? That's the *club championship*, man. Early mornings and late nights. Who'll be around to babysit over a holiday weekend if Penn's in Capri?"

Hugh's boxing came to a halt. "Well, I'm sure not paying for Deedee to go gallivanting. So she better start sellin' more brassieres. And before headin' off, she better find a stooge to take her mama. That done, I'm not gonna say no. Sure could use a break from that sick biddy!"

Ken Jr. finished the last of his beer. He crushed his can underfoot with a brisk stomp. Droplets of beer hit Dirk's hairy calf. Dirk whirled around, glowered.

Ken Jr. feigned remorse. "Oops! Sorry there, sweetheart! And I could use a break from Amelia. Just kidding."

Penn looked at Amelia, who flushed bright pink.

Ken Jr. went on, "Anyways…I can always count on Amelia to line up a sitter."

"We'll see about that!" Amelia whispered to Penn.

Penn cringed; George's anger was on the rise. She backed away from the window and into Lily's arms.

"Hey man, like when were they going to ask our permission?" George's harsh voice bounced around and around in Penn's skull.

Dirk took a mock Napoleon pose. His buddies hee-hawed. "You're all losers. I'll nip this in the bud right now."

"This is best discussed in the p-p-privacy of our homes," Pietro snapped.

Deedee sashayed onto the patio, minus her apron. Penn thought she looked like an angel fresh from heaven. "Who's gonna dance with me?"

Penn turned up the volume on the stereo. She peered outside to see if the situation had changed. Hugh was lustily pulling Deedee close. Cat was two-stepping onto the patio and giving Pietro the high sign to join her. The purple bougainvillea fluttered. *Thank you, God*, Penn whispered.

Feeling bolder, Penn carried a platter of T-bone steaks to the barbeque. George handed her the cooked wieners and the now-crusty buns. She kissed his cheek timidly.

"Kids, come eat!" she hollered in her loudest voice.

Marc took Dirk aside, and the two had some private words by the partially rusted swing set. The birds of paradise looked upward and sighed sweetly. Afterward, Dirk seemed to be buoyed by a new idea. He danced like a wild man with Lily, who had been very quiet up until then. The tension broke. Penn resumed her role as proper hostess and served the sangria. The steaks sizzled as fat melted into the coals. Amelia finally joined the others. What a beautiful salad she had prepared, they all agreed. How hungry they all were.

By the next morning, each of the six was assured of her escape to Italy. A round of telephone calls confirmed it. Each had a few concessions to make, a few favors to grant, but nothing beyond the realm of one's wifely duties.

9. DEEDEE

The Nordstrom lingerie department was bustling. Deedee had yet to take her midmorning break. The manager pointed to her watch and arched her eyebrow at Deedee.

"Yes, ma'am. I'm goin' right now." Deedee reached under the counter for her clear plastic purse—the regulation one all the salesgirls carried, ostensibly to prove they weren't secreting any company goods out of the store. As soon as she reached a corner in the back room, she fished out a small notebook and pencil and made some entries onto the pages. Deedee's sales had skyrocketed these past couple of months. She was sure to make sales associate again. The bonus would help pay the airfare to Rome. That would get Hugh off her back about the cost of the trip.

Heck, with a little loan from Nanette's child support check, she'd be home free. That Ryan White hadn't been good for much, and he'd never shown any interest in seein' Nanette, but he always sent that check on time. Ever since she took him back to court for ditchin' his daddy responsibilities, that is.

The manager's voice broke right through Deedee's thoughts. "Deedee, Mrs. Dawson is here and refuses to let me assist her. She says you're expecting her. Are you making appointments with the clientele? That's highly irregular, and I'm not so sure you aren't in code violation."

"No ma'am," Deedee assured the manager. "No appointment. She calls first to make sure I'm on duty." It was just a little white lie. She'd called Mrs. Dawson and the rest of her regular customers to remind them of the sale. If they bought somethin' and helped her to reach her goal, was that so awful? Deedee called herself motivated.

Lordy, it was no kind of picnic to be squeezin' women into brassieres that pushed their bosoms up to their neck, makin' 'em look like they had a baby's butt on their chest. And how about compressin' over-plump bottoms into foundations in hopes of enticing husbands? Of course there were some fun times. Those shy young men who bought sexy panties and garter belts to match lacy bras for girlfriends, and cute young teens who were embarrassed in the try-on room. Deedee was a master at putting them at ease. Then there were the newly pregnant women who simply refused to believe that in just a few months, their sore breasts were going to fill the gigantic cups of the maternity bras.

Deedee regularly tickled her friends by imitating her customers. She knew she was good at her job. If she took the initiative and contacted customers, well, they sure never complained. Why on earth would the company?

Deedee closed her eyes and dreamed of Chianti and pasta before getting back to work. But once on the floor, she was all business.

"Good afternoon, Mrs. Dawson." Deedee smiled at the well-put-together woman who had more money than she needed and time on her hands for shopping, then she started pulling intimate items in dove-grey silk from the drawers under the counter. "My goodness, I believe you are gettin' younger every day. How do you do it? One of these visits, you just have to tell me your secret. In the meantime, look what I put away for you. Positively delicious, aren't they?"

10. AMELIA

Amelia knelt in front of an open file drawer in her sewing room. She sorted through and pulled out several used pattern packs. The styles of McCalls, Simplicity, and Butterick usually served her purposes. Finding nothing she already owned inspiring, she determined that a Vogue pattern would offer something smarter, something a little more continental for her trip. Amelia checked her watch. It was still early. Hopefully, Lily had spare time today—her advice could make all the difference to Amelia's project. She brushed up the beige shag carpet where her knees had left their imprint, then picked up the phone.

"Lily, sweetie," Amelia crooned into the telephone, "any chance you could meet me at that fabric store on Ninth and Main?"

Less than an hour later, Amelia and Lily sat at a counter and pored through pattern books and wrote down the numbers of the contenders.

"I found a winner." Lily pointed to an open page. "The strapless version is adorable, and you can wear the little bolero jacket over it as well as the halter style. Very Italian. Let's go look at fabrics."

Amelia piled a bolt of black cotton sateen onto the cutting counter, along with thread, zippers, buttons, and the real find of the day—the much-sought-after Vogue pattern with its seven variations of the same basic dress. The salesclerk went to work cutting the fabric and tallying up the purchases.

Lily handed the clerk her resale card. Turning to Amelia, she said, "Using this will save you a bit."

Amelia laughed. "Thanks, sweetie. I'll put it toward the trip."

That same afternoon Amelia sat poolside at the YMCA. Typically she would stay in the lounge and read a Harlequin romance, but her trip was getting close and she felt obligated to give her children a little extra attention.

All four kids were taking swim class in different sections of the pool. Jennifer was showing promise as a diver, and Kenny had finally gotten the timing correct on taking a breath between strokes. The twins were cannonballing in the shallow end despite their instructor's pleas that they stay inside the pool with the rest of their class.

Had Amelia been focused on the children, as was her original intention, she would have intervened and disciplined Don and Andy for their rascally behavior. Instead, uppermost on her mind was the bolt of black sateen that sat on her sewing table begging to be fashioned into something stunning.

11. GRACE

Marc McCrea's viewing room was a technological wonder and the envy of all his golf buddies. Watching sports was never the same in their own living rooms. And while the men cheered for their team or golfer, the wives sat around Grace's kitchen table for a hen session and iced tea. Or wine—preferably wine.

It had been Grace's idea to put the large maid's room to use. Marc didn't complain when she suggested a theatre, and was thrilled when she purchased theatre-style seats for their tenth anniversary. He handled all the other details. Upon completion, it may not have rivaled Coppola's, but most guys would have been proud to own it.

Grace regularly invited her parents over to watch themselves on reruns of *Murder Between the Sheets* and the new nighttime edition of *Hollywood Squares*. Hope and Jimbo Derringer, a very attractive couple in their late fifties, looked every inch the movie-star couple they were. As frequent guests on the show, they shared the same square. The nighttime version was a tad racier than the daytime show, and the Derringers had a saucy sense of humor. Grace didn't allow Jemima access to that program lest she hear her grandparents' improper but comical responses.

Jemima did, however, get to watch reruns of *Murder Between the Sheets*. That night Grace dimmed the lights just as the title and cast names of *Murder* began to scroll.

"Oh, Grammie Hope, I like this one," Jemima said. "It's one of my favorites."

"You've already seen this?"

"Twenty times," Jemima exaggerated and rolled her eyes. "It's the one where the police dog finds a bone and brings it to Grampa Jimbo, but it's not a dog bone, and you and Grampa find a dead person who lost a bone and solve the murder."

Hope and Jimbo laughed delightedly.

"Oh Lord!" Grace groaned. "Marc, we may have a problem here."

Marc entered the room with bowls of buttered popcorn. "I told you she was advanced. Have some popcorn."

"Advanced? She has trouble recognizing the alphabet. I never knew she was such a little sponge about this show," Grace whispered. Then, in a normal tone, she said, "I wish I could, but I can't eat popcorn. I have three more pounds to lose before Capri."

"My mistake, Gracie," Marc sympathized. "But you'll look great by the time you go."

"He's right, darling," Hope added. "I know you're hungry, but it'll pay off. Remember what Wallis Simpson always said, 'You can't be too rich or too thin.'"

"So I've heard. When my stomach growls, I repeat your mantra, 'Hungry means thin; thin means beautiful; beautiful means happy.'"

Hope and Marc smiled at Grace encouragingly and tucked right into the popcorn.

Jimbo frowned. "I'm not so sure about that, Gracie, sweetheart. You're too scrawny now. I can't see you losing three ounces. Honey, I'm afraid you're gonna vanish." He reached over, lifted Grace's thin arm, and shook his head. He was tall and well built. He came from a family where strength and muscle counted.

"Oh, for heaven's sake, Jimbo. You know how much weight the camera adds. I've taught Grace all the tricks I use. You never thought I was too thin."

"Excuse me, Hope, dear, but you've always had some T & A," Jimbo replied. "Gracie never got any. What you taught her was to diet, and she's been doing it since she was twelve."

"You guys are so noisy," Jemima squawked. "The dog already found the bone. Isn't *anyone* gonna watch this show with me?"

"Jemima, sweetie, come sit with Grammie. Let's cuddle and eat popcorn. I'll watch the show with you." Hope patted the space next to her.

"Okay." Jemima gathered up her blanket and climbed onto the wide leather chair. "But first I just gotta tell you what Mommy's bringing me back from Italy." She paused before delivering the shocker. "A baby brother."

"That's wonderful, sweetheart," Hope commented. Her tight voice belied her words. Marc's jaw clenched.

"Jemima, I did *not* promise that." Grace giggled. But Hope's intention of discouraging a second child who might interfere with Grace's figure and career was not lost on her daughter.

▪   ▪   ▪

The next afternoon Grace picked at a bowl of iceberg lettuce, tomato, and lemon juice at Musso and Frank Grill on Hollywood Boulevard. Amelia and Penn sat across from her. They'd been served the restaurant's signature chicken potpies, which oozed a steamy fragrance, sorely tempting Grace to request just one bite.

As a distraction Grace relayed Jemima's antics of the previous evening.

"You don't give that child enough credit, Grace," Amelia advised. "All kids are 'little pitchers with big ears.' I swear, Jennifer is only eleven and knows things I wasn't aware of till my late teens. You must admit, Jemima needs a sibling. You know what it's like growing up an only child. And so do I. Time's a wasting, you're already thirty-one."

"I want another baby, but Marc isn't so sure," Grace began.

"Kids, kids, kids!" Penn interjected. "I'm sorry, but why do we always talk about kids? I've got kids up to my uvula. Let's talk about Capri." She paused a moment. "Or Cat. What's up with her and that psychic?"

"Penn, sweetie, we all know Cat doesn't walk on terra firma. I just ignore that psychic babble when she starts it." Amelia changed the topic to one more interesting to her. "You both have to come over and see the dresses I've made for Capri. And Penn, give me a call later, I've got some ideas to make our trip easier on our menfolk."

"Speaking of kids and Capri, have you two worked out who'll watch your children?" Grace asked. "My parents are going to take Jemima when Marc is working—which is most of the time. I wonder how Deedee plans to resolve her Mama issue. I can't quite see Hugh helping her out on that one."

12. DEEDEE

The temperature in the den was uncomfortably hot, but Deedee tried to smile and be reassuring and upbeat for Mama. But it was so danged hard when Mama was on one of her rants. There was almost no calming her.

"Now, Mama, just settle down. I'll get this all figured out. Don't you worry about one single little thing." Deedee set a glass of water and a couple of pills down next to her mother.

"You don't need to be trekkin' across the ocean for no good reason. You're plannin' on leavin' me here with that no-good, no-count, baseball bat-swinging kid you call a husband. I know you, Daphne Denise. You're only thinkin' of yourself and your own good time!" Mama accused. An afghan was pulled up to her chin. Her La-Z-Boy chair was set in a half-reclined position.

Hugh chose that inopportune moment to enter the house. Looking from Deedee to her mother, he put his hands up and shook his head. "That ain't happenin'! No way, no how." Hugh contemplated leaving and backed up a few steps. "Deedee, I said it was okay for you to go, but you're not stickin' me with her. Why, she's downright nasty. Ain't no love lost on my side either. You're gonna hafta work somethin' else out."

"I can hear you," Mama hollered. "I'm sittin' right here in front of you."

"Can you two just quiet down? No one said anything' about Hugh takin' care of you, Mama. And Hugh, don't you think I know what I'd be comin' back to—fur flyin' and maybe a dead body or two."

Only slightly mollified, Hugh continued, "All right, but don't be thinkin' you're gonna leave that sourpuss teenager of yours here with me either. I'm not in the babysittin' business. I'm lookin' forward to some quiet time."

Exhausted with the effort, Deedee turned to Hugh and smiled brightly, "Yes, poopsie." Then she strode off to the bedroom, tossing her hair.

Hugh wasn't sure how he should take it.

■ ■ ■

In the Nordstrom fitting room, Deedee updated Cat a few days later. "I put a call in to Aunt Bea. I was hopin' she'd take pity on me. If anyone can handle Mama, it's her baby sister. Mama never gives Aunt Bea any guff."

"So what happened?" Cat prompted.

"Thankfully, it's all under control now. Mama and Nanette will be goin' to Aunt Bea's. She says she's got nothin' important on the calendar and she might as well knock some sense into Mama."

"Figuratively, not literally, you mean," Cat clarified.

Deedee hung a dozen or so bras on the dressing room hooks. She organized them by sexy to sexier.

"Well, of course. Aunt Bea's bark...It used to scare me when I was a kid, but I know she'll take good care of Mama. See she gets her medicine and take her to any doctor appointments. I can't tell you how mightily relieved I am." Deedee sighed. "Now let's get to work on you."

"I hope you can help, but I don't know what buying a new bra can do." Cat looked in the mirror, her eyes beginning to water.

Deedee knew Cat's moods could go up and down, and judging by Cat's lackluster attitude, it was apparent she was in a slump. "What's up, Miz Cat? Is it Pietro or that wicked witch, Noni, that's got you feelin' so low?"

A single tear rolled down Cat's cheek. Her lips started to quiver.

"Enough of that. It's time for you an' me to stop feelin' sorry for ourselves. Heck, we should be celebratin'."

Deedee picked out a lacy bit of lavender frippery and handed it to Cat.

"We're gonna have us the time of our lives on that Capri. Now you try this on, an' if you don't like it, you try on another. I'm gonna give you a little privacy; give me a holler if you need help. An' if I don't hear from you, I'm gonna bust right in here and see why the heck you're bein' difficult." Deedee winked at Cat, then closed the door.

Cat laughed—she couldn't help it. Then she set about trying on every brassiere Deedee had left her. When Deedee returned, brassieres and hangers were strewn about the room. Cat was standing at the three-way mirror gawking at herself as she turned front to side to back, confidence renewed.

"Who knew?" she asked.

"That foundations could make such a difference? Well, me, for one. Just see how perky you feel when your bosom looks great. I dare Pietro or Noni to dampen your spirits now, sister."

13. CAT

Pietro was in the Cantina's small office, around the corner from where Cat dusted bottles. She could hear him talking on the telephone.

"But we ordered c-c-cabernet '74," he was saying firmly. From the sound of it, he'd be complaining about that last shipment for a good while longer.

Cat wore the Italian peasant costume with theatrical flair. Dressing up for the job seemed pointless, yesterday. But today, assisted by a Wonderbra, she actually looked radiant. Sexy. In fact, the whole world looked different to her. Everything, except Beppe's Cantina.

Sure, Beppe's Cantina had its charm. Used brick walls and floor, wine bottles stacked on dark wood shelves. A tasting bar to one side. But after all these years, the same routine was uninspiring. But. If she could change, the shop could change.

Cat dragged three boxes out from under the draped tables. She quickly sliced through the tape and opened them. From the first she unpacked pottery goblets and arranged them on a shelf with artificial bunches of grapes. She stood back and admired her work. Then she looked around the shop again. No customers waiting outside, no Pietro. Cat hurriedly unpacked the second box. Printed linens from Tuscany. She folded and stacked them, just so, to make a display. She was good at this and she knew it. Lily had even told her so.

Pietro's annoyed voice grew louder. "I'll hold."

"Good, more time," Cat told herself. She stealthily set out wine, glasses, crackers, and chocolate from the third box.

The shop bell jingled as the door opened. In came Noni, her gray hair pulled tightly into a braided "business day" bun.

"*Buon giorno*," she said to Cat. Just like she did every day.

Noni turned the "Closed" sign to "Open." Jason and Leo ran to Cat.

"Mommy, Noni got us jelly donuts." Jason held out his crumpled waxed paper. "Here, Mommy." Cat deftly avoided Jason's sticky hands. She kissed little Leo's sweet brown fingers, one by one.

Noni advanced to Cat's display, picked up a pottery goblet, and shook her head in disgust. "Pietro!" Her voice lingered in soprano on the last syllable.

Pietro scurried in, wearing a grocer's apron. Cat thought he looked older than his thirty-four years, with those sad brown eyes and waxed mustache. He spotted Cat's new displays. Stopping midstride, he waved his arms frantically. "You ordered all th-th-this?"

Cat hated the indignant tone of her husband's voice. Of course she had. Who else did he think would have used any creativity in regard to the shop? Defiant, she crossed her arms and stared at Pietro.

Leo clung to Cat's leg.

"Our cantina, wine only. Is family way." Noni wagged a finger in Cat's face. She spoke oh, so slowly. As if Cat were a child.

"Cat, you know your p-p-place," Pietro pleaded. "Now what are we going to d-d-do with all this?"

Cat, seething, turned on her heel. Once in the storeroom, she sat on a on a wine barrel and fumed. She pulled a pack of Salem cigarettes from her apron pocket and lit up. She needed a new career. And Lily was her best hope. A phone call followed.

"Lily, I'm dying on the vine here."

Cat pleaded. She cajoled. She whined. Finally, Cat used flattery.

"Lily, you have so much influence, with Quinton—and obviously with the editor. All it would take is a tiny word from you on my behalf."

"Oh, Cat, at the very least, we'd need to show the editor some prints of your fashion styling," Lily countered. "And you know, well, you don't have any."

That's when Cat knew how easy it was going to be.

Cat San Carlo glowed in anticipation of assisting Lily as the photo stylist. She slyly purchased a Hasselblad and film. When not in use, she hid the contraband on the top shelf of her closet behind hatboxes. She shot 140 irresistible shots of Leo and four of Jason. Twenty-two of the glossy prints were displayed in a handsome portfolio. How could she be denied the opportunity now? A few prints, displaying her "concept" for styling Lily's fashions, would be kept under wraps; she'd surprise Lily and Quinton on Capri.

Cat liked having secrets. Secrets brought new happiness into her life. She felt sweeter toward Pietro knowing he didn't have a clue. One evening when Noni burned her fingers stirring bubbling arrabiata sauce, Cat took over the entire meal without complaining. She'd tell them both about her new career *after* the trip. Getting Pietro's permission for a wives-only spree had been enough for the time being.

14. LILY

Details presented a snarl of time management issues. Making patterns, grading, cutting, and sewing for the shoot had taken the full cooperation of contractors and her minimal staff. Lily contemplated her final to-do list—tasks for herself, Darleen, and Dirk.

Lily looked up, startled, as Darleen flew into the workroom—tan trumpet skirt, floral blouse with ecru faggoting, cinched waist. Lily barely managed a smile, stressed beyond affability.

"I need to send you out on a few errands," she said. "Write this down."

Darleen gave a thumbs-up expressing her willingness to cooperate, and wrote out Lily's directions. Her manicured fingernails matched her violet belt. Lily noticed Darleen's hands with a start. What was it? What was the image she suddenly recalled? Violet nails. Madras shorts. Descending bubbles. An encounter at the watercooler? No. No point wasting time on fragmented impressions.

"We pack cartons tomorrow, so come dressed comfortably," Lily said.

Darleen streamed out of the workroom in her open-toed, high-heeled Candies, off on her mission, feet flying like a carhop on roller skates. Her willingness to please rated an A plus these days. She was paying excellent attention to Lily's schedule, for a change. Any earlier snippiness had vanished. *Good timing*, Lily thought.

Lily cut out xeroxed images of the Antonio Caldo Mediterranean Collection, her latest creations, yet to be revealed. Xeroxes? Something about the Xerox machine. Lily sliced through the mind debris with the precision of an X-Acto knife. She had a talent for staying focused. She repeated to herself, "No time to waste."

She pasted the copies of shirts, vests, jackets, slacks, and shorts into ensembles. Combinations for the models to wear on the Capri photo shoot. Planning ahead would save precious time. Complications were to be expected, but she did not want her components to be at fault. She took her finished pasteups to the copy room. The copy room? Something disturbing flared. Had the door been partially closed, allowing an unwelcome view? But when?

Feeling slightly off kilter, Lily returned to her workroom and her list. She wrote:

Me
Have Dirk cut bonus check for Darleen
Call Vivian at H.I.S *re an extra assistant on site (?)*
Pull out suitcases
Sort Dirk and Callie's laundry

Lily stopped. Callie's name brought a lump to her throat. Tears pooled in her eyes; she brushed them away. She glanced up and caught the compassionate stare of an otherwise inanimate mannequin. Leaving Callie? Lily felt apprehensive. This would be their longest separation. Callie's incessant chattering and giggles invigorated her. She stood straighter and smiled more in Callie's presence. Mornings without Callie? Hard to imagine. Would she miss Dirk? Lily shoved the question aside and started her review.

She had already scheduled the Antonio Caldo sales reps' meeting for mid-September, allowing the office a lull during her absence. She had collected brochures for SeaWorld, Busch Gardens, and La Brea Tar Pits. Perhaps Dirk and Callie could share a few days of exploration. Perusing the information she felt a pang of jealousy. She determined to share a fun outing with Callie in the fall.

She'd confirmed with Marlys, Callie's summer nanny, that yes, Marlys was flexible about her schedule, soon to be directed by Dirk, but weekdays only, per the initial arrangement, because Marlys took evening classes at UCLA and *needed* her weekends. Dirk would be responsible to tend Callie every evening from five o'clock on.

Lily frowned. Dirk tending Callie? The reality of that arrangement often turned into a fiasco. Usually because Dirk's gift of junior golf clubs had strings attached. Callie "owed" Dirk sessions at the driving range. Although Callie would submit to whacking a bucketful of balls, one by one off the rubber tee, her lack of enthusiasm brought consequences. Dirk felt slighted and retaliated with lectures and withdrawal of privileges. Withdrawal of privileges translated into days with surfing denied, and surfing was Callie's passion. Lily sighed. She would not be there to intercede on Callie's behalf.

Fortunately, Dirk needn't miss golf. Over the past few years, Lily and the neighbors—Jimmy's folks, the Suttons—exchanged "parental lifeguard watch" as the kids rode waves. Sometimes the adults spent a Sunday afternoon all together enjoying the young athletes and conversation. Mrs. Sutton admired and followed Lily's career enthusiastically, claiming not to have a creative bone in her own body. Hearing of Lily's opportunity on Capri, she generously offered, "Callie's welcome here while you're away. Treat her like my own, I will."

Mr. Sutton, a marathon swimmer, added, "You tell Dirk we're surefire serious. Knowing he's not much for watching the youngsters of a weekend, eh?"

Lily congratulated herself. No need for Dirk to miss out on any golf, especially not the Labor Day club championship, if he took the Suttons up on their offer. Feeling calmer about her husband's happiness quotient, she tackled the last items on her list.

> ### *Callie*
> *Have a pep talk about being apart* and *about being positive with Dad*
> *Make rice crispy/marshmallow treats together*
> *Wrap gift for Jimmy:* Illustrated Guide to Sea Creatures

Lily covered her list casually as Dirk entered her office. His voice was soft and sexy. "Hey, Lily girl, watcha need me to do? I'm your willing slave for a little while longer." Dirk came around behind Lily and massaged her shoulders. Lily relaxed. Dirk was in one of his good moods.

That night Lily spent longer than usual with Callie's bedtime routine. While Dirk settled into watching the Dodgers, Callie read aloud from one of her favorite books, Perrault's *Little Red Riding Hood*. Doré's engravings delighted Callie as much as the story. And Callie's observations always intrigued Lily.

"Red Riding Hood *knew* it was that wolf in bed! Why didn't she bonk him with her basket, or kick him with her hiking boots? Then she could have run away!" Lily had never thought to question the story in her youth.

Lily tucked Callie into bed, turned out the light, and sang one verse of a song. It was a ritual from Lily's childhood; her mother also sang it, romantically rim lit by the hallway light.

15. PENN

Aprons tied, groceries organized, Amelia joined forces with Penn. "Doesn't even seem like work in *your* kitchen," Amelia said as she watched tomatoes whirl in the blender. Penn responded by singing a song about whistling while one worked.

The cooking had been Amelia's idea. A brilliant one. It enabled Penn to cross chores off her previous "while I'm gone" list for George. (Less for George to complain about meant less for her to stress about.)

From ten o'clock on, the wives worked, eager as Girl Scouts earning merit badges, while their seven children built a city of blocks and dominoes from the rumpus room to the kitchen. By three that afternoon, duplicate offerings of tuna casserole, chicken potpie, lasagna, beef stew, and cheesy chili mac were set to cool. The children, restless now, were placated with orange 50/50 pops. By five o'clock the entrées were transformed into well-marked portion packages. One set for each family's freezer. The children watched cartoons, whining just a little, hungry for dinner. Amelia spread peanut butter on Ritz crackers and Jennifer doled them out.

"One by one, please," Penn directed.

"Now we'll get no complaints about grocery shopping," Amelia said defiantly as she dried cookware and utensils.

Penn put the dried items away in the proper shelves and drawers. She preferred doing this herself.

Work accomplished and feeling celebratory, Penn and Amelia shared a light beer. The beer gave Penn a headache immediately; she blinked like a mermaid struck by sunshine.

■   ■   ■

Penn passed out hymnbooks, her eyes misted with pride. How fine her redheaded sons looked, all dressed up, alongside her parents. Phillip, nine, wiry, tin medals pinned to his jacket, resembled the Admiral, who was a daunting figure in full dress regalia. Charles, eight, had inherited Mummy's golden skin and stature. Mummy in a brocade cheongsam, gloves, and veiled hat sat beside Henry, the youngest, just seven. She allowed Henry to hold her fan *if* he would be still for the service. Henry unfolded and folded the ribbed paper, exposing birds that lived amongst cherry blossoms in a world between the ivory guard sticks.

Sunday church anchored Penn's week. Hers was a life of tradition, where birthdays and holidays were ritualized, where manners, defined by a military code, were to be obeyed, implicitly. She and George agreed about raising three sons with this tenet, and that was a blessing.

After prayer and hymns, Pastor Barnes began the sermon. His topic: the duties and dangers of marriage.

"The Bible encourages young women to love their husbands, to love their children, to be sensible, pure, workers at home, kind, being subject to their own husbands..." Surely she was a good wife. Penn patted George's thigh. He was wearing the green and blue striped tie that the boys had given him for Father's Day. George was a good husband. Well, he had his faults, but he was not nearly as difficult as Lily's Dirk.

Penn would never have said it out loud, but she resented Dirk's sarcasm. If it wasn't Lily's dreaminess, it was her haphazard budgeting or lack of meal planning he berated. Unfairly so. Wasn't Lily the *Little Red Hen* and Dirk the paper tiger with a brass title plate?

As newlywed couples, the George Pines and the Dirk Whites took turns hosting laid-back, laugh-filled dinners. But when the foursome played card games late into the night, each husband's temperament was revealed. Penn and Lily began to share frequent phone conversations; being young wives was new territory. Penn had mastered the entertaining arts, thanks to Mummy's example as hostess of navy base bridge parties. Even laundry and housekeeping were a snap. It was keeping a husband happy that presented a challenge. To both Penn and Lily. And keeping a husband happy was, of course, a priority.

Pastor Barnes's voice broke through Penn's musings—"and quoting from Galatians, 'Now the works of the flesh are manifest, which are these; Adultery, fornication, uncleanness, lasciviousness, idolatry, witchcraft, hatred, variance, jealousies, wrath, strife, seditions, heresies, contentions, murders, drunkenness...'"

Penn bit her lip. She stared straight ahead and picked at a thumbnail. Pastor Barnes continued, "Romans 6:21 sums it up this way, husbands and wives, my fellow sinners: 'therefore what benefit were you then deriving from the things of which you are now ashamed? For the outcome of those things is death.' Let us pray."

During prayer Charles kicked the pew ahead with his new tan sandals. *Thunk, thunk, thunk.* George whapped Charles with a hymnbook. A loud disrupting *whap.* Mummy, head still bowed, opened her eyes and glowered at George.

The congregation filed past Pastor Barnes, shaking hands, exchanging pleasantries. The Admiral and George walked on ahead to the foyer and out into the sunshine.

The Admiral was first to speak. "Penn tells me you're off to Greece. That's fine, young man, travel is fine. Did I ever tell you about my time in Tripoli?"

George's voice seemed weaker than usual. "No, sir. You haven't. I mean, yes, sir. But actually, sir, only Penn is. I mean, only Penn is taking a trip to Italy."

The Admiral seemed shocked. "Without her husband? Didn't raise my daughter to go gadding about, now did I? Does her mother know?"

Penn and Mummy followed a few yards behind with the boys.

"When do you leave for Corsica, Penelope? How many weeks will you be away, dear?" The silk petals on Mummy's hat danced in the slight breeze.

"Not even two weeks, Mummy, and it's the Isle of Capri, off the coast of Italy." Penn answered casually as if the trip were just some offhand event (so Mummy wouldn't overreact).

Casual event, hardly. On Penn's calendar the weeks were highlighted. Penn's closet was organized with travel items hanging in dry-cleaning bags. A purse-sized tablet was filled with details: the lira exchange rate, historical sites, arts events, travel tips, and important phrases translated into Italian. After hours of research, Penn had convinced Amelia and Deedee to spend three days in Sorrento, shopping, while Lily's photo session was underway. Cat was still non-committal, frustrated with Lily's indecision, actually. After that the shoppers would board a hydrofoil and meet up with their working friends.

"Two weeks, that's a long time." Mummy looked away and sniffed.

"But Mummy, we'll make up our missed outings at Babcock's Tea, I promise. And I'll bring you back something very, very special from Sorrento."

Penn was sincere. She believed she would have renewed energy for her family—after the trip. Penn could hardly wait. She would arrive at the legendary Isle of Capri, late afternoon, August 28, 1979. Unless something sadly unexpected were to happen, as it almost always did.

16. AMELIA

Amelia set a crystal bowl of low-cut hydrangeas on the dining room table. She'd used her good china and sterling flatware. The table was large to accommodate the family, but she'd placed candles and two cozy place settings at the end. She'd planned a very romantic dinner the night before her flight to Italy.

Amelia had managed to get all four kids bathed and bedded down. Nothing would spoil her last night with her husband. When Ken Jr. arrived home, he was greeted with soft music and a quiet house. Amelia led him to the dining room. She gave her backside an extra swish to make sure he was paying attention.

"Whoa! What's all this?" Ken Jr. grabbed Amelia around the waist and planted a lover kiss on her lips.

"Have a seat, handsome. I've got our night all planned." She held out his chair, then went to the kitchen to retrieve the awaiting dinner plates displaying the boeuf bourguignon, from Julia Child's cookbook, that had taken hours to prepare.

Ken Jr. smiled appreciatively as Amelia placed her masterpiece before him. Oh yes, this would be a night to remember. He reached for the wine bottle and poured two servings.

When the phone rang, Amelia got up. "It's probably one of the girls about tomorrow. I'll just be a second." She went to the kitchen to take the call.

What Ken Jr. heard from the dining room wasn't reassuring.

"Excuse me, Sarah! I haven't left yet!" A loud slam, which could only have been the receiver hitting the wall, caused Ken Jr. to jump up. Damage control was obviously required.

"Amelia, sweetheart," he appealed, unconvincingly. "It's just business. I swear."

Amelia sweetheart had grabbed the dinner plates and busied herself throwing the contents down the InSinkErator. The water ran full blast, the disposal ground away. Amelia stormed off, calling out, "Blow job cancelled!"

17. DEEDEE

The mirror held no pleasure for Deedee. She could see puffiness below her eyes. And were those fine wrinkles at the corners? She sighed, convinced that nobody needed this vacation more than she. A sweep of mascara to cover her blonde lashes, a quick brush of blush, and ruby gloss on her lips—there now. Much better. Deedee had never allowed Hugh to see her without makeup. Although exhausted by the effort to prepare for the trip *and* by the effort to keep Hugh and Mama from killin' each other, she'd always keep up her pretense of natural beauty. The makeup would come off after Hugh was sleeping deeply, happily exhausted by his effort to keep Deedee satisfied.

The bedroom door opened and was kicked shut. A half-dressed Hugh threw his shirt on the floor and stripped off his jeans. Deedee caught her breath, her temperature rising at the sight of his abs and the path of hair that went from his belly button and disappeared into his briefs. Yep! He may act like a kid most of the time, but he was all man.

She shimmied up to him, swishing her peignoir, prancing in high heels. "Ready to unwrap your goin' away gift now? It'll be gone tomorrow."

Delighted, Hugh spun Deedee around and slipped the silky robe off her shoulders. Deedee danced away, exposing sexy lingerie beneath the filmy gown. Hugh pulled her close, hands on her bottom, straining to feel her, to make sure she felt him. She reached around his neck and tugged his handsome face down to her level…

"Deedee, I needs help. Now!" Mama screamed, slaying the mood.

Deedee cupped Hugh's crotch and whispered suggestively, "Hold that thought, I'll be back lickety-split."

"For chrissakes! Baby, ignore her."

"You *know* I can't." Infuriated, Deedee pushed Hugh away. She picked up his shirt, threw it on, and hollered, "Comin', Mama!" then strode out. Behind her, she heard the crunch of wood and correctly surmised that Hugh had put his fist through the wardrobe door.

Four minutes later Deedee returned. Hands on her hips, she marched up to the wardrobe and inspected the hole. "Your temper is outta control!"

Hugh threw himself onto the edge of the bed, abject. "I'm sorry, baby, but your mama is intent on squashin' all our fun."

"Ah, that's plumb nasty, Hugh. You're the one squashin' my fun. I was only gone a couple a minutes. You still got a hard-on."

Hugh cheered up markedly. "Say, baby, how 'bout we make up?"

18. GRACE

"I think it's perfect. It has 'Grace' written all over it." Marc smiled across the Nordstrom lingerie counter at Deedee. He fingered a silk and lace peignoir that Deedee had spread before him. "Wrap it up." He pulled his wallet from his pocket.

"Looks like someone's gonna get lucky tonight," Deedee said with a wink.

Marc wished he could think of a bawdy reply for Deedee, but nothing came to mind. "It's for Capri. I wanted Grace to have something beautiful to take."

"I'm sure I'll be hearin' all about how good you treat her, and not just from Grace, you know—all the girls talk about it. But heck, Marc, I can't think of another man who'd send his wife off for a couple of weeks with sexy lingerie. If Hugh has his way, I'll be takin' Dr. Denton's."

Marc gave a rueful smile. "After all her effort to shed those few pounds, she deserves something special."

▪   ▪   ▪

Grace's half-packed luggage was lying on the bedroom floor. Alternate clothing and shoe choices were stacked on the comfy stuffed chairs and beside the suitcases—decisions to be made in the morning, under pressure. Grace did her best packing under pressure.

▪   ▪   ▪

Marc looked around the room as he lay on the left side of the king-sized bed. He could hear Grace singing in the bathroom, as she tidied herself after lovemaking. Her pristine hygiene was only one of the many things he appreciated about her. She could barely carry a tune, but she was sweet, witty, generous, and a wonderful mother to their daughter. His heart squeezed.

■   ■   ■

Grace looked at herself in the mirror. She wore only a diaphanous robe loosely around her shoulders—part of the luscious peignoir set Marc presented earlier. Her body was lean and hard from exercise; her breasts hardly had any plumpness to them. Lots of models were getting breast implants, and her agent recommended she consider having the surgery. An idea she rejected.

Marc hadn't seemed to enjoy her more womanly figure after she gave birth and nursed Jemima. He liked her best just the way she looked right now and he'd proven it tonight.

She entered the bedroom still singing. Marc shut his eyes, feigning sleep, but there was no ignoring Grace as she jumped onto the bed, slipped under the covers, and snuggled up to his back.

"Gosh, I needed that. Thank you. It's been such a long time—months."

Marc winced, but made no response.

"You enjoyed it too, right?" Grace pushed up against Marc's back.

Marc grimaced, then rolled over to face his wife. He tenderly put a hand on either side of her face. "Gracie, you know I love you, don't you? You and Jemima mean everything to me."

"For goodness' sakes, Marc, I won't be gone that long." Grace was puzzled by Marc's unusually emotional show of affection.

19. PENN

Penn detested the smell of a martini on George's breath. Even though they had stood side by side brushing their teeth, she in a blue teddy, he in his boxers, the smell persisted. It persisted when he kissed her during foreplay. Why was he humming the seven dwarfs' theme while he toiled above her? Arm over her nose, Penn participated like a good soldier, knowing their sexual exercise would be over quickly. And tomorrow she would be leaving, without him.

The anticipated morning came. George and Penn entered the boys' room; they flipped the lights. On, off. On, off.

"Wakey, wakey, Mummy's leaving," Penn said sweetly.

"Good morning, troops! It's gonna be just us guys, having a little R & R." George sounded jovial, or was he putting on a good act? George sat on the junior bed with Henry. He tousled Henry's red curls affectionately. Charles and Phillip hung from their bunk beds.

"I've got a little surprise for Daddy," Penn said. She presented the colorful platter-sized Chore Wheel. "You boys remember what I taught you. Rules here in the middle. Number four is very important, 'No clothes to be left on the bathroom floor.' Next, just like a game, everybody spins the arrow to find his chores. Daddy too."

George frowned. "Whoa, I didn't to agree this." He sighed like a schoolboy.

Penn gave her husband a cold, hard stare. George's red hair stuck out sideways. His robe yawned below the belt. His ankles looked ridiculously white below his tanned hairy calves. Penn's annoyance crawled up into her craw like a large black spider.

"I'm not coming home to a pigsty." Her voice sounded stern, even to her. Then, with new control, she said sweetly to the boys, "Don't disappoint your mum."

A taxi honked. Penn kissed and hugged her family good-bye, her entire body tingling as if circulation were reaching a deprived extremity.

2 0. CAT

Pietro followed Cat, hauling two Samsonite suitcases and a garment bag. Cat proceeded down the five steps, hatboxes stacked in her outstretched arms; she minced as if she carried a multitiered wedding cake. Pietro managed the stairs with some difficulty, his sad brown eyes looking more melancholy than usual.

Cat was dressed for business travel, a jaunty silk rose pinned to the lapel of her raw-silk summer suit, which she wore unbuttoned. The draped blouse beneath allowed a hint of cleavage. Today Cat felt every inch a photo stylist.

She'd been given an opportunity! The first she could recollect. In high school she had been wrongly kept in *business classes*—which for teenage girls meant *secretarial courses*, while others, no smarter than she, strode the fast track to college. While the college girls met aspiring professionals and were given matrimonial choices, she had taken the first proposal of marriage offered. Pietro's. Catholic guilt played some part in her decision. She had allowed him certain intimacies. This she had never admitted to anyone, however.

Pietro put his hands on his hips and offered no assistance as the scrawny taxi driver loaded Cat's luggage.

"Careful with the hat boxes," Cat said firmly.

As the driver slammed the trunk closed, Pietro grasped Cat's shoulders.

"Well, Mrs. San C-C-Carlo, please work this *skifezza* out of your s-s-system. Because when you get home, it's back to n-n-normal."

Cat wrenched free. "Well, Pietro, what's normal? Wearing the San Carlo straitjacket? With no room for ideas? Dusting wine bottles? Babysitting the cash register? Kowtowing to you and your, your..." Cat was at a loss for the appropriate insult. She stood tall, turning her back to Pietro.

Noni lost her restraint on Jason and Leo, who squirmed to get free. The boys ran down the walkway and hung on their mother's legs. Cat tousled their dark wavy hair. She had already kissed them—inside, before applying her lipstick. "Be good boys," she said.

Noni came face to face with Cat, shaking her head.

Cat extended her face toward Noni's and gave an air-kiss to each cheek. "*Ciao*," she said without emotion.

Noni's mouth rolled into a crooked snarl. Cat smirked, thinking that Noni looked like a taunted Doberman.

"*Si sposa ingrata! Si può essere puniti!*" Noni hissed. Pietro looked shocked at first. And then he chuckled. Noni continued to mutter in Italian as she turned, walked back along the sidewalk, up the five steps and into the house.

"What did she say?" Cat asked Pietro angrily.

Pietro answered without hesitation, "She said, 'You ungrateful wife. May you be punished.'"

Cat scoffed. She and Pietro exchanged a hard unyielding stare. Pietro tugged at his mustache. And then he caved. He held his arms open to Cat, his chocolate eyes melting.

If you asked Cat to describe that moment, she would have compared it to, well, growing a rose more perfect than Amelia's; having a more voluptuous bosom than Deedee; outscoring Penn on an IQ test; owning a home more impressive than Grace's; or, the best, having a career far grander than Lily's.

Cat allowed Pietro a quick kiss and a hug. Pietro felt warm and firm. Cat caught a faint trace of English Leather. *He used aftershave,* she thought.

As the taxi pulled away from the curb, Cat parade-waved out the passenger window. Her sons ran alongside, calling out, "Good-bye, Mommy." She shifted in her seat and waved out the back window as the taxi outdistanced the runners. Cat turned away abruptly as Pietro caught up to their sons and knelt between them.

21. LILY

*In retrospect, maybe I never…*Lily thought to herself.

The Pacific Ocean blurred like an indigo brushstroke as the shuttle breezed down the Coast Highway. Lily checked her watch. It seemed she'd been awake for hours. But it was only 6:46 a.m. What time was it when Dirk cuddled up to her back? Nuzzled her neck? Slid the hem of her lilac batiste nightie up over her hips? She had allowed his penetration, too sleepy to find pleasure herself. Heat and stickiness between her legs. His grunting. His sighs. She must have dozed after that until the alarm buzzed at 4:45 a.m.

Dirk's silhouette outside the foggy glass as she showered. His smile as she dried off. His unwrapping of the towel around her head. The towel tucked around her body falling to the bath mat. His lust at the sink. *No, I didn't, it's true,* Lily thought. She spied pelicans gliding over the water looking like prehistoric scavengers, awed as a single pelican dived into the blue, sleek as a sword.

She recalled Dirk's anger at 6:00 a.m. She'd been sitting at her vanity. Her hair was dry then, and styled, blunt, shiny. Her minimal makeup almost complete. In the mirror Dirk all but blocked the view of her crisp white shirt and black slacks on the bed. He wanted her again. Just like that in her flesh-colored panties and matching bra. He was unhooking her bra. He was tonguing her ear. She had said it, in a most unwifely tone. In an irritated tone. "Not again, Dirk, I'll be late."

"You never get turned on, Lily! You never get turned on, do you?"

The shuttle stopped with a jerk. Busy intersection and red light. Lily's satchel fell against her seatmate's legs. He wore khaki gabardine slacks, nicely creased. She pulled her patent satchel into her lap.

"I'm sorry," she said. He nodded and kept reading the folded *LA Times*. *Never. In retrospect. Maybe I never do anymore*, Lily thought to herself.

CAPRI

AUGUST

1979

THE GETAWAY

22. QUINTON

Quinton and Lily watched Vesuvius recede from view. "Foreboding, ominous, sinister," Lily said in her *famous author's voice*. Quinton smiled. He enjoyed Lily's play with words.

"Just decided," Quinton said. "I'm exploring Pompeii on the way home."

"I'm envious," Lily sighed.

Cat returned to the table with coffees and cello-wrapped cookies. "They don't serve cappuccino," Cat said grumpily. Grace declined the crisp almond cookies and ignored Cat's complaints.

The ferry's downstairs concessions area was crowded and stuffy. It smelled of brine and lavatory chemicals, but morning rain had left the deck too damp for comfort. A bank of windows allowed passengers a sea-level view from the side tables. Seated at one of these, the foursome sipped the dark coffee without conversation. They watched the Port of Naples slide away behind rolling swells as the hydrofoil navigated the Tyrrhenian Sea.

Quinton was eager to reach the Isle and dock at Marina Grande. He had specific locations for the photos in mind. Now he wanted to make observations firsthand, in order to be well prepared. As the hydrofoil approached the southeastern cliffs of Capri, Quinton pulled out his binoculars.

"There she is," he said, zooming in on ruins of Villa Jovis perched high above. "That's tomorrow's location, I hope." He handed the binoculars to Lily.

"Let me see," said Cat, reaching for the binoculars. "Oh my, there's a statue up there! Look!"

■   ■   ■

Edwin wore a sleeveless Nehru shirt and pleated trousers, Antonio Caldo fashions. He spun for Lily's approval, which she gave enthusiastically. "Thank you, sweetheart," he said.

Edwin calls everyone sweetheart...when things are going well, Quinton thought to himself.

Edwin, photography editor of *H.I.S.*, drove the foursome up a dusty road in the rented mini-vehicle. "We're basically paralleling Via Sopramonte," he said, the self-appointed tour guide.

"Via Sopramonte, road over the mountain," Lily translated. Cat and Lily sat in the back, knees up to their chests. Their climb was greeted by panoramic views over the rooftops of Capri and the sea. Quinton was armed with his camera and notebook. He held Edwin's overflowing ring binder on his lap.

"Amazing hike to Villa Jovis. You must take it while you're here, but for a worksite, it's a logistical nightmare." Edwin was well travelled, and Quinton respected his opinion. "Transporting equipment and people, you see, all this way. But an afternoon session might work, eastern side. We'd spend our morning in the medieval section of Capri proper, as we've discussed. Lunch break. And up the mountain. Well, you take a look my sweethearts, and you tell me." Edwin bounced in his seat, as if enthusiasm rubberized his body.

Quinton still felt jet lagged, but he smiled, gaining energy.

They parked a short distance from the entry and walked. At Villa Jovis they were greeted by a caretaker, who seemed as ancient as the imperial villa before them. He sat at a rickety table under the shade of coastal pines and offered to answer their questions. Quinton strode forward in awe, lured first by the courtyard with its crumbling columns and playful shadows. And next, by the rock arch opening to a mysterious interior. *Travel brochures have not done this place justice.*

Edwin talked with his hands in motion. Palms together, arms in opposing circles, ten fingertips tapping together. He gestured wildly as he related the ordeals of pulling permits, casting the male models, hiring assistants, and making catering arrangements. Quinton laughed. *Glad Edwin came ahead. He's invaluable.*

Quinton could tell that Lily also accepted Edwin's lead. He was, after all, a seasoned editor with a keen eye. Cat trailed behind the trio, interjecting her thoughts from time, but receiving little response. They explored the site's levels terraced along the slope of the land. Edwin pointed out potential problems as they discussed the merits of different views: juxtapositions, angles, texture, color, light.

"What are these?" Lily asked, looking down into room-sized rock basins.

"Cisterns. They held rain water for drinking and bathing purposes," Edwin said. Newly inspired, he waxed professorial warbling about the *frigidarium, tepidarium,* and *calidarium* areas.

It was in the midst of this lecture that Quinton heard a shriek. *It came from a distance. Cat?*

Lily cried out. "Where is Cat? Oh no!"

Edwin's hands stopped moving. "Was that Cat?"

Some distance behind them, only a quaint wooden fence bounded the walkway from the mountain's edge. *More scenic than lifesaving, that fence. But wasn't Cat with us just moments ago? Surely, she's not back there. No, she passed us and went on.*

Quinton took off running and rounded the corner ahead. He spied Cat, all but hidden by scrub and trees. She balanced on the ruins of a rock wall, looking up at a Madonna statue atop a small chapel.

"Oh, Cat, there you are!" Lily screamed, catching up with Quinton.

"I feel them here." Cat twirled unsteadily on the rubble and mortar.

"Cat, stay still, I'll help you down," Quinton called as he dashed across the uneven surfaces.

"No! I'm overwhelmed with the sense of eternity…I can't possibly budge from this fabulous spot. I'll be right here. Pick me up on your way out."

Edwin windmilled his arms. "This is a very large site, dearie. It's not like we can holler for you."

Quinton turned to Lily and asked quietly, "Who in the hell is 'them'? Who is Cat talking about?"

"Spirits, Quinton, spirits," Lily answered.

Cat pouted on the return trip; Edwin drove downhill like a local; Lily watched the terrain fly by. Quinton wrote in his notebook, "Only minor complications, so far."

Little did Quinton know.

■   ■   ■

Hiring Cat proved to be a huge mistake. Cat showed an uncanny ability to snafu the moment by distracting the models; by repositioning accessories; by rearranging Lily's charted, organized-by-model combinations. When Lily would gently redirect Cat's activity, Cat's outbursts were disruptive.

Lily vented to Grace in the privacy of their room at the Villa. "Why can't she just stick to helping you change outfits and repair makeup? She knows the magazine didn't hire her. She knows I'm giving her a chance to learn by watching."

"We're behind schedule, get her out from under my feet," Quinton protested to Lily. He wanted to tell Lily, "Get Cat off the set." But he knew the girls' relationship too well to expect compliance. Finally, driven beyond concern for female emotions, he told Lily flat out, "Cat is compromising the shoot. And our careers with it. Edwin can blackball us, and who could blame him!"

Quinton appreciated Lily's levelheaded reaction. Lily sent Cat on errands for inconsequential items, opening windows for serious accomplishment. Cat remained oblivious, chatting it up over their late dinners. She glowed, glass in hand, as she reminded Edwin of the "amazing" details she'd supplied, all of which perfected Quinton's "fabulous photos." And Edwin hadn't called anyone "sweetheart" for three whole days.

23. AMELIA

Amelia, Penn, and Deedee lugged their suitcases up the ramp to board the ferry. Amelia couldn't remember why they'd all made so many purchases in Sorrento. They had easily half-again the amount of luggage they'd started off with, and they hadn't even gotten to Capri and begun their shopping mission there.

She pushed her pragmatic self aside, and smelled the salty sea air. "Listen to the engines winding up. We'll be seeing the girls in just about an hour." She smiled. Amelia lurched a bit as the boat took off.

"Where are the life jackets?" Penn asked. Amelia sighed. Already Penn was fretting about the rocking waves.

"Let's grab a seat on the deck," Amelia suggested.

"Oh, I think we should stay close by our luggage," Penn cautioned her friends. "I don't see any security around here—after all, this is Italy, and the taxi driver warned us to keep a close watch."

"But I want to see the island when it comes into view," Amelia complained.

"We can stand at that rail right there and see everything." Penn gestured to a spot about a yard from where they stood.

"Listen here, ladies, I am not sittin' around lookin' at a bunch of bags." Deedee did not hide her exasperation. "My hair will turn into spun sugar in the wind and this muggy air. I know there's a bar down below. If y'all care to join me, I'd love to have you. If not, I'll see you when we dock."

"We're asking for trouble if we don't stick together," Penn said uneasily.

"And I'll get seasick if I go down below," Amelia added.

"And one of these days, I'm gonna teach y'all how to have fun!" Deedee threatened.

Amelia shook her head as Deedee flounced off. Deedee did what Deedee pleased—most of the time, anyway. In Sorrento Deedee had led the party. During the day she'd dragged them from shop to shop, encouraging them to make purchases for themselves and their families.

"When y'all think you're gonna get to Sorrento again in this life? Lordy, we'll be lucky if we get to go downtown once we're home. Let's do it right!"

After a late-afternoon rest, necessitated by the humid, hot weather, Deedee would coax them to stroll in the warm Italian evenings and nights. The shops along the streets would still be open, with colorful scarves and pottery, men and women's clothing, artwork, all set out to tempt tourists.

"Let's stop for a drink," she'd say and pull them into small *trattorias* and flirt with the waiters, asking for wine recommendations. Always charmed, the waiters would bring appetizers to the *bella* American ladies—appetizers that mysteriously did not appear on the check. "Heck, I could do this all night," Deedee would boast. And a few nights, they did.

Standing at the boat's rail, Amelia listened to Penn's little history lesson about Augustus and Tiberius and the early days of Capri. Penn had done her homework. She always did. Just like her parents had taught her.

"Sounds like Capri was quite the destination for those Romans lucky enough to get an invite. I think Deedee would have been in her element during those days." Amelia laughed.

Penn shivered. "Maybe I'm feeling a little over protective, but you should go check up on Deedee. It won't be long before we dock and we should be together. I'll stand guard."

"I'm sure she's fine, but I'll go check."

Amelia went downstairs to look for Deedee. The bar was a small space with some tables and a bar top with several stools. Sure enough, when Amelia peeked in, there sat Deedee on a bar stool, legs crossed, back arched—holding court. Three attractive men surrounded her, several umbrella drinks lined up on the bar counter behind her. Deedee laughed beguilingly. When she turned back around to the bar to sip her drink, one of the guys snapped her bra strap. Deedee shook a finger at him. Amelia could read her lips. "Naughty, naughty."

For a moment Amelia was reminded of her own mother, but she quickly rejected the thought. Deedee was a hardworking, sensible, stable girl. At times it was tough to deal with Ken Jr., but Amelia would never want to be burdened with Deedee's life.

"Deedee's doing just fine," Amelia reported back to Penn as the boat slowed and approached Marina Grande in Capri. White clouds punctuated the deep blue sky. Groups of birds soared above the dock and over the ocean, occasionally diving for food. The hydrofoil docked, and chains rattled as the gangway was lowered.

The captain's voice could be heard over the racket. "We are safely docked at Marina Grande. Passengers for Capri should disembark at this time."

"We're here, Penn. After all our planning, we're finally here. Capri!"

As the boat docked, passengers filed past Amelia and Penn, grabbing suitcases, walking down the ramp. The pile of baggage dwindled, the line of passengers disappeared.

"Where's Deedee? We're going to be the last to leave. Lily and Grace will think we've been shanghaied." Amelia bit her lip in consternation.

Penn softly mimicked Rosemary Clooney singing about being on a slow boat to the Far East, then checked her watch. "'Scuse me, but she really should be here by now. The girls will be waiting for us and sure to worry."

"Shall we grab our stuff and go? We can connect with Lily and wait for Deedee on the dock."

"No! We're supposed to stick together. We need to wait right here so she can find us." Penn wasn't budging.

A few minutes later, when theirs were the only suitcases remaining, Amelia was aggravated. "Okay, she's pushing it now…"

Before Amelia could finish, a glowing Deedee emerged. She held up a cocktail napkin and assured her three beaux, who appeared behind her, "I've got the name right here. See y'all real soon."

Joining her friends, she said, "I've got a special feelin' about this trip."

24. GRACE

Grace stood alongside Lily and Cat, watching their friends disembark the ferry. Grace thought Lily seemed to shimmer with excitement at the reunion, and noted that Cat had adopted a nonchalant European air these last few days. Grace was glad the others were finally here. Work was behind them and an exciting adventure was ahead.

Hugs were exchanged, a flurry of comments and questions ensued: "How was the job?" "How was Sorrento?" "You look beautiful." "Tell us everything."

Finally, Grace announced, "Enough of this here. We can catch up at the Villa."

Lily gave her friends another hug. "We have refreshments waiting. The gardens are just lovely. There's even a romantic trysting spot with a fountain and a bronze statue of Pan. Water flows from his pan pipes as he plays. He's enticing the local nymphs, I suppose."

"That would be us!" Cat said laughingly as if she had become a young nymph there amongst the trees and flowers of Capri.

"I can't wait for you to see it all," Lily added.

"Ummm…there any chance we can see it just a wee bit later?" Deedee asked.

"What do you mean, later?" Grace quizzed. "You've got somewhere else to be?"

"Kinda sorta. I thought it'd be nice to stop at this place called the Tavern first and have a drink and do some socializin' there. I met some interestin' people on the ferry. They're gonna be there, and they invited me to bring my friends."

"What an excellent suggestion," Cat quickly responded.

Grace knew how eager Lily was to share Villa Bianco with their friends. Turning to Lily, she asked, "Are you okay with that?"

"If that's what everyone wants to do, of course it's fine with me. We have time for a drink."

"An authentic tavern on Capri—sounds quaint," Penn said. "And something else to check off my list of things to see."

Grace signaled for a taxi.

▨   ▨   ▨

"Can you take all of us and our luggage?" Amelia asked the driver, who stood waiting next to the open taxi door. He shrugged. Lily translated for him. He smiled and motioned everyone to jump in, then set about loading their suitcases.

Grace squished herself tighter against the taxi door. She tried to make some breathing room for Lily, who was sitting next to the driver—the driver who must've consumed a considerable amount of garlic shortly before picking them up. The road, not a term Grace would use for this donkey path, was narrow, cobblestoned, and bumpy, with a splattering of side-view mirrors along its edges. Like most of the taxies in Capri, its mirrors had been clipped off during some other harrowing ride.

Penn, Amelia, Deedee, and Cat all sat in back: half-cheek on the seat, half-cheek on the person next to them. Amelia was the recipient of Penn's sharp nails in her thigh as the taxi careened around the corners.

"Yow!" Amelia hollered out, momentarily halting Lily's tour tips. "Stop it, Penn! We are not going to die—we're on vacation."

Grace rolled the window down farther and stuck her head out, hearing Cat begin her spiel. "This is nothing. Believe me, this guy is good. You'll get used to it." Cat, ever confident in her own limited experience, loved being the voice of reason. "We've had real scares since we arrived. Wait till you ride the buses!"

"Do y'all think they serve Jack and Coke in this country?" Deedee poked at Grace to get her attention. "I could use some refreshments about ten minutes ago. Where the heck is this place? Bob made it sound like it was real close to everythin'!"

"Almost there," Grace called back over her shoulder.

At Piazza Umberto the taxi screeched to a halt with such force, it threw Penn right into the back of Lily's head. "You still think this guy is good?" Penn shot at Cat as she made her getaway from the taxi.

"We're safe, sweetie; now you can relax," said Amelia as she shepherded Penn into the piazza. "I need a bottle of wine!"

Grace watched Cat lead Amelia, Penn, and Deedee off to the Tavern, while the taxi driver unloaded suitcases. She looked over at Lily, who was paying the driver, and shook her head.

"Yoohoo, ladies. We're not your personal porters," Grace reminded the newcomers.

"What? We gotta walk with our suitcases? To the bar?" Deedee asked in surprise.

"Uh, yeah," said Grace with a hint of sarcasm. "There are no cars allowed in the piazza, and you chose to come to this dive to meet some 'interestin' people' instead of going up to the Villa and having wine and antipasti like Lily had planned." She and Lily helped the others carry their suitcases past the clock tower to the bar known as the Tavern.

The proprietor stood just inside the door. He informed Lily of the cover charge, who then translated the news back to the women. "You've got to be kidding me!" Grace exclaimed. "How much? Just to go in and spend more money on wine?" This was never part of her plan.

Penn did some calculations and made a notation in her small note-book, then informed the group, "It's the equivalent of fifteen dollars per person. Somehow lira doesn't seem like real money. It looks like play money from a kids' game."

After collecting the admittance fee and accepting a large tip from Deedee, the proprietor agreed to keep a close watch on their luggage at the coat rack.

Once inside the dark smoky establishment, they found a large table in the corner to accommodate them. The Tavern housed a variety of patrons: local men, who'd been working all day but weren't ready to face wives, children, or Mama just yet. And tan, sophisticated young couples, whose clothing and jewelry Grace found impressive—very European, very fashion forward, very expensive.

Penn and Amelia, the least traveled of us, must find their style intimidating, Grace thought.

"Bring us chips and pretzels with our drinks," Cat directed the waiter. He nodded and smiled, but no chips and pretzels accompanied the drinks. Cat tried again, asking for chips and pretzels while mimicking munching motions. The waiter smiled and nodded.

"Bob! Bob! Hey, Bob! I'm over here! I brought my friends!" Deedee stood on her chair and waved her arms. Surprised by the power of Deedee's normally calm Southern drawl, Grace had a quick thought to duck under the table, while Cat surreptitiously plumped her breasts in her Wonderbra and sat up a little straighter. Three American men made their way over to Deedee, now standing on the floor with outstretched arms. "I want y'all to meet my friends."

"Have you been holding out, Deedee?" Cat pouted. "Hi, I'm Catherine San Carlo. Get a glass, have some wine. Now me, I prefer Campari; Italian bitters aren't popular in the States, but they're a staple here." More glasses, more wine, more chairs. The newcomers settled easily into the circle while introductions were made.

Deedee sat close to Bob. Mick positioned himself between Amelia and Lily; Jax dragged a chair over and sat himself between Grace and Penn. Grace could tell from her friends' posture and quiet demeanor that they were as ill at ease as she. But not Deedee and not Cat. Cat shone, sitting next to Bob, her back toward Grace.

"A photo shoot," was Cat's response to the inevitable question.

"So, you're all models?" asked Mick.

A knowing "We could see that coming a mile away," look passed between Amelia and Penn.

"Heavens, no! Lily is a men's clothing designer—Antonio Caldo! Ever heard of it?" Grace was indignant that anyone should cast her friends as mere models. After all, their talents far exceeded hers, didn't they?

Attempting to further the conversation, Jax tried another tack. "We're staying on Anacapri at the San Michele. How about you?"

Deedee jumped in. "A villa, somewhere, kind of in that direction... right, Lily?" She waved vaguely in the air.

"Anacapri, you say? Home to Axel Munthe's Villa San Michele." Penelope knew her facts. "And just what *is it* you do?"

"Delta, Delta, United! We navigate the friendly skies!" Bob indicated each man in turn.

Grace silently scoffed; she thought these guys looked the epitome of pilots, with their styled hair and mustaches!

"You're male stewardesses?" asked Penn slyly, provoking a smirk and small snort from Amelia.

Not as unsophisticated as she pretended, Amelia commented, "We had a couple of them on the flight over. So much more accommodating than the women. Didn't you think, Penn?"

"They're pilots, ladies." Cat turned to the men. "I knew that as soon as you walked in. Sorry, they don't get out much!" Cat wasn't one to let a male ego lag.

A local fisherman approached Cat, then whisked her off to dance. Deedee and Bob followed a moment later.

"You're one hot number," Bob blurted out to Deedee, trying to be heard.

Grace heard him alright.

Deedee slipped her arms around Bob's neck, giving him a sexy smile. Her hands slid down his back, stopped at his butt. Deedee pulled Bob closer and their hips gyrated together, answering the primal demand of the Euro disco music.

Grace leaned to Lily. "Look at this, will you." But Lily seemed not to hear. She sat immobilized, staring at the pockets on Bob's tight jeans. Staring at Deedee's brightly manicured nails digging into Bob's undulating buttocks.

Mick leaned in closer to Amelia and gazed into her face. "Julie Christie's got nothing on you, and she's a ten in my book." Amelia turned away, embarrassed, but flattered.

Jax turned to Grace. "So you really are a model?"

Grace's spine stiffened. "And you really are a stewardess?"

Grace felt cantankerous. Amelia and Penn were engaged in one-on-one conversation with Mick and Jax, no longer offended by their attentions. As her friends' unease declined, hers increased. The Tavern was starting to feel claustrophobic to her. It was harder to breathe as the smoke grew heavier and the press of dancers tighter. Passing time brought more patrons, more heat, more smoke.

Grace reminded herself of five-year old Jemima, who knew better than to squirm, but had difficulty holding still. Rising, she slung her purse over her shoulder and signaled to Lily by slicing a finger across her throat. Lily nodded, then announced, "It's time to leave. Quinton is coming for pre-dinner drinks, and I've instructed Marie Elena to serve dinner at nine. I know you must be famished and exhausted."

Deedee returned to the table with Bob. "It's early. Can't we stay a little later? There'll be live music in a little bit."

"I can bring any of you home later," Bob offered.

"No, thanks," said Grace.

"Deedee bug, we're all ready to go," said Amelia. "We have lots of days ahead, honey."

Bob lifted Deedee's hand, kissed it, then pressed her hand to her own lips. Grace tried not to snort. Did Deedee even notice what a smarmy move that was?

▨   ▨   ▨

The taxi ride to the Villa did little to alleviate Grace's discomfort. Her friends were abuzz with talk about the pilots. She certainly hadn't seen anything special about any of them, nor had she been looking. "Barhopping wasn't on my to-do list. I'd be crushed if Marc was out flirting with starlets."

Penn discreetly nudged Amelia, who rolled her eyes. "Sweetie, that's the least of your worries."

"This whole thing was Deedee's idea," Penn defended herself. "And I wasn't flirting."

"Go ahead and blame me, but I can hardly believe how this trip is goin'. Simply thrillin' and I'm lovin' every minute of it."

"Acting like giddy geese, if you ask me," Lily said.

"Don't listen to Lily, she's been the taskmaster from hell," Cat announced. "Kudos, Deedee. You brought some fun. Finally."

"Yes, but that kind of fun could lead us fundamentally off track," Lily declared.

"Ahhh, now Lily, don't get your knickers twisted. Shoot, it's been a coon's age since a gent took the time to rev my engines."

"Deedee, you don't have to listen to Lily," Cat said, a bit smugly. "After all, this is *your* vacation too."

Grace wished she'd kept her mouth closed. She hadn't meant to start a discussion, she simply wanted it known that *she* wasn't on board to repeat this evening's activities. The taxi came to a quick stop.

"Here we are. Villa Bianco." Lily gestured proudly to the ornate entrance gate.

2 5 . LILY

Each of the six, Lily the eldest at thirty-five, shared twelve years or so years of friendship, motherhood, and Southern California addresses, and each found her passion quickening in the fierce orange sunset. Something about the familiar-—the aromatic scent of lemons, the delicate tint of hydrangeas, the brilliance of birds of paradise—exuded the exotic here, set against the reflective expanse of sea far below.

Lily surprised herself. She felt strangely possessive, almost proud, as if Villa Bianco held the most significance to her. Luminaires lit a meandering path toward the Villa's terrace, where tall glass doors glowed with a promise of hospitality. Lily savored the approach while hauling Deedee's duffle. Grace walked beside her, carrying Amelia's garment bag and Penn's Dopp kit. Penn, Amelia, and Deedee, giggling like teenagers, followed Cat, who hurried ahead, urging them on.

"This hacienda is breathtakin'," Deedee gushed, dragging a new suitcase filled with purchases from Sorrento.

Grace corrected her. "It's a *villa*, Deedee. We're in Italy."

Mario met them in the entry and began carrying their luggage upstairs.

"We can settle in after dinner," Cat said. "Come look at our work now."

The wives greeted Quinton warmly. He was, after all, a familiar face in this distant land and a good friend to boot. He continued spreading Polaroid prints on the long sideboard. Responding to their interest in these, he differentiated between the locations—Marina Piccolo, the Phoenician Steps, Villa Jovis, and Medieval Capri.

Cat began rearranging the photos, but was overcome with coughing. Quinton turned to her, looking concerned.

"Are you okay? Need some water, Cat?"

Marie Elena, the young uniformed domestic, scurried into the dining room with a tray of water and wine. She poured Cat a glass of water; she lingered, also intrigued by the photos.

Lily grabbed an HB pencil and tablet from her multi-pocketed vest. She began sketching. Her friends and their days of relaxation ahead were erased, temporarily. Pure geometry spoke to her from the captured images. And it ensnared her.

Penn, Amelia, and Deedee, wine in hand, chose their favorite shots, exclaiming favorably about the Italian models, Lily's fashions, and Grace's appearance.

Amelia picked up a photo. "Look at Grace in this embroidered midi. And I love that scarf on you, Grace, twisted into a rose."

"My styling, my styling, thank you, thank you!" Cat curtsied right and left, expecting applause.

Quinton joined Lily, startling her. "It will be interesting to see which ones the magazine prints," he said quietly.

Lily looked up from her sketch, trying to read Quinton's face. Was he pleased? She answered, but not too quickly. "Hard to say. Because they all look exceptional." And after another pause, she continued sketching.

Penn held up three photos. "Grace, you look ethereal in these."

"That diva, Edwin, almost ruined the airy effect, but I stood strong," Cat piped up. "Grace, you can thank me anytime. God, am I good."

Cat curtsied again. Lily's pencil point snapped off from the pressure she applied to it. Cat's behavior rankled her, to say the least. Grace and Quinton shared a look of exasperation.

When Marie Elena headed into the kitchen, Lily and Grace followed.

"Remind me. Just how *did* Cat convince you to hire her?" Grace asked peevishly.

Lily looked heavenward and rolled her eyes.

Marie Elena looked heavenward and rolled her eyes—as if she could understand the situation, even with *her* brief history with Cat.

Lily spied a carpenter's pencil on the counter. She picked it up and resumed her sketching again, thinking out loud. "Pockets angled just so, and yes, double topstitching along the fold."

Grace dipped a heel of crusty bread into a bowl of olive oil. She ate slowly, and finishing, licked the slick drops from her fingers. Then joining Marie Elena, who stood spoon in hand at the stove, Grace inhaled the risotto's steaming aroma.

The back door opened with a friendly squeak. A gentleman entered. So Lily thought, although the *supposed* gentleman wore a ribbed undershirt tucked into rumpled trousers. A humble workman's outfit. He withdrew his straw hat, exposing a tumble of black wavy hair. He was fortyish, Lily presumed, but carried himself with the elegant posture of a young gymnast.

He nodded courteously to Lily and Grace before he addressed Marie Elena in Italian.

"Marie Elena, *hai visto il mio matita?*"

Lily understood the man's question; he was looking for his pencil. Lily looked at the pencil in her hand. She gasped softly. She had picked this one up just moments ago. A flat carpenter's pencil, not her own HB. Embarrassed, Lily extended the pencil to the stranger.

He nodded to Lily. "*Scusi*, where are my manners? My name is Angelo, and I thank you for the return of my writing instrument."

"*Mi scusi!* My name is Lily, *non era niente*," she answered, apologizing too, and accepting his thanks. Angelo reached out to take said item. Lily noticed darkness under his eyes. His face was creased with smile lines, but he wore no smile just now. Their hands touched as they exchanged the pencil.

Inexplicable electricity charged the room. Grace and Marie Elena turned in unison, called by the same thunderous silence. As if the pencil were a lightning rod, Angelo and Lily stared at each other with a soul mate's connection.

From the dining room, Deedee's voice broke into the space. "Lily, Grace, can y'all get your backsides in here? Quinton's fixin' to leave."

■   ■   ■

"*Il pranzo e preparato*, dinner is ready, shall I serve?" Marie Elena asked Lily. Lily sensed that the four loud-talking, foreign young women in the dining room intimidated the domestic.

Marie Elena set the meal buffet style on the table and backed into the kitchen, wiping her hands on her apron.

"No salad bowls?" Amelia asked, heading for the kitchen. "We can't put everything on one plate."

"Lily, is this the only wine available? I thought something a bit heartier, less fruity, you know." Cat examined the bottles with what appeared to be a touch of disdain.

"Yup, that's it!" Lily's tone was undeniably curt.

Penn hugged Grace. "You can eat now, okay? Eat hearty," she said, and then to Cat, "because as gorgeous as she is, she looks skeletal."

"I could eat risotto every night of the week! Where'd Marie Elena learn to cook?" Grace took a dainty spoonful of the rice and vegetable blend.

"If she's not careful, those caverns around her clavicle are going to fill in," said Penn, who placed a thick slice of crusty bread on her plate before passing the basket on to Cat.

"Her mother and grandmother," said Lily.

"What?" asked Cat.

"That's who taught Marie Elena to cook."

"Oh, right. Some people have mothers who care, take time with them, show them how to do things." Cat reached for olive oil.

Deedee shook her head. "Some of us have mamas who were never well enough to teach us." With a nod to Lily, she continued, "Some of us didn't have a mama at all, but we learned anyway and are none the worse for it."

Dinner continued with the back and forth chatter usually present among the group. At Cat's request Marie Elena was about to open a fourth bottle of wine when Lily suggested they settle into their rooms first and then rejoin for Limoncello in the sitting room.

"Bob said he'd be callin' me this evenin'. I wonder what time he was thinkin' he could call till? It's almost eleven o'clock. I'd say that's too late, wouldn't y'all?"

■　　■　　■

Cat and Deedee each had a room to themselves. Cat appeared from her private haven, makeup removed and hair flattened by a barrette, Wonderbra back in the drawer. New pink satin pj's, purchased just that afternoon, flattered her green eyes. "First minute I've had to relax in days. Lily's a tough taskmaster." Peering into Amelia and Penn's shared room, she added with authority, "Gnats are vicious at night, best to close your shutters."

Penn flared, mouthing to Amelia, "If I wanted her advice, I'd—" as she continued to make tidy stacks of neatly folded polo shirts and tailored Bermuda shorts. Each of her drawers was now lined with scented striped paper, which she'd generously supplied for Amelia's bureau as well. Three cardigans, khaki, navy, and white with matching belts, and new white socks folded in pairs, lay on the bed awaiting their assigned spaces.

Amelia, seven black dresses draped over her arm, seemed oblivious to Penn's irritation., "I can't believe it, we're here on the Isle of Capri!"

A bit later, Lily, looking refreshed in a white peasant dress with Mount-mellick embroidery, gathered her friends in the salon.

"C'mon, Deedee! A toast to our long-awaited fantasy vacation." Marie Elena served dessert and Limoncello; she also placed a carafe of wine and glasses on the liquor cabinet. She hovered quietly.

"My dream, getting to Italy with George," Penn mused. "But here I am with you. And there he is with three boys, twelve casseroles, and a Chore Wheel."

Deedee, dressed in red lingerie, zydeco danced down the stairway, sing-ing. "I'm wantin' one, y'all. A toe-tappin', washboard-strokin', harmonica-squealin', crazy on the bayou, buzzin', son-ova-gun. Gumbo jumbo, Grace, come dance with me." Deedee and Grace danced a two-step, side by side, clapping and singing.

Lily raised a small chilled glass filled with lemony nectar, saying, "A toast to our Enchanted August."

"And luscious Limoncello, yum!" Grace added.

Deedee downed the small glass of Limoncello and poured herself another.

"Deedee, why are you so chipper? If the shine you've taken to that pilot is any indication, you're practically on the verge of your second divorce!" Cat spoke her mind with no restraint.

"Oh, hush up. Is it all that obvious?" Deedee asked. "It's dang hard dealin' with Hugh and my mama. Accordin' to him, I'm a fabulous daughter but a less than mediocre wife."

"He said that to you?" Grace looked shocked.

"Oh, that an' more, to be sure!" Deedee drained her second glass of liqueur.

Lily observed Deedee's blithe drinking. "You might want to slow down on that Limoncello, it's meant as an after-dinner digestive. Combining it with all your wine at dinner could prove disastrous."

"I've only been gone a couple a' days, and already I'm feelin' this big weight off my chest. I haven't felt this free since before…"

"Great! Maybe we can get a two-for-one at the divorce lawyer's." Cat found the wine and poured some into fresh glasses, one for Deedee and one for herself.

"Divorce?" Lily whispered. "Cat, don't joke like that!"

"Joke? You think I'm joking? Pietro is no saint. You see his charming side. It's an act. A good one, but an act nonetheless. If you could hear the way he talks to me in private; scolds me for shop improvements, tells me that Noni has had it with me spending the profits! Had it with me? Beppe's would be *nothing* without me. Who designs the amazing windows? Who arranges the tables and shelves? Who imports quaint crockery to dress it all up? Do you think Pietro ever once praises me?"

"Just a shot in the dark here, but I'm guessing not," Penn quietly commented to Amelia.

Cat's tirade, which had begun in anger, dissipated into discouragement and hopelessness.

It was painful for Lily to witness.

"Well, none of our men are flawless, but *divorce*? That's pretty drastic. Don't you think it's important to keep the family together? What about counseling?" Amelia offered.

"Obviously *you* think it's better to be stripped of your pride!" Cat retorted.

"Hey, if it's that bad, dump the baggage! Take it from me, it doesn't get better!" Deedee pushed the carafe across the low coffee table to Cat.

"Maybe I'm wrong…but I think Cat has it pretty good. Pietro may not be without fault. Who is? But he *is* an attentive father."

Penn sounded both apologetic *and* antagonistic to Lily.

"You don't get it do you? I have talent and Beppe's showcases it. Those doors would close without me! Lily, look at the difference I made to the shoot—even Quinton was impressed. My first job as a stylist and I kicked ass!"

"You do have talent and we're all in awe of your styling; you set an unequaled table, for sure." Lily chose not to address Cat's work on Capri.

"With all of his calls, Pietro has never mentioned missing me at the store!" Cat pouted.

"Seems to me that men are just men, Cat, I think we expect too much from them. Like I said before, maybe we wives bear some blame as well." Lily's voice of objectivity triggered a loud scoff from Cat.

"Really, Lily? So you believe if you were a better wife, Dirk would... what? Stay off the golf course? Spend more time with you and Callie?"

"That blond pilot Jax sure has a cute ass," Deedee piped up.

Lily flinched. An unwanted memory pushed its way through a cocoon of haze. A memory was unwrapping itself like bandages winding away from a wounded limb.

Penn ignored Deedee and addressed Amelia, who hunkered on an oversized tapestry pillow. "Jax said he worked for Delta, so where were his wings?"

"What's wrong with you, gal? Checkin' for wings?" Deedee challenged.

"I love it, I love it, I love it! Getting away from Ken Jr., talking about cute asses." Amelia took several swallows of her Limoncello.

Penn obviously knew the latest about Amelia's domestic situation. "Maybe I shouldn't say anything, but Ken Jr.'s so blasted lucky to have Amelia—"

"Sweetie, you have no idea how much I need this getaway. *And* Ken Jr. needs to know how good he's got it with me. Absence making one fonder and all that."

"*Again?*" Deedee moaned. "I thought Ken Jr. promised to call it off with her last—"

"He did. We cried and made up. He broke it off, but here she is calling the night before my flight. Oh, he knows how upset I am, didn't give him what he wanted in bed before I left."

"Aren't you worried about him now? I wouldn't leave Marc horny." Grace's voice dropped an octave with her last sentence.

"Doll face, with four kids in tow, he can't stray far!" Amelia sounded tough. "I lined up a sitter daytimes only. He's on duty nights and the entire Labor Day weekend too. Tough patooties."

Amelia shifted the focus to Lily. "So what's Dirk up to in your absence?"

"Golf, what else?" Lily disciplined her voice; it sounded convincingly matter-of-fact to her. As she intended. But a riptide of fear was threatening her composure.

"Barely made it to the hospital for your hysterectomy," Grace spoke up. "Golf's his mistress!"

Lily defended Dirk. "I know. It hurt my feelings. But maybe I don't give him enough attention. Do you think we wives create, generate, in a way, our husband's behavior? I'm always so busy."

Deedee stopped dancing and stomped her foot. "Y'all are treadin' on my last nerve here. When are you gonna wake up?"

"Ah, come on, Lily," Cat said.

"Sweetie, men do cheat," Amelia added.

Penn, looking angry, turned to Cat. "Maybe I shouldn't say so, but I could never be married to Dirk! The way he criticizes Lily, and look at her, here on Capri. Dang, she deserves…"

Lily ignored Penn's loyalty. Dirk was Dirk. She'd married him for better or worse, mostly worse. These past few years she cringed more frequently under his raging temper and looked forward to his long absences from the office; was she not somehow to blame? Business and raising Callie took her best energy.

Lily stiffened. She could not escape the hazy image that suddenly floated free. There was Darleen. Darleen squeezing Dirk's ass at the watercooler. Darleen stroking the plaid on Dirk's madras shorts, twisting the button on his hip pocket with her long, painted nails.

Lily put her hands over her face. Something else troubling appeared.

"Lily. Lily?" Grace scooted in beside Lily on the settee.

Lily looked up. Her friends gazed back, their faces contorted with concern and curiosity. "I found a note," she began. "Dirk was taking Darleen to MoonShadow. She'd been working so hard to help me get ready. I told myself it was just a bonus."

"Shoot! I think *bone* might be the only part you got right," Deedee said.

Shyly, Marie Elena refreshed everyone's drinks.

Deedee knelt in front of Lily and took her hands. "Lily bug, I'm gonna fess up. Remember how we always declined hot tubbin' at group therapy? Well, one night when you stayed home with flu, I found the light in that hot tub."

Years ago, Deedee had strong-armed Lily, and the two had embarked on group therapy. Lily was strengthened by the gruff Bohemian guru who led the sessions in his modest living room; from his unflinching use of Freudian and Gestalt techniques, Lily grasped the concept of personal responsibility for her problems. Deedee related better to his young, witty assistant, whose hugs and backrubs brought comfort. If not revelation.

Lily and Deedee had both modestly eschewed the invitation for group nude hot tubbing that followed each emotional session. Until one night Deedee—without Lily's prudish influence—agreed to enter the swirling foam. She discovered a pertinent truth about life's choices. And Deedee spared no details describing the event now.

"You all undressed in the living room?" Lily asked, shocked. "Weren't you embarrassed?"

"Honey chile, I'm tellin' you, it felt *fine* going bare assed. I divorced number one and stepped off my cross. You can tug those nails out too."

Lily pulled her knees up to her chest.

Grace rubbed Lily's back. "Shh, shh, shh," she repeated softly.

Deedee rose; she reached out to hug Lily. Without explanation she turned pale, leaned over the antique vase beside the settee, and vomited loudly into it.

Marie Elena, looking aghast, rushed from the room. Lily could only hope the domestic went for cleaning supplies.

Deedee fell to her knees. She wiped her mouth with the back of her hand.

"Dang! Bob doesn't have our number."

2 6. CAT

It was 3:22 a.m., the very first night of their Enchanted August. And Cat was awakened by the sounds of moaning. "What could possibly be wrong?"

Throwing on her silk kimono, she followed the distress signals. They led her to the large blue-tiled bathroom down the hall. She knocked softly once, then opened the door without waiting for an answer.

Amelia and Penn were on their hands and knees wiping up the floor with large towels. Grace and Lily flanked the toilet and bidet. The moaning came from Deedee, who lay curled up in a tight ball on the cold tile.

Cat felt alarmed at first. And then left out. "What's going on?"

"Forgive me for stating the obvious, but everyone is sick," Penn said.

"Everyone? Is it a bug? I feel okay—well, a little the worse for being woken from a good sleep—but okay."

Amelia began to fill in the blanks. "We're not feeling great ourselves, but we aren't sick, just helping out. They woke us too."

"Deedee looks half dead; you drank a lot tonight, huh?" No answer. Cat moved on with her interrogation. "Grace, are you sick?"

Grace shook her head, eyes downcast. "My stomach is upset, that's all."

Well, of course your stomach hurts! Cat thought to herself. *You ate a meal for once.* But she kept the allegation to herself and nodded sympathetically.

"Lily? How are you doing? Sick?"

Lily nodded. "Not at my best."

"Grace, get off your rump and come with me," Cat ordered. She knew that fresh air and a little walking would help Grace more than hanging over a toilet.

"What are you going to do, sweetie?" Amelia asked. "Need any help?"

"No!" Deedee squeaked out in a small voice. "Don't anyone leave! Y'all be talkin' about me and I'm dyin', I'm really dyin'!" Amelia and Penn immediately hovered, soothing her.

Cat led Grace to the kitchen. Grace leaned against the door frame holding her belly, while Cat gathered a scant bowl of ice and several tea towels. "Take some deep breaths," Cat said. "I know it's painful to overeat. But you'll survive."

Grace remained silent.

Cat posed a question, as if Grace had more answers than she. "What do you suppose is wrong with Lily? It's not like her to drink too much. Do you think she's got the flu…or is it something she ate?"

"It's Dirk. Little things are adding up, making sense."

"She needed to be thousands of miles from home to see what's been right in front of her face? It's been obvious, but none of us would say it." Cat's tone softened with compassion for her friend. "Our sweet Lily. She'll need to take action."

Once back in the bathroom, Cat tended to Lily, wiping her face with a cold, soft tea towel, urging her to sip water, gently patting her back.

"It'll be okay, you'll see. Everything's going to be fine. We're all here for you. You know that, don't you?" Cat put her arm around Lily, who nodded and leaned against her. Lily was pale and limp.

Cat hadn't expected this response. What would accompany Lily's discovery of Dirk's perfidy? Cat assumed there'd be anger, outrage. Some fiery discourse. This was *Lily*, after all. Strong, independent, smart Lily. But there she was, beaten up with sadness.

Now they all sat together on the intricate mosaic of tiled floor, pouring out love and support.

"Sweetie, I know how badly this hurts," Amelia said.

Cat knew that Amelia was addressing Lily's pain from firsthand knowledge.

"It feels like a violation, a rape of your spirit," Amelia continued. "I know about piecing trust back together. It doesn't happen without a price, sugar. It's a sacrifice I've made for those four little miracles Ken Jr. and I created. But knowing Ken Jr. might be digging his spade in another garden…the anger I push down, it all takes its toll."

"My God, Amelia! Where *is* your pride? Don't you know you deserve better? You've let Ken Jr. treat you like old carpet!" Cat was exasperated by the inequity of it all. She had a few ideas of what she might do to Ken Jr. if she were in Amelia's position. Her friend was a loving, faithful wife and homemaker, a wonderful mother. Ken Jr. was a first-class moron.

"Cat, honey, I'm the only one who can decide what's best for my children. What comfort is pride if I can't provide food for the kids? What kind of a mother doesn't put her kids and home first?"

"Maybe it's just me, and I could be wrong, but doesn't it seem like men are born to be unfaithful?" Penn asked. "Not that it's right, of course. I mean, I'm sure we all think cheating is despicable. At least I do. But don't men seem to have a predilection for it? I don't see that trait in women, do you?"

"I wish Ryan *had* cheated, I'd've been able to bail out sooner. But no, ol' Ryan was home every night, 'bout as excitin' as farina." Deedee was returning to normal, sitting propped up against the tub, an ice-filled tea towel at her forehead. "Lily girl, you know I love you better than my own sister. When're you gonna listen to me? Look at Amelia here. She can tell you, once the stud gets a taste of a different mare, his appetite is never gonna be the same."

"And that's a mouthful of wisdom if I ever heard one!" Cat clucked.

"I think I'll make some coffee and wait for sunrise in the garden. Anyone care to join me?" Grace seemed anxious; she looked around for a willing companion.

"I'll join you," Cat said, feeling generous, "and I know how to use the espresso machine!" But Cat was filled with questions she chose not to voice—not right now, anyway. *What's bothering you besides a full stomach, my skinny friend? Has the conversation stirred up something? Would Marc ever cheat on you? Fortunately, Pietro will never cheat on me. He's not built that way.*

But about Marc cheating on Grace, Cat had her suspicions.

27. AMELIA

Marie Elena stood at the door, hesitant to break up the breakfast conversation. *"Me scusi, è importante. Signora San Carlo, c'è una telfonata per lei. Il signor."*

Just how many times could Pietro call? Amelia wondered. She knew he'd never agreed to his wife traveling to a foreign country, and Cat complained that he'd called several times since their arrival. Amelia was glad Ken Jr. wasn't keeping tabs on her.

Cat slapped her juice glass down; sticky drops splattered the table. "That's just great! Pietro's called ten times with stupid questions that any father could answer. He probably can't figure out which soccer field Jason's playing on. Wait till he gets the phone bill. He won't be so quick to criticize my spending." She stomped her way to the telephone.

In the other room, Cat's voice rose. "How could you let it happen? Why didn't you call me sooner? Oh, *now* you have it under control!" And in a final crescendo, "I'll call you tomorrow!" There could be no doubt the receiver had been slammed into its cradle.

Cat's return to the room was marked with sobs. "Jason and Leo were sword fighting. With palm fronds. Jason has a tear on his cornea! He's at Valley Presbyterian Hospital."

"Will his vision be affected?" Grace asked, sounding afraid of the answer.

"Thankfully not. He'll have to wear a patch till it heals, though."

Amelia put her arm around Cat soothingly. "I'll call the airlines and make a reservation. Lily has the ferry schedule; we can coordinate this for you." She couldn't imagine the angst Cat must be experiencing. Why, if it were one of her four darlings...

"I'm not leaving. Jason's going to be fine. He'll be released in a couple of hours." Cat recovered rapidly.

"But dear, don't you think Jason will be asking for you?" Amelia queried.

"Noni San Carlo is there to nurse him when he gets out of the hospital; there isn't much I can do for him."

Penn piped up with an appropriate song—some verses about a home where the mother-in-law left the couple alone. Amelia frowned at Penn for being insensitive and was glad when Grace, who normally accompanied Penn in song, did not join in on this occasion.

"Cat, sweetie, I'm sure you'd feel better if you were with him," Amelia advised.

"I've worked my backside off for Lily. I deserve this time. It isn't fair if I have to leave now. The rest of you get to stay and I should go?"

"An accident is hardly Pietro's fault," Penn quietly remarked. "I mean, who can watch a kid every single second? Especially wild boys. It's not for me to say, but Cat's a far cry from my mother." She pierced a slice of banana with her fork.

Amelia hoped Cat hadn't heard. If so, it wouldn't go well.

But Cat had not missed Penn's aside. She was ready to spar. "I *am* a good mother. I'm certainly a better mother than I had."

Lily tried to soothe Cat. "Well, it would be very sad for us all if you were to leave now. Mothers are important, but dads can step up to the plate when they have to. I know that from experience. Pietro will do fine."

Amelia didn't agree with Lily—no way could Ken Jr. do her job. She had inherited the nurturing gene that entirely missed her mother.

"Cat, honey, we know you're a good mother. Heavens, everyone had a better mother than mine. My mom could drink a NASCAR driver under the table. She was proud that six-year-old *me* did my own laundry."

Personally, Amelia thought Grace had the least to complain about, with a beautiful mother who supported Grace almost unconditionally. Hope could be a little tough on Grace when it came to the weigh-in, but she'd certainly understood when Grace decided she was in love with Marc. Why, she'd even convinced a skeptical Jimbo that young Grace *was* ready to be married. And although Grace was beautiful and undoubtedly a catch, Hope had almost certainly given Grace a tip or two on how to lasso her man.

Penn didn't have it too bad either, Amelia reflected. Penn's Mummy just wanted to spend more time with Penn. So what if Mummy called on the first of each month and scheduled dates to get together with her only daughter? It was so vexing to Penn, she wouldn't answer the phone, but Mummy wouldn't give up. At least Mummy had her health.

Then there was poor Deedee. Amelia wouldn't know how to deal with Deedee's mama. If there were a more sour face in Southern California, Amelia didn't know where she'd seen it. Deedee had been stuck with sickly Mama for years.

Deedee never admitted it, but Amelia was pretty sure Ryan White was thrilled when Deedee gave him his walking papers. He no longer had to put up with Mama's screeching and whining about all her aches and pains. Amelia had even overheard him complain to his brother, Dirk, that Mama was an albatross around his neck. As sick as she was, she was too ornery to just die. No doubt, even the devil didn't want her.

Amelia had a theory about Cat's relationship with her mother. Cat's sense of entitlement was a simple survival mechanism. Cat had a blonde, blue-eyed, dimpled, younger sister who was the sunshine in her mother's life. Petite Anne Michelle got to wear pinks and blues; chubby Catherine was stuck in yellows and greens. Anne Michelle wore matching ribbons in her long Alice-style hair; pixie-shorn Catherine got bobby pins to tame her cowlick. It was no mystery to Amelia why Cat felt she deserved the brass ring.

Amelia sadly looked at Lily. "You lost your mom so early, Lily bug. How hard that must've been for you."

"I was just twelve," Lily said softly. "If I'd known, understood how sick she was, maybe I wouldn't have been so sassy to her. Every so often I'm caught off guard by a song. Like someone singing 'For All We Know' on the radio. Well, Mother hummed while we washed supper dishes. And that was a favorite. I'd give a lot to hear her sing once more."

"Oh, I've heard *my* mother's voice," Cat informed her friends. "I've even *seen* her."

Amelia's sense of pragmatism was offended; she couldn't disguise her sneer before Cat caught her skeptic look. Penn's face also reflected disbelief.

"How come y'all didn't think to bring it up before this?" Deedee probed. "Seems like seein' an' talkin' to your dead mama might be worth a mention. When did this all start? I'd like to know, just in case my mama decides she wants to come back and haunt me."

Sensing undesirable territory ahead, Amelia tried to change the topic. "So what's the plan for today?"

But Cat wasn't ready to give up the floor. "Deedee, cut the wisecracks! Lily and Grace know all about it. They were with me when Daulphine came to my house. Weren't you?" Cat looked to both for corroborating nods. "I knew the rest of you wouldn't believe it!"

"So what did this psycho gal tell you?" asked Deedee.

"*Psychic*," corrected Grace. "Tell about the funeral dress," Grace egged Cat on with a wide grin.

Amelia didn't believe in spirits. It was wrong of Grace to goad Cat. She tried to change the subject again.

"Shall we take our coffee to the garden? It's a lovely day." Her voice made no dent. Cat spoke louder.

"Daulphine said my mother hated the dress I'd selected for her to be buried in; she also wished I'd let my sister make the choice. Anne Michelle couldn't even pick out her own panties to wear to the funeral—Mother would have been wearing a hospital gown if I'd left it up to Anne Michelle."

"Just skip to the part where y'all see her an' talk to her now. Do y'all just call up her spirit when you want?" Deedee continued her quizzing.

Couldn't Deedee just give it a rest? Amelia put her head in her hands.

"It doesn't work like that. The dead possess the power to communicate; those of us who have the *gift* need to keep an open line for them. That's what Daulphine did for me—opened that line." Cat's experience sounded vast.

"Mother would appear to me when the boys were napping in the afternoon, when I'd have my first chance of the day to relax for a few minutes. She had the nerve to tell me to keep my eye on Anne Michelle, help her out, as she wasn't getting along with her husband, or she had money troubles, or she had the flu. Nothing had changed! Mother alive or dead was solely concerned with Anne Michelle, who apparently doesn't have enough talent to speak with the departed. After several visits Mother continued to whine that I was the only one who would receive her. I shut communication down, refused to acknowledge her presence. She finally gave up. She's probably still knocking on Anne Michelle's thick skull, but she's too dimwitted to answer."

Cat's nattering had worn Amelia out. Turning to Lily, she said, "You started to tell us about how you wish you could hear your mother's voice one more time, sweetie. You never talk about her and you shouldn't keep it all in, no matter how long ago it happened." Amelia's voice was soothing and persuasive.

Lily opened up. "I didn't know the last time she hugged me would be the *very last time ever*. Have I told you that after she died, I'd hide out in my father's closet? Just feeling the fabrics of his suits and ties somehow brought me comfort; running my hands along his rows of white starched shirts would bring up a vision of my mother at the ironing board, with the water bottle with holes on top. You know those bottles, right? I haven't seen one since I left for college. Aunt Maude used one to dampen the laundry before she ironed it."

Marie Elena entered the dining room discreetly. Quietly she set about removing the used dishes and flatware.

Our sweet Lily is becoming somber, Amelia thought. Time for action. "Penn, dear, why don't you retrieve your must-see list?"

Penn dashed off obligingly.

28. THE GROUP

"What shall we do today?" Cat asked. All the girls, save Penn, sat in the garden. The Pan fountain splashed in the background.

"I need to get out and about!" Deedee exclaimed. "I've had so much coffee, I could teach an armadillo the jitterbug. Heck, let's hit some shops. How long will it take all y'all to get ready?"

"Thirty minutes is all I need. What about the rest of you?" Cat asked.

"Whoa! I was imagining a lovely day relaxing in the garden; maybe a walk and a gelato later on would be nice." Grace stretched her back, lifting her arms upward. "Lily, are you as thoroughly spent as I? What do you feel like doing?"

"What I'm feeling like is to *not* be in charge. I don't want to plan one thing for the rest of the trip. This is everyone's villa and everyone's vacation, and I am officially resigning from director's duty." Lily sat back in her chair.

"I've got my list." Penn joined her friends. "Did I miss anything? You didn't talk about me, did you?" she added with a little laugh. Best not to be out of the room when the group was together had been the running joke for the past several years.

"Your reputation is safe," Cat answered. "Lily was just stepping down from the throne. And not a minute too soon. What've you got on your list?"

Penn began to count off restaurants, shops, art galleries, Villa Jovis, Mount Solaro, as places of interest they *had* to see.

"I believe Lily and Grace would enjoy a quiet day around the Villa," Amelia countered. "I think they're ready for a little break."

"Oh well, sure. We can play tourists tomorrow. Anyway, I want to work on my crewel. It's for Mummy's birthday. Can't have too much excitement in one day," Penn joked.

Deedee and Cat nixed the lounge-around day. Both colorfully attired, they waved gaily as they walked down the path toward the taxi whose unmuffled engine polluted the morning hush.

Penn and Amelia rested on a bench in the arbor, peacefully chatting. Their needles worked quickly, darting in and out of their fabrics.

"Let me see your silks. I need a few strands of yellow to finish this corner." Amelia reached for Penn's bag.

"Remember when we talked about opening up a needlework shop?" Penn asked.

"Honey, it seems like a hundred years ago. We were going to call it A Stitch in Time. Didn't we think we were the cleverest?"

"We were so young, me newly married, you pregnant with Jennifer. My George always taking cocktail hour meetings, your Ken Jr. working all those late nights. Didn't it just seem like everything was possible back then?"

"A hundred years ago, anything *was* possible, sugar. Now, with the kids, the house and yard, all the activities—being den mother for the Boy Scouts, hospitality committee on Sundays at church, and let's not forget Ken Jr. snipping long stems from someone else's rosebush. Things don't seem so possible anymore."

"Don't I know it! I'm in charge of the teenage Candy Stripers at Valley Pres; George expects to entertain twice a week; the boys are getting older and needing me more than ever. I had to resign my volunteer position at Sunrise Seniors. I felt so guilty, but I couldn't spread myself any thinner. Not that I'm complaining; I love what I do…just wonder what life would've been if we'd opened up that shop."

"There's no going back, is there?"

"What if we'd burned our bras like they did in the sixties?"

"Never happened!" was Amelia's answer. "Just a myth. Symbolic."

"I know, but what if we'd taken that route? Decided that we deserved careers and equal salaries. Didn't want or need a man and a family."

"Sounds dreary, doll. I'd have hated it. So would you. The choice was there. I always knew what I wanted. We made the right choice, didn't we?"

"Sure. Except I wish George didn't have so many cocktail meetings, and I wish you didn't have to put up with Ken Jr.'s philandering. Things haven't changed much in all these years. We're thirty-three years old, and we've lost our future."

The pupils of Amelia's eyes dilated as she spoke the lie. "I'm fine. I have everything I didn't have, everything I wanted."

■   ■   ■

Lily and Grace wandered the garden. They stopped at the Pan fountain, where Grace splashed her fingers in the basin. Lily stretched out, reclining on a chaise. Grace shook her fingers, sprinkling water on Lily.

"That's refreshing. You're not bored, are you, Grace?"

"This is just the type of day I'd hoped for. Our first real day to do nothing. I'm going to lounge in the tub for a bit with my book."

"Still working your way through *The Flame and the Flower*?"

"Not working my way through, Lily. I'm savoring it."

"You're such a romantic, Grace."

"Will you be okay here?" Grace was concerned—Lily rarely required looking after, but she had every reason to be in a contemplative mood. Grace knew it wasn't solely exhaustion, or the "mother" conversation at breakfast. It was Dirk.

Lily placed an arm over her eyes. "Go ahead, I'm fine here," she said languidly. "I don't plan to move for hours."

29. LILY

Midmorning lethargy. It felt foreign to her. Foreign to her, Lily of vigor. Foreign to her, Lily of accomplishment.

I'm an alien, drifting away, drifting far, far, far, in a foreign place. Listening. Listening…Penn's voice from a distance, muted, rising, falling, "George, if only…" Amelia's voice, atmospheric, sour, sad, "Ken Jr., Sarah…" And a buzzing grew louder. Wiped across her like smooth, peppery leaves. Cicadas, rustling trees, a humming helicopter overhead. She opened her eyes. *Cerulean sky.*

She wiped away a tear that dared trickle onto her cheek. Looking down, a lizard, blue, lazy too, sunned himself on the smooth round lip of the fountain pool. Listening. Listening. The fountain chuckling, trickling, its cool mist flirting with the breeze.

Gentle breathing. Breathing in the perfume, perfume borne by inland winds, perfume practicing its wiles, on her. Breathing in, fragrance of unnamed scents, scents conspiring to drug her, balm of aromatic woods, of herbs, of wild rockrose, of wild carnations, of citrus, crisp, comforting. Intoxication. Drowsy. Sluggish.

Sunlight warming, creeping down her neck, across her chest, warming, softly, softening her fingers, crawling the length of her arms, circling her breasts, sliding across her belly, inching down her legs, wrapping around her toes, one by one by one. And the inland wind sighing as the sunlight found her, owned her. Time passed, and passed, and passed…and she forgot to remember. Forgot to remember her name. Her name that was his name. Forgetting, forgetting. Sirens of Capri coming to snare her, calling, singing, seducing from the rocks. Odysseus too, seduced, once upon a myth ago. And later—*how much later, how much time wasted?*—guilt consumed her. But her heart throbbed wildly, like some machine, unbalanced. And she did not know how to calm it.

■   ■   ■

Lily heard Cat and Deedee returning; their footsteps crunched and clicked on the stone walkway. They chattered and giggled, sounding as breezy as the late afternoon had become.

When Lily rejoined her friends in the Villa, plans for the evening were already underway. Deedee was advocating dinner at a seaside restaurant on the other side of the island. Cat was filling in with glorious details they'd learned from "two studs at the most awesome bar."

Penn began to sing, emphasizing the word *paradise* in the refrain. Grace joined her; she swayed beside Penn, air microphone in hand. They all burst into laughter. Even Lily.

The truth is, they had each anticipated a vacation to magically renew their zest for "life as usual." Or at the very least, they imagined a drawn-out duplication of their birthday luncheons—eight-hour gourmet offerings with much laughing, wine drinking. And, yes, a little crying. Where conversation began with updates on their twelve collective children, and progressed to the airing of resentment toward their variously offending spouses. All of which suspended their marital frustrations until the next good phone call.

But once that they were together so very far from home, something unexpected was happening; a strange giddiness was setting in.

30. GRACE

Grace was proud of her friends. They all looked darned good, never mind they were in their thirties, and mothers too. Who would guess? She took a quick assessment as the girls moved through the narrow streets in their own cloud of color. Deedee wore a sleeveless jumpsuit of true red. Its wide belt nipped her waist, bringing attention to her femininity. Penn wore a crush-proof, knife-pleated skirt of teal with a coral blouse and matching leather sandals and purse.

"I didn't see you unpack that," Amelia commented. "Where are your khaki bermudas?"

"I packed a few surprises. I love your sundress! Can I borrow it when we get home?"

"My pleasure," Amelia nodded. Her sundress was black. And strapless. She was continental and sophisticated.

Lily was crisp and cool in white slacks, sandals, and of course, a white shirt that she had uncharacteristically tied at the waist, exposing a narrow margin of flat stomach. Grace thought Lily finally looked care-*free*. According to Cat's assessment, Grace was looking a little care-*less*. Wearing no makeup other than lip gloss, long hair pulled straight back in a ponytail, and a nondescript linen blouse/slacks set, she'd acquiesced to Cat's suggestion that she at least wear some colorful hoops and a chunky matching necklace and bracelet.

Cat herself was sporting a large Versace scarf in vibrant colors of orange, yellow, and pink. This was tied bandeau triangle style in place of a blouse. Paired with pink capris, she looked fabulous. How easy to overlook Cat's fuller silhouette, Grace realized. She knows how to disguise it with her uncanny sense of style.

The shade of a Cinzano umbrella protected the six wives from the smoldering sun as they dined outdoors at a local restaurant situated in the bay of Marina Piccola. Even as it set, the sun's glow was uncomfortably warm.

A little pasta and a few bottles of wine had been consumed when Grace turned to Cat and quietly asked, "Did you still want to visit that lingerie shop? Whispers?"

"I'm planning on it. Thought I'd look for some interesting combinations to concoct for Pietro in the bedroom. Why?"

Grace spoke softly. "I thought I might go with you. See what Capri has to offer in lacy stuff—might be different than in LA." She looked around to see if anyone had heard. She shouldn't have bothered.

"Girls, did you hear that? Our Grace is looking for sexy," Cat called out in a singsong voice. "She wants to go with me to Whispers."

Grace cringed. Although accustomed to being photographed in various states of dressed up to almost undressed, from Chanel suits to tiny swimsuits, Grace still preferred to maintain modesty in her personal life.

Cat grinned—a little lasciviously. "Have you girls ever given your man a fashion show? It's Pietro's favorite. He gets hot quickly and things move fast."

Cat's bragging again, thought Grace. *This time about sex, of all things. She's pushing too far. We don't talk about this, at least not in detail.*

"Oh boy, I tried that with Ryan on a few occasions," Deedee said. "I could've been struttin' the sexiest stuff, and he wouldn't even look up from his book. Once I had on some real high heels, with stockin's an' a garter belt with a lacy bra. I walked this way and that. Finally, I stood right in front of him and put one leg up on the arm of his chair. Do you know what that dead lump did? He put his finger under the line he was readin' in his book and said, 'Yes?' That's what he said, like I was interruptin' the good ol' time he was havin' with himself!"

Holy heavens! No one seemed put off. Grace's curiosity was in high gear. She took a deep breath and moved ahead with resolve. "What about when you were actually in bed? It was good then, right?"

"In bed? Oh sure, sometimes it was okay! Like on *his* birthday, when he'd let me give him a little somethin' extra. I was always hopin' he'd give me somethin' back! Mostly he didn't. Mostly he'd just curl up on his side and start that dang snorin' of his. I tell y'all, the nights I lay in that bed just wishin' he'd get frisky. Well, at least Hugh is much better in that department, and that's about all I can say for Hugh."

"Sorry to be so blunt, but if I were to parade like that for George, I'd never get anything done," Penn stated. "The laundry would pile up and we'd have dust bunnies under the beds. My house would be chaos. It's all I can do to keep up with him. Forget sleep! Why, some nights, when I'm sleeping great, I feel this hard thing. Mister George! It's got its own agenda. Pushing at my...my thigh...my back...my stomach. Mister George doesn't much care where it's poking me, and it doesn't care that it already got what it came for two hours ago. It won't stop till I'm awake enough to push back..."

"But it's a nice way to be wakened, isn't it?" Grace said dreamily. She couldn't remember a time Marc had ever woken her with lovemaking on his mind.

"Nice? Grace, it just means I need to perform once again. Hopefully, George is very excited, and Mister George doesn't take too long if I pretend I'm excited too. I need to sleep sometime!"

"But you do like it, don't you?" Grace's question was considered, but went unanswered by Penn.

"Listen girls, the thing is, Pietro is so fast, it's over before I know it, and I'm not sure if I've ever had a climax. If I haven't, it just isn't fair. I deserve it!"

"Oh, sweetie. You'd know!" Amelia assured Cat.

"And you? What about Ken Jr.? We all know he's a crowd pleaser! Does he do as good a job at home?" Cat prodded Amelia.

"Ken Jr. wants it in the morning. He's all revved up! I hate turning him down...I'm sure you get my drift. Unfortunately, that's the main reason I run late in the morning. I find if I go along with the program, once I get started, I can't turn back. I wish his engine ran a little warmer at night. I like taking a hot fragrant bath and putting on pretty panties and a matching bra and seducing him once in a while, kind of like I did the first time—when we went to that conference in Seattle."

Grace's eyes widened. "Are you saying you *planned* to, to—"

"Go on, don't leave us hanging!" Cat demanded.

"Oh, I was young back then. I'd never been with a man, but I'd seen Mama in action. Now she knew how to get a man. When the company selected me to attend that conference, and I knew Ken Jr. was going to be there, I blew my whole paycheck on lingerie. Had to take a salary advance to meet my rent that month. I'd seen the way Ken Jr. looked at me when he was dictating letters and landscaping proposals. If I ever was going to have a chance at a good life, it would be with him."

"That sounds so cold and calculatin', not at all like you, Amelia," Deedee stated.

"Amelia, the planner?" Penn said to the ceiling. "This doesn't sound like her?"

"Does it sound cold? I don't see why. I had a huge crush on Ken Jr., and he couldn't keep his eyes off me. You *know* when a man wants you. We were already on that track. I just moved us over to the fast one!"

Grace couldn't imagine Amelia having the gumption to plot and carry out her scheme. How did she get so brave? After all, he was her boss—she could've lost her job. "So how'd it happen?"

"First, I made myself indispensible to Ken Jr. at that conference. Then on the last night, I told him I wasn't up for the big crowd at the company dinner and was going to make an early night of it, back in my room. He asked if I'd be amenable to a quiet meal with him. Of course, I had to think about it, but ultimately I agreed, and we went to a little Italian restaurant near the water. We had wine and shrimp scampi, a little coffee, and way too much Amaretto. Before I knew it, we were back in his suite with lovin' on our mind, and I had a chance to show off that lingerie I'd gone into debt for. As it's been said, the rest is history. Enough about me. It's someone else's turn." Amelia reached for her wineglass.

"Grace, how's Marc? Can an older guy still do what someone your age wants and needs?" Cat asked with her usual lack of tact.

Grace gasped, surprised. "Marc? You act like he's my parents' age. He's only forty-nine! Hardly hurtling toward AARP!" Did everyone see Marc as an old man? He was certainly the most fit of all the husbands. He jogged and went to the gym frequently. Marc didn't rely on golf as his only exercise.

"But Grace, you're only thirty-one." Cat spoke to soothe. "Eighteen years can make a difference. Have you noticed that he's slowed down at all?"

If Cat was trying to make nice, Grace wasn't buying it, but now wasn't the time to be offended. There was information to be gleaned. "Umm…not exactly slowed down. How often do you all make love?"

"Once a week," Cat replied. "But if Noni's playing mahjong with the neighbors, then we get to sneak a little party while the kids nap."

"Depends on what extracurricular activities Ken's engaged in, but between two and four," Amelia said a bit dryly.

"A week?" Grace asked, eyebrows raised.

"Five, maybe seven times," Penn said. She thought a moment, then added, "And I think it's six too many!"

"It varies with Hugh. And of course how Mama's doin'," was Deedee's answer. Lily observed, but didn't contribute.

"Wow! That's a lot." Grace needed to explain. "I mean, probably, if I were about five pounds thinner, Marc would be more attentive. He just doesn't appreciate extra inches on me. Wouldn't come near me when I was carrying Jemima."

"Grace, you dieted yourself into waif mode for the shoot. How attentive was Marc before you left?" Lily asked.

Amelia refilled Grace's wineglass and handed it to her.

"Well, he was pretty busy with that feature he's directing," Grace hurried to clarify. "Lots of night shoots; he had to catch up on sleep in his trailer on the set."

A look passed between Penn and Amelia.

Grace took a sip of wine, then continued, "I must confess, I wouldn't mind Marc being more assertive that way. He's very sweet and gentle toward me when we are together, though."

"Have you tried salsa? George is crazy about it."

"What do you mean, Penn? Latin dancing? Marc *is* a good dancer."

"I mean salsa. Hot spicy Mexican dip with tomatoes, onions, cilantro…"

"Wouldn't that burn his…you know?"

"Feed it to him! Not…" was all Penn could get out. Visions of putting salsa anywhere near the male species' most revered appendage caused a fit of contagious hilarity.

Grace had never felt so foolish and exposed. Eager to be out of the spotlight, she turned to Lily. "Tell us, how's Dirk?"

Lily wilted.

Grace covered her face with her hands.

LOS ANGELES, CALIFORNIA

AUGUST

1979

THE "BACHELOR" HUSBANDS

3 1. GEORGE

While the wives conversed, lured uncharacteristically, even boldly, to the topic of marital sex, the husbands, exposed but ignorant, consoled themselves by playing golf. And after that, they drank beer at the 19th Hole. George sipped vodka from his flask; his score today required a stronger form of consolation than beer. A young waitress drew the blinds against the sun and turned her attention to the bartender. They flirted at the empty bar; George recognized their playful tone. A fly buzzed, hovering nearby. How annoying. George looked across the table at his five buddies. Ken Jr., Marc, Hugh, Pietro, and Dirk stared back. Were they all feeling as abandoned as he?

Dirk's mood had obviously lightened since Lily left, but he complained now anyway. "Well, they did it again! Dumped the kids on us just like those four long days of hell when they went to Sequoia."

Pietro wiped the beer off his mustache. "Cat knows this is the last t-t-time."

Marc brightened. "I think it's super for Gracie and the gals to be included, and Dirk, what an opportunity for Antonio Caldo."

Dirk flipped Marc off. George laughed; it felt good to laugh at Dirk's expense.

Dirk shot back, "Easy for you to say, Marc. You're not stuck dealing with a passel of whining reps. As if handling the finances isn't a full-time job."

"Full-time job, your ass," George said, snubbing his freckled nose at Dirk. Then turning to Ken Jr., he asked, "Whose idea was it to introduce our wives to each other? Ken Jr."

Ken Jr. scoffed. "The Golf Widows Club? Yeah, but you gotta admit, it bought us a lot of free time. Been a dozen years, hasn't it?"

George thought Ken Jr. seemed pretty flip for a guy with four kids underfoot. George continued to whine.

"I used to think it was brilliant. Now they gang up on us. Capri, yet!" He sighed and turned to Hugh. "You think Nanette could watch my boys during the club championship? Penn left me holding the bag."

"Sassy Nanette? She and Mama are staying with Aunt Bea. And I'm flyin' under the radar." Hugh performed some curious hand jive to underscore his position. "But *you* can call her if you want." Hugh signaled to the waitress. His mug needed a refill.

"Gracie's parents are giving me a break," Marc volunteered. "They have Jemima." George thought Marc sounded mighty chipper—looked it too, dressed like he owned the dang pro shop.

"I'm enjoying a little *time-out* from Amelia!" Ken Jr. snorted. "Just kidding."

The waitress sauntered over to check on the husbands. "Another pitcher, boys?"

Ken Jr. reached out and patted her butt. "You bet your sweet…"

Dirk flapped his scorecard. "By the by, I'm begging off the Labor Day event. Time for you losers to pay up."

George took several swigs from his flask. "Go on, hit me!" he said angrily. "How much do I owe?" Was he the only one suffering?

32. KEN JR.

"I'll be right over, sweetheart," Ken Jr. whispered into the phone. His reassurance was required outside the home. Looking around he could see that Jennifer had his three sons under control. *Sesame Street* was a good diversion. He grabbed his keys and motioned to Jennifer to join him for a powwow. She put down her mom's Harlequin Romance and gave a "What now?" sigh.

"I'm going out to get ice cream for you all," he said conspiratorially. "I'll be back when the *Electric Company* is over. Keep a close eye on your brothers." He patted Jennifer's shoulder. She looked up at him, head tipped to the side as if to assess his veracity. More like Amelia every day.

Ken Hawkins Jr. was a proud man. Senior VP of a solid architectural landscape firm in Los Angeles, he'd worked his way up and was well respected in his field.

Ken Jr. was a family man. He loved his wife. Beautiful Amelia could cook up a storm, keep the house spotless and the garden magazine perfect (in fact, it had been featured in local glossies). He adored his children:

Jennifer, a perfect miniature of her mother. It was going to be some big job keeping the wolves away from his baby girl, but none would get close while he had breath left in him—he knew what was on young men's minds. Kenny was a little sensitive, but would toughen up as he grew older—the wrestling class, tae kwon do, and water polo would stomp all that sissy behavior right out of him. Then there were Andy and Don, twins with nuclear energy, sure to set the world on fire—if they didn't blow it up first. Amelia needed to impose consequences on those two grenade launchers. A time-out now and again would be helpful.

Ken Jr. was a virile man. Thankfully, his wife had some real skills in what he and Amelia privately referred to as bedtime "gymnasties". But it simply wasn't enough. Ken Jr. needed more. Willing female flesh was so luscious. He'd had flings throughout the years, but Sarah Rosenberger had stayed by him, wouldn't give him up. And soon he would be the father of another little Hawkins. He hoped it would be a girl. He loved little girls.

It was going to be a mite tricky telling Amelia. But heck, she was a trooper. Hadn't she always forgiven him on the occasions she'd discovered him straying? Yes, she had. Ken Jr. knew Amelia valued the well-being of his children above all else. And this was his child.

33. HUGH

Hugh, in boxer shorts and a bowling shirt, swaggered to the den couch. Dang, it was sure nice and quiet at home without the women. In one hand he carried a bucket of bottled beers on ice and in the other, a bag loaded with cartons of Chinese take-out. Looked like he was set for the evening. He pulled a church key from his shirt pocket and popped off the lid of his brewski.

The home movie video was all queued up in the VCR. Hugh turned up the TV's volume. A driving seventies dance club song pounded the wood-paneled walls of the room. He watched his Daphne Denise, who was a surefire Fourth of July sparkler. She was the cutest and most sexiest cheerleader for the softball team. Hugh missed her at the games now. She was too tied up with Mama the shrew and Nanette the sasser to come much anymore. Where was the carefree Deedee he'd met a few years ago? Who knew her family would suck the romance right outta her? Ah shoot, he missed her bad.

Almost time for Hugh's favorite part. Yup, the background music was changing to a sexy Rod Stewart song. *And here she comes, folks. Dancin' and prancin' and smilin' at the camera.* Deedee blew kisses and winked and flirted. It was almost like havin' her right there.

He picked up the phone and dialed. "Operator, I want to make a long-distance call to Capri." When the operator asked him to repeat the city, Hugh got testy. "I said Capri! You know, that island in Italy!" Was this operator a moron? "Ah, just forget it!"

He shoved the receiver back into the cradle, then rewound the video and started it again. Hugh sighed, took a long draw on his beer, then leaned back into the couch and slipped his hand under the waistband of his shorts.

34. PIETRO

Pietro tended Beppe's Cantina, anxious for Cat's return. He missed having Cat around—on a good day, so charming in her costume, so convincing behind the tasting bar. Where were customers today, anyway? Pietro glanced at his sons. Jason busied himself decorating a long stretch of computer printout paper. He colored around the words Pietro had written, "Welcome Home Mommy." Leo sat on Noni's lap, listening as she read a storybook. Pietro choked back the bile. Why can't *my* wife be content caring for her family, helping with the family business? What's wrong with the San Carlo tradition…time-honored by my mother, my grandmother, and my great-grandmother before her?

Pietro knew Cat's argument; she'd been deprived of opportunities. She wasn't offered the college track in high school, despite her intelligence. *Of course* she'd married too early, because she was given no options. She'd ing to go to Capri and surprise Mom?" Negatory. "Then where are just us going?"

If he were honest, her innocence created discomfort right in the pit of his stomach. He had answered her straight up, putting his cards on the table with no hedging. She deserved that. She was having a vacation without Mom or Dad, with other kids, at a very cool camp. Callie had looked incredulous. No tears, though. But he had saved the very best stuff about that camp for the moment of her arrival. And taking in the reality of that camp, Callie had once again looked incredulous. But she'd get used to it; Dirk felt certain.

Back at the office, Dirk finished cutting the Antonio Caldo payroll checks. Behind him, the mannequins smiled their painted smiles. Dirk made a few extra calculations, fingers adeptly striking the keys of the calculator, tore off the curl of paper, reviewed the figures, and grinned. Lily would never miss the funds, or him. He'd ducked every call of hers so far! Next, Dirk chatted with Suzy, the travel agent, who confirmed his accommodations. He cut himself a check and pocketed it. Feeling debonair, Dirk dialed the phone once more. Behind him, the mannequins, dressed in Lily's creations, glowered.

CAPRI

AUGUST

1979

TEMPTATIONS

missed out on a career. And she was making up for lost time. Now! Pietro felt helpless in the face of Cat's determination; he'd already tried everything he could dream up to keep her happy.

35. MARC

Marc jogged along the beach. It felt good to be outside, in the sun, breathing the briny air of the Pacific Ocean. He'd had a long stretch of days and nights in the studio and looked forward to the next few days on location. The company would be shooting in Malibu and Paradise Cove. Marc would be able to take a break and get some exercise in.

He turned to his jogging companion, a handsome well-built man in his midthirties, "Glad you could get away for a run." A wave rolled in and over his running shoes. Marc smiled. "Always nice to have company."

"Hey, man, I needed this as much as you. Appreciate the invite."

A mile or so down the beach, Marc heard someone calling his name. Looking around he spied a waving Pietro San Carlo up toward the dunes.

"Kevin, excuse me. An old friend. Run on ahead, I'll catch up." Marc changed directions and loped up the sand to the mound where Pietro and his family had pitched an awning.

Pietro's boys, Marc couldn't remember which was which, drank Coca-Cola from cans and shoveled the sand into a racetrack for their Tonka toys. A kite with a large rip in the tissue sat next to the littlest guy. The older boy sported a pirate-style patch over one eye. *Guess I was a theatrical kid too.* Pietro's mother sat in the shade, wearing a large-brimmed hat. All flesh, save her face and knobby hands, was covered. Her knitting needles clicked away furiously, attached to some frilly pink thing. She didn't look up.

In his hairline Pietro had beads of sweat that dripped to perch atop his eyebrows before escaping down to his mustache. *He should be down by the water where it's cooler—and wear a hat*, Marc thought. He reached out a hand for Pietro to shake.

"Marc, my man, have you talked to G-G-Gracie?" Pietro asked, his concern apparent.

"I haven't. Been in the studio night and day. First time I've seen the outdoors since she left. Why?"

"It's just that I haven't talked to Cat for a couple of d-d-days. I've left messages, but she hasn't returned my c-c-calls."

"I'm sure everything is fine. Don't worry, buddy. They're just having some fun."

"Let me know if you h-h-hear anything, huh?"

"Will do. Gotta run. My assistant director is waiting for me." Marc sprinted across the sand and down to the water. He waved at his companion, who was running in place.

36. DIRK

Dirk inhaled, taking a deep breath of Malibu Canyon air; the scent of sycamore pleased him. *Nice vacation spot*, he thought. He headed back to his car, dodging parents who hauled duffels and youngsters who dragged their equipment through the gravel.

Sliding onto the leather seat of his Porsche, he glanced into the rearview mirror. Callie wasn't in sight. Of course not. The counselor had her in tow and pointed in the right direction. He backed out carefully and sped away, the auto's tires kicking up dust. Just had the dang car detailed too. Oh well.

Dropping Callie off hadn't been the hardest part of the deal. Callie was no emotional sissy, not attached to her Baby Beans and her *Mommeee* like other little girls. Callie could be called a tomboy in the best sense of the word. She outran and outswam most fellas her age. Neat little physique developing. However, this camp experience would reorient her focus. Actually, Callie reflected the best of him. She faced facts and adjusted to new situations, once she understood.

But she didn't understand this new arrangement at first. Yes, the tough part had been Callie's inability to grasp the situation. "Well, are we pack-

37. PENN

Penn waited in line with her friends; she checked the arrival/departures leaflet again. The bus should appear any minute. A day of inactivity had seemed to bolster Lily, enough anyway. Conversation at dinner had sparked a new brightness in Amelia. And Penn was eager to see Capri, as much as they could take in. With a few exceptions. She still wasn't sure about ascending Mount Solaro.

"As long as we don't take the funicular, I'm in. *Nothing* could terrify me more." Penn was emphatic. She saw Lily and Grace exchange a quick glance, like they knew something ominous was ahead, but wouldn't speak up. But then, who could read Lily? And Grace always spoke her mind. So maybe she was just imagining the worst. After all, Mount Solaro had rated high in the travel books, so how bad could transit be?

Only a moment later, the Orange Bus destined for Anacapri City Center pulled to a stop at the small station. Passengers spilled out, chatting casually. Penn noted that none looked to be in distress; she stepped aboard behind Amelia and paid her fare. Amelia hustled Penn into the lone available seat; the four other wives stood holding onto the vertical bars or overhead straps.

The bus doors didn't close until the vehicle was overstuffed with people and under-supplied with oxygen. Penn relaxed as the bus began its uphill journey, but once the twisting streets narrowed and the gravelly shoulder revealed a long drop to the ocean, Penn shut her eyes.

"Oh God," she whimpered. "I don't think I can do this."

"Of course you can, honey. I'm right beside you. Here, let's open this window. You can squeeze my hand." Motherly Amelia spoke in the same voice one would use to calm a frightened child.

"Visiting Capri without seeing the view from the top could prove to be one of life's regrets!" Cat offered her opinion whilst eyeing the attractive man standing beside her.

Penn noticed the fellow's distress, feeling validated, but the scant distance between Cat's hip and the placket of the man's jeans jolted her upright. Penn stared at the two bodies, leaving her terror on autopilot.

Cat addressed the nervous passenger. "Are you okay?" she asked.

"I thought the bus trip from Naples to Sorrento prepared me for anything," he said, beads of sweat in the springy curls of his black hair and gleaming on his dark brow. "I'd no idea what my friend was getting me into here."

"Ramón, you are the biggest sissy!" his companion jeered. "Miss, you should have seen him in Sorrento. Praying like God might actually be listening! Talk about *coming to Jesus*! He was down on his knees promising he'd call his mama every Sunday if he could only *just not die yet!*"

Penn almost smiled, seeing Cat's compassion kick in. Cat was probably sparked by the embarrassing accusations. Or maybe Cat just had a weakness for athletic-looking young men. There was no denying that Ramón was gorgeous. His velvety deep-chocolate skin accentuated a muscle definition Penn had never seen on George. Or Ken Jr. Of course George would never wear a tank top like that either.

Cat continued. "I know what you mean. I've been here awhile, and I haven't seen an accident yet, but it *was* a little off-putting initially. How long are you staying?"

Penn couldn't resist giving Amelia a nudge and a there-she-goes-again signal with her eyes. Amelia turned from the window and joined Penn in observing Cat at her best. It was hard to hear the words, but there was no mistaking Cat's flirtatious lingo. And body language. Cat momentarily shifted into an enticing pose, but lost her balance. Finally, despite the violent swaying of the bus, she managed to shift her position and face Ramón. Cheek to cheek they remained, eyes modestly cast down as their bodies jounced capriciously together.

Bumping along at an unlikely speed, the bus wound its way up the incline, sending small rocks skittering over the rim of the road to the abyss below. A loud, long horn sounded, and the bus skidded, screeching to a stop. A large package from the overhead bin was projected missile-like forward, striking Ramón squarely in the back. He yelped and lurched into Cat, forcing her to let go of the leather strap. With lightning speed she grabbed Ramón around the neck; both hit the floor, miraculously not taking anyone else down.

"*Porcellino! Lo pensa possiede la strada!*" the bus driver exclaimed.

Grace looked at Lily. "Translate?" she asked.

Lily answered while sinking to the floor beside Cat. "Called that driver a pig who thinks he owns the road!"

Deedee pulled Lily back. "She's dandy! Why, look at that smile on her face. Like a big ol' Cheshire cat. I'm thinkin' she won't want you botherin' her just yet."

The bus came to a squealing halt. The passengers pushed and shoved out the small folding doors. Once safely on the pavement, Ramón gave Cat a casual hug.

"Thanks, doll, you saved my terrified ass!" He strode away arm in arm with his companion, leaving Cat dazed.

Penn felt euphoric to have survived the ride; she jokingly called Cat an opportunist. Cat laughingly denied the charge and cited her quick reflexes as both lifesaver and culprit.

Cat trundled ahead to catch up with Deedee. Conspiratorially, she admitted a very private truth (which did not escape Penn's ears). "You can't imagine how incredible it was, all the points of contact where Ramón's body touched mine—I deserve more, now I know it for sure."

3 8. LILY

Lily looked forward to the day's outing, determined to make the most of her vacation, despite the sorrowing realities she'd been forced to confront. She led the wives along, commenting on the sights they passed.

A brisk walk took them through the tourist center of Anacapri, up the stairs, past the currency exchange, alongside the outdoor restaurant with its large photo menus, left, heading away from Capri Palace Hotel, and straight ahead to the gondola ticket house.

Before purchasing tickets, Grace was straightforward with Penn—about the chairlift, about being alone on it, about swinging high over the terrain.

"But Penn, the view is magnificent!" Lily cajoled. "On the ride, and up on top. Or, I'll stay here with you here, if you'd rather." Lily hoped Penn wouldn't take her up on the offer.

"I just hope I'm not making the biggest mistake of my life." Penn was shaking.

Lily smiled at Penn, hiding her astonishment at this newfound courage.

"I'll go first," Deedee said. It's easy, you'll see." She stepped into the painted green footprints that marked one's position for accessing the gondola chair. The swinging chair turned the corner and approached. The attendant steadied the chair while Deedee plopped into the seat. Amelia and Lily made a safety sandwich of sorts, herding Penn between them, and each one boarded safely.

Amelia turned to see Penn, whose eyes were squeezed shut. "Penn, look at the garden!" Earth, rocks, and trees slid below. Grace snapped photos, charmed by a humble masonry house with a small trellised vineyard, a furrowed vegetable garden, and off to the left, a rock surface covered with trinkets, thousands of them. A farmer waved. He was clad in baggy shorts with a knotted bandana on his head. An aria swelled from his yellow boom box, permeating the space for a few seconds. Deedee blew him a kiss.

Holding onto the vertical pole, Lily turned around and called to Grace, whose long legs dangled from the metal chair, "Puccini."

Cat, from her chair behind Grace's, hollered informatively, "La Bohème!"

Arriving at the top, Penn tumbled off the chairlift, assisted to balance by the attendant. Deedee greeted her with congratulatory hugs. Eyes wide, hands only slightly shaking, Penn managed to ask, "Now what?"

"Let's hike the perimeter," Lily suggested.

"Ah, I'm gonna beg off, my sandals sure gave me some nasty blisters yesterday," Deedee said. "Let's find a nice place to sit and take in the view."

They strolled, following the metal guardrail, amazed by the sheer drop to the sea. As they climbed the ancient rock steps toward the ruins, a concession stand and bistro tables could be seen.

"I'm tingling," Cat said. "The spirits are here too, like at Villa Jovis." She twirled ecstatically, falling into Amelia. "Whoo, I'm a little dizzy, must be altitude." Amelia helped Cat to settle on a rock bench. Penn sat there too, taking sidelong glances at Cat's flushed cheeks. Lily shut her eyes and tried to feel the supernatural presence Cat kept sensing. *Spirits, are you truly here?* she wondered. *Give me a sign.*

"There must be a God! Look, there's Bob." Deedee waved energetically, stepping out of the group. Bob waved back and approached the wives. Deedee headed in his direction, hardly slowed by her blisters.

"Not that it's my business, but it looks to me like she's chasing his trousers!" Penn said. "Am I the only one who thinks so? Lily? Grace?" She looked to each for her opinion.

"A little fun isn't such a bad thing…she's practically said she's *had it* with Hugh! Still, it does seem a bit precipitate to…uh…act like she's single. But, that's just me."

Lily noticed that Grace attempted to be nonjudgmental, but had found little success.

"Probably just a little harmless flirtation going on," Lily temporized. "We might all be doing the same thing if we were in her sandals."

"Excuse me, I'd rather be wearing that double D bra of hers; those sandals didn't do her any favors, far as I can tell," Penn said.

Bob made the sign of the cross when he reached Deedee. "You again, angel. Thank you, God! Join me and the guys for a Coke?" Bob seemed to be including all six wives. He signaled, motioning as if they were teammates being called to the field. Amelia and Penn exchanged a "Shall we?" look.

Bob put his arm around Deedee's waist and led her toward the concessions, with Cat, Amelia, and Penn following. Grace scuffed the dirt. She stood with her arms crossed. Lily shrugged her shoulders, raising her eyebrows at Grace. Finally, they both tagged along.

"Two chairs over there," Grace observed, stepping onto the terrace. She headed off to buy colas while Lily spread out their sandwiches. Colas purchased, Grace and Lily relaxed at their own table in the shade, waiting out Deedee's encounter, such as it might be. Their seats overlooked the white Faraglioni rocks rising from the turquoise sea. Lily felt no need to talk; the view was compelling. Besides, she and Grace could overhear the conversation going on at Deedee's table.

The four other wives shared their picnic with the pilots, who reciprocated by buying colas. Marie Elena had prepared sandwiches of crusty bread with tomato, mozzarella, and basil—lots of basil at Cat's request.

Wiping the crumbs off her bosom, Deedee remarked, "It's a wonder these Eye-talians haven't figured out a way to make liquor out of this green stuff. It's darn good, that's for sure. But does anyone believe Cat when she says just the smell of basil is orgasmic? I mean, didn't you just say the other day you don't even know if you ever had one? Huh, Cat?"

Lily cringed. How audacious of Deedee to use the word *orgasmic* with strange guys. And speaking Cat's secrets aloud to these pilots…Where were her loyalties?

"Good grief, Deedee, thanks for nothing." Cat made a wry face. She pulled her chair over to Lily and Grace's table.

After that Deedee and Bob flirted ridiculously, obliviously; Cat pretended not to notice, although Lily thought Cat's face was a dead giveaway.

At an adjacent table, Jax gazed into Penn's face. "Your eyes are lapis blue," he said. "What fool let you out of his sight?" Lily could see Penn blush, a flattered, eyes-down sort of blush. Her shiny black hair swung over her face, catching the sunlight like an oil slick. Jax went on. "Oh, I'm dead serious. You're dazzling."

A few steps away, Amelia leaned against a column, looking like a goddess bathed in dappled light. Mick moved in close and ran a finger along her ear, along her cheek, and down her neck. Amelia did not stop him; she trembled visibly.

"Anyone for a walk or a little hike?" Lily proposed, a bit loudly. Grace stood up and stretched, indicating she was in. Cat shook her head. The other three seemed not to hear the invitation.

Lily ventured to a cliff with Grace. Ancient vases sat on the ends of an equally ancient fence. Through the fence's opening was a sheer drop to the sparkling Mare Tirreno. Grace, attempting a photo, stepped beyond the fence. A fraction of a second later, Grace lost her footing; she slid precariously downward on the shale. Grace planted a foot as Lily reached out to catch her extended hand. Together they managed to stop Grace's descent. Lily's heart thumped, her veins burning with excess adrenaline. Grace was breathing hard. Hand in hand they retreated a respectful distance.

"Only one step too far, and we'll fall into forever," Grace said in a barely audible whisper.

"Then we'll both walk carefully," Lily answered, wondering if that was even going to be possible. Then with some urgency, she added, "We'd better get back to our friends."

■   ■   ■

Mick and Jax were excusing themselves; they were "expected somewhere." Lily scanned Penn and Amelia's faces. No particular reaction was evident.

Deedee stepped into her sandals. She winked at Bob, who waited confidently a few paces away.

"Y'all just go on ahead to Gus's Garden," she said.

"It's the Gardens of Augustus, Deedee," Grace admonished. "Listen, aren't you on vacation with us? It's more fun if we experience all the sights together."

"Oh, Grace. You're such a good little schoolgirl. Doin' ever'thin' by the book. I'm ready for kickin' my heels up a little. I'll see y'all back at the hacienda in a couple of hours." She waved merrily and sashayed over to Bob.

Lily wondered if this was how it would feel when Callie began dating; the thought began to twist back on itself, presenting more questions and memories. The thought began illuminating Dirk. Dirk in their dating years, Dirk with his tender, passionate whispers.

39. DEEDEE

"So, angel, what's it going to be? Shall we window-shop the Via Vittorio Emanuele? Or how about checking out the Carthusian Monastery by the Gardens of Augustus?"

"Heavens, Bob, keep me away from those gardens. I vote for shoppin' in the Via." *Lordy, I cannot envision runnin' into the gals while I'm havin' a little free courtin' time,* she thought. Putting her arm through Bob's, she beamed up at him. "Carry on, handsome. Time's a wastin'!"

■　　■　　■

Wandering the narrow streets of the Via Vittorio Emanuele, Deedee took every opportunity to investigate the fashions in the shops and on the women.

"Just look at these ladies here. However do they walk in those high, high heels and such skinny skirts?" She thought herself quite competent in heels, but on these cobbled streets? That took some serious finesse. Not one to linger on her shortcomings, Deedee poked Bob in the side. "How about gettin' some ice cream?" She led Bob down the lane to a little café that advertised gelato and espresso.

A few minutes later, as Deedee alternately took bites of her gelato and pondered why the spoon was so tiny, fat heavy raindrops began to fall—hard and fast. Deedee abandoned her gelato, tried in vain to cover her hair with her hands. "Get me out of this," she wailed.

Bob sprang into action. He helped her get under the awning of the café, then disappeared inside. He was back in no time with a newly purchased umbrella. "The proprietors are always ready for quick weather changes."

Deedee flashed her widest smile. "You're my hero!"

Bob flashed his own charming smile back. "Why don't we go back to my hotel? We can dry off and have a drink there."

Deedee considered.

40. AMELIA

Amelia watched Grace, Cat, and Penn stroll away, down the terraced path, seeking an aerial view of the Via Krupp. She'd noticed a not-so-subtle change in Penn. *I believe she's found a hideaway from her fears. Look at her so close to the cliff's edge. It's this island. She'll be a daredevil before we leave*, Amelia predicted. Of course, she didn't say this aloud. She'd stayed back with Lily, who sat in silence on a stone bench, gazing out at the sea. Lily didn't need to hash out Penn's phobias right now. No, Amelia's experience and counsel was what Lily needed—she didn't know that yet, though.

Amelia put her arm around Lily and gave her a little squeeze. "I know that not everyone of us respects my decisions."

Lily looked at Amelia, confused. "Respect? You can't think I don't respect you, Amelia, because I do. I'm in awe of your talent. I wish I had your green thumb and your kitchen witchery."

"No, precious, I don't mean you. I guess I'm mostly referring to Cat and Deedee. They don't understand. They think I'm a sucker for Ken Jr."

"Oh, right. But how *do* you endure it? Ken Jr. with Sarah and the others?" Lily shook her head.

"Like I said the other night, I have four children who need their father. I know what it's like to not have one. When I think about Jennifer and my boys growing up without Ken Jr., it breaks my heart. They are why I stay. That, *and* Ken Jr. is a good father." Amelia sighed. Her tone hardened slightly. "As to the moral compass attached to his pecker…it got demagnetized a long time ago."

"You sound so convicted, Amelia. Could anything change your mind?"

"I can't think what it would be. I'm in it for the long haul. Cheating isn't the *worst* thing men can do to us. But I want you to know that whatever you do—be it work through things with Dirk, or split the sheets, I won't judge you. I'm on your side whatever you choose."

The clouds that had threatened to break open chose that moment to do so. Amelia and Lily jumped up and dashed beneath a grove of cypress trees. They laughed at the spectacle of their friends squealing and scurrying toward them, seeking to share the protection offered by the enormous foliage. They squished together into a tight ball.

"It's a good thing Deedee went off with Bob," Cat remarked. "There isn't a square inch to spare under here. You know she'd be whining about her hair getting wet."

They giggled like young girls.

41. GRACE

Grace found Lily's lethargy disturbing. She was lying on her bed with a cloth over her face. Grace went into the bathroom, took a small clean towel from the shelf, and soaked it in cold water.

"Here's a fresh cloth, it's cool. Let me take the old one."

Lily uncovered her face and handed Grace the towel. "Thanks, Grace. I'm fine, okay?"

Grace sat at the vanity, took the elastic from her hair, shook out her ponytail, and began to brush her hair with long efficient strokes. Time for a heavy-duty conditioner, she decided. Behind her, reflected in the mirror, Grace saw Lily stir.

"Lily, do you feel like talking about it? About Dirk, I mean?"

"I guess I shouldn't be surprised that Dirk hasn't called and yet I am. If there *is* anything going on…it would seem he'd try to keep up the masquerade. He'd call, pretend, *something*."

"I know just how you feel. Well, not exactly, because Marc isn't…but I haven't heard from him nor have I been able to reach him. Mom says he's very busy with his show." Hope had assuaged Grace's concern, briefly, but Grace had been uneasy, almost from the time their friends had joined them.

A knock on the door interrupted Grace's thoughts. She turned her head toward the door to watch Penn enter, displaying the omniscient Chore Wheel. *Penn treats that fancy poster board like it's a Bible.* In all fairness, Grace reminded herself she'd never actually seen Penn with a Bible.

Penn strode in and dropped a heap of damp clothes on the floor next to Lily's bed. She pointed to the multicolored, pie-charted Chore Wheel.

"Lileeee, you left these in the bathroom. You've disregarded rule number four!"

Lily sat up, her gauze shift slipping off her shoulder. She looked at Penn apologetically.

"I wonder if George and the boys are observing rule number four," Grace asked no one in particular.

"Well, of course they are. How else would they manage?" Penn retorted and strode out much as she'd entered.

And they call me *self-righteous*, Grace mused.

The telephone in the hallway rang. Looking at each other, Lily and Grace spoke simultaneously, one apprehensively, "It might be Dirk!" and one eagerly, "I hope it's Marc!"

Deedee's Southern tone sang out in the hall, "Hello? Girlfriends? Where the heck is everybody? Someone's got a phone call."

Grace, Lily, Penn, Amelia, and Cat all poked their heads out their respective doors.

Marie Elena rescued the shrill bell. "*Prego…Signora* Penn, for you."

Grace sighed in disappointment and not a little envy. She turned to Lily. "At least Penn's husband misses her."

Lily returned to her bed, but Grace lingered by the door, hungry to hear a moment's worth of affection between Penn and George.

"Bob? Oh, hi there…" Penn gushed.

"Lily, it's that wolf in pilot's clothing. Penn is all giddy and blushing! You've got to see this," Grace whispered, motioning Lily to join her.

"Stay away from the door, Grace. She'll see you. Eavesdropping isn't what friends do to each other!"

Penn's voice rose a notch in response to Bob's query. "Well, it's a little uncomfortable, there are six of us and only three of you. I don't *know* who to pick! You decide."

Lily raised her eyebrows, her mouth a perfect O.

"Well, it doesn't take a mastermind to get her drift." Grace was flabbergasted. She stuck her head back out the door.

"Look at that! She's telling Amelia that Mick and Jax picked them to go to dinner, and she said it's like being voted to the cheerleading squad. Lily, why would she think *we* even cared about going out with those guys? Not everyone wants to be on the squad!" Grace couldn't keep the repugnance from her voice.

Lily came to the door just in time to see Penn and Amelia holding hands, jumping up and down—like cheerleaders. Deedee smiled at their enthusiasm, Cat shook her head.

"Wait a minute," Lily called out. "I've already made reservations for tonight, and Quinton is joining us."

"I'll call Bob and tell him where he and the boys should meet us. Where're we goin'?" The problem was solved to Deedee's satisfaction and apparently to Penn and Amelia's.

Penn put her arm through Amelia's. They walked toward their room singing like Frank Sinatra about black magic.

Grace was indignant. "No one better be feeling sorry for *me* because I wasn't picked. Those guys are strangers. I don't understand wanting to be with men you don't know. I'm not going."

"Grace, we need to be there. Besides, Quinton isn't a stranger. How many years have we worked with him?"

"It isn't Quinton I'm worried about. Pilots? Please, we all know their reputations! It's not what I expected from a girl's trip!" She wanted to be tolerant, but didn't this cross the line?

"Bubbly, ladies?" Cat strutted in carrying a bottle of champagne and three glasses. She held an empty glass to Lily and one to Grace. "I'll trade you for Sophia Loren?"

"Okay, but pour heavy. I can use a drink." Grace guided Cat to the vanity and began to dig through her sizable makeup kit. Deedee, Penn, and Amelia sneaked in behind.

A glass of champagne later, Grace was in a much-improved mood. She congratulated herself on the Sophia Loren replica sitting before her.

"You could be twins," Grace laughed. She handed Cat a pair of huge sunglasses. "These will fool anyone, darling."

"I'm next," Amelia called out.

Lily handed Cat a lavender scarf. "Cat, I think this will perfectly complement the neckline on your dress. Maybe throw one end over your shoulder *a la Loren?*"

"Oh no." Cat dismissed Lily's suggestion. "I know just the knot to make." She took the scarf and began a complicated twist that ultimately resulted in an intricate rosette.

It was not long before a bevy of movie stars gazed at themselves in the foyer's tall mirror: Deedee smiled—Marilyn Monroe in a strapless red dress smiled back; Amelia posed, a Julie Christie with thick honey hair fluffed, lips soft pink; Penn gasped to see herself as Nancy Kwan.

Marie Elena looked on mesmerized.

"Wouldn't it be just my luck if George showed up?" Penn looked stricken.

"Worse yet, Pastor Barnes!" Grace murmured to Lily, who elbowed her to be quiet.

"Hush, Penn. You're wadin' knee-deep in cotton!" Deedee warned.

"Lord, what if our husbands *could* see us now?" Amelia asked.

Still in awe of the beautiful *signore*, Marie Elena didn't hear the knock at the door. But Cat did. "I'll get it."

Quinton stood waiting, dressed casually in linen slacks and his customary loafers. "Wow, did you study knot tying?" he asked Cat in surprise, eyeing her scarf choker.

Cat blushed with pleasure, presuming a compliment. When a taxi honked twice, the starlets scrambled out the door, leaving Grace and Lily with their own moment of reflection in the mirror.

"We look an unholy mess," Grace said, horrified. Lily laughed—a rich, carefree laugh.

Quinton smiled encouragingly. "I'm guessing you two need a few more minutes? I'll wait."

42. QUINTON

Quinton waited like a gentleman for Lily and Grace. He sat on the terrace watching the sky turn to fire. Honestly, he'd been taken aback, seeing the wives just now.

Grace and Lily looked bedraggled, while the other four—well, they were knockouts! Of course he'd seen them dressed up before, but not looking like this. *Capri must be having quite an effect. What if their husbands could see them this way?*

Quinton had socialized with the couples over the years. Enough to have formed some opinions. He'd golfed with the husbands, heard them brag about introducing the gals, brag about the ingenious Golf Widows Club. The wives had bonded immediately, buying these husbands lots of "guy time"—best of all, with no complaints. But had the arrangement just backfired? *Do the husbands pity themselves now, stuck with the kids for days on end? Stuck with the kids over Labor Day Weekend, same weekend as their biggest golf tournament?* Quinton didn't have answers, although he had his suspicions. Suspicions about Dirk for sure.

He'd known Dirk quite a few years. Early in the Whites's marriage, Dirk wearied of peddling his *croqis* (dozens upon dozens of painted textile designs in various color combinations). He lost incentive.

"Freelancing pays diddly squat," he complained. "And working in the sweatshop of a textile factory? Never."

Not to belittle the guy. Dirk was clearly a math whiz. Dirk could keep count of cards at bridge and blackjack. He even performed algebraic calculations in his head. Lily preferred numbers that related to thread count, yardage, chest, waist, hip, and inseam measurements. Logically then, when Lily's opportunity appeared, Dirk dumped his chosen profession. He hired himself as the Antonio Caldo CFO, reminding Lily of his sacrifice.

The bottom line for Dirk was time. Time for golf and other hobbies. Quinton feared his current hobby was Darleen, Lily's eccentric, but efficient assistant. Quinton had recently spied a brochure for a children's golf camp on her desk. Malibu Little Links. Darleen had covered it with her tablet when she saw Quinton looking. *Now, Darleen doesn't have children. Callie doesn't like golf. What's going on?*

Quinton was hard-pressed to have similar suspicions about Grace's Marc. Marc advocated Grace's career while he worked tirelessly, earning a nice paycheck. Just some niggling worry bothered Quinton. With the oddest basis.

Quinton remembered images in photos. He remembered Marc's face alongside Jemima's on her third birthday; she was untying ribbon. In this photo Marc's face is captured as a twist of fear and pride. And in another photo, Marc balances a paper plate of cake with its shapeless glob of ice cream escaping over the edge. He gazes wistfully as helium-filled balloons—released by a gust of wind—fly into the distance. Quinton frowned with a conclusion; *Marc wasn't remotely present.*

Marie Elena approached Quinton on the terrace. "*Scusate, questo è per te.*" She handed him a bottle of beer with a smile and disappeared before he could say thanks. Quinton took a refreshing swallow and let his mind resume its travel.

What about Pietro? Quinton could almost feel sorry for the man. Pietro's feet were firmly planted; he played it straight on the golf course and on his scorecard. His values were traditional, unshakable. Cat was equally stubborn, but unlike Pietro she floated along on the ethers. *I'd say Pietro's chosen the wrong gal. Unless something changes, life will be an ongoing battle for those two.*

Quinton checked his watch. Seventeen minutes had passed since Grace and Lily horrified themselves in the mirror and scurried off. He didn't mind waiting. He preferred their company to the others'. Preferred it to Deedee's company, for sure.

Deedee's probably way too much woman for the average fella. Probably was for Ryan. Lily had told him a little about her brother-in-law's failed marriage with Deedee. Quinton savored his beer and remembered the story.

Deedee and Ryan White relocated to LA from Baton Rouge, just after Nanette's birth. Deedee soon trusted Lily enough to grouse about her faltering marriage.

"A spankin' new start in Tinseltown, and wouldn't ya just know it, Ryan's still the same ol' pig in a poke." Deedee divorced Ryan shortly thereafter.

When Deedee met Hugh, she claimed it was love at first sight. His gym-toned body didn't hurt things, according to Lily. Seeing Deedee just now in that seductive dress gave Quinton chills. She didn't look very married. Hugh might be batting five hundred tonight for his beloved softball team; he might be feeling like a winner…but he didn't have a clue. *Poor Hugh, you'd better step up your game in another department.*

Amelia's Ken Jr. was a conundrum. Talented landscape architect. Good looking, if you fancied the ever-smiling, vigorous-handshaking sort of a guy. A respectable golfer with an eleven handicap. But there was no denying this report; Ken Jr. consorted with a petite interior designer. Amelia's physical opposite. Sophisticated vs. homespun. *Go figure.*

What was George up to without Penn? George was a church deacon and expressed his belief in and fear of a fiery hell. As far as Quinton knew, George conscientiously observed the Golden Rule. Skills? George could flip a burger and mix a mean drink. But George was hardly domestic. Maintaining a household of three boys for any length of time? *Hope Penn lined up full-time help or else there's trouble—with a capital* T.

Quinton looked at his watch again. His stomach was growling.

43. GRACE

Grace watched her friends while she sipped iced tea. Her mood was as flat as the bubbles in the champagne she'd enjoyed earlier. That same champagne, which had lifted her spirits and impaired her judgment, had also gifted her with a slight headache. There sat her friends at their most alluring, looking beautiful and flirting their hindquarters off. Grace was embarrassed for them and highly aggravated at them.

"This meal is taking forever," she whispered to Lily. "Are we in a contest to see how long we can drag out each course?"

Lily half smiled in sympathy. "Hang in there. We're closing in on dessert."

Grace observed a coquettish Cat, who knew she was looking good. Grace's makeup and hair handiwork had boosted Cat's self-image, and she was putting all her skills to work.

"Look at that, Lily! Cat is practically sitting in Quinton's lap. She's oblivious that he's only being polite. I saw him scootchie his chair away from hers."

"We've both seen Quinton under attack before. He's in no danger of Cat's guile."

"Right. I've got to credit him with enormous tolerance—considering how she messed up the photo shoot, then took honors for the styling of his layouts."

Lily took a sip of her barely touched wine. She was having no better a time than Grace.

Grace, Lily, and Quinton had arrived forty-five minutes behind the others. The party was already rolling and the wine had been flowing. Amelia and Mick were paired, Penn and Jax sat next to each other, Deedee was cozied up with Bob, and Cat was next to Deedee, an empty chair on her right. Was it an oversight that there were only eight places at that table? Grace thought not. Without apology from their friends, two chairs appeared, and two settings were laid out by the attentive waiter. Grace and Lily were crammed together at the end of the table.

"Do they even know we're here?" Grace nodded her head toward Amelia and Penn, who were so caught up in the pilots' attention it was possible they did not.

Lily shrugged, perplexed, brooding.

Grace had been the last member to be admitted to the fold. She was freshly married to Marc and eager to meet his golf buddies and their wives. The entire group had made her welcome, but the wives had been especially warm and included her immediately. In thirteen years, she had never seen them behave like this. Her friends were excellent homemakers, doting mothers, and attentive spouses. The gushing and blushing Grace witnessed was alien conduct.

Grace passed on dessert. Lily drank espresso. The pilots nuzzled and smooched with their dining partners and still managed to order Grand Marnier without taking a break from their advances.

"Grand Marnier for Angel Face and me," Bob called out.

"Make that two more," Mick added. He took a small nip of Amelia's neck. She giggled.

"We'll do the same." Jax, jittery, gazed into Penn's eyes and nibbled her fingers.

Grace reached for her purse. "I'm done. We're not welcome."

"Me too," Lily agreed.

Both women stood to leave. Understanding their intent to depart, Quinton stood and announced, "I'll see you ladies home. I want to get an early start in the morning, anyway."

Cat jumped up, became quite pale, then sat quickly. "Whoa. I'm a little dizzy."

"Are you okay, Cat?" Quinton put a hand out to help steady Cat's descent into her chair.

"Nothing a Courvoisier won't cure. Join me at the bar, Quin? It isn't all that late, and these two have no sense of nighttime adventure. Please, just one drink, and then I'll let you bring me back. I promise."

Quinton hesitated. Cat didn't notice, but Lily and Grace did. "Go ahead, you don't need to see us home," Lily encouraged. "We're perfectly capable of catching a taxi on our own, aren't we, Grace?"

Quinton shook his head slightly and gave Lily and Grace a parting kiss on the cheek. "She won't be long, don't worry. I've got another sunrise to photograph."

"How many of those do you need, Quinton?" Grace asked. "You've been at it since we got here."

"I'll know it when I get it!" He reached out and tugged her hair, and smiled at Lily. "'Night, see you two in the next day or so."

Lily pulled Quinton aside. "They look pretty wild, right? But they won't let it go further than dinner."

"How long have we all been friends? I know they're just letting their hair down."

Grace saw that Lily was relieved by Quinton's reassurance.

Cat and Quinton headed for the bar. Lily and Grace attempted to catch Penn and Amelia's attention to no avail.

"So much for good-byes," Lily said. She and Grace turned to leave just as the waiter served the liqueurs.

They could hear Bob's toast as they departed. "Grand Marnier, up your end!"

■   ■   ■

Lily awakened to Grace, moaning. "Grace, are you awake? Are you having a nightmare?"

"I have a nightmare of a stomachache. That sweet potato gnocchi is sitting like a rock in my gut. How could I eat so much of it? Why didn't you stop me?"

"*Me*? Stop *you* from eating?" Lily scoffed. "Grace, the most enjoyable thing about tonight was seeing you take pleasure in the food. And you didn't eat that much anyway."

"Ohhhh, I hurt so much."

"Get up. I'll make some chamomile tea. It should help settle your stomach."

The two padded barefooted down the stairs to the kitchen, where Lily put a kettle of water on to boil. "Odd. The lights are on down here. Wouldn't you think the girls would have turned them off when they came in?"

"It's after one. They must be home by now. Want me to go check?"

"No, of course they're home. Probably didn't know how to do it. I'll show them tomorrow." Lily spooned tea leaves into a yellow and blue crockery teapot.

Grace pulled her hair back and used the elastic band on her wrist to make a ponytail. "I don't know what's come over me. I have such an appetite and no discipline."

"Oh, bother! You do realize that even with such an advanced appetite, your food consumption is still minimal, don't you? The shoot is over. Try cutting the fabric on the bias and give yourself a little slack!"

"But Lily, what if I'm bulging out of my clothes when we go home? What will Marc think? You know how he dislikes…" Grace used her hands to make a curvy figure in the air.

"You'd have to gain twenty pounds to bulge out of those baggy pants you wear. I don't think there's the least danger of that. Here's your tea. Let's go sit in the garden, I bet it's still nice out there."

Once settled in the fan-backed wicker chairs, hands cupping their mugs of hot tea, Grace turned to Lily. "What the heck was Cat up to tonight with Quinton?"

"She did seem particularly frolicsome." Lily took a sip of tea and considered further. "She's been quite clear regarding Pietro and how she's feeling about him of late."

"I'd bet money she never drooled over Pietro like that. Even in the early days." Grace thought about Pietro and how hard he tried to please Cat. And Noni.

"Grace," Lily spoke softly. "Quinton isn't only *our* friend. He's known our group for years."

Grace sat up, taking umbrage at the perceived implication. Was Lily thinking that she, Grace, might be feeling possessive of Quinton? No, that was an overreaction.

"Right. Okay. Fine." Grace put her hands up. "But what about the others? Wouldn't you say they're trekking off center?"

Lily didn't answer. Grace chastised herself for being insensitive. Lily had her own quandary to resolve. Hashing over their friends' actions was silly. Lily was in pain; expecting her to participate was childish. She reached over and patted Lily's arm.

A cheerless smile crossed Lily's face. "Look at that moon! Too bad the girls are sleeping through it. You don't often see a moon like this in LA."

44. LILY

Lily considered a gray ship far below. From her perch on the balcony, it looked as tiny as a bathtub toy; it reminded her of a misplaced piece in a puzzle of blue. *What am I going to do? What* can *I do?* She had not the slightest notion of possibility. A cold straitjacket of grief and anger immobilized her.

The ship melted into a blur on the pastel smear of horizon, and Lily's face twisted into a frown.

"I feel so betrayed," she said, hearing her voice crack.

Grace looked up from her book sympathetically.

"Think I'll take a shower," Lily said, trying in vain to smile. It was not her intention to burden Grace further—Grace, who would attend her distress like an enormous Saint Bernard. Lily looked at her slender friend. What a contradictory image. She smiled despite herself.

Lily tied her robe and passed the vanity mirror without looking.

Cat, treading slowly upstairs, coffee in hand, saw Lily headed for the bathroom. "Forget a shower. Plumbing problem. There's a man in a wife beater under the kitchen sink."

"Oh? Then I'm going to the garden for a while," she said quietly.

The Capri morning greeted her with familiarity. The air was dense with humidity. Birds twittered their refrains, over and over. Moths, humming-bird-like, drank from fluted flowers. Lily relaxed in a fan-back chair facing the bronze Pan. He was predictably impish and gay. Water barely trickled from his musical pipes, denting the sky-bright pool. Lily closed her eyes, unable to recapture the languor she'd found here before.

Angelo plopped into a fan chair with a loud sigh. Lily's presence caught him unawares. Startled, Angelo and Lily both jumped up. Then, recognizing each other, they sat back down.

"Oh, Angelo, I thought I was alone," Lily said. Her hands fluttered to her unbrushed hair.

"I'm sorry, I thought *I* was alone!" Angelo gestured wildly as he attempted further explanation. "The plumbing has gone cuckoo."

Lily found some amusement in this. "My life has gone cuckoo," she said, trying to be clever.

They shared a little laugh. And then Lily looked down sadly.

"You carry some sadness, I see," Angelo said gently.

"I've lost my husband to a senseless affair." She paused and looked into Angelo's solemn face. "I see sadness in you as well."

"I lost my wife to a senseless disease."

Lily was mortified. Had she appeared insensitive to the gravity of his situation? She cringed, hands covering her mouth.

"*Alora*, we are like two trees. We bow to the same wind."

Lily broke down in sobs.

Angelo nodded, understanding. "Go on…The tears must come before we stand straight again."

As if cued by Angelo's compassionate words, Pan's pipes sent freshened streams of water bubbling into the pool.

There were more words to be shared. Angelo and Lily continued to talk.

45. MARIE ELENA

Sprinkles of morning sunlight formed dancing patterns on the heavily waxed surface of the dining table until Marie Elena pushed the lace curtains aside, allowing the sun to flood the room with its warmth. She set out sliced fruits, yoghurt, hard rolls, and wedges of cheese—all on a variety of colorful platters and bowls. Cotton napkins, which she'd just ironed, sat at each place, along with the old cutlery, which had been in the owner's family for generations.

Normally the napkins would have been smoothed out and folded once dry and off the clothesline, but one of the guests insisted that they be ironed crisply. Maybe in her country, it was rude. Oh well, it only took a few extra minutes. But what of this guest, this *signora* Amelia? For that matter, what of all of them? She'd had more opportunity to observe the *signore* Lily, Grace, and Catherine; yes, she'd already formed opinions of them.

Lily was an easy guest. She understood the difficulties that she, Marie Elena, encountered attempting to please everyone. Lily was soft-spoken, always wearing *camicia bianca*, always considerate. She smiled and asked about Marie Elena's life and family, always interested, but never spoke about herself.

Now that other one, *signora* Cat! They could send her home anytime. Demanding her sheets be changed every day. Not a common practice here that caused ample extra work for Marie Elena. Speaking loudly to her as if that would assist Marie Elena to understand whichever language she was trying to speak, English or Spanish. Forget Italian! If Cat's Spanish was better, it mightn't be so difficult, but she was a butcher of languages, that one. And feelings too.

Then there was *signora* Bones. Tall and slender like a laurel tree, but no wonder. The woman didn't eat much, and when she did eat, well, Marie Elena knew what came next. A bellyache. And guilt. Why, if it were up to her, Marie Elena would put some weight on that *signora*, and she would get some breasts in the process! Still, she was always sweet, and generous. Look at the beautiful bracelet Grace had given her—large beads of amethyst and aqua-colored glass. Marie Elena had never owned anything like it. Grace was hungry for something, but what?

Pausing in her reflection, she poured cream into the pitcher, hoping the skinny one would splash a bit onto her sliced peaches. She filled the carafes with dark rich caffé, began steaming milk, and continued her reverie inventorying the personality traits of the three women who arrived at the Villa just a few days ago.

Signora Deedee. No mystery there. Golden hair and a figure like a film star. She was warm and friendly. It was easy to see that she knew how to enjoy herself. She spoke with an odd accent, almost a different type of English than the others. She was a bird of paradise, colorful and grand, stretching out her wings.

The other two *signore*, Penelope and Amelia, did not look alike but acted like sisters. Both were polite with fine manners. They shared a room and they shared each other's clothes (which looked to be well made and expensive). How *did* American women keep their figures after babies? From what she could gather, these two had multiple children and still looked like girls. Maybe they shared a very close friendship because they shared the same problems.

If Marie Elena had to guess, she would say that all these *signore* had to work very hard to keep their men happy. She believed there was a longing in them, these women who seemed to have everything, but who could say? She might be seeing in them what she felt within herself.

And that was all she had time to think about as Grace and Lily entered the dining room begging for a caffé.

46. GRACE

Grace was animated that morning, looking forward to being on the boat that would take them around the island. She'd forgotten her stomachache of the night before, eating two of the hard rolls to which she'd added large chunks of cheese. No one commented when she accepted Marie Elena's offer of a second latte, not wanting to bring to her attention the calories she was unconsciously consuming.

"What time did you guys get home last night? Lily and I were up around one o'clock this morning, and all the lights were on."

"Not sure," Amelia responded.

"Not much later than that," Penn answered simultaneously.

"We were having hot tea in the garden around then; there was a gorgeous moon," said Grace. "I don't know how we missed you. What about you, Cat?"

"I was in bed before that. Quinton wanted to stay out longer, but I was more tired than I'd realized. Just an after-dinner drink, and I was back here less than an hour after you two bailed out."

Grace polished off the remaining fruit on her plate and stood up. "Finish up, everybody. Our boat reservation is in an hour." Noticing Penn and Amelia's heads together, she asked, "What're you two huddling about? No secrets. What's up?"

Amelia was defensive. "Nothing's up. We're ready. Lily, what time will we be back?"

▪ ▪ ▪

In the end there were just the five of them on the tour. Deedee had ultimately declined. "I'm not so interested in gettin' myself all tanned up. I'll fry out there."

"That's why God invented white muumuus." Penn scooped up the last bit of foam in her cup and examined the spoon.

"An' another thin', my hair can't tolerate bein' out in that sun and ocean air. I'll have a sticky mess to deal with. Besides, I'm gonna be spendin' some time with Bob today. Go along on some errands he's runnin'."

"If Bob weren't so good looking, I bet a hat would solve the problem, maybe a scarf," said Cat as she looked around the table for the group's reaction to Deedee's announcement.

Lily was distracted, and only Grace did not disappoint. She was surprised anyone would give up seeing the island by boat to do chores with some guy. Crazy! "What happened to 'We're all on vacation together'?"

"I *never* said that. It was Penelope. Besides, y'all know I'll probably never have another opportunity to leave Mama. I need to cram a whole lotta fun in these next few days. Thinkin' about gettin' back to Hugh and his complainin' about Mama just gives me a bellyache."

"Admit it, Deedee, you've simply got a bigger name on the other line," stated Cat.

▨　　▨　　▨

The small boat rocked across the water, staying close to the shoreline, darting in and out of coves and a multitude of colorful grottoes, each bearing an appropriate name. Amelia sat on one side, dangling her arm over the edge, catching the wet spray that shot up as the hull slapped the waves. Penn sat back, surprisingly relaxed, but with a life jacket on her lap, just in case. Upon boarding, Lily and Grace made for the bow and positioned themselves on the cushions provided, leaning against the mast; sails tucked away, the boat was powered by an engine. Cat sat in the back with the young captain, Luciano. In his accented English, Luciano recited facts and myths about the Isle of Capri and answered questions about its history.

At the entrance to the Blue Grotto, several tour boats bobbed about in the water, awaiting the dinghies that would transport the passengers from the Mar Tirenno into the mysterious blue of the cave. With no more than three tourists allowed to a dinghy, the girls were separated into two groups. After a precarious transfer from small to tiny boat, the oarsman who would pilot the dinghy directed the girls to lie back and make themselves flat to accommodate the low opening. The oarsman grabbed the overhanging chain and hand over hand pulled them through the rock portal. No doubt a common sound to the rowers, sighs of awe escaped from all who entered. Once inside, it was impossible to miss the cathedral-like atmosphere where talking was done only in whispers.

Lily gazed around the large cavern. Grace saw longing reflected on Lily's face and gasped when Lily quietly stripped off her gauze shift and slipped so quickly into the water their oarsman was unaware, her cerulean blue swimsuit indistinguishable from the phosphorescent water. Lying on her back, hair fanned out like a mermaid, Lily looked peaceful. Taking note, Grace understood it was Lily's need to cleanse herself of Dirk's lies and unfaithfulness, a way of rebirth, a way of forgiving, a fresh start before returning home.

Cat did not succeed in distracting their oarsman when the tiny dinghy dipped sideways with the displaced weight of Lily half climbing, half being pulled in by Grace. His consternation at this infraction was apparent as he vehemently, but quietly, hissed at her, "*Signora*, no, no, no! You must not! My job! Ayyyy! You want to swim—you go Green Grotto!" Lily was immediately repentant and apologized.

Who wouldn't act out like that? Grace thought. How easy to be overcome with the magnificent colors as the rowers' collective voices singing "Santa Lucia" echoed over and over. Lily had concluded an important photo shoot that culminated months of work and dedication. Here she'd fulfilled a dream, only to have it instantly overshadowed with the realization of Dirk's dalliance with Darleen.

Cat handed Lily a small towel from her bag while Grace quickly tossed the shift over Lily's head. Grace could not ignore the glow on Lily's face. Surely Lily had achieved what she'd hoped for.

Only moments later the sun's bright light made them squint and grab for sunglasses, its warmth penetrating Lily's wet hair and damp shift as they rejoined Amelia and Penn.

47. AMELIA

Amelia and Penn were having a different type of tour in the grotto that prevented them from taking in its beauty. The age-old high-school question had surfaced—whom to choose? Their girlfriends or the guys? *What a dilemma,* Amelia thought. *Neither of us has had much experience with a pickle of this sort.*

Once situated back in their tour boat, they continued their conversation while awaiting the arrival of Lily, Cat, and Grace. No longer needing to keep their voices low, they spoke loudly to compensate for the sound of all the motorboats idling awaiting their passengers.

"How are we going to tell them we're going out again tonight?" Amelia did not relish the idea.

"We can avoid it by staying in," Penn suggested.

"We don't know how to reach them to cancel, even if we wanted," Amelia rationalized, but even as she said it, she knew that wasn't accurate. They could always leave word at the Hotel San Michele.

"Good point. We *can't* reach them, so how 'bout we just tell the girls? We're adults, after all. On the other hand, what're they going to think of us? I made such a big deal about all of us being together and staying together. I wish I'd kept my mouth closed, who knew we'd…"

"Meet men? Get to feel pretty and sexy again? Think about it, Penn! I've got four kids and a cheating husband. It's not like we went out *looking* for excitement, and it's not like we're *really* going to have sex with them."

"Admit it, Amelia, you know we both came awful close last night!"

"Admit it, Penn. We had a good time! And no one says we need to repeat last night. We'll just have a nice dinner, a good wine, and some nice conversation and go home to our own nice beds. I promise." Amelia believed it.

"It sounds *nice.*" Penn laughed. "I don't know why I'm worried about what any of them think of us. Deedee didn't waste any time finding some fun."

"That's true, sweetie, and you know Lily doesn't judge," Amelia mused. "She's able to justify almost anything anyone does. She can always find an excuse. Just watch. She'll get home and instead of dealing head-on with Dirk, she'll find a way to give him the benefit of the doubt, maybe even make it her fault."

"Don't forget Grace! Is it my imagination, or is she more of a goody two-shoes than ever? It's not so much what she's said, but she seems to act more strait-laced every day."

"She's always been a bit of prude. More ludicrous is her blaming her *weight* for her lack of sex. Remember how cute she looked pregnant and for six or eight months after? She was adorable with boobs and booty." Amelia would never find a scrawny figure appealing.

"I won't lie, I was taken aback by her surprise when we revealed how many times a week we…"—Penn searched for the right term, but gave up—"you know, with our husbands. I doubt it's her weight that's interfering with their sex life."

"Grace seems oblivious to Marc's…whatever you want to call it," Amelia frowned, causing her brow to furrow. "Ever wonder why Hope and Jimbo encouraged her to marry him? She was so darn young and naïve, and he was so much older. She'd been chaperoned and sheltered nonstop on all those print jobs in New York. Back then I never dreamed I'd be friends with a girl who was on the cover of *Glamour* and *Seventeen*. Grace always says they were supportive of her, but it seems to me they practically pushed her into it, him being their director and all. Did they want him in the family that badly? Do you think they know?"

"We could be wrong about him, you know. But then even George has commented, and he's one of Marc's biggest fans—the last person you'd expect to gossip. I don't know what Grace would do if she found out. But she shouldn't have to live like this." Penn sounded deeply concerned for Grace.

Amelia contemplated the past several years. There was a time when Penn and Grace were closer, spent more time together. It was a phenomenon within the group, a changing of partners, a shifting of the level of commonality. At this time Penn and Amelia seemed to bond, as did Lily and Grace. At one point it had been Deedee and Lily, and Grace and Cat. It was ever changing, depending on each woman's needs.

Penn broke into Amelia's thoughts. "We all should have perfect lives. No one should have to live with infidelity."

Amelia winced.

"Oh, Amelia, I'm sorry. I was thoughtless. But, do you think we should tell Grace?"

"Tell her *what*? I'm not having that conversation." Amelia stopped suddenly. Just as she'd been distracted and missed the beauty of the Blue Grotto, she was caught unaware by the dinghy that gently bumped up alongside their boat to unload their friends.

"Honey, you're all wet! What happened?" Amelia gathered her composure, wrapped a large towel around Lily like a mother hen clucking comfort.

"She took a dip!" Grace stated dryly. "You two were so deep in conversation in the cave, you didn't even notice. What gives?"

"We're just deciding whether or not we're going out tonight," Penn responded with the slightest hint of defiance. "Mick and Jax have invited us to dinner."

"Again?" Cat directed her question to Penn, who looked away, not answering.

"Are you mad at us?" Cat asked Amelia when no answer was forthcoming.

"Not mad, they just don't want to be with *us*," Grace assured Cat. "They prefer flirting…with guys who want exactly what?"

Amelia matched Grace's distasteful tone. "Grace, let your hair down for once."

48. LILY

On the return trip, Luciano stopped at the Green Grotto, where the wives swam through the tunnel. After the splashing, with laughing and teasing, the tension dissipated. And, after their continued boat tour, they were air-dried and feeling gentle in each other's company. Walking along the marina, they passed colorful fishing boats tugging at their lines in response to the freshened breeze.

"You go on ahead," Lily told her friends. "I'll take the bus later." She felt buzzy after her submersion in the grotto. It was a big step, a positive step. She wanted time for the reality to sink in. *I've forgiven Dirk, I've released my anger. If he'll agree to drop Darleen, we'll have a fresh start.*

"I'll stay with you. We can get a caffé before we head home," Grace suggested.

"No, you go on with the others, I'll be fine," Lily said. She felt Grace scrutinizing her.

"Ummm, I think not. I am staying with you." Turning to the others, Grace asked, "What time is your dinner date?"

"It's not a *date* date. It's dinner—" Penn stopped midsentence.

Lily recognized Penn's defensive tone.

"What kind of an answer is that?" queried Cat. "Dinner? Guys? Sounds like a date to me." Cat paused for a reply. None was given. Cat scoffed, "Whatever."

Cat is irked, Lily thought. *And Penn doesn't want us to judge her. But apparently on this occasion, Penn wants to go out more than she cares about our judgment.*

"Speed it up, the bus is about to leave." Cat quickened her pace, never bothering to see if Penn and Amelia followed.

Grace and Lily watched the threesome disappear into a cluster of tourists.

"You don't need to babysit me," Lily said emphatically. Grace gave her a squint-eyed look.

"Come on, Lily! You're not usually impulsive. Taking a dive in the Blue Grotto?"

"It was a lark. I felt like it, and I didn't want to stop myself." It was a glib comment and Lily regretted it instantly.

"No need to qualify. I get it completely and I can't blame you. Let's forget the caffé—that was an excuse—and grab a taxi for Anacapri. I'll treat you to a drink at the San Michele bar. We need potato chips and olives. Sounds good, doesn't it?"

"*If you're* eating chips, count me in!" Lily laughed. "I don't want to miss that."

"Just the olives. I'm dying for salt!" Grace confessed.

▪   ▪   ▪

Seated at a table on the hotel's terrace, they overlooked the narrow winding road and the whitecapped sea. A waiter took their order and reappeared with drinks and munchies. He set a scotch and soda in front of Lily and positioned a martini glass with icy vodka in front of Grace. He looked around at incoming guests, impatient while Grace counted lira and paid the tab.

Lily looked out the window. A road maintenance man in neon bright overalls caught her eye. He was bent over, picking up leaves off the street. "*As if* his orange pants could save him!" she quipped.

"What?" Grace was confused until she located the man Lily mentioned. "Whoa! His entire hindquarters are hanging in the street, simply begging for a bus to come along and smack him! A gnat's ass would be squashed; they drive so close to the walls and rails."

Both began to giggle like teenagers, unable to stop themselves. Although aware of the horror to witness such a disaster, and feeling badly for their reaction, it still took several minutes to suppress their laughter.

Lily took a sip of her drink, smiling, and rattled the ice cubes round and round. Her expression changed. Her smile melted.

"*As if* my little baptism could save my marriage." The insight felt like a tsunami racing from the Pacific to the Mediterranean with no mercy. "*What if* Dirk actually doesn't want me anymore? What can I do?"

"Oh, Lily, I don't know. Don't know what I'd do either. I mean, I'm sure Marc would *never* cheat, but if he did…"

"What? If he did, what would you do? When you start thinking about it, it isn't so simple, is it? What a mess everything might turn into. A divorce? How could I separate Callie from her dad? Old Aunt Maude and my father, what would they think? And Antonio Caldo? What about my company?" The floodgates opened quickly, and Lily's fears refused to cease flowing. An edge had crept into her voice, giving it a slightly shrill sound.

"I should never have married Dirk. That makes all of this my fault." Lily closed her eyes. Her memory sharpened. It felt like a vise had clamped down on her skull. "But I just couldn't disappoint Aunt Maude by calling it off."

"You thought about it?"

"Yes, yes, I did. But by then Aunt Maude had the church, the country club, the caterers all booked. No children of her own, only me. We went to bridal shop after bridal shop until she found the perfect gown."

"It *was* an exquisite dress," Grace interjected.

"Yes, maybe not what I'd have chosen, but lovely, and how could I put the brakes on and wreck her joy train?"

"No way, Lily! You went through with it because of Maude? You never said. She was very proud of you, like she'd birthed you herself. I remember the first time I met her, out came the wedding album. I got the idea that all her hopes and efforts culminated right there at the altar."

"You're right. So you see, I dug in, trusting I could make the marriage work and love would follow. Well, Dirk and I shared common goals. He was the wonder boy of Parsons. I was the envy of most of the girls, snagging a talented straight man! I chose to ignore that black snake winding itself into my dreams at night and slinking under my daytime door. No, I can't blame Aunt Maude for that."

Lily had never made this admission to anyone. Her stomach clenched. Grace sat in respectful silence, hearing the long-withheld truth.

Lily mustered a smile. "I want Callie to be smarter than I was. I'll do everything I can to guide her and show her that she has choices."

"Lily, if you want to go home now, I'll go with you."

"And leave the others after all their planning? I can't do that."

"Finish your drink, let's go back!" Grace made sure Lily drained her glass, then threw an arm around her shoulder and guided her to the porte cochere at the front of the hotel. Signaling for a nearby taxi, she bustled Lily and herself in, and gave the address of the villa. Before the taxi took off, Lily's shoulders began to shake with sobs.

"It'll be all right, everything is going to be all right," Grace said. Lily knew that Grace did not believe what she was saying.

By the time the cab rolled to a stop at the Villa, Lily had quieted and made only the softest sound with her remaining few erratic sobs. Grace tossed some lira notes at the driver and helped Lily out.

"Thanks for the drink. We didn't even get our second bowl of chips." Lily smiled wanly. Her face was blotchy and tearstained. Her hair was stiff with dried salt water; the tops of her shoulders and the tip of her nose appeared to be sunburned.

"Go upstairs and take a nice bath. I'll see about some iced tea or something for you," Grace offered.

49. GRACE

Marie Elena whacked at garlic, then diced a few tomatoes and sliced an onion. A mountain of tomatoes and a pile of onions remained on the large kitchen chopping block. She signaled to Grace. "Your time. Cut small."

Grace picked up a knife and smiled excitedly at Cat, who sat at the table savoring a juicy peach. Grace wasn't a complete stranger to the kitchen. She cooked for Marc and Jemima and with the help of a favorite caterer, often threw dinner parties. Her skill, while good, was not gourmet.

Grace was in love with Marie Elena's cooking, even fascinated by it. She did not equate food with sensuality, yet here she was seduced by Marie Elena's sauces, risottos, eggplant. The spices, the fragrance—surely were a taste of heaven.

She'd timidly approached Marie Elena to ask if she could watch. Marie Elena had smiled and just as shyly said, "Why watch? I can teach!"

So began Grace's cooking lessons. Tonight was manicotti.

Deedee breezed into the kitchen as chatty and colorful as a macaw. "Hi y'all! How y'all doin'? I can't begin to tell what a day I had. I went all over this island on a scooter with Bob!" Her windblown hair made it easy to envision her sitting on the back of a Vespa holding tightly to Bob's washboard abs while he dodged in and out, between buses and taxies.

"You daredevil, you!" Grace tried to laugh.

"I thought you didn't want to mess up your hair by going out on the boat?" Cat sniffed.

"Oh my goodness! Y'all got *your* panties in a bunch, don't ya? I thought we been all over that! I'll be back home scrappin' with Hugh and dancin' attendance on Mama before God gets the news. I'd like a little slack from my best friends, if y'all don't mind." Deedee sniffed back at Cat.

"Deedee, have you been drinking?" Grace asked, agitated.

"Drinkin'? What gives you *that* idea?"

"You've got a mile-high buzz on, that's what."

"I'm guessing Jack and helium," Cat deduced.

"Don't sneer at me, Miz Cat. Toodles, toots. I'm gonna go get ready for dinner with Bob tonight, *if* you two got no objections?"

"Leave your conscience in your suitcase, Deedee?" Grace inquired, tightening her grip on the knife.

Deedee grabbed a peach, tossed her head, and flounced out of the room, leaving Grace gaping after her.

"Grace, Grace, Grace, aren't you Sister Mary Immaculate?"

"What do you mean, Cat?"

"Never mind, keep the choir girl thing going, it's working for you."

Stung, Grace smacked down the knife.

Marie Elena reached out and placed a calming hand on Grace's arm. "We just begin. Now we make pasta," she said soothingly.

50. PENN

Deedee sat at her vanity setting her hair with hot rollers. Cat was stuffing cotton between her toes in preparation for painting her nails. Penn and Amelia lounged in kimonos, coiffed, manicured, makeup perfected. They all giggled listening to Deedee's tales of an *excitin'* afternoon.

Penn felt keyed up, jittery, exhilarated. What would tonight bring? A luxurious restaurant on a dramatic cliff? Italian wine? Grand Marnier? A stroll under the enormous moon? Gentle caresses, male body heat, intense lingering kisses? Yes, she craved Jax's attention; this was a man who took the time to appreciate her.

And then, interrupting, there was Lily. Lily standing in the doorway. Lily looking fragile. Lily ruining everything by asking, "Can we please get back to our Enchanted August?"

Lily sounded firm, like Mummy talking to a teenage Penn, like Mummy affirming the Admiral's rules of conduct. Penn creased the tie of her kimono nervously.

Lily spoke again. "Look, *Grace* is cooking. *And* we've been invited to a champagne dessert event."

Penn's thoughts crisscrossed like a gopher trap around her. *I don't want to disappoint Lily, but she's not my mother. Somebody please, just this once, give me a break, I'll make it up to Lily when we get home. Lord knows we'll have hours and hours to spend, especially if she and Dirk...*

Deedee spoke up. "Sorry, Lily bug, but I've got my own plans for enchantment."

Lily put her hands on her hips. "Girls, I'll see you at dinner." Penn and Amelia stared at Lily and nodded noncommittally. Lily gave them a long pleading look, after which she turned abruptly and headed for the blue-tiled bathroom.

Cat mimicked Lily, "'Girls, I'll see you at dinner.' She's just jealous. I'll probably catch up with Quinton, maybe join you." Amelia and Penn left for their room without responding to Cat.

Penn and Amelia leaned on the rail overlooking the arbor. The silence was broken only by the crickets and cicadas.

Penn spoke quietly. "I don't know, Amelia, Lily makes me feel guilty. Maybe we *should* just stay with the rest of the girls."

How Penn abhorred being made to feel guilty. Penn never wanted to be judged; a low score would cause immense angst, followed by immediate justification for whatever test she'd failed.

Amelia sighed. "Penelope, sweetie, we've only a few days left here. Let's make it memorable. Deedee has the right idea. Anyway, it's just dinner!"

Penn picked her cuticles. Silent.

Amelia continued, speaking slowly now. "Look, we haven't done anything wrong. It's not like we're cheating on Ken and George."

"Not that *Ken* doesn't deserve a little retaliation, pardon my saying." Penn's shaky resolve softened, and she sang a few familiar bars, tromping as if in boots over an offending male. She looked at Amelia for a reaction.

"That's the spirit, honey. We'll go out for a meal and be right back here before we know it." Amelia seemed relieved to have Penn on board again.

But Penn was still wavering. What was she doing? Why, she wasn't doing *anything*, just a little partying. She deserved some time off after all. Her three boys, nine, eight, and seven, were exhausting...but oh so sweet when asleep, drooling slightly on their pillows, lashes resting upon their cheeks, hair tousled from the shampooing at bath time, faces kissably soft. She always thought she'd have daughters, one at least. But she wasn't taking any more chances. Besides, she loved those boys...and George.

George. *Did* she love him anymore? Did he love her, or was she just someone to have sex with? Legitimately. The sin of infidelity would probably never occur to George. A deacon in church, he observed the Golden Rule, mostly. At that she shook her head. If she observed the same rule and did unto him what he did unto her, they'd never get out of bed. And that she could not stand. It was bad enough that he expected her to have the kids bathed, fed, and ready for bed when he got home. Oh, she would do that whether or not he expected it. It made things right with her world to be orderly, but he got home so late anymore with his after-work cocktail meetings running longer and longer, how could she *not* have the kids all pajama'd and ready for bed?

A quick meal (which had taken ten times longer to prepare than George would take to eat), and then watch out! He was ready for the bedroom waltz. If it was a good night, the alcohol on his breath wasn't too bad, and he'd dance just once, but on other nights she'd awaken from an exhausted deep sleep to him demanding release from his sexual demons. It was like a drug to him, if there was such a thing, but she'd never heard of anyone being addicted to sex.

Last fall she'd taken herself to the ob-gyn requesting to be put on the pill. The night before George suggested they live dangerously and she not use her diaphragm, Penn refused and damned if he didn't break right through it that very night. Terrified she might be pregnant, flooded with relief when her cycle began, ecstatic when she swallowed that first tiny baby-preventing tablet, she never allowed herself to think about what she might or might not have done had she conceived that night.

"Earth to Penn? Anyone in there? Have you heard anything I've said?"

Penn grimaced guiltily. "Sorry, I was just thinking about…the boys."

"I know, I miss Jennifer and my little guys too," Amelia said, leaving the balcony. She opened the armoire. "What do think about this dress? It'd look great on you. Want to try it on?"

"Are you wearing black too?" When Amelia nodded, Penn said, "Wish I could ask Lily if she has something I could borrow…probably best not to now, considering…"

"No great loss, Penelope, white shirts aren't your *forte*. What would you wear with it anyway? We can't all pull off the fashion statement Lily makes with her *signature white shirts!*"

"True. I'll just dig deeper in my own closet. I wish I were better prepared…I never expected to be dining with anyone except the girls."

"Let's not go over that again. Can you please relax and commit to having a good time?"

"Amelia, what if things get out of hand? What if we don't—"

"What if, what if? Penn, we're in charge here. We make the decisions. What's going to happen? We'll be together."

"Right. I'll go as long as you promise me we won't split up. No matter what Mick and Jax want, right?"

"Of course we won't split up, honey. I promise. Why would we?"

There was a brief knock on the door and in came Deedee. "Hi, y'all! All ready for our big night out? Won't it be fun? The six of us havin' a little party. An' Bob's got a surprise for y'all. I can hardly wait till y'all find out. Goodness! I can't remember the time I had so much fun three days runnin'. Must've been when Hugh took me to the Hollywood Bowl Jazz Festival last year. We brought wine and bought some fancy box lunches in a Japanese bento-somethin' or other. Aunt Bea took care of Mama and Nanette, and we stayed over in a motel. Come to think of it, it wasn't all that fun. Not too excitin' neither." With that she left the room.

Penn looked at Amelia expectantly. "What are we going to tell Lily and Grace?"

51. GRACE

Marie Elena had arranged a festive table in honor of Grace's meal. The flowers were freshly cut from Villa Bianco's garden; the beeswax candles were flickering; wine from a local vineyard was breathing in a crystal carafe; the napkins had been ironed and folded into bishop's mitres. Marie Elena set out the better china instead of the whimsical pottery plates she normally used. The *signore* would surely be pleased with Grace's efforts and the ambience of the evening.

Grace had selected earrings, amethyst and moonstone drops, to complement her cotton wraparound sundress. Lily wore a white linen dress, wide straps with a tight bodice and full skirt.

"Can you believe we only have a few more days here?" Grace asked Lily as they descended the stairs.

"Yes and no," was Lily's response. "Seems like I've been away from Callie far too long."

Both girls drew in their breath upon entering the dining room. Marie Elena stood at the kitchen door, awaiting the wives.

"How wonderful," Lily exclaimed.

"So fancy! Thank you," Grace said modestly.

"Holy cow! Are we having a party?" Cat strutted in, looking impressed. Marie Elena motioned for them to sit and poured wine.

Cat moved to make a toast, but Lily stayed her. "Let's wait for the others. Then we can make a special toast."

"Gosh, I didn't expect anything so elaborate, did you guys?" Grace asked.

Cat reached for the breadbasket, but Lily again requested she wait. "I'm certain they'll be down any second."

Cat gave a skeptical look.

Ten more minutes passed. Lily, Cat, and Grace found little to talk about.

"Shall I go on a roustabout?" Cat offered.

Lily nodded. "It's getting late, and we have the San Michele Benefit to get to."

Cat returned and sat. "We've been abandoned. Looks like the lure of the guys trumped us."

Lily straightened in her seat. "Marie Elena, it'll just be we three. Please serve. I believe we're famished." She turned to Grace. "Let's make the most of your dinner, okay?"

Grace nodded, but the party atmosphere could not be summoned.

52. PENN

How clever of Deedee to scope out an exit plan using Marie Elena's back entrance. The door creaked only a little. The stone stairs leading into the yard were moss stained, steep, and narrow, with no handrail. Penn noticed they had not been swept for some time. Descending cautiously, she fought off guilt. Nonetheless her heart fluttered in anticipation; blame it on Amelia (who was obviously reveling in bravado).

Amelia turned to hurry her up. Before she could say a word, Penn gestured, ten fingers spread rigidly, as if pushing all sound downward. "Shhh! Shhh!"

Luckily the Villa didn't have a barking watchdog to give them away. But their high heels seemed to click like mammoth typewriters spilling the news: "Look who's sneaking out!"

Penn had snuck out before. High school days. With her crush, Johhny Hammond, star quarterback, a senior. He was "too old for her." Mummy and the Admiral never found out. No one back home had to ever find out about tonight either.

Penn and Amelia minced along the uneven sidewalk trying to catch up with Deedee. Penn shushed Amelia's giggles, while giggling herself. A taxi waited by the shrine where Virgin Mary surrounded by rose petals looked heavenward. Then off to Anacapri and sweet exhilaration.

Call it a conspiracy of temptation, with Capri in collusion. The cypress trees sighed; the moon, mysteriously veiled by clouds, flirted; a blood-red strip of horizon panted heat; and all the while, planets winked.

53. GRACE

Tea lights surrounded the gate at the Axel Munthe Villa, San Michele. Grace was captivated by fairy lights twinkling in the trees. The arriving guests were greeted by a waiter at the entrance with a tray of champagne in tall flutes, while a quartet played soft classical music in the courtyard. Uniformed staff passed out hors d'oeuvres on silver salvers to the elegant group assembled.

"Ritzy," Cat said. She took a sip of champagne and lifted her glass to Lily. "How did you wrangle invitations for us?"

"Actually, the owner of Villa Bianco extended the invitation."

Grace noted with satisfaction that Cat was quite impressed.

"Is that Quinton I spy?" Cat asked. "What's he doing here? You know he treated me like the queen's pajamas over our Courvoisier."

Grace bristled at the proprietary note in Cat's voice. "Yep. That's Quinton. But look! Lily, is that the plumber he's talking to?" Lily laughed at Grace's surprise. "Whoa, he cleans up well," Grace whispered.

Lily grabbed Grace's hand and pulled her through the crowd to Angelo and Quinton. "Come on. I'll introduce you."

"The museum was a pet project of my wife's." Angelo looked sad for a moment, then continued, "I volunteer when I can."

"Well, it's a lovely evening, Angelo. Thanks for including me." Quinton put his hand on Angelo's shoulder just as Lily approached. "Looks like you have some other guests to greet."

"Quinton, Angelo, hello." Lily smiled at her old friend and introduced her new friend to Grace and Cat.

"You *own* Villa Bianco?" Cat queried. Angelo smiled.

They all made small party talk for a few minutes, then Angelo excused himself.

"I'm so glad you were able to attend. I have some hosting duties I must see to. Please enjoy yourselves." He walked away into the crowd.

"It's time for me to make my exit as well. Busy program in the sunrise department," Quinton explained with a laugh.

"Let me meet you in the morning. I can help," Cat offered.

"Sit tight, sister. Tomorrow is our hike to Villa Jovis." Grace smiled but clenched her jaw tightly. Hard to believe Cat would pass up a chance to commune with the spirits just to assist Quinton. Evidently it was true.

"I've seen it," Cat replied brusquely to Grace. She turned to Quinton to plead her case. "You know I've got a good eye."

Quinton smiled, gave each an innocuous kiss on the cheek, and left.

"Great. So what are we going to do now? There's no one interesting left here," Cat complained.

"Cat, darling, thanks for the sentiment. We love you too, don't we, Lily?"

"Actually, I'm a tad worried about our friends who shinnied down the fire escape and tiptoed through the tulips to an assignation." Cat's smirk belied her words.

"Fire escape? Tulips?" Grace questioned sardonically.

Cat rolled her eyes, then slowly, as if to a child, explained, "It's a metaphor."

"The idea is disturbing me too." Lily ignored her friends' verbal sparring.

"It's just wrong, them on a date," Grace declared.

"We could crash the party and play chaperone, if you two are willing," Cat said with a self-satisfied smile. "*I* know where they went."

Grace looked at Lily to see if she too understood what Cat was implying. Lily let out a breath and put a hand to her forehead.

"*You knew they were sneaking out?*" The betrayal Grace felt was reflected in her voice.

"Why didn't they just tell us?" Lily spoke reasonably.

"Tell you two? Seriously? Nah!" Cat shook her head.

54. LILY

Lily walked ahead of Cat and Grace; she looked up at the waxing full moon, appreciating the sky's transformation; the cerulean of dusk had dissolved into evening's cobalt, revealing a swath of stars across the cathedral-like arch above. Lily shivered and pulled her pashmina tighter, although the air was still balmy. Strangely, she felt cold. And alone. She found herself regretting the minimal conversation this evening with Angelo. She surprised herself by wishing he had not excused himself so quickly.

Soon they stood in line for the bus to Punto Faro with a few weary locals. "How long before our bus comes, Lily?" Cat asked impatiently, breaking into Lily's thoughts.

"One will be here in a few minutes, read the schedule up there." Grace pointed to the overhead signage. "Relax, this is Capri, not Hollywood."

An orange bus pulled into the adjacent lane, offering a strange sense of intimacy with the noise from its sputtering engine. Cat sidled up to Lily. "So Angelo's the owner of the whole place? Whew, and I thought he was just a handyman."

"So much for assumptions, Cat," Grace said frostily. "He's an educated and cultured man."

Lily looked dreamy for a moment. "He has the kindest face and eyes."

The trio climbed into the bus, paid their fare, and chose seats; the driver waited for more passengers with the engine idling.

Cat sat behind Grace and Lily; she leaned forward into the space between them. "Where does he live? What does he do?" she asked, always on the alert for intrigue.

Lily turned, placing her back against the window, and engaged happily in the conversation.

"Angelo lives here. Most of his family does too, although he splits his time between New York and Italy. Just think! Angelo was visiting New York frequently while I was going to Parsons. Villa Bianco was built in the early nineteen hundreds; its architecture is the Liberty style. Angelo's grandparents offered the Villa to be used as a hospital during the war. Can you imagine? Anyway, he's in leather goods—gloves, bags, and shoes. We didn't get too far into what he does because he kept asking questions about me and Antonio Caldo."

"Is he married?" Cat asked bluntly.

"He was," Lily answered, irked, "weren't you listening? He said as much at the reception."

"So are you, you know, kinda going to see him again?"

"Catherine San Carlo! Are you loony? Why would I *kinda see him* again? I'm married, and not looking."

"Sorry-eee, I don't know." Cat sat back and folded her arms.

"Rules don't seem to be applying right about now—to anyone but you and me," Grace whispered to Lily.

Lily hadn't intended to sound harsh. She turned back to Cat. "Not to say Angelo won't be around the Villa. The Villa's handyman vacations in August and September, so Angelo fills in. No doubt we'll see him again before we go home."

The small bus wound down the steep, unlit roadway. It stopped in a circular drive next to an unexpectedly remote restaurant. Lily, Grace, and Cat stepped out and the bus drove off. On an adjacent cliff, a lighthouse threw beams of brightness into the choppy ocean.

"Are you sure this is the right place, Cat?" Grace asked.

Inside the restaurant, a display greeted them: fresh seafood on ice, all silvery-lilac and orangey-red, garnished with parsley and lemon. Waiters bustled serving the crowd. The searchers glanced about for the deserters.

55. PENN

Out back on the terrace, sharing a round candlelit table, the pilots dined with their dates. Deedee and Bob cozied up, snuggling, smooching, setting the mood. Mick and Amelia nuzzled. Penn felt euphoric, actually beautiful in Jax's company. Best, she shared this adventure with two of her dearest friends.

Bob snorted (again) from his tiny vial. Then shaking it, he offered the vial to Deedee. She snorted, showing no inhibition. Earlier, Penn had tried just the tiniest bit when Jax offered some. Amelia had too. Not enough to hurt anything, surely.

Just now, Mick stroked Amelia's arm and gazed into her eyes.

"Ever been to San Torini?" Mick asked.

Amelia shook her head, intrigued, holding the gaze. Mick whispered into Amelia's ear, "Come with me."

Penn, overhearing, blushed but openly watched as Mick French kissed a yielding Amelia. Jax was watching too. He worked his hand up Penn's thigh. She laughed and pushed his hand away, but she enjoyed his attention. Jax lit a cigarette for Penn. She took a drag with cocky bravado—and in that moment she saw a host leading Lily, Grace, and Cat toward them. Penn hurriedly stubbed out her cigarette; she nudged Amelia, mouthing, "Oh crap!"

"Helloooooo, everybody!" Cat sang out. She signaled a nearby waiter to bring more chairs. "What're we all drinking?" she asked.

"Jack and Coke," smirked Bob, looking around the table at his buddies and Deedee.

"Just wine," Amelia answered in a voice lacking enthusiasm. Penn knew that her flat tone was not due to the unexciting nature of the beverage (because Mick had splurged on a fine bottle).

"I'll have a Jack and Coke too," Cat informed the waiter. "How about some bruschetta before dinner?"

"Dinner's on its way. We ordered twenty minutes ago. What're you guys doing here?" Penn looked at Grace and Lily.

"Group trip to the *Ladies*. Come on, girls," Grace ordered.

Now you're a warrant officer? Penn didn't want make a scene, but she seethed as she followed along to the bathroom.

The sign may have said *Signore*, but it should have been singular. There had been comments throughout the trip on how small and inefficient the restrooms were in Italy, and this one was no different. It was tiny, with room for one lady only.

Once all six were squeezed in with the door closed, the agenda became clear to Penn. Lily and cohorts came to perform anchor watch. *As if we three, the ones actually having fun, have cast ourselves adrift.*

Amelia spoke first. "Cat, sweetie, thought you could keep a secret." And then to Lily and Grace, "What the fudgesicle are you doing here?"

"We're here to take you home," Grace answered.

Deedee shook her head. "Not me."

Penn fished in her purse and avoided eye contact.

"Penn, what about our early sunrise hike tomorrow?" Lily pleaded. "All your months of research and fact finding…We might not have another opportunity. It's already pretty late. Come on home with us now, please."

Deedee primped, admiring herself in the mirror; Penn envied Deedee's detachment.

"We'll be up early, Lily, honey," Amelia spoke. "If not, give a little knock."

"We'll wait in the bar till you're finished," Lily bargained.

"We are *not* leaving you here," Grace said impatiently. "Can't you see you're in over your heads? Sheesh! It's not just tumbling you out of bed in the morning. We're a little concerned about these guys."

"Don't be silly, they're gentlemen. We'll be just fine," Amelia reassured.

Cat, as if she were a proud co-conspirator, spoke discreetly to Penn and Amelia. Nodding toward Lily and Grace, Cat said, "I told them they were buzzkills."

Amelia smirked and opened the door. "Let's go, Penn." Penn appreciated Amelia's resolve in the face of this confrontation.

Penn wanted to lighten the moment. "We look like we're piling out of a clown car!" But then a carp on the seafood display seemed to roll a wary eye in her direction, and she hushed up.

"What do you think?" Lily asked Grace as they watched their friends hurry away.

"I saw *things*. Bob has drugs. What should we do?"

"We can't drag them out by their hair." Lily sighed. "Let's get Cat and leave. There's nothing to be done except hope for the best."

56. CAT

Gears grinding, the bus climbed the steep, bumpy road. Cat, Lily, and Grace, the only passengers in the dimly lit vehicle, were jostled about.

Cat could not contain her displeasure. "Cocktails and a taxi, I said. No, we had to wait outside forever, only to take this rattletrap."

"I had to get the hell out of there. Bob and his vial!" Grace sounded so self-righteous to Cat. Cat felt like taking her on.

"What? Coke? Is it so shocking to experiment? They'll be fine."

Lily shook her head. She leaned forward holding her stomach, her eyes closed.

57. AMELIA

Amelia was charmed by the Hotel San Michele. At least a hundred years old, it overlooked the coastal road and ocean. It didn't have the warm intimacy of Villa Bianco, but she found the lobby quite appealing, if a bit ornate. The reception desk was a large semicircle of polished wood with letterboxes and a key bank directly behind.

The foursome waited for the desk clerk to return. Amelia giggled quietly as Mick nipped her ear. She noted that Penn allowed herself to succumb to the little kisses Jax was plying upon her neck—thankfully, she'd overcome her earlier reservations.

Jax, suddenly impatient, stopped his advances upon Penn. "So where is everybody?" He heaved himself over the counter and grabbed the appropriate room keys attached to weighty metal identification tags. He checked the room numbers and tossed one to Mick. "See ya later, buddy."

Amelia looked up at Mick coyly and smiled.

"Amelia, come with me. To the *Ladies*. Now." Penn's voice had a shrill edge. And there was no mistaking the exasperated eye rolling that passed between Mick and Jax.

"Of course, dear," Amelia said. It was critical to placate Penn. She'd promised Penn they'd stick together. She smiled a little lamely at Mick as she departed.

Once inside the ladies room, each went into her own private stall. An elderly tourist entered the room and began to powder her face in the dim light.

"What is it now, Penn, dear?" Amelia was careful to speak serenely, as if she weren't every bit as keyed up as Penn—just in a different way.

"Amelia, I'm scared...but when Jax kisses me...it's exciting."

"Well, that's a good thing, isn't it? Besides, we're the ones in charge here. We decide how far we let them go."

"Yeah, but what will we tell the girls *if* we don't show up till tomorrow?"

"There are a thousand things we could be doing. There's music to go listen to and parties. That's it! Mick and Jax know people here." Amelia waxed creative. "Someone could be having a party—and of course, they'd want to go. And if we get home too late, sweetie, we'll say we went to sunrise services. Goodness, everyone will believe that about you." Amelia congratulated herself for thinking of church as an alibi.

"Promise, on your honor, we won't split up...We'll leave together."

"I already have, sweetie." Amelia emerged from her stall and caught the tourist's reproachful stare in the mirror. She blushed and went to the sink to wash up. The tourist handed Amelia a folded linen towel, embroidered with the San Michele crest, sniffed disapprovingly, and left.

Penn opened the stall door. "Was there someone in here?"

"What makes you think that, sweetie?"

Just a couple of minutes later, they walked down the hall to join their dates. Penn stopped, then plopped herself down onto a chair beneath an etching of St. Michael, the archangel. *If Penn isn't the picture of guilt,* Amelia thought as she pulled out her hankie and began dusting a little bronze statue of St. Michael, in armor with sword in hand, which stood on the console next to Penn.

"Amelia, stop it right now!" Penn's voice was laser sharp. "I'm a wreck!"

"Fine! Let's leave. Now." Amelia knew she wasn't done having fun, but if Penn was going to put the brakes on every five seconds, there wouldn't be any fun left to have.

"Leave? I don't exactly want to leave…"

58. CAT

Cat wandered down the hall, holding her abdomen. Lily and Grace, dressed to hike, scanned Penn and Amelia's room: beds made, clothes strewn about, armoire open, empty wineglasses on the vanity.

"I can't hike," Cat whined. "I've got cramps."

"Look, the girls didn't come home," Grace said, pushing the door open.

"I'm calling the police." Lily headed to the hall phone.

"The police? Don't be silly." Cat felt sorry for Lily and Grace. Such naiveté. She heard Lily on the phone, all emotional, speaking in Italian.

Cat followed Grace; she plunked down on Lily's bed and waited. Grace brushed her hair vigorously and made a tighter ponytail.

Lily returned, upset, and threw herself into the armchair. "We have to wait forty-eight hours. Can you believe it? Now what?"

"You go take your hike, they'll be back before you are." Cat curled up on Lily's bed and moaned a little. "Anyway, I'll be here if they need anything."

■   ■   ■

A slight breeze cooled the terrace as the morning fog lifted. Cat, still in pj's, dozed on the Egyptian chaise. She roused, hearing footsteps again; she thought it might be Penn this time. Opening her eyes, she saw Quinton climbing the stairs carrying a bag of eggplant.

Cat, befuddled, wondered if she had misinterpreted Quinton's response last night. He must have intended for her to go along on his shoot. Yikes, here she was, totally unprepared.

"You're early. I'm not ready yet."

"Hey, appreciate your offer, but I have to beg off. You aren't looking too spunky anyway. You okay?"

"Ah, just cramps. Some gorgeous eggplant you got there."

"I brought it for Marie Elena. Say, where is everyone this morning?"

Cat was happy to be the gossip columnist, as it were. "Deedee and Penn are MIA. Lily and Grace are hiking. Amelia only just crawled in."

A flash of relief crossed Quinton's face. And then a look of concern. "Cat, do me a favor? Get yourself checked out once you're home."

After Quinton left, Cat wandered back to her room with a fresh latté. Now she was sure—Quinton liked her best, as much as Lily, for sure, probably more. He paid her such sweet attention. All of this brought confidence to Cat. Maybe she didn't want Quin. But when she divorced Pietro, she'd have no trouble attracting a professional who would value her as a co-equal.

59. GRACE

The rising sun soaked up the remaining coolness of the dawn chill. "Maybe we should have waited awhile longer," Lily said, questioning the early departure. "It wouldn't have made that much difference to us. We're almost there and it's not even hot; Penn will be very disappointed."

"We left a half hour after we'd planned," Grace grumped. "The ground will be baking around here soon. At least we'll be heading downhill during the worst of the heat." Lily was always so accommodating. After all, wasn't this little excursion at Penn's insistence?

"Grace, I hope they're okay. I admit I'm worried."

"Me too. A little. But when I think about them all cozy and cooing with those smarmy guys…it's irritating." Grace tried to balance concern with anger. "And you know, Lily, they are smart and capable."

"You're right, of course," Lily agreed as they walked past postcard-like gates and entryways to the homes that flanked the path.

"But they did promise they'd be back and up on time. 'Give us a little knock, just in case,' says Amelia. Damn! I almost knocked my knuckles off before I opened the door. Penn didn't enforce her Chore Wheel; the room looks like it did before they left last night. What the heck is going on?" Grace frowned as she gave a cursory look at their surroundings.

Every home had a visible garden with flowers and vegetables.

"Maybe Amelia will help me put in a small garden when we get home. Something Callie and I could tend together…tomatoes, basil."

The sun was hot and there was very little breeze atop Villa Jovis. The rising temperature only served to increase Grace's ire.

"I hope they can manage to get to the airport. I'd *hate* for them to miss our plane," Grace continued, working herself up into a good mad.

"Smell the air, Grace. Mmmm, it's sweet and lemony." Lily became pensive for a moment. "Pay attention. We'll remember this hike and talk about it later. Did you bring your camera? I want a picture of you right there, at those old columns."

"Hold on, let me put it on the timer. We can both be in it. Would've been nice if everyone were here with us. Three are MIA and Cat's got cramps. Oh sure, buddy! 'We're going to take a girls' trip. Just the six of us. What fun we'll have,'" Grace mimicked as she fiddled with the camera settings. "'We'll sightsee and shop and eat wonderful Italian food and best of all we'll be together. No husbands, no kids; footloose for the first time in years.' Some vacation!"

She continued to grouse as she set the camera on a rock and ran over to join Lily. The two leaned together and smiled, one whose smile didn't reach her eyes, the other with a look so practiced, no one would ever see the disappointment and anger that roiled within her, just the brilliant blue sky and the ancient ruin in the background.

Lily took off her hat and fanned her face. "Built by Augustus, you know. Tiberius inherited after he died…" Lily began, but was stopped by the gloomy look on Grace's face.

"I miss Marc and Jemima. Wouldn't you like to be home with Callie? Our friends are so absorbed with themselves, they aren't even sympathetic to you about Dirk. And that woman!"

"Enough, Grace! I don't want their sympathy." Lily's voice softened. "I know how you're feeling. Yes, I'm sick with longing for Callie, and I don't know what to say about the girls. I simply want to enjoy the last little bit of vacation we have left." Lily paused. "I'm scared to confront Dirk."

"Lily, did you ever have suspicions about Dirk? About infidelity?"

"It has crossed my mind, and I've heard it said that if you think it's true, it probably is true. But that saying can't *always* be true. The thing about Dirk is that he's calculating, shrewd. He'll have a good reason for writing Darleen's name next to his reservation for MoonShadow."

Lily sat on a low wall and tied her shoe. She looked up at Grace, who was winding her ponytail into a bun. "Did you know Dirk has always been jealous of our six-some? He thinks I'm more loyal to the girls than to him. Well, if you think it's true, it probably is true," Lily ended with a rueful smile.

"Do you think Marc could be seeing someone?" Grace looked away, fearful of Lily's answer to her niggling question.

"Grace, don't be ridiculous," Lily said. "Marc adores you. He treats you like a goddess. With the turn our group vacation has taken, it's no wonder you're having doubts. Try to forget about it. You'll be home in a couple of days, and everything will be fine. Come on, let's get some more photos and see the rest of this place. I don't imagine we'll be back anytime soon."

■　　■　　■

Marie Elena could be seen dusting in Penn and Amelia's room as Lily and Grace came up the stairs and approached the door.

"Where've you been?" Grace's voice contained a harsh note that she hoped was not lost on Penn as she strode down the hall with her hands on her hips. "We waited for you to come home! You could've called us. I thought you wanted to go with us. It was all you talked about before you got here. So much for sisterhood!"

Penn collapsed against Amelia in tears.

"There, there, sweetie. No need to cry, everything is fine now," Amelia comforted Penn. Turning to Grace she said, "Back off! We were in way over our heads. It took some planning to get ourselves out of there and back home intact. They weren't too cooperative."

"We're thankful you're safe," Lily said. "We'd no idea what happened to you."

60. PENN

Penn fell against the door, her elbow striking the hinge.

"Oww," she wailed.

Her heart pounded. Pounding just like before. *Eerie fog. She's running, terrified. Is her dress torn? The way it trails on her legs. It's wet. She's wobbly. Her high heels snag on the cobblestones. Six bells ring out, from the distance. She turns to look over her shoulder. Am I being chased?*

"Terrifying!" Penn wailed as Amelia pulled her into the bedroom, with Lily and Grace following.

61. GRACE

Marie Elena discreetly picked up a stack of fresh towels and carried them into the bathroom.

"Where's Deedee?" asked Grace.

"She's with Bob," Amelia responded. "We haven't seen her since we left them at the restaurant. Penn, honey, I'm going to draw you a hot bubbly bath." She bustled Lily and Grace out the door. "I think we'll take a tray in our room tonight and see you tomorrow."

Marie Elena began to strip the beds. Grace thought it an odd time for her to tackle the job.

Once back in their own room, Lily grabbed a brush and gave her hair a few quick strokes. "Poor things, it must have been terrifying for them. They should have called us; we would have rescued them."

Grace sat on her bed, pulled a pillow onto her lap, and leaned against the wall. Water being run for Penn's bath rumbled softly through the pipes.

"Let's not forget whose fault it is they were ever in that position." Grace reflected a moment. "You're right, Lily. I'm ashamed of myself. Thank goodness they're safe."

Sitting next to Grace, Lily unlaced her boots and leaned back and closed her eyes. The low murmur of Penn and Amelia's voices could be heard. Occasionally Penn's voice rose, but the words were indistinguishable.

"What can't they tell us? Do you think they were, you know?" Lily cringed.

"Do you mean raped? Oh no. I can't even imagine!" The idea turned Grace's stomach.

"Oh, Grace! How can we help them?"

Moments later, waves of laughter could be heard through the wall.

"Laughing? *They're laughing*!" Lily said with disbelief.

Furious, Grace jumped to her feet. "We've been chumped!" Grace spat out. "They had a damned good time!"

PUERTA VALLARTA, MEXICO,

AND LOS ANGELES, CALIFORNIA

AUGUST

1979

HUSBANDS LEFT TO THEIR OWN DEVICES

62. DIRK

"I'm having a damned good time, Mr. White, sir." Dirk tugged Darleen's side ponytail affectionately. Dirk was having a damned good time himself. The two lounged by the ocean clad in revealing swimsuits, their bodies glistening with oil.

Dirk closed his eyes against the ultra brilliance of the Mexican sky. Lily never had to know about this escapade to Puerta Vallarta complete with five-star boudoir, mariachi music, margaritas, lots of margaritas, and lots of TLC from a willing partner.

"Whatcha thinkin' about?" Darleen asked.

"Thinkin' how clever you were, finding that junior golf camp. They've got bona fide pros on staff." Dirk sucked the margarita's lime wedge and made a silly face. Darleen laughed. A bright, sparkling, unrestrained laugh.

With that laugh Dirk felt even more adored. No guilt attached. Callie was just fine. Malibu Little Links, with its focus on golf, offered plenty of *worthwhile* activities for one eight-year girl, considering the reasonable fees. As for Lily, she was selfishly spending leisure time on the Isle of Capri, get that, the Isle of Capri, with her supposed friends. Why shouldn't he have some relaxation too?

63. KEN JR.

"Aren't you just mad about Nordstrom, Hawk?" Sarah Rosenberger asked Ken Jr. He liked her nickname for him. She thought it illogical that a grown man would continue to be referred to as Junior. It was cute that she didn't get the whole senior, junior, and III concept. He didn't mind that his family and friends added the junior. Once his dad passed away, maybe he'd drop it. Become just plain Ken Hawkins. Or maybe by then he'd be known to all as Hawk.

"Nordstrom has the best selection of nursery furniture and baby clothes. It's by far the most elegant department store in Southern California. Come over here so you can see the crib I want." Ken Jr. was firmly guided toward a massive display of baby equipment. Ken was struck by how big Sarah was getting. Not too much longer till the little tyke made an appearance. Ken Jr. always enjoyed the anticipation of the due date. The Mr. Toad's Wild Ride to the hospital, the first time he held his baby, it was all exciting.

"It's all nice, but I'm partial to the Jenny Lind. I like the spooled crib bars." Ken Jr. immediately noticed he'd made a mistake.

Sarah's face fell. "I like a more modern style. Jenny Lind is nice, Hawk, but so old-fashioned."

A Shirley Temple pout, if Ken Jr. had ever seen one. But he knew better than to tangle with an expectant mother.

"Modern it is, then," Ken Jr. announced magnanimously. "Let's take it to your place now, and I'll get it set up."

Sarah perked up. "Oh, thank you. Let me just select some sheets, and a few little outfits, some booties, receiving blankets—"

"Whoa, whoa, whoa! Save something for the baby shower."

▓   ▓   ▓

Sarah's home was a small but appealing little Spanish, impeccably decorated, south of the Boulevard. Ken Jr. reflected briefly on what a brilliant purchase Sarah had made. And she a single woman. He pieced together the crib and tightened the screws. He set the mattress on the coils, then began to make up the bed. When the last bunny-covered bumper was in place, he turned to Sarah and grinned proudly.

Sarah sat in a rocker, feet propped up on a cushion in the same bunny print as the bumpers. "Nice. Thank you. How about a foot rub? My feet are screaming!"

Ken Jr. knelt down and picked up a swollen foot, attached to a swollen ankle. He imagined her skin splitting like a cooked sausage. Good thing it wasn't up to him to give birth.

"Why don't I call for some takeout? Italian, Mexican, Chinese?"

"Mercy! What time is it? I've got to call the kids." Ken Jr. went into the hall, dialed the phone. "Jenny? Are you kids all right?" He sighed with relief. Once back in the nursery, he knelt back down to pay the necessary attention to Sarah's feet. He remembered Amelia having the same complaint and unwisely commented upon it.

"I'm not interested in the trials of Amelia's pregnancies." Sarah's voice was clipped. "What I am concerned about is getting Amelia to agree."

64. HUGH

Hugh sat on the bench in the dugout, waiting for his turn to bat. Why, before ol' Mama came to live with 'em, bringin' her walker and a basket of prescription bottles, his Deedee used to park her cute self in the stands and cheer for him. Tight purple team T-shirt, flauntin' her bazooms. Who wouldn't wanna slipstream her velocity? Now his best girl was workin' her ass off at a department store and actin' as a hands-and-knees slave at home too. *What's left over for me? Slim pickins. Oh, don't get me started*, he admonished himself.

Hugh, Hugh, Hugh! his teammates called. He was up. *Hugh, Hugh, Hugh!* He grabbed a bat and got himself in position. *Hugh, Hugh, Hugh!* He watched the pitcher spit, grab his crotch, glare at him, then pitch. Hugh, poised to bat, eyed the ball spinning toward him. The ball transformed into Mama's head and her sourpuss face. He swung that bat with all the force within him. *Crack!* Mama's head sailed beyond the field into the clouds. Hugh loped proudly around the bases and slid home to a thunderous cheer: *Hugh, Hugh, Hugh!*

Back in the dugout amidst backslaps and congratulations, Hugh made a promise to himself. He took charge of that ball he just hit; he would take charge of the household too.

65. PIETRO

Noni slit open envelopes. She blew into each before passing to Pietro. Pietro unfolded the contents, reviewed the bill, okayed with a red pen, and passed it back to Noni. She had a pile forming beside the checkbook. And then one item in particular caught Noni's attention.

"How much? For airplane ticket?" Noni wagged the bill at Pietro.

Pietro took another look at the figure. His sad face grew livid. In one swift move he slid from his chair and slammed it back under the table disrupting Noni's tidy pile of envelopes. "Charges! And more charges! First the German camera, then film lab f-f-fees. That alone cost us more than a m-m-month's groceries. Now a first class t-t-ticket?" Pietro pulled himself erect, resembling a legendary colossus. "If these charges indicate the cost of Cat's personal growth…Cat's going to remain st-st-stunted."

Noni heaved herself to standing. "Pietro, *mio figlio, guarda tua madre!*" Noni lustily produced a series of hip thrusts. "Plant a seed in her belly. A baby will stop her."

66. GEORGE

George Pines shook another martini. "The last of the olives," he groused. "Penn should keep a backup in the pantry. I've told her repeatedly. Lists, lists, and lists, and not a thought for me."

Phillip's bossy voice penetrated from the playroom into the den. "Give me some alone time!" A door slammed. Labor Day weekend and George was stuck at home with his sons. Darn it all, he should be on the links. None of the babysitters on Penn's list was available. Nanette said no, and he hadn't a clue who else to call.

The younger boys came screeching into the room. Charles yelled, "Henry hit me, it's my Lego's, and I didn't give him permission."

Henry sniveled, "When's Mommy coming home? You didn't give us lunch yet."

George gritted his teeth. *This is the last, the* very last *time Penn is going to head off into the wild blue yonder. She belongs at home taking care of her responsibilities; that's what consumes her anyway—laundry, shopping, vacuuming, de-fingerprinting every freaking surface as if the Mr. Clean police might pounce momentarily.* Finding the pretzel bowl empty, he scrounged the last peanut from the salty can.

"Phillip," he called out, "make your brothers a sandwich, for heaven's sake." George opened the under-bar fridge in search of more olives. "Damn! We'll see who's in charge of this outfit when she gets her world-traipsing butt home."

He strode down the hall, crunching army men underfoot. Angrily he ripped the Chore Wheel from its perch of honor next to the wall clock. He struck a match, lit the offending item, and at arm's length, the Chore Wheel flared, burning to ashes. The boys watched aghast.

"What are you doing, Daddy?" Phillip squealed, spoon poised over the grape jelly jar.

67. MARC

Marc McCrea sat on a shady park bench and watched Jemima tear around the sandy play center. She slid down the curly slide, climbed up ladders, swung on the monkey bars. Lots of energy; his little mouse's battery seemed charged up to infinity. He'd been a father for five years, a husband for thirteen. He'd never meant to marry, knew marriage wasn't for him. But Grace, his sweet Gracie, had enchanted him. Made him think that maybe, just maybe, he could be a husband. And maybe even a dad.

"Jemima, time to go," he called out to the little blonde scamp. She was on the rings and let go at the sound of his voice, falling into the sand and onto her face. Marc rushed to her, helped her up, and hugged her.

"Oh, sweetheart, are you okay? Sure you are," he assured the whimpering child as he brushed sand out of her hair and off her face. "So brave. Let's get all that sand off you. Grammie Hope won't want to vacuum it out of her carpet, will she?"

"Daddy, I never went on the rings before. Mommy says I need to be taller. She'll be surprised." Jemima glowed with accomplishment.

Later, Marc McCrea sat on the edge of the bed; how quiet the house seemed, with Grace away in Italy and Jemima situated with grandparents. From this perch he could see his reflection in the round mirror behind Grace's dresser. The porcelain hand on the oaken surface wore his wife's favorite rings, gold and silver creations crowned with hefty iridescent stones. The frozen hand beckoned him closer.

Pushing himself from the bed, Marc withdrew one of the scarves that hung in streams from the outstretched fingers and wrapped it twice around his neck, mock hanging himself. *She'll be home soon. A noose, my beautiful noose*, he thought as he viewed his drawn face. Lifting the rope of silk to his nose, he inhaled and shuddered as he caught a waft of Grace's perfume.

CAPRI

AUGUST

1979

DISENCHANTMENT

68. GRACE

"It's almost our last night. Let's go somewhere. I don't want to sit around here waiting for my period," Cat said with enthusiasm.

"I thought you had cramps this morning. That's why you didn't hike to Villa Jovis with us." Grace was testy, easily piqued.

"I did. Sometimes it takes longer to get here. I can have cramps for three or four days before it comes. I've been home all day. I need to get out," Cat complained.

"Good idea, Cat," Lily said. "I know a little place that serves a superb thin-crust pizza. We don't need to change."

"Not change? Don't you want to get a little dressed up? Go to a nice place? Celebrate?"

"Celebrate what?" Grace growled. "Cat, you can come or not. Your choice. I'm going, and I'm not changing, and I'm not putting on makeup."

Cat looked to Lily as Grace walked out the door. "She's a little bitchy, isn't she?" Lily shrugged and followed Grace. Of course Cat followed Lily.

Lily ordered their pizza; Cat ordered their wine. Grace surprised them both. "I'm craving sweet cream. I'm having cannoli. After a slice of pizza, that is."

Lily looked at Grace in disbelief. "What's up with you? No salad?"

"Who knew real food was so delicious?" Grace grinned.

The waiter brought a bottle of wine to the table. When he began to pour, Cat stopped him, claiming the duty for herself. Once he'd walked away, she said, "They always pour light. I think wine tastes better when you have a healthy serving!" Grace disagreed, but said nothing. A big glass of wine sounded fine.

"That Midol from Marie Elena fixed me right up," Cat continued. "I was doubled over this morning, but felt much better when Quin showed up."

"Quinton? He was at the Villa today?" Grace asked, surprise slipping into interest. "When was that?"

"Oh, I don't know. I didn't check the clock. He brought back his photography gear. Stayed on for quite awhile. We had caffé. He was rather chatty. Thank God I'd gotten around to showering and making up my face."

"Yes, thank God!" said Grace. Her hint of sarcasm was lost on Cat.

"If I had to guess, I'd say there's some electricity between us."

Grace gulped her wine before asking Cat which manifestations might be indicative of this crush.

"The way he looks at me. Makes eye contact. Reaches out to touch my hand or arm when he's making a point. He stayed on and on. It's cute. Flattering, you know."

Grace's eyes narrowed as she listened to all the symptoms of Quinton's affections. "Cat, don't put too much value on those things. Quinton has loads of girlfriends. His models are always attracted to him. He's a flirt."

"I think I can tell the difference between flirting and real interest, Grace. By the way, has Quin ever been married?"

Grace hesitated, then responded with a clipped yes. She didn't feel like giving Cat the lowdown on Quinton.

"When? For how long? What happened? Does he have kids?"

"Cat, you're the one who had such a lengthy chat with him today. Why didn't you play twenty questions then? You'll just have to ask him yourself."

"My, oh my, aren't we touchy tonight. Lily, what do you know about Quin?" Cat persisted.

"No more than Grace told you," Lily answered. She stood up, telling Grace and Cat that she wanted to check out the art in the shop next door and would be back before dinner was served. Lily walked away from the table with a little wave. Grace knew she wasn't interested in being drawn into Cat's quest for information.

"Fine. Play it close to the vest, if you must, but I'm willing to bet I'll hear from him when we get back to LA." Cat poured another healthy round of wine and held up the empty bottle, signaling the waiter to replace it.

"Don't count on it," Grace stated in a flat voice. This was too much. Cat had stepped on her last nerve.

"Don't underestimate me, Grace. You think being skinny entitles you to Quin?"

Grace's eyes widened, and her voice, though no longer flat, was no louder. "Have you lost it? What are you talking about?"

"Don't pretend to be shocked. You think being emaciated makes you attractive to men. I'm going to tell you differently. Quinton likes women with meat on their bones. He's sick of all those doe-eyed, hollow-cheeked skeletons he has to photograph. I hadn't planned on telling you, but he made it ever so clear that he prefers my fuller figure to the usual x-rays." Cat returned fire with an equally quiet voice, but her conviction was clear.

"Cat, you aren't serious!" Grace was appalled.

"He's attracted to me, and you're jealous!"

"We're married women! I don't need to be jealous! What are you playing at? We'll be home soon—with our husbands and children."

"Don't throw that at me, Grace. I haven't heard you scolding Amelia and Penn or Deedee for dallying with the pilots. Besides, you have no idea what I've missed out on being married to Pietro. I deserve more. You don't think I can attract handsome, interesting, intelligent men. You think only Pietro could want me!"

"Please, stop it! I didn't mean it that way. You're taking it all wrong. I'm sorry. I apologize. I'm sorry." Grace was beginning to tear up. Why did Cat refuse to see there was nothing wrong with Pietro? Pietro, who loved Cat and Jason and Leo? He worked hard at being a good husband and father. It was all too much.

Hearing Cat talk about what she deserved and what she wanted was causing Grace to look too closely at her own life. Tears spilled over her cheeks as she thought about Marc. What had she missed out on? What did she deserve that she wasn't receiving? There was a persistent ache within her that even lovely little Jemima couldn't fill; only Marc had the power, but he was not so inclined. It had nothing to do with him being a good husband and father. He performed those jobs admirably, at least to the onlooker. He was good and kind to Grace and Jemima; no one could fault his devotion. But she needed more than being treated like the duchess on her fifth birthday. She craved for Marc to touch her, love her.

"Grace, calm down, don't cry. It's okay, I forgive you. Obviously you can't understand what I'm feeling. I've had more time to think about everything since I've been away from Pietro, and I know I don't want that life anymore. Distance and time alone have given me clarity."

Grace didn't tell Cat. *Couldn't* speak of her humiliation. She simply let Cat think her tears were an apology.

"Goodness, *signore*! What am I interrupting?"

Thank heavens, Lily the intuitive peacemaker, is back. Grace was relieved. Cat could wallow longer in the misery of her marriage and unsatisfying life, but Grace didn't want to think about her own situation.

■　　　■　　　■

"I wonder if Deedee ever made it home," Grace worried as the three walked the narrow streets back to the Villa.

"We know Deedee can take care of herself," said Cat. "She keeps telling us how much she dreads going back home; she's simply making good use of her time here."

"But what if we needed to reach her? What if there were an emergency or something?"

"Those things only happen to me," Cat said. "Do I have to point out Jason and his scratched cornea? I could have run home when Pietro called, but what would've been the point? Noni San Carlo is ensconced in my house with all she needs: my husband and our two children. There's no room for me in that happy quartet, believe me!"

Lily protested Cat's jaded words. "Don't discount the love of your husband. It's hard to replace."

"Oh, right. Maybe you refer to Pietro's fumbling lovemaking; his jackrabbit starts finish the race before my slow and steady tortoise ever begins. Or is there something else I should be grateful for?"

Grace clenched her jaws. Pietro was a hardworking, good man. "How about the security Pietro's income provides?"

"Funny how you completely ignore my contribution to the equation. It's not like he's hanging on a limb by himself, solely responsible for putting bread in our mouths," Cat reminded Grace. "I could run the Cantina."

Grace, fatigued by Cat's sparring, dreamed about a more pleasant topic. "Now I wish I'd had the gelato too."

Lily sighed. "If only my life were as simple as selecting lemon gelato."

The Villa was quiet when Lily unlocked the door, stepping aside for Cat and Grace to enter. "I guess everyone's in bed already. Maybe that's not a bad idea. We can sightsee all day tomorrow if anyone wants. We only have one full day left. Then home."

Cat decided to make a pot of tea and stay up awhile longer. Climbing the stairs, Grace saw the trays scattered with scraps from dinner in the hall outside Amelia and Penn's bedroom.

"They must think they're in a hotel and it's Marie Elena's job to clear up after them," said Grace. "They couldn't walk their trays down to the kitchen?"

Lily didn't reply. Lily did note, however, that Deedee was not in her room. "Where the heck is she? What is she doing? Is she okay? Should we do anything?"

"Like what? Call the police?" Grace thought Lily's earlier lack of success with the police would discourage that suggestion.

"I don't know. But why hasn't she called us? If she isn't back tomorrow, we have to do something. This is her second night gone."

"Damn! She should know better! She's a mother, for heaven's sake! She must know we're worried about her! I'm going to tell her just what I think about her scaring us this way. And she isn't single yet either!" Grace felt like lashing out. Except for Lily, everyone else was tending to primal needs and throwing away vows and promises. Grace had never felt so different from her friends.

6 9 . CAT

Cat suddenly felt superior. How ignorant were Grace and Lily? Acting so shocked over Deedee's maneuver. As if Southern California suburbia cloistered wives from extramarital attention these days. This wasn't the fifties, anymore, if anyone was paying attention. Cat abandoned her idea of having tea; something more exciting was afoot.

"Let's stay up and talk," Cat said. "You won't sleep anyway, being worried and all."

Cat savored the elegant satisfaction of a front-row seat. She had grasped the unspoken back home; obviously Grace and Lily were snoozing through the play and had not. Now she could awaken her friends and watch them squirm. How to start?

Once settled on the terrace, Grace with chamomile tea, Lily with lemon water, Cat with a crystal snifter of brandy, the conversation could begin. But Cat hesitated. Moths circled the Venetian lantern and cast fleeting shadows against the wall. Somewhere off and away, a crow heckled.

Cat finally led with, "Lily, what did you wear to Pat and Ted's character party?" Cat had moved to Chatsworth in May of '78, and the twelve had begun socializing with her energetic neighbors. Parties were held monthly, always with a costume mandate.

"Hmm, oh yeah, I had made myself an elaborate Snow Queen costume. Nice change from tailored projects. Why?"

"What did you wear, Grace?"

"I dressed as Wendy in a flannel nightgown. Marc dressed as Peter Pan; he wore green tights and a pointy cap with a feather. But I felt so stupid! Talk about being out of step."

"Yeah, you sure were. That was the party when what's-her-name did the hoochie coochie in a harem get-up," Cat said, feeling her way to the punch line.

"Oh Lord, now I remember," Lily said, disgusted. "What's-her-name hoochied her coochie right in our guys' faces. Tantalizing one husband after the other."

"So like, did you know *switches*, by *mutual consent*, were in progress?" Cat leaned forward to fully view the impact of her words. "What's-her-name was soliciting a partner for later."

Lily jolted, spilling her water. "No way!"

"Did Deedee or Amelia or Penn catch on? Hell, do you think they got caught up in, well, permissive morals and never said?" Grace began to pace.

"Makes sense now, doesn't it?" Cat said, trying to imply a rationale for the new behavior.

"No, heavens, no!" Lily said emphatically. "I can't believe it." Cat enjoyed how shaken Lily looked in that moment.

Conversation halted. The crow's raspy voice scraped the blackboard of night again.

"Well, hit me over the head," Lily said. "I'm slow. I thought it was about dressing up ultra sexy for theme parties. Any excuse for making a costume, you know me."

"I remember the luau party, nipples and belly buttons on display," Grace chimed in. "Husbands dancing close and sweaty, reeking of pineapple juice and rum. After that Marc said he didn't want to go anymore."

"Grace, it makes me sick. Couples believing the grass in another bedroom is greener, and then a turn on for their marriage."

"You're awfully quick to judge," Cat said in a newly philosophical voice. "Maybe our trio of swingers will be happier in their own beds after this!"

"That's a loaded *maybe...*," Lily whispered.

70. AMELIA

Amelia wakened in the still, dark, early morning. Penn sat Indian-style on the floor folding and refolding her clothes in the dim glow of the nightlight. Amelia sat up and assessed the scene before her. She knew most of Penn's moods and expressions. She had no difficulty interpreting the worry she saw on Penn's face. Amelia was only somewhat bothered by the same thing—a Christian conscience. Her stomach gave a little flip when she considered the last few days of excitement and their daring behavior.

"Penn, sweetie, you're obsessing," Amelia said softly.

Penn looked up. "I'm going to hell! How can I be forgiven? I've never been with anyone but George."

"Yes, but George was surely with someone before he met you," Amelia reasoned.

"Well, of course he was. He's a man, isn't he? How does that make it right? I'm damned, for sure."

"Sugar, the Lord forgives all manner of sinners. We know that from years of Bible study. We simply need ask His forgiveness and He grants it." Amelia wasn't thinking that she would ask any favors of the Lord for herself at this time, but maybe it would bring Penn some relief.

"This might be the only time I've wished I were one of those Catholics! They go into that little booth behind the velvet curtains—they're hidden from view, and they confess to a priest who never sees them. Then they walk out of there feeling just fine. Oh, they have a few little prayers to say for penance, but otherwise their souls are brand new. I've always made fun of that exercise, but it sure sounds better than telling Pastor Barnes."

"Penelope, you don't need an intercessor to obtain forgiveness. Go directly to The Source. There's no heavenly reason to discuss this with Pastor Barnes."

Crikey! Penn blabbing this to Pastor Barnes was alarming. And ridiculous. "I must admit, it's harder for me to forgive Ken Jr. than it is to forgive myself. Not that I don't believe what I did was wrong, and I *do* feel *some* guilt, but not nearly what I'd have expected."

"Amelia, you're subscribing to the eye-for-an-eye philosophy, aren't you? Can't blame you. Seems to me you've got little to repent for, considering what you've had to put up with. I have to admit, there are times that the *turn-the-other-cheek* stuff is just too hard to swallow." Penn was quiet for a moment. "I'll tell you what I don't look forward to. In fact, I'm dreading it…"

"The flight home? Don't be scared, I'll be with you." Amelia didn't relish the long flight ahead with a twitchy Penn in the seat next to her.

"No, I was thinking about facing our very own *Sister Mary Grace*. Principal of the school for goody-goodies! I can just imagine…"

Amelia extended her hand to pat Penn's shoulder. "My rings! Where did I leave my rings? Penn, have you seen them?"

"What rings? I thought you only had your wedding rings here."

Amelia's face was blanched. Her full lips turned downward, a very recognizable look when she was upset. "That's what I'm talking about."

71. LILY

Lily opened her eyes. It seemed she had only just fallen to sleep after a restless night. There Grace stood at the foot of her bed, silhouetted against the open window. Lily checked the clock—pre-dawn of their last full day on Capri.

"Lily, I brought you caffé," Grace said.

"It's not even daylight yet."

Grace set the tray with a pot, two mugs, and a pitcher of hot milk on the table. "I can't sleep. I've been awake for ages. I'm worried."

"Is it Deedee?"

"No, no. I peeked into Deedee's room, she's finally come home. Cat's snoring like a dog. I can hear Amelia and Penn whispering."

Lily propped pillows against the headboard, turned on the bedside lamp, and leaned back before accepting the rich Italian caffé, Grace's peace offering for awakening her. "It's a big relief to know Deedee's back. So what are you worried about now?"

"You. Me. The group." Grace sounded hopeless.

"Alter your list, Grace. Take me off."

Grace sighed. "Why hasn't Marc called?"

"You know how hard international calling is." Even though she answered calmly, Lily felt alarmed by this new anxiety in her friend. A friend who seemingly led a storybook life: home in the Hollywood Hills, husband in the entertainment business, enviable career, two doting parents, one spirited daughter.

Previously, she could categorize Grace's problems as the everyday variety. Problems easy to patch, mend, or withstand. But Grace's face just now, pinched and pale, exposed turmoil of a different category. Newly acquired, or newly exposed?

"So forget the phone calls. Something's been missing in my marriage." Grace's voice trembled, but she looked Lily in the eye.

"Like what? Marc's always so complimentary, pointing out what a great hostess you are, what an attentive mother you are, how photogenic you are. He couldn't *be* more proud of you!"

"I know! I wish he felt the same about me in bed. And you know something weird? We have three friends who within hours of landing in Italy all happily found themselves trysts. But as deprived as I feel, I couldn't possibly look at another man. I only want Marc."

"Isn't that just as well, since you're married to him?"

Lily thought of her own situation, and Amelia's, now possibly Grace's too. "We escaped the seven-year itch. Maybe our husbands are simply overdue."

Grace jumped up in exasperation, almost spilling her coffee. "Christ on a crutch, Lily!"

Lily tried to explain. "I think every relationship has its own challenges. Don't you? And I suppose we weary mothers don't always offer much excitement."

"Excusing our husbands? Come on, next you'll be excusing our friends, who seem to be forgetting their marriage vows."

"No. We don't know that our friends have exactly broken their vows."

Grace's eyes grew steely, Lily noted, matching the Prussian blue of the embroidered coverlet. *Am I sounding sanctimonious*? she wondered as she traced the satin stiches with a finger.

Grace stiffened. Her sharp tone drew Lily's focus back to the conversation.

"Marriage vows mean something, don't they? Where exactly does sin begin? I hardly recognize my friends. What about Deedee? Gone missing for a couple of days—and nights." Grace was taking no prisoners. "I don't care what kind of act Penn and Amelia pulled yesterday afternoon. You can't tell me something didn't happen. They didn't get out 'just in time.' Sitting around laughing about it when we left the room. What an eye-opener this has been. You think you know someone! At least I thought I knew them."

"Grace, we do know them. For years we've known them. Just name one time when something like this has happened." Lily paused to give Grace a moment to think. "You can't! Twelve years, and our friends have never even joked about it. So why now?" Lily asked, not expecting an answer.

Grace continued, her tone changing, her face filled with sorrow. "Lily, we're like something icky stuck on Penn and Amelia's shoes. They've been trying to ditch us since they arrived."

Lily knew Grace's words were true. Worse, she couldn't help feeling somehow responsible for these personality changes now manifested by her friends.

"I never imagined my invitation would set us up for temptation. It's as if this island breathes some life of its own into us."

Grace scoffed. "Yeah? Four of them got a different whiff than you and I."

"Stop it, Grace! I hate to think it's my fault we're pulling apart." Lily sat still, very still, lured by another thought. "Maybe we haven't escaped it; we've changed too."

Grace fell into the chair, curled up with hands over her face.

Lily hesitated, knowing that Grace's next words could not be withdrawn. "Grace, is there something else?"

"We almost never have sex. I have to beg for it. Marc says he likes me bony, so I stay skinny. Doesn't help. We've barely had sex a dozen times since Jemima's birth. What if it is someone else? Could I be wrong about him?" Grace began to sob. "Lily, am I so unlovable?"

72. PENN

Once inside Hotel San Michele, Penn pushed Amelia toward the front desk. She and Amelia must look a sight. They had thrown on rumpled clothes and forsaken makeup in the interest of haste. Penn hid behind a potted palm and tried to smooth her tangled hair.

Amelia approached the uniformed desk clerk with determination. She pointed to her ring finger. "Lost. Rings. Room 321."

The clerk clucked, amused. He twisted his thin mustache. He licked his finger and flipped pages in a leather-bound book. "Room cleaned. Nobody find."

"Give me key. I look." Amelia sounded ridiculous to Penn, the way she mimicked the clerk's stilted English. The clerk shook his head, closed the book, turned away.

Amelia spoke louder. "I want manager!"

A short while later, Penn and Amelia followed the disgruntled manager out of an antique lift cage and down the dark hallway. Penn held Amelia's hand, sniffling, on the verge of tears. *Let me out of here, I can't be here again.* The manager opened Room 321 and haughtily gestured them in. Amelia made an increasingly frantic search of the bedroom and bath. Penn repeated each of Amelia's examinations, unable to think objectively. She avoided eye contact with the manager, who leaned against the door watching, suspicious-like. *What awful lie is he thinking about us?*

■   ■   ■

There on Anacapri, a short walk from the hotel, Penn and Amelia found the Phoenician Steps. They leaned against a rock wall looking out at the Tyrrhenian Sea far, far below. Penn turned around to gaze at the Sphinx guarding the villa above. Did he know her secret? She looked back at her friend, hoping this would all be just a bad dream someday.

Amelia's face had never looked more morose. Penn felt bad for her; their search of the hotel room (trysting spot for Amelia and the fast-talking-fun-loving-seductive-pilot Mick) had proved futile. Since no errant pair of rings had been returned to the reception desk, and Amelia's scouring on hands and knees had been unproductive, Amelia would indeed return home without her wedding ring set.

Penn had prayed a little discreet investigation might reveal if Jax was all right, if he had returned to his room or maybe checked out. But when Penn got the nerve to inquire, the haughty clerk could find no Jax in the register. Penn didn't know Jax's last name. (This couldn't be happening.)

Penn felt a surge of undirected anger. She turned to Amelia.

"How could you lose them? Whatever possessed you to take your rings off? Your wedding band, not to mention that engagement ring, gone! Over two carats, and it's gone. Ken was continually reminding you to take it in for cleaning, so any light would 'refract just so and throw a prism.' What will he say now?" Penn focused on Amelia's troubles, shoving her own off the hot seat.

"Stop it, Penelope! I'm sick, just sick about it. I feel like throwing up right here. I don't know what I'm going to do."

"But why did you *ever* take them off? You dig in the garden with them on, and I've seen you elbow deep in meatloaf with them on. I can't imagine what you were thinking!"

Amelia's flush increased as she confessed, "As stoned or, or drunk as I was, I knew what I was going to do—I *wanted* to do it—but not with, you know, that reminder of Ken Jr., of my vows, right there on my finger! What am I going to tell him? He's bound to notice they're missing the minute he sees me!"

Penn didn't have a good answer for Amelia. At least her own crimes would be invisible to George, thank God.

"I suppose I could tell him they slipped off while I was climbing into the dinghy at the Blue Grotto…and while listening to the vibrant strains of 'Santa Lucia,' I watched my precious rings sink to the bottom of the phosphorescent water."

"Who knew such poetry lurked within you?" Penn mocked. "At least you didn't murder someone!"

"You didn't murder anyone, sweetie. Stop saying you did. Don't put it out there, just scrub that thought from your mind." Amelia's voice sounded impatient. And in return Penn felt impatient with Amelia, who didn't seem to sense the gravity of her less tangible misery.

"Amelia, what are we going to tell everyone? You know Cat will probe and dig until she gets some kind of answer that will satisfy her. And can't you just see Grace's face all pinched in disgust at us?"

"No one ever needs to know. I'm not telling anyone anything; promise me you won't cave in. We'll stick together, right?"

73. DEEDEE

T*his might just be one of the dullest scenes I've ever had the misfortune of viewin',* Deedee said to herself as she strutted onto the terrace. Lily relaxed on the Egyptian chaise, a book in one hand, the other flung over her forehead. Cat leaned back on a lounge admiring her freshly painted toenails, while Grace stood at the balustrade, listless and apparently entranced by the birds attacking fruit on the trees.

She adjusted the green belt she'd paired with a red halter top and white pants before she called out to her friends, "What the heck is all y'alls' problem this mornin'? I know why I'm feelin' low—havin' to go home tomorrow and face the music." Deedee was feeling cheerful despite her words. "But I thought ever'one else would be beaver-eager to head back home, since y'all been here so long."

"*Eager beavers.*" The correction was made by a lethargic Grace.

"Great—whatever! So what gives?" Deedee persisted.

"Look, girls, it's Miss Flag of Italy…" Cat began.

"I hoped y'all would notice. I thought it was fittin' since it *is* our last day here. I picked this belt up day before yesterday in the cutest little leather shop. These tricolored sandals too. What d'ya think?"

"Where the *hell* have you been? We haven't seen you for the last two days—and nights. You sure didn't need that room to yourself, since you've hardly slept in your own bed!"

Cat's voice caught the attention of Lily and Grace, snapping each out of their brooding. Cat put on her sandals and flounced down the terrace stairs.

"Goodness gracious!" Deedee mocked. "I'm feelin' distinctly monitored."

"Deedee, we've all been concerned about you," Grace rebuked, her voice sharp. "We had no way of knowing if you were all right or where you were. Lily and I talked about calling the police! You know better than to scare us that way."

"I think I'll park next to Lily here. At least I don't have to worry about gettin' a scoldin' from her!" Deedee sulked for only a second before continuing, "I need to get me some espresso. Dang! Havin' fun can sure take the starch out of you."

Contrary to Deedee's expectation, Lily had a little admonishing to add. "Deedee, all we needed was a quick call. You could have let us know you were okay. It would've only taken a few moments to reassure us and you'd have spared us the worry."

"Heavens! I can't believe y'all are making such a big deal over this. How could any of you think I wouldn't be fine? But, since you *are* havin' such a hard time with it, I'm sorry. Awfully, truly, sorry I ever caused you a minute's worth of grief. There now! All better?"

Deedee looked at Lily's glum face and Grace's slumped figure at the terrace rail. "Come on. A little smile won't cost a nickel. I don't know if I'm ready for the funeral y'all look to be plannin' on attendin'."

Lily sighed and returned to her book. Deedee walked over to Grace at the rail. "Well, lookee there! If it isn't the two dancin' queens." Deedee pointed toward the grape arbor where Cat had joined Penn and Amelia. "Man, were they somethin' to behold the other night. Who knew they had that kind of fun in 'em?" Deedee chuckled.

"They secreted themselves away in their room, had dinner trays delivered. *And* they missed our hike to Villa Jovis! They promised to be *up* in time! They never even made it *back* in time!" It was apparent that Grace was still holding a grudge; Deedee could hear the petulance in her voice. "This is the first time they've graced us with their presence since yesterday afternoon."

"Well, don't be gettin' used to my presence, 'cuz I'm catchin' a ride with Bob back to Rome." Deedee turned away, gave a little smile, then headed indoors.

Lily dropped her book and gave a palms-up shrug.

"Oh, that's just dandy!" Grace blurted.

■　　　■　　　■

Coulda gone worse, Deedee thought, pleased that her friends hadn't obstructed her plans. She stuffed a suitcase with the last of her lingerie. Ah shoot! Her self-congratulations were halted by a knock on the door and the quick entry of Lily and Grace.

"What a couple of fussbudgets y'all have become." Deedee frowned.

"A minute's relief and now we get to keep on worrying about you," Lily said.

"Now, don't y'all go gettin' mad at me. This is somethin' I wanna do! I'll meet up with y'all at the airport."

"We're not mad, Deedee, we just think going off with Bob might not be the smartest thing to do," Lily cautioned. "You hardly know him."

"Maybe he's *married*!" Grace added.

"Grace, honey, you just crack me up! *I'm* married. Listen to me, would ya? Ever'thin' is goin' to be fine. I'm only leavin' about twenty hours earlier than all y'all. Bob's rented a Ferrari. We're gonna spend a little time in Sorrento and drive up the coast. I'll be at the airport when I need to be there." Deedee locked her suitcases and attempted to move them from the bed to the floor.

"Deedee, the thing is, we won't know everything is fine until we see you at the airport," Lily said. "We'll have no way of contacting you; we'll be en route ourselves. If you have any kind of a problem, you won't be able to reach us. Did you think about that?"

"Let me tell you somethin'! I'm returnin' to what might as well be a death sentence. Do you think goin' off with Bob could possibly be scarier than that?"

"Are you going to see Bob once you're home?" Grace asked.

"You never know. I might like to, but he's based in Atlanta, and I got a mind to find someone a little closer once I get the mess all sorted out with Hugh. Even though Bob's excitin' as all get out, an' I think he's got money too, that long-distance stuff doesn't hold much charm! But I'm not rulin' anythin' out at this point."

"Deedee, maybe things will work out for you and Hugh. I'll keep my fingers crossed," Grace promised.

"Don't ya dare! Quite frankly, I'm lookin' forward to some relief. I know folks think your husband should come first, but I gotta honor poor Mama too! My taxi's honkin'."

"Deedee, wait! Please change your mind, stay with *us*. We all need to reconnect."

"Gotta go. I'm meetin' Bob at the jet boat. *Ciao, ciao*, girls. It's been fun. See you in Roma."

74. GRACE

When Marie Elena announced dinner was ready to be served, Cat clipped up the stairs to roust Penn and Amelia, who hadn't descended from their ivory tower since Deedee left.

Cat returned with Penn and Amelia's regrets.

Lily's face fell. Her disappointment caused Grace's heart to squeeze. It was all too much. Look at the opportunity Lily had provided to the group. First Deedee took off, now the other two were dumping on her with no regard for her feelings. Personally, Grace didn't give a flying fig if they came to dinner or not. But she did care about Lily and Lily's hope the friends could reconnect and return home feeling as close as when their adventure began.

Grace took the stairs two at a time, stopped at the holdouts' bedroom, and rapped sharply on their door. When there was no answer, Grace turned the handle, only to find it locked. Now riled, Grace banged on the door like a five-year-old.

"Open up, you two. What do you think you're doing? Open up this minute!" Her tone brooked no resistance.

The lock clicked and Amelia opened the door six inches. Penn was visible just behind her.

"Grace, dear, we'll just eat in our room tonight," Amelia stated quietly and reasonably. "We aren't up to socializing."

Grace was too offended to notice Amelia's red eyes or Penn's white face. "Socializing? That's what you're calling common courtesy now?" Grace took a deep breath. She needed to regain a sense of calm. She brought her voice down to match Amelia's quiet and reasonable level. "You both need to come down to dinner. Please don't hurt Lily. She's missing her friends, she's missing you. So get over whatever you two are nursing up here and come to dinner."

At that she turned around and sped away, giving Amelia no chance to rebut her request.

▪   ▪   ▪

If the mood were any icier, we'd be in the Arctic, Grace thought as she surveyed the faces assembled around the dining room table. There was Cat, waxing verbosely, philosophically, about making a responsible decision to leave Pietro. Knowing Cat as she did, Grace knew all her analyzing simply meant that she'd figured out a way to justify her future actions.

Lily was much too quiet. No doubt weighing, yet again, just how at fault she might be for Dirk's conduct. And this upsetting vacation. Grace thought about shaking her, but knew that she could say nothing to sway Lily's perception. She would have to come to her own conclusion, in her own time.

Marie Elena entered with salad, momentarily diverting Grace's attention from her friends to her plate. Grace picked up her fork and speared olive, cucumber, tomato, and feta cheese. As sensuous as food had become to her, Grace couldn't take the bite. Her stomach clutched with tension.

Penn was edgy, evidenced by her pushing lettuce around her plate, reaching for her wineglass, then putting it down before ever drinking. Amelia appeared calmer than Penn, but just as silent; she wore her brooding look. And all the while, Cat nattered on and on.

Grace sat still and tried to manage her volcanic thoughts. She'd been pushing feelings down almost since the arrival of Deedee, Penn, and Amelia. She'd swallowed her irritation at their initial flirting, but was having a more difficult time keeping that aggravation inside, once the innocent turned deceitful.

"Well, you two church ladies certainly pulled a switcheroo! Who'd a thunk it? Leave hearth and home for a week and have a fling!" Cat chortled as she held her wineglass up in a mock toast to Amelia and Penn.

Lily sucked in a deep breath, no doubt appalled by Cat's audacity. "Cat! For heaven's sake! Is that necessary?"

Grace realized that no one had so boldly confronted anyone in the group—ever!

"Oh, come on. What's the big deal?" Cat was nonchalant about her allegations.

It was this specific instant in which Grace's insides began to warm.

"You have no idea what you're talking about, Cat, dear." Amelia sounded sensible as she placed a reassuring arm around Penn's shoulders, but it was too late; Penn would defend herself.

"It was awful, just awful. I don't know how you can joke about it." Her voice trembled, tears brimmed.

Grace felt the warmth in her gut turn molten as it slowly began to rise and spill out when she addressed Penn.

"How awful was it? Let me count the ways. First you meet these scummy guys and all of a sudden you forget about us. The group! Our vacation together becomes a time for you to trollop around meeting weird men for drinks and dinner and drugs. You refused to listen to Lily and me when we tried to get you to come with us. Then you limp home like quivering cocker spaniels who've peed the carpet and retire to your room to lick your wounds, probably praying you aren't diseased."

"Grace, calm down." Lily's shock at Grace's dramatic performance was evident.

Grace knew that none of her friends had ever witnessed this behavior from her. She was biting, contemptuous, and angry; she did not care what they thought.

"Lily, you heard it too. You heard them laugh. Amelia couldn't push us out of the room fast enough. She had to take care of 'poor Penn.' By the time we were back in our room, they were laughing. We heard it through the wall."

Lily didn't respond, but Cat did. "You're making too much of this, Grace. Wherever did you learn this puritanical crap?"

Turning on Cat, Grace pointed a finger and said, "Why the hell are you sticking up for them? And in case you didn't notice, Lily and I were the only ones who didn't go out on the prowl like common cats!"

Penn stood. Grace could tell Penn wouldn't let the fighting words pass. She braced herself for the attack.

"Take a look at your own life for once, Grace."

"Penn, dear, be careful," Amelia cautioned.

Grace went cold. She instinctively understood that Penn knew something that would change her life forever.

"The perfect older man marries the perfect young girl, and they are perfectly happy for years. Well, almost." Penn stopped with the cliffhanger.

"What're you saying, Penn?" Grace's voice was a low growl. She prepared to defend her marriage, bile rising in her throat.

"Get off your cloud, angel; come back to earth and see what you've married!"

"What *I've* married?" Grace selected the sharpest arrow in her quiver, "At least Marc isn't a habitual drunk, Penn. He doesn't run over Jemima's toys in the driveway. How many bikes have you replaced for the boys?"

"And how many times have you been replaced by the boys?" Penn's point pierced even deeper.

Mouths gaped, except Amelia's. She put her head in her hands and moaned.

Marie Elena dropped the tray of dessert in the doorway, but the crash went unnoticed.

Horrified, Grace sank to her knees, retching repeatedly into her napkin.

Penn, shaking, fled the dining room, with Amelia close on her heels.

Lily knelt down, gathered a keening Grace her into her arms, and rocked her.

Cat looked on, paralyzed.

75. PENN

Penn ran up the stairs. She heard Lily cry from below, "How could we be doing this to each other?" As the blue-tiled bathroom came into view, Penn heard only the sounds coming from her own chest, throat, mouth; raw, unbidden wails circled her exploding head. Penn, frantic to hide, to be alone. She slammed the bathroom door behind her. Now she felt frightened to be hidden, to be alone.

She tore at her arms with her manicured nails, hunching into the tiniest Penn possible. She leaned against the porthole window, her breathing rapid and shallow. She stared into the sky, at the mare's tail clouds trailing upward. *Get me out of here, get me away from here, I want to go... home. Home? No! How can I go home?* Penn wailed anew.

Amelia opened the door without knocking. She carried Penn's kimono and a candle, a lavender pillar; its flame wavered and smoked. Perfume immediately filled the small space.

For Penn the scent conjured lavender fields and grass and a childhood moment at an aunt's knee. *Cutting flowers, yes, we were carrying flowers in a basket for Mummy*. Penn's breathing calmed.

Amelia closed the door and set the kimono and the candle on the marble-topped chest. "I'll start you a bath, sweetie," she said kindly.

Soon Penn soaked chin-deep in the claw-foot tub. Amelia sat on the closed toilet and stared at her friend's mascara-streaked face rising from the froth of bubbles. A few straggly locks of Penn's hair trailed into the water. Penn brushed at them from moment to moment, but Amelia didn't offer assistance.

"Penelope, sweetie, I told you to be careful, but you didn't listen," Amelia began. "You could hardly expect Grace to be overjoyed with your news."

Shut up, just shut up! How dare you!

Amelia and Penn had not shared their recent misgivings about Marc's sexual preference with the group. They'd had that conversation with their husbands, who would neither confirm nor deny the allegation. George and Ken Jr. liked Marc. They were impressed by his vocation as well as his golf game. Marc was no sissy; he was a real guy. George wouldn't have become skeptical had he not seen Marc leave the club (more than once) with one of the young caddies who was known to be, well, swishy. But who was he to hitch an uncertain thumb at a good golf buddy? He was content to shrug it off. Not so Penn who enrolled Amelia. Together they'd enumerated all the clues that supported their suspicion until they had convinced themselves.

Penn's anger rose. She sat up and pawed at hair tickling her eye. "Excuse me, Cat started it all. With that wretched toast to us!"

"Yes, sweetie. She certainly *was* stirring the pot, but you have to admit, Cat had no idea where it would lead." Amelia shook her head.

Indeed, after this shocking clash, how will Grace and I even look at each other again? In all their years of friendship there'd never been a fight like this. Sometimes one or the other might get their feelings hurt, but it always worked out after a little venting to someone in the group—other than the perpetrator, of course. With kids' and husbands' continuous demands, the wives chose to keep close a steady friend even if it meant forgiving an injury quickly. But this exchange had gone beyond unintentional hurt feelings. Both women had hurled words intending to wound a once-loyal friend.

Amelia continued to chew on the event. "In some ways, we shouldn't be surprised by Grace's actions. As hard as she tries, she's never been good at hiding her holier-than-thou attitude. Imagine what she felt hearing about Marc! I feel sorry for her, if only she hadn't been such a bitch. But if she hadn't been so bitchy, you might have held your tongue."

Penn nodded, gray tears streaming, her upper lip glistening with snot. "I would *never* have said anything if she hadn't...Oh, drown me, right this minute!"

Amelia ignored Penn's protracted victim role-play. "And what about Lily, reporting the news to us?" Amelia mimicked Lily's literary voice, "'And so, the friends slink into separate camps—forgetting how much they need each other in the foxhole back home.'"

Penn thought Amelia's face had never looked more witchy as she spit out her declaration. "She said that? Slinking? Foxhole?"

"Yes, actually. Like, who does she think she is, Edward R. Murrow or some such? Anyway, didn't you hear her?" Amelia's irritation with Penn showed in her tone.

Penn seethed. *Of course I didn't hear her say that, you bitch. You have no idea how I've been feeling. I can't even think straight!*

"Guilty, okay, I'm guilty," Penn blubbered, turning away from Amelia.

"You're feeling guilty? What about me? I'm going home without my wedding rings!"

The two spent a few silent minutes reflecting on the disaster at dinner. And then a new reality bashed Penn. *Oh dear God.* "So, like all of you have talked about *George*, but nobody had guts enough to tell me?"

76. GRACE

Grace and Lily wandered the garden. Gusts of wind played with the sheets pinned to the distant clothesline; leaves were whisked to the base of the Pan fountain. Lily stopped to stare at the never-ending stream of water splashing from Pan's pipes. Grace stared at Lily. Minutes passed. Lily barely moved. Only her hair lifted by the strong breeze showed life.

Grace felt her stomach flip, twist, knot. "It was a vile lie! Lily, you know it was a lie! She said it to get back at me!"

Lily glanced at Grace, then began to toss coins from her pocket one by one into the fountain. A cloud passed in front of the moon, throwing eerie shadows.

"Okay. She was mad because I blew open her cover about George. She couldn't stand hearing the truth. Like nobody had already figured it out. Wow, big surprise. *But to attack Marc like that?* After all the years we've been friends? Despicable."

Penn's betrayal was unfathomable. Hadn't they been closer than sisters?

Lily turned to Grace and put an arm around her shoulder. She spoke gently. "It's getting chilly out here. We should go in and finish packing."

"Are you patronizing me? You don't believe it. You don't believe Penn's lies…Do you?"

Lily gave Grace's shoulder a squeeze and tried to guide her back to the Villa.

Grace stopped short. "Lilleee, please answer me." Grace heard her own voice and was sickened by the pleading tone.

"Grace, I'm shocked by Penn's words. I don't know what to say. I only know that you need to talk to Marc."

"*Talk to Marc?*" She shrugged Lily's arm from her shoulder. "One of our dearest friends turns on me like a viper, and that's all you can say?" Anger pricked every nerve.

The wind picked up, soughing through the trees, sending droplets of water from the fountain spattering to the ground.

"Grace, I'm not the enemy. Don't focus your anger on me. I'm here for you." Lily's voice was soft, soothing. She put her arm back around Grace's shoulder.

Grace did not rebuff Lily's care. She began to breathe more easily.

"It makes no sense. Think about it, Lily. If it were true, and it's not, wouldn't it be in every rag sheet? Something like that can't be kept under wraps. The gossip columns would have a field day. Marc isn't some unknown in the business." Grace was starting to feel better. "There hasn't been a hint of scandal. Penn said it because there was nothing bad to say. Nothing as bad as George being a drunk. So she had to make something awful up."

Lily made no response. Grace also was quiet, but she began to form a plan. It suddenly came to her how to make everything right. She would prove Penn's accusations false.

"A baby."

"What did you say?" Lily fairly croaked.

"A baby. I'll have another child. We'll get started as soon as I get home. Marc has put me off long enough. If anyone suspects that he isn't anything but all man, a new baby will put it to bed." Resolution, relief, and a little bit of peace surged through Grace. She could fix this.

"Right," was all the response Lily could muster.

The ever-increasing wind tore a sheet from the clothesline. It whipped through the air before settling in the garden's dirt.

77. LILY

Lily sat on the bed looking at Grace, who finally slept. She'd fought against the effects of the sleeping pill Lily had talked her into taking, but within a half hour, she lay against the feather pillow, looking pale and defenseless, mouth open slightly. Salty tears had dried on her cheeks, forming matte blotches against her complexion. Lily gently pulled her hand out of Grace's. Lily was filled with foreboding for her friend.

It was time for this trip to be over. Lily longed to hug and cuddle with Callie, to paint her child-size toenails shell pink. To poke through the jewelry box side by side, the one that had belonged to a grandmother Callie had never met, Lily's mother. To stay up late together watching TV, drinking hot chocolate, eating popcorn, on Dirk's poker night, of course. Criminy! She almost made it through a whole hour without thinking about Dirk.

What would Grace encounter on her return? Lily forced herself to ponder, once again, Grace's dilemma; she hadn't known how to answer. Tell Grace that she, Grace, had transgressed the boundaries of friendship? That she'd pushed Penn into a corner from which fighting in kind was the only form of escape? Or maybe level with Grace. It had never occurred to Lily that Marc was gay. Hearing Penn speak it, Lily was astounded by the realization. Things fell into place, made sense.

Along with the knowledge, though, came many questions. Who else knew? How long had they known? Did Grace's parents suspect? Probably not; they practically worshiped Marc and had been thrilled when he joined their family. On the other hand, who knew Marc McCrea better than Hope and Jimbo Derringer? They'd worked with him for years. Had there never been a whisper of his predilection around the set? Wouldn't the gossip columnists have hinted at it in their rag sheets? Maybe not; the shame of it all could shatter a career.

This inquiry helped Lily keep thoughts of Dirk pushed way down in some dark corner.

78. CAT

Cat wandered the quiet hallways of the villa. She felt closed out. Deedee had the right idea ditching this scene early on. She should have gone with Deedee.

Ever since the fight, Penn and Amelia were acting like six-year-olds, Flossie and Freddy. *The Bobbsey Twins*. After hogging the bathroom, they skulked to their bedroom. Never even saying good night.

Grace and Lily had ducked her too. They just took off. If they had returned from the great outdoors, she wasn't aware of it.

What was the big deal? Was Penn actually shocked to hear that George had a drinking problem? Or was she devastated because Grace had been so frank? These friends of hers never spoke the whole truth to each other. They played slippery games of partial truths and withholds. Maybe they weren't even straight with their husbands.

She and Pietro yelled, called each other names, got fuming gall-darned angry, then let it all go. Pietro never had to wonder what she thought. Oh, except for her secrets, but that was different.

Then it was pretty obvious. Penn just wanted to wound Grace after being hurt. Marc was an artistic sort, a dreamer, just like she was. How cruel for Penn to call him a blasted queer out of the blue. But why was Grace so upset by that dirty lie? Why did she melt? *Grace didn't melt.* Grace was a fighter. Why didn't she stand her ground?

Cat entered the kitchen; it still smelled of garlic and lemons. She peeked into the covered cake dish and found it empty. Something sweet would help her mood. Vexed? Irritated? Yes! Husbands! Just look at the lot. An alcoholic, a suspected homosexual, a cheater, a goof-off jock, and a dictator. Hers, well, a traditionalist. She opened the biscotti tin, and finding it almost full, she indulged. She stood at the counter and let the chocolate crumbs fall harmlessly into the sink. She could rinse them away. All of a sudden, Pietro didn't look so bad.

About her friends, when she got their attention tomorrow, she had secrets to share. She could entertain them, yes, shock them. And they would all rally around her again. She had that talent.

79. LILY

This must be Angelo's uncle with his bride, Lily thought. The groom's hair rose into a curly pompadour. Both his smile and his silky tie had a jaunty mien. She opened her sketchbook and drew the wing-tipped lapels of his suit. The bride wore a suit also, the skirt tailored with four well-placed pleats. The jacket with its triangular lapels bordered a silky blouse and supported a corsage. "Benedetto Bianco and Gianna DeGaudio, November 7, 1942," the plaque read.

Lily turned her attention to a pink-cheeked boy child. Never mind the photo was black and white; Lily knew the color of his skin and eyes. He sat on a lady's lap, his mother no doubt, from whom he had inherited deep-set eyes. A round, brimmed hat framed her face; she wore a fur jacket and sat with crossed ankles. She held the child gently, but firmly, with both hands on his middle as he leaned forward, his fingers cupped like a piano player's. She leaned forward also, close enough to smell the sweetness of her son's blonde curls.

"Angelo," Lily said aloud, "that's Angelo, at maybe two." Lily's heart raced at her recognition of a virtual stranger, this oddly mixed with thoughts of Callie.

Marie Elena opened the double glass doors and entered the library slowly. Dawn's light coming through the clerestory windows surrounded Lily with a pinkish glow. The domestic stopped to gaze before she placed espresso and biscotti on the long table. Lily, who had been studying the array of family photos, turned with a grateful smile. She thanked Marie Elena for the breakfast *and once again* for ironing her shirt. Line drying had left the white garment looking crumpled and unattractive. Marie Elena had even managed to starch it.

Lily took up her sketchbook and turned back to the classic photos. First one and then another caught her attention. She made notations for future use, her brain thankfully engaged in cruising gear, realities forgotten. Until the sight of a young man in a particular wedding photo stopped her—Angelo wearing an elegant dark suit, his shoulders broad, his posture upright. Lily studied him—a proud, sure, unsuspecting Angelo. *How we can never see the future*, she thought.

Seated beside Angelo was a delicate beauty, her gown styled like the twenties, as was her be-flowered cloche hat, its lengthy veil moving from behind the chair and fanning into the foreground. A mixed bouquet filled her lap, so large that it covered much of one gloved arm. Lily memorized this face as if adoring a lost friend's image. The dark almond eyes, the upturned impish mouth, the fair skin, and the blonde hair. "Angelo Bianco and Inge Zorn, May 5, 1965."

"So this was Angelo's wife, Inge," Lily whispered, feeling little chills run up her arms.

She peered into the glass-topped chest just below the display, catching sight of calligraphy nibs in an ivory box. Beside the box rested nib holder pens and a bottle of India ink. Further along she saw handmade paper in small stacks, deckle edged, dove gray. *Who was the calligrapher in the family?* she wondered. And why was she feeling significance in her discovery of these heirlooms?

On a sudden whim, Lily returned her now-empty dishes to the kitchen and headed for the garden. She revisited the fan-back chairs facing the Pan fountain. Pan was predictably puckish, one hoof lifted in a high step, his horns glinting in the sunlight. Water trickling from his pipes—musical pipes forever silenced in bronze—rippled the shadowed pool. She stroked the curvature of the young satyr's cheek and smiled easily, here in the company of his mischievous grin.

Across the way she caught sight of several people. Yes, one of them was Angelo. He led his group past the apple orchard, the pear orchard, and toward the property's east boundary. Lily dashed along the winding path, following them to the rock wall, where a vista of the sea could be enjoyed. She wanted to say her good-byes. No, she wanted to have more. She wanted more.

As she drew closer, her pace slowed. Blood rose to her cheeks, and a strange timidity overpowered her. Angelo held the elbow of a striking blonde who wore stiletto heels and a sleek, grey, jersey dress. A scarf, grey with chartreuse and purple blossoms, fluttered at her throat as they walked along. Lily readjusted the combs holding her hair back. Was her lipstick still intact? If Angelo had not caught sight of Lily, she might have turned away.

Angelo called to her, asked her to join them. He explained they had gathered for a meeting in Capri, as they always did in September. He introduced her to his companions, two designers and a sales manager for Bianco Leather.

"You must join us at Fashion Week, Milano," he said, suddenly struck with the idea. "Begins just this *lunedi*."

"This Monday," Lily repeated.

"Lily's Italian is *multo buona*," Angelo said proudly. "She's a menswear designer from California."

If only she could attend, but no, she must return home, today. Lily said her good-byes, feeling awkward in the presence of these sophisticated foreigners.

"Maybe next year you will come to Italy, we will show you Milano," Angelo offered. The blonde designer and the other equally exotic designer nodded congenially.

Lily nodded too, as if this were entirely possible, hiding all her doubt and sadness. She headed back to the Villa alone, feeling cast adrift from something intangible.

■　　■　　■

The evidence of last night's misery reigned. Amelia spoke with Mario as he gathered their baggage, but Penn leaned against the console, her back to the mirror, her head hanging. Neither dear friend managed to greet Lily as she approached. Lily encountered Grace in the kitchen.

"Are you all speaking?" she asked, pointing to the entry. "Because they sure gave me the cold shoulder." Grace shook her head, back and forth, back and forth. Marie Elena made eye contact with Lily, expressing her concern for the state of affairs.

Soon Mario had each guest's luggage stacked beyond the wrought-iron entry gate. The gate cast circular shadows, visually joining the pairs of unconnected women. Cat wheezed as she bustled down the path, finally making an appearance. From the looks of it, she had overslept. She faced Marie Elena.

"I have to say, my time on Capri, well, mind-blowing. Quite an island for showing off my best." Marie Elena patted Cat's shoulder. Cat turned to Lily. "Hey kiddo, when's the next get-together?" Penn and Amelia sniffed disdainfully and hurriedly seated themselves in the taxi's backseat.

The driver crammed the last possible item into the trunk. He threw his hands in the air, "*Abbastanza, è troppo per la mia!*" Half of the suitcases remained on the pavement. Mario volunteered to drive the overflow down to the marina in his mini truck. Lily, who had been distracted by the drama, finally answered the hanging question. "Cat, the party's over." Cat raised an eyebrow and tried to catch Penn's attention, with no success.

The time had come; Grace hugged Marie Elena. She removed her chunky glass necklace and clasped it around her cooking mentor's neck. *How mindful*, thought Lily, *here's Grace suffering and she's thinking about someone else.*

Marie Elena reached out to Lily, and the two embraced for a long moment. When they stepped apart, Marie Elena, with a hand over her heart, whispered, "I pray your next visit to Villa Bianco will bring tears of happiness only."

80. CAT

None of the original tourist attractions claimed the attention of the taxi's occupants. Even the sunrise filling the dawn sky with a citrus glow caused no comment. Cat wriggled for comfort, happily occupying a window seat. Without Deedee, there was more room in the back she shared with Penn and Amelia. Lily and Grace had resumed their seats in front with the driver, of course.

Cat sighed loudly. A strained silence hovered between the back and front seats. Oh, Cat had given it a shot, cheerily remarking on what a fine time they'd all had, but her observations went unheard, and eventually she stopped searching for a topic to spark conversation.

Cat observed the back of Lily's head, her dark hair still pulled back severely with combs. Cat preferred to see it worn loose; today's style wasn't flattering. And she had told Lily so. Lily confounded her in other ways. Why had Marie Elena spoken privately to Lily this morning? Standing in the gate's shadow, the two had embraced. How had they grown close so quickly? Cat wondered about this. After all *she, Catherine San Carlo,* had been the dynamic one in the group, hadn't she?

The jet boat to Naples was no icebreaker either. Once aboard, Cat offered to bring back breakfast-time mimosas from the bar.

"Not that it's my business, but isn't it a bit early…?" Penn remarked to Amelia as they took a seat near the luggage. Lily thought Cat's idea of a morning bracer was unusually good. She followed Cat down to the bar and purchased caffés for Grace and herself. Caffés nicely laced with some dark liqueur. Grace joined them downstairs, opting to forego her preferred seat atop the boat; the early-morning wind off the Mare Tirreno was too chilly to enjoy.

Lily left Cat at the bar, found Grace, and held a steaming cup out to her. Cat trailing along behind, eavesdropped covertly. Were they talking about her?

"How're you doing?" Lily asked Grace.

Grace smiled crookedly, an answer of sorts. "You?"

"I'm about the same," Lily said. "Drink this. We can both use some medicinal fortification."

"It's going to be a long trip home," Grace replied.

Boring, Cat thought. Mimosa in hand, she looked around for someone to talk to.

The train sent plumes of steam up from the track. Passengers milled about, saying good-byes, tending truculent children. The wives, luggage in tow, found a *No Fumar* car and prepared to board. In that moment, Cat observed a brouhaha in the making. Lily was pointing out the stamping device. Did Penn and Amelia know to stamp their ticket before boarding the train? Penn was haughtily stating that she and Amelia had passes, pre-purchased in Rome. Lily continued to explain, with interruptions from Penn.

Cat, fed up with Penn, boarded, followed by Grace. They heaved their luggage into the racks and found seats.

The lengthy train trip from Naples to Rome did nothing to relieve the strained atmosphere between the five friends. All were returning different, changed from when they'd arrived in Italy, some not so spotless, none as naïve.

Cat's green eyes glittered with determination. Her time spent in Italy was akin to an epiphany. She had married an Italian man for a good reason. It had simply taken her this trip to understand it. Leo, darling artist incarnate, was the product of their union. She was paving the path for him. Someday they would dance together atop Mount Solaro, celebrating with the spirits of times past, their creations acknowledged by the world.

Instilled with a new sense of her creativity, a fresh career called. Having Quinton in her pocket, and with Lily whispering recommendations into the right ears, Cat would soon be the photo stylist *du jour*. Maybe for Italian *Vogue*, who knew? She'd show that egotistical Edwin. And Pietro? Pietro would concede. He'd have to; she could ignore his sad eyes without missing a beat. But, if she ever felt the need to divorce him—no rush—and remarry, it would be to someone with status and money.

The train ride seemed lackluster, even monotonous with the constant grind of wheels. Looking out the window, she spied ruins of the Via Appia. Big deal! On the other hand, what a conversation starter.

"Hey Grace, see the Via Appia out there?"

Grace looked, nodded, and looked away. Clearly she wouldn't be interested to learn there had been 53,000 miles of road during the peak of the Roman Empire. Grace looked like a corpse, mum, hollow, and pale. If possible, she'd lost weight overnight. Cat had been envious of Grace many times in the past, with her famous parents, an exciting career, a handsome and well-known husband, and her slim frame that didn't require calorie counting. Grace had everything Cat wanted. Or so Cat used to think. After last night, Cat wouldn't give a rat's rump to trade places now.

She looked across the aisle, thinking to start a conversation about her new vocation with Lily. But Lily seemed completely absorbed by her book, *A Delta Wedding* by Eudora Welty.

81. LILY

Lily felt Cat's eyes on her, but refused to break gaze with the page in acknowledgement. The words in front of her danced and jiggled with the movement of the train's wheels making their way along the track. Lily had no hankering for conversation; Eudora Welty was merely a ruse, a privacy insurance policy. Ordinarily, Lily loved getting lost in the prose of Eudora, but as her arrival at home neared, her concentration was marred.

How glorious it had been to be out from under Dirk's rule for a stretch. Had her friends done her a favor? She'd awakened to Dirk's deceit. Deedee hadn't meant to hurt Lily, going on and on about divorce. Deedee was addressing unspoken solutions for marital disenchantment. But Lily knew better. Feelings of dissatisfaction, which wax and wane in all relationships, aren't to be trusted; they feed on other emotions.

No, Lily wouldn't allow herself to be tricked by those emotions. Dirk was Dirk; he may not have fulfilled the potential Lily had seen in him. It was her shortsightedness to have predicted so bright a future. Sadly, his affair delineated her shortcoming as a wife.

Lily tried to sum it up. Important things had not changed: not her commitment to her marriage, not her resolution to expand Antonio Caldo, and above all else, not her dedication to Callie. But somehow *she* needed to change—after firing Darleen. And *if, if Dirk still wanted her*, she'd be less passive in her role as a lover. She'd find a way.

A uniformed conductor came through the car collecting tickets and passes. Penn and Amelia had not stamped their tickets. Despite Lily's warning. Lily fidgeted. It was an "I told you so moment," and she knew it. But somehow Lily felt sympathetic as she listened to the duo's plaintive excuses and pleas. The conductor would not be put off. Money was needed now.

Amelia and Penn dug through their purses, scrounging up their last dollars and lira. They came up short. Would this be enough? No. The stern answer was repeated; they must look better! Penn burst into tears. Amelia glanced at adjacent passengers, obviously embarrassed.

Lily opened her bag and offered the difference. Penn took the money from Lily and looked away, muttering about paying her back. Lily's throat tightened with a wretched realization. The group's friendship was over. She wished she had never invited any single one of them along! An annoyed steward bustled down the aisle, having been held up by the ticket infraction. He hastily served caffé and small hard cookies to the frowning women.

82. DEEDEE

Grace and Lily sat a little apart from Penn and Amelia in the airport lounge. Cat had just returned with a cup of coffee; she stood between the two groups as if she couldn't decide whom best to join. Deedee strutted into the lounge, high heels clicking on the tiled floor, full-skirted sundress swishing about her knees.

"Yoo-hoo! Ladies!"

Five faces turned toward the familiar Southern drawl, all with an expression of surprise.

"What? All y'all can't be that shocked I'm here. I said I'd be on time." Deedee stamped her foot with indignation. That indignation soon changed to delight once her friends greeted her with hugs and declarations of relief at her appearance.

"Oh, you cuties, the fun we had. I can hardly believe it. We drove a Ferrari all the way from Naples to Rome. That Bob has got some serious connections. Lordy, does he know how to show a gal a good time! I can hardly take in how quick ever'thin' is over. Seems like I just kissed Mama and Nanette good-bye."

The group's initial relief soon evaporated, and the ensuing temperature of the troop was like a blast of cold air to Deedee's thermometer. Delight now turned to dismay.

"Good heavens. Fess up. Who died? All y'all are gonna step on your faces if you don't pick up your heads. What the heck is goin' on here?"

"Everyone is tired," Cat responded for the tongue-tied group. "None of us relishes the flight home." Deedee allowed Cat to escort her to a vacant section of chairs, away from the others. Dang, no way would she let their pity party spoil her last few hours of freedom. Deedee happily complied when Cat begged for her to tell all. She filled in some of the details about her coastal trip and the road north to Rome in the bright yellow sports car.

"First off, you've never been in a Ferrari, have you? Well, I can tell you, that is one fast pony. Better than a day at the Kentucky Derby. And Bob is one heck of a driver. You gotta know these Eye-talian drivers are nuts. Even at ninety miles an hour on the autostrada, they are ridin' your tail and tryin' to pass you up. Well, believe me when I say Bob wasn't gonna allow that to happen."

Privately, she savored the more intimate particulars. Like what she did to Bob while he was driving. To share those exceptional moments wouldn't be ladylike now, would it?

■   ■   ■

Boarding for the flight was called; Lily and Grace were seated together; one row back on the opposite aisle were Amelia and Penn, just a few rows ahead of Deedee and Cat.

At an altitude of thirty-thousand feet, Cat spilled the story about the all-out attack between Grace and Penn. Deedee alternately showed disbelief then nodded knowingly as the gory minutiae were revealed in customary Cat fashion. She started with Grace demanding Penn and Amelia join them at dinner for Lily's sake, and ended with Penn dashing from the room and Grace huddled on the floor sobbing. The one fact Cat left out was her responsibility for the explosion, how she'd taunted her friends by toasting their uncharacteristic behavior.

"I just knew there was somethin' off with Marc. He was a little too perfect to be for real! Poor Grace. Well, it's a good thin' she found out while she's still young and good-lookin'! Could've happened years from now when no decent man would give her a tumble."

"There's the old glass-is-half-full spirit."

Deedee smiled, pleased with Cat's compliment. "I'm nothin' if not optimistic. Besides, Grace can still have more babies, though Lord knows one is a good enough number in my book," she added with her down-home practicality. Heck, she did love Nanette, but kids sure made life more complicated. Deedee suspected it was Leo's cherubic face Cat was thinking of when she nodded her affirmation. Jason rarely rated thought.

Frustrated by her attempts to recline her seat, Deedee gave up and instead tried to envision the dinner scene from the night before. What Cat described did not sound like any one of Deedee's five friends. She turned to Cat.

"What I *cannot* picture is Grace tearin' after Penelope like that. Seems dang mean-spirited on her part to be startin' somethin' up. So what if George tipples a bit? Least he's there bringin' in a decent paycheck and keeping the fire stoked in the bedroom. A man's gotta have some refuge, don't ya think?"

"I guess so," Cat agreed. "It's not like he's out *chasing* other women. He is kind of cute when he's tossed a few back. And he can be funny—a little flirtatious, but I'm sure that's only with me."

83. AMELIA

Amelia sat quietly, plunging and pulling her needle with its bright orange silk through her fabric. Once the jet reached its cruising altitude, the passenger in the seat ahead reclined—practically into her lap. She repositioned her legs, dreading the long flight ahead, but eager to get home. Amelia had made peace with herself about the aberration in her conduct. It was folded tightly and tucked away in a nook she named "anomalies".

She would unpack the memory every so often in the years ahead, but not to berate herself, rather as a reminder that she was a woman with value whom men found appealing. She was more than a cook and a gardener, more than a chauffeur and housekeeper. She was sexy and attractive and her week on Capri was proof. Amelia would return home with a sense of self she'd never before possessed.

The time spent with Mick was akin to taking an interesting class about herself. She'd had no complaints about her former sex life with Ken Jr., but she was now better equipped. Convinced that he'd missed her, pined for her, and was just as eager to reunite, she swept aside the two problems that wanted to plague her—the lost wedding rings and Sarah Rosenberger. Ken Jr. would never learn the truth about her rings; he would believe they were lost at the bottom of the Blue Grotto, having slipped off her finger due to suntan oil. And Sarah? Well, he wouldn't need Sarah or any other woman. He would have his hands full with the new, improved Amelia.

Now if only Penn could box up her irrational fears and guilt. Amelia would first tackle the infidelity aspect. Men had been breaking vows since the invention of marriage. So what made it so much worse when women did? Why flog yourself needlessly over a little harmless fun? And Penn *had* had fun. Sharing the adventure, watching Penn flirt with Jax, both of them stepping right over the line of their limited thinking—it just wouldn't have been the same without her.

Second, Amelia would address the part that wasn't fun. Once again, men have been taking advantage of women's weakness since birds learned to fly. Jax tried to rape Penn. What did that moron expect? That Penn should feel any remorse for fighting back was absurd. It simply wasn't possible that she'd inflicted any injury on that jackass. Whatever kicking or punching was administered in self-defense could not begin to take down a big, well-built guy like Jax.

84. PENN

Penn had taken the window seat, but only because Amelia said she must; the aerial view of Rome, Elba, and then the sight of the Alps as they crossed to Switzerland would be lovely. But Penn swallowed a sleeping pill with the last of her water. She threw her forearm over her closed eyes and waited for unconsciousness.

Before sleep was granted, Penn's mind dragged her through a nightmarish labyrinth. The golden thread of Amelia's voice offered protection, as demons, with enormous heads and legs for necks, sprang up at every turn. Grace's triangular face scowled at her, mouth twisted. Jax's face with oversized lips taunted her. Lily's face, with sad, disappointed eyes, turned away. George's enormous face flashed orange, then red, orange, then red, like some broken traffic signal.

Like a traffic signal. What did that mean? George's drinking! Danger if she didn't stop him? But how? Penn opened her eyes and looked over at Amelia. Amelia seemed absorbed in her needlework. Penn closed her eyes again. Nothing hasty. No, George didn't take well to change. Slow. She'd take it slow. Gentle. Penn's mind clutched for lyrics that floated at the surface of her mind like unwanted flotsam. She'd take it gently, day by day. *I'll take my time.* Penn's mouth twitched as associated song lyrics whirled. From nowhere a Chamber Brothers song from college days surfaced and spun.

Stop it! Focus! she told herself. Penn's mouth drew into a tight frown again. *Say how you fear for his health. Say how much you love him.* Another song interrupted her self-lecture and caught her attention. *Is love a splendored thing?* she was forced to ask. *Do I love George? Do I deserve him? Who am I to tell him what's right and wrong? George Pines doesn't deserve a wife who, who...* Words for what she had done vaporized.

Finally, Penn slept. She twitched. She snored, a soft nasal snore with an open drooling mouth. When she called out—crow-like croaks, "No, no, no, no"—Amelia roused her. On these occasions Penn stood shakily. She looked up and down the aisles as if searching for some missing person.

85. GRACE

Grace stared out the window at the tops of the clouds below. She leaned back in her seat and allowed misery to enfold her. She felt gutted—like a rainbow trout. One day she was swimming merrily along with her friends, and the next she was hooked, reeled in, and sliced open. Vicious words flying around and no one defended her.

Grace knew she'd been a harsh judge this trip. But hadn't she been a good friend for years and years before? She'd been understanding when the girls vented their problems. She'd been kind and supportive when they needed a little boost. How many times had she piled Jemima in the car and driven to one of their homes to do makeup or to help with their hair for a special event? And loaned jewelry too. Was her care and concern for them that easily forgotten?

Grace twisted in her seat, straining to get a look at her friends behind her. They carried on what appeared to be normal conversation, which ceased when they noted her looking back. She didn't recognize her friends, and they pretended to not know her. A guilty silence was strung between them like last Halloween's cobwebs. Tears slipped down her cheeks. Lily reached over and squeezed her hand.

LOS ANGELES, CALIFORNIA

FALL OF

1979

CONSEQUENCES

86. GRACE

Grace was seated in the back of the black Lincoln Continental Marc had sent to collect her. *Well, that was awkward*, Grace thought to herself. *Our luggage was circling on the carousel and still no one was speaking.* And those tight little good-bye waves Penn and Amelia made with no eye contact. Oh, Deedee had been effusive in her leave-taking. "Gotta get goin'. Hugh promised to be curbside. Talk to all y'all real soon!" she'd called out with a grandiose wave.

Cat seemed deflated—as if she couldn't comprehend the schism in the group. Lily had walked with Grace over to the uniformed driver, who held up a sign with Grace's name.

"We'll talk tomorrow," Lily said and gave her a hug. Grace didn't want to let go.

"Lily, I'm scared."

"I know," Lily replied. "Me too."

Grace stepped into her entryway. It was late, and the house was completely dark. Setting her suitcases down, she carefully made her way along the hall to the bedroom she and Marc shared. How good her own bed would feel tonight. She made up her mind to let her customary bedtime routine wait until morning.

Quietly she opened the door and tiptoed to the bed. It was empty. Marc must be working late. Damn. Disappointed, she flipped on her bedside lamp and gasped. Marc's armoire was open and empty, as was his closet. Grace pulled open each of Marc's drawers only to find them all void of his possessions.

Breathe, Grace, *you need to breathe*, she reminded herself as fear compressed her lungs. Propped against the china hand holding Grace's rings and scarves was a note. Marc's heavyweight stationery, pale, pale blue.

The room swirled about Grace like a tide pool as she reached for the note. She ripped it open, read it, and sank to her bed. No, please, noooooo! Grace reached for the telephone, punched in a number, and sobbed, "He's gone. Only a note. He left a note!"

"Calm down, Grace. I'm on my way now."

Grace fell back against the fancy shams and European pillows. Lying on her side atop the satin comforter, she looked around the room. She watched as the upright china hand went limp. The rings and scarves slid from its fingers. Grace cried.

87. LILY

Lily squinted as she viewed the McCrea's dimly lit master bedroom. A sense of desertion struck her. Armoire doors and open dresser drawers cast shadows at odd angles, exposing vacant spaces. Grace, curled up on the bed, looked more like a victim of Pompeii than a glamorous model, shoulder and hipbone protruding and casting more shadow.

When Lily stepped into the room, Grace sat up slowly; she inched to the edge of the bed and dangled her long legs to the floor. Lit by the nightstand's amber glow, her face looked blotchy, her nose runny, her hair tangled. Grace smoothed the sheet of paper she had been clutching. She held it out to Lily.

Lily took the note. Grace's eyes clarified as much as Lily could bear to know. But she scanned the note at Grace's insistence. Several lines struck her. She read them aloud, each as a question. Her voice faltered.

"'I can no longer live the lie? Nor should you be forced to?'" Lily choked. "'You and our precious Jemima will want for nothing?'

"Oh dear," Lily moaned, "it sounds so final." She looked into Grace's brimming eyes, her own heart constricting even more tightly. "And he signs it '*Affectionately*, Marc?'"

"How am I going to tell my parents?" Grace sobbed again—hard, convulsive, uncontrollable sounds erupted from the depths of her gut. Lily put her arms around Grace and rocked her gently.

"It's okay. Everything will be okay."

Finally spent, Grace slumped back. Lily turned off all but the nightstand lamp. She sat on the bed stroking Grace's hair until Grace slept soundly. Confusion crept in. How did she feel about Grace's plight? Angry?

Sad? Relieved? No wonder Grace had been deprived all these years. Well, Marc had come clean. Now Grace had faced the unthinkable. It was a start. Lily headed home. Time to face her husband and her own mess.

▪   ▪   ▪

Lily drove into the beach house garage and checked the clock as she parked. Three a.m. She was still dressed in traveling clothes, a loose linen jumper and lightweight cardigan. Entering the kitchen, she encountered Dirk—to whom she had barely given a "hello" before Grace's call sent her running. That was hours ago; she imagined he would be asleep by now.

But there he was, wearing boxer shorts and T-shirt, angrily dumping out a drawer, scattering fabric swatches, sketches, and magazine clippings. As Lily entered, he reached for his snifter of brandy and downed it. Lily sank to her knees and picked up a sketch. Flabbergasted.   "What are you doing? This is my inspiration drawer."

Dirk kicked at the contents of the drawer, grazing Lily's hand. "I'm sick of all this shit," he said.

Lily rose from her knees and rubbed her hand, shaking. Fury caught like a wedge in her throat. She fought it off. But anger addled her brain.

"Well, I'm sick too. Tell me it's not true about you and Darleen. You didn't...did you?"

Dirk's voice lilted with braggadocio. "It's true and I did."

She had known it was true. But hearing it from Dirk, like this? Lily doubled over and clutched her stomach. She fell back against the stove. "Why?" she asked, fearful of the answer.

"I need more than you give, Lily. Not that you'd notice." The sarcasm stung. "Where do I show up on your list? Fourth? Fifth? Let's see, one and two would be, hmm, Antonio Caldo and Callie—"

Lily interrupted, her words rushing, driven like a set of waves.

"Antonio Caldo? We started the business for *us*...you and me, for *our* future. We wanted to design *together* and make a splash in this world, *together*. Dirk, when you gave up on designing and took over the finances, well, it left me doing both our jobs. I know I'm spread too thin, and I shortchange both you and Callie. But..." Lily cautiously put her arms around Dirk's shoulders and laid her cheek on his chest. She was breathing heavily.

Dirk removed her arms and stepped back. He regained an air of control as he leaned against the counter and poured himself another brandy.

"I'll buy that you're working for our future, but you allow your friends to monopolize your free time. You know you weren't home five minutes before you ran out on me. Because your precious Grace called."

"I couldn't *not* go. Grace needed me. Marc was gone. Took all his belongings and left a *sorry* note."

"Someone always needs you, that's the problem. Anyway, Grace is better off without Marc."

"You knew?"

With momentary softness, Dirk answered. "I had my suspicions, poor guy, trapped like that."

Heartened by Dirk's empathy, Lily hesitantly approached her husband and placed her hand on his cheek.

"Callie needs us. We're a family. Dirk, we can iron this out if you cut it off with Darleen."

"I can't promise anything."

"I will do better. You'll see."

Dirk swirled like a dancer, Lily held tight to his torso. He forced her onto the kitchen table, with her legs straddling his hips.

88. DEEDEE

Deedee spied Hugh's souped-up truck in the passenger loading zone. She was relieved he'd made it on time and she wouldn't be waitin' at the curb. She was tired of travelin' and not lookin' forward to this last leg. Didn't matter that she could be home in less than an hour—she was ready for her bed right now. Well, maybe a quick Jack and Coke before hitting' the sheets.

Hugh jumped out of his truck, waving and hollering, "Deedee, baby!" In his excitement, Hugh knocked over a suitcase and almost took out

Deedee too. He wrapped his arms around her and tried to plant a sloppy kiss on her mouth, but she held him off.

"Cool your jets, hot stuff! Let's get movin'."

Deedee looked around and gave an embarrassed smile to all who stared. She gathered her Southern dignity, and asked Hugh to please put the suitcases in the truck and get the show on the road. As she climbed into the truck cab, she could swear the wheels were new. A lot fancier than when she'd left.

"Hugh, did y'all get new wheels?"

Hugh grinned. "Yeah, baby. Aren't they bitchin'? Kinda surprised you even noticed." At Deedee's frown, he continued, "And don't be worryin' about the cost. I traded in my last two sets—the shiny ones and the ones with all the spokes, and that old radio set of your other husband's—so these didn't set us back hardly at all!"

"Great balls, Hugh, those shiny ones were just fine. If I didn't keep an eye on y'all, we'd have nothin'!"

"Ah, baby, don't be mad. I missed you so much, I even changed the pillowcases. I needed somethin' excitin'. Not like you weren't spendin' money over on your ritzy island."

"Hugh, you know I worked extra and saved and saved for that trip. Hey, where're you goin'? This isn't the way to Aunt Bea's. We gotta pick up Mama and Nanette. They'll be waitin' up for us."

Hugh groaned and Deedee saw the dejected slope in his posture. He slowed the truck, pulled over to the side of the freeway, and stopped. He turned to Deedee and reached out to hold her.

"Daphne Denise Stone, you're my wife, and I love you with all my heart. But your mama's killin' our marriage. And you know it's the truth. She runs you ragged till you got nothin' left for me. I'm gonna tell you straight. Mama stays on with Aunt Bea startin' right now...or I'm gone."

Well, how easy could this be, Deedee thought to herself. She looked at Hugh, took in his boyish, handsome face, and thought for a moment about their brief marriage. Time to cut bait.

"An' now I'm gonna tell *you* straight. You're gone."

89. AMELIA

Amelia checked her watch when the taxi stopped in front of her house. Exhausted as she was, she felt confident that Ken Jr. would be waiting up for her, even if it was 1:12 a.m. She was not disappointed. Ken Jr. flung the door open and ran down the driveway to greet her. He picked Amelia up in a bear hug and swung her around.

"Darling, you're home. It hasn't been the same without you."

Amelia was delighted. She'd known that her absence would be good medicine for Ken Jr. Life was just about to get better.

"I missed you. How are the children? Isn't international calling the pits? And astronomically expensive. What've you been doing since I left?"

"Kids missed you like crazy, but they're all great. We survived with the help of Jennifer. Sorry I didn't call more, just awful darn busy. I'll fill you in tomorrow."

Later, cuddled up to a softly snoring Ken Jr., Amelia felt pretty and sexy and important; she had pleased him mightily. She did, however, find it odd that he was the one asleep when she'd spent all those hours traveling and still had enough energy to perform bedtime tricks. Men!

90. PENN

Picking her broken thumbnail (her nails always got wrecked traveling), Penn began in whispered breaths. "*Now I lay me down to sleep.*" No, it doesn't go like that. "*There are four corners to my bed, Four angels round my head, One to watch, and one to pray, And two to…*" Her voice broke with an involuntary gasp of air.

"*Our Father who art in heaven…*" Penn tried to pray. But couldn't. How could she pray to him? How could she expect angels to protect her? She, an adulteress. She hated that word. She had always hated that word. Poignant yearning spun and glimmered like a school of sardines: if only Amelia hadn't egged her on, if only she hadn't spilled the coke, if only, if only the feel of him moving inside hadn't thrilled her. Yes, she had wanted him, again and again. She had moaned and called out and begged for everything he did to satisfy her lust. This errant wave swept away her last illusion of decency.

Penn startled herself with an involuntary gasp as the taxi pulled up to her house. She was arriving home wholly changed. She was an adulteress, she was a murderess. Was there such a word? Mur-der-ess? Noun. Murdress? Dress?

Penn paid the driver, calculating the tip carefully. He followed her up to the porch, her luggage in tow. She stood on the porch as he sped away. (Did she look okay?) Penn shook, hyperventilating. She fished out her compact and flipped it open. There under the amber porch light, she looked frightful. Her mouth gaped open like a fish's. Her eyes were glassy, with puffy bulges below and smudges of mascara. Her heavy breathing continued. (George might hear her and come looking. She had better go on in now. To greet George. How could she look George in the eye? Allow him into her again? He'd know, he'd just know. She couldn't bear to be touched by any man again, not even George, never. Never.)

Penn lugged her suitcases into the laundry room and then tiptoed into the family room, where George reclined on the sofa watching TV. *Oh, South Pacific on the* Late Show, Penn thought. The familiar song brought momentary comfort. She and George loved musicals.

"Remember seeing *Jesus Christ Superstar*?" Penn blurted nervously.

George raised up on an elbow. "Oh, my wife paying me a late-night visit. This calls for another drink. How about a making us a fresh pitcher, Penny?"

Penn stood still staring at her inebriated husband as if she had never seen him before.

George staggered to Penn, and hung onto her for stability. He French kissed her forcefully and kneaded her breast; he drew back, self-satisfied. "'Bout time you got your world-traipsing butt home. Where's that pitcher?"

Penn, disgusted, pushed George back down on the couch. George landed with a thudding "Oomph," but smirked and flipped Penn off.

"You are a disgusting *drunk!*" Penn snarled. She delivered her angry ultimatum with no restraint, blood plumping the green veins in her temples. "Your drinking days are over."

George pushed himself upright and lifted his empty glass in a mock toast. "Oh, Lieutenant Pines finds me disgusting? For your information, *Lieutenant Pines*, you've been AWOL for the last time." He hocked a loogie into his glass and continued. "You march back to the barracks and insult *me?* Alcohol is the only thing that makes your military encampment here bearable. So if you think I'm gonna stop drinking—I mean drinking *what I want when I want*—you've got another thing coming! Dismissed."

"Get out now!" Penn shouted at the top of her lungs.

91. CAT

Pietro's jackrabbit start and quick finish satisfied Cat. Her "slow and steady tortoise" responded quickly—and noisily—surprising both of the eager spouses. Cat's success on Capri had warmed her up to new possibilities. No need to be hasty in ditching Pietro.

Jason looked solemnly at the art books Cat brought home. He asked questions and turned the glossy pages carefully. Leo enjoyed the books too. He scribbled on one page with a Bernini self-portrait and another page with Bernini's St. Teresa in ecstasy. Cat made a note in her journal, "Tell Daulphine about Leo's connection."

Cat returned to work with the intention of soliciting both Lily and Quinton's referrals. She'd call during her first break. That morning Beppe's Cantina seemed to have reverted some twelve years, duplicating the cantina when Noni was monarch. Gone, the goblets, the glazed pottery, the colorful imported linens, the aromatic cheeses, the chocolates. Never mind pricing and tagging a jillion bottles; that could wait. Cat retreated to the storeroom and slumped on a wine barrel. She smoked one cigarette and lit a second with the fiery butt of the first.

She heard Pietro's soles grind along the floor. She pictured his expensive shoes, leather wingtips, custom-made by a Florentine cobbler. Don't tell her Pietro didn't pamper himself. So could she. She could take a breather, if she wanted one, and right now she did. Pietro flung the storeroom doors open with some urgency.

"Th-th-there you are! You haven't even started, and it's t-t-time to open."

Out front, the shop bell jingled. Cat heard Noni, Jason, and Leo chatter as they entered. She imagined Noni flipping the sign from "Closed" to "Open".

"Mommy, Noni got us donuts!" Leo in pure delight.

"Chocolate with sprinkles!" Why couldn't Jason ever let Leo hold the stage? And another thing, it was a wonder her boys weren't butterballs, the way that woman stuffed them.

Pietro again. "Are you all right, Cat? C-C-Cat?"

Annoyance in her voice. "Give me a minute, I'm exhausted."

Noni and kids burst into the storeroom. Leo dived for Cat's lap and held his donut up to her face. "See. Mommy, see?"

Noni gave Cat a disparaging glance. "What is problem with her now?"

"She's feeling f-f-faint."

Cat felt grateful for Pietro's defense. Yes, she was feeling faint.

Noni stood tall, thrust her bosom forward. She patted Pietro on the back, cackling a little. Bending down to the boys, she said sweetly, quietly, "Little sister coming."

Before Cat could react, Noni took her face between two, soft, mother-in-law hands. Cat smelled coffee on Noni's breath and tried to wrench away. Noni squeezed the flesh on her daughter-in law's jaw, tenaciously holding on. "Time you be good San Carlo wife."

Infuriated, Cat stood up, pushing Noni away. She ground her cigarette into the floor. Just then, her family blurred into abstract pinholes of shimmery light. A traumatic thought seared her being. What if she *were* pregnant?

92. GRACE

Grace hated afternoon traffic, especially on the parking lot officially known as the Hollywood Freeway. It could take an hour to travel ten miles. Callie and Jemima sat in the backseat of the BMW playing cat's cradle with a piece of string. Grace turned on the radio just as Rod Stewart scratched out a sexual solicitation. Grace switched the station when both Callie and Jemima chimed in, their little-girl voices singing along with Rod.

Save me, Grace thought. No such luck. The next station was playing Blondie lamenting past love. Once again the backseat duo couldn't control themselves and crooned the chorus. Grace lowered the volume.

"My stars, girls. Do you know all the inappropriate lyrics?"

"I don't know any 'propriate lyrics, Mommy," Jemima informed her mother. "Just the ones on the radio."

Callie and Grace laughed. Jemima grinned, revealing a space. She'd lost her first baby tooth while Grace was on Capri. *That's not all we lost, kiddo,* Grace thought to herself. Her parents came to mind. *How could they?* she asked herself for the hundredth time as she exited on Ninth Street.

Having the worst week of her entire life, she was hardly able to believe her good fortune—there was a parking space directly in front of the building that housed Antonio Caldo. She parallel parked and fed the meter.

"Jemima, leave your book bag in the car. Callie, wait up for me!" Grace called out to the two girls racing for the lobby. It was futile. She arrived just as the elevator door was closing on the little wiseacres, who gave a chipper wave.

A few minutes later, Grace entered the reception area of Lily's company. The girls were hugging Lily, bragging about leaving Grace in the dust. Lily looked sternly at them and shook her head.

"Listen, little ladies, it isn't a good idea to go on elevators alone. Promise you won't do that again." Callie and Jemima nodded solemnly before scampering off to the supply room to investigate the variety of buttons and fabric scraps.

"Thanks for picking up Callie. I'd never have made it on time. Thought my meeting would never end."

"I'm happy to do it." Grace nodded toward the reception desk, where a middle-aged woman in a no-nonsense business suit signed off paperwork for a delivery man who stood next to several stacks of boxes. "I see you've solved *your* problem. I still have one, aside from Marc, that is."

Lily tilted her head quizzically.

"My parents. I still haven't told them, and I haven't returned any of their calls. How am I going to get through this? I'm feeling helpless without Marc. And cut off from my folks."

Lily looked at Grace sympathetically. "You're going to be fine, you know. You're like denim. And that's a compliment."

Grace felt a lump swell in her throat. Eyes filled with tears, she turned to a mannequin and adjusted the pose.

"I know how you're feeling, Grace. But our girls need us to be strong, especially when their fathers aren't. And your parents will be supportive. You need to tell them. Soon. "

Grace turned back to Lily with resolve. Hands on her hips, she tossed her head.

"You know what? They sacrificed me! For their *careers*! Made sure I married the director. How could they? I'm going over there right now and let them know—"

"Whoa! Grace, we've talked about this. I'm certain you're wrong. That is *not* the Hope and Jimbo I've known all these years. Let's take this a little more slowly, go through it again," Lily cautioned. Grace had revealed her suspicion earlier in the week, but Lily couldn't reconcile it.

"Uh-uh. Nothing to talk about. I'm going now." Grace adjusted her purse strap on her shoulder and called out, "Jemima? Time to go!"

"Wait, Grace. If you're that determined, I'm going with you. I'll stay with the girls in the car."

Grace pulled the car into her parents' driveway. The front of the house was filled with fall blooming flowers, but Grace didn't notice. She pounded the steering wheel, fuming. Jemima and Callie sat in the backseat wide-eyed and silent, holding hands.

"Grace, you have to calm down. You cannot go in there like this. Just take some deep—"

"The fuck I can't! Just watch me!" Grace fairly blasted out of the car, slammed the door.

"Auntie Grace said the *F* word!" Callie squealed gleefully.

"Mommy said the *F* word!" Jemima giggled, then turned to her buddy. "Callie, what is the *F* word?"

"Hey, little ladies, how about if we all draw mermaids?" Lily proposed. "Get your colors out. The best two get ice cream."

As Grace stormed up the walk and barreled through the front door, she couldn't recall ever feeling such anger at her parents. But there was no pushing it aside or down or anywhere. It was a powerful burn deep inside her, and she would spew it back at the people responsible for ruining her life.

Hope and Jimbo sat reading under an umbrella by the pool in the backyard. Both looked up as Grace pushed open the sliding glass patio door and stomped out.

Hope smiled brightly. "Darling, what a delight to see you. Where's my granddaughter? You've been home almost a week and you haven't called us. Well, no matter. Come sit down, and I'll get you some iced tea."

"Gracie girl, what's that scowl about?" Jimbo moved to get up for a hug, but Grace shoved him back into his chair.

"You want to know what's going on? Well, so do I!" Grace spoke harshly to her parents, who sat openmouthed in surprise. "Why did you encourage me to marry Marc? Was marrying me off to your director a way to keep him in your hip pocket? Obviously your damned careers were more important than me, your daughter."

Hope and Jimbo stared at Grace, their only child, their beautiful, brilliant light.

Grace saw utter confusion and hurt upon their faces. She reached into her bag, pulled out a ball of pale-blue paper, and thrust it at them. Unable to speak, she tried to stop trembling. She did not want to let go of her anger. If she did, she'd cry like a two-year-old.

Hope and Jimbo stood together and read the note. Hope clutched her heart. Jimbo sank back into his chair. "When did this happen?"

"The night I came home. You always knew, didn't you? You *wanted* me to marry him. Even though he was gay." Grace finally found her voice, but it was raspy, cold.

"Gracie girl, you don't know what you're saying. Think back. Your marriage was never our idea. You could not be talked out of it. And you know how hard we tried. You told us if we weren't with you, then we were against you, and you'd elope." The normally unflappable Jimbo spoke, the wound Grace had inflicted apparent.

"Darling girl, of course we didn't know. There's never been a breath of scandal about Marc. And if there had? Who believes those trashy rag sheets anyway? According to them, your father and I have been divorced seven times. And only two weeks ago Raquel Welch gave birth to an alien." Hope pleaded, "Grace, don't you know there is nothing more important to us than you?"

Deflated, Grace sagged onto a chaise and crossed both arms over her face. For the umpteenth time that week, she sobbed.

Jimbo sat beside her and put his arm around her. "Gracie, the truth of it is, our movie careers were well established long before we met Marc. There was nothing Marc could do for us. If anything, we provided an opportunity for him on our TV show, pulled him into success."

"This is agonizing for us too, darling." Hope began to sniffle. The effects would be far reaching. "We love Marc as a son. We never dreamed he would hurt you. Oh dear, little Jemima…We should never have allowed you to… We should have fought harder."

"Well, one thing I do know. Marc is an honorable man," Jimbo stated with assurance. "Look at his note. He has no intention of deserting you financially. Take a deep breath and count your blessings. You have a beautiful daughter and two parents who love you dearly."

Grace looked up at her parents. In the harsh sunlight, without the benefit of makeup and lights, they looked old and defeated.

93. AMELIA

Amelia found the week following her homecoming positively dreamy. Her time on Capri had galvanized her. Dealing with her unruly boys was hardly the task it used to be; they were cute and sweet, albeit more than a little naughty.

Mother-daughter special time happened on Jennifer's twelfth birthday. Jennifer called Amelia to come into her bedroom. She sat on her canopy bed wide-eyed and pale, bottom lip trembling.

"It's come, Mommy! What a rotten birthday!" She burst into tears and ran into Amelia's arms. Amelia's heart squeezed with sympathy, but at the same time swelled with pride. "Oh, honey, it *is* a rotten birthday, but a wonderful one as well."

Ken Jr. had never been so attentive. Amelia thought she should go away at least once a year. Maybe the girls would enjoy Hawaii next. Never mind. Scratch that. Hardly likely they'd ever go anywhere together again. But back to Ken Jr. Tonight they would finally enjoy the going-away dinner Sarah Rosenberger had spoiled by calling. Amelia felt only a little guilty about having sent that meal down the disposal. It was an expensive dish to make in dollars as well as time. Nonetheless, Julia Child's *boeuf bourguignon* was simmering on the stove.

She decanted the wine and put a record on the hi-fi stereo console. Andy Williams's velvet voice promised the delights of love. Amelia hummed along, her pulse quickening as she listened to the romantic lyrics. The table was set, the candles lit. Lost in her own world, Amelia twirled to the music and right into Ken Jr. bearing pale lavender roses. She had no doubt that this evening would be unforgettable. And it was.

Hours later, curled up in their king-sized bed, Ken Jr. stroked Amelia's cheek and pushed her thick honey-toned hair away from her face.

"Your vacation did us both some good. You've been one hot date this whole week. I can hardly keep up with you—but don't quit. I'm having the time of my life."

Amelia glowed. She was saturated with love for her husband. "I can promise you this, it's only going to get better. We've made a fresh start, and from now on, I'm all the woman you're going to need."

Ken Jr. took a deep breath. In a soothing tone, he spoke softly into Amelia's ear. "With one minor exception, darling. We have another baby on the way. You, my sweetness, are a fabulous mother, and knowing that, I'm sure you'll want to do the right thing. Sarah isn't—"

Amelia felt the oxygen being sucked from her lungs. Surely she'd misheard. Ken Jr. would clarify everything momentarily. Blood pounded in her ears for a million minutes while she waited for him to continue. When he didn't, Amelia somehow summoned the courage to whisper, *"Sarah? Sarah Rosenberger? A baby? What are you saying?"*

In a frantic voice, Ken Jr. blurted out the crushing words. "Yes, Sarah. *My* baby. She isn't asking for much. Just a little monetary support." He spoke more quickly. "Nothing more than you can easily save by chopping here and there on your household budget. And a bit more of my time, a child needs to know its father. You of all people understand that, and I'm so proud of you!"

Anger, rising from years of being duped, engulfed Amelia. She flew out of bed, yanking the sheet around her. Ken Jr. lay in bed, exposed and shriveling before her eyes. Her voice was a terrible sound to hear.

"Asshole! You moronic mothersucking sack of manure. Get out of here before I kill you!"

Ken Jr. grabbed a pillow, covered himself, and escaped.

Amelia clenched her jaw, held back her tears. She went into her bathroom, turned on the tub, and dumped an entire box of bath salts into the steamy water. She would show that cur that she was worth more without him than she ever was with him.

94. PENN

How had things escalated so quickly with George that first night home? Penn mulled it over, perplexed each time she remembered his anger—and hers. What could she have done instead? Well, if she hadn't been so jet lagged, she might have formulated a plan. Thought it through. Better to have made a sweet wifely request of George first, nudging him toward sobriety.

Next, perhaps, she could have explained how important maintaining his health was to the family; or she could have said how his relationship with their boys would develop into real father-son appreciation once he got to know them better. In fact, he could have taken over the Scout duties that so encroached on her time. Yes, she could have handled it better, if she hadn't been so jet lagged.

What if that hadn't worked? Well, she'd have given it time, but before the holidays, if he were still unreformed, she'd have laid down the law. *George, you simply have to quit drinking,* she'd have said. No more cocktail meetings. To clinch it, she might have promised a much better sex life once he wasn't drinking. Wait a minute. Would she have? That's all she needed, George pawing her even more than usual, anticipating a racier type of romp if he got sober. Especially since she was grossed by the thought of male body parts right about now.

Truly, George could be so very, very stubborn; perhaps she'd have resorted to the Big Ultimatum after all. He would either give up the bottle, or she and the boys were going to leave, right after Christmas. Better, he would have to leave! That's what she'd have threatened.

But no matter how Penn mentally twisted and turned the situation, the reality of her separation stayed constant. The split up had happened in less than five minutes. Reconciliation in this lifetime seemed impossible. How in the world could she tell Mummy and the Admiral? Divorce was a four-letter word, to her family's thinking.

It had been nine days now. Penn stressed, she lost sleep. She forgot to make lists, and the boys had no milk for cereal one morning. She called Amelia for advice, feeling close to a nervous breakdown. Amelia came over with her kids and several bags of groceries; she made two meatloaves while encouraging Penn to face her parents and get it over with.

Penn held up the large square of crewelwork, a gift for Mummy's imminent birthday. "Thank goodness I finished it on Capri," she said for the seventh time.

"I know, sweetie," Amelia said. She listened but her eyes had a faraway look.

Penn hoped Mummy would adore the pillow slip and then put it away like all the other mementos Penn had gifted her. That reminder of the Capri nightmare could be happily out of sight forever.

"Give it to Mummy at lunch. *Before* you tell her," Amelia said. "And then just out with it. Don't explain, don't expect her to understand."

"Okay, okay." She'd say it simply, straightaway. Penn rehearsed for Amelia, "George and I are getting a divorce. George and I are getting a divorce."

Mummy would be shocked speechless. But the intricate Edwardian crewelwork might monopolize further conversation if Penn was clever.

"Your military upbringing taught you a few maneuvers, sweetie," Amelia reminded her. Penn agreed, although her brain still felt like mush. And even if Mummy could be calmed, what about the Admiral?

Penn made it to lunch, only eleven minutes late, the gift perfectly wrapped with a perfectly tied bow. Mummy looked exactly the same, gray silk blouse with that triple strand of rice pearls and tailored pearl earrings. *Her uniform*, Penn thought. *Do I look different to her?* Mummy gave Penn an up and down, scrutinizing hair, nails, hem length, and shoes. Mummy smiled and Penn did too. After which Mummy opened the package, careful not to rip the paper. She inspected the backside of the crewelwork, then the front, and thanked her talented daughter. Next the pair ordered their usual: clam chowders with extra oyster crackers, side salads with Thousand Island dressing, and two large iced teas with lemon, please. Then, before the food arrived, Penn gathered her courage and began confession.

"Mummy, please forgive me for having to tell you this. I'm so, so sorry I'm going to have to upset you and the Admiral, it's just so out of my control."

Penn continued exactly as she had not intended. Amelia would disapprove, but she couldn't help herself. Mummy sat openmouthed hearing that George's drinking had become so intolerable; that he wouldn't even try to sober up; that he called Penn dreadful names and made horrid accusations; that he neglected the boys while she was gone, as well as the house (left it a pigsty she was now cleaning up); and, pause, that she had asked for a divorce, and George had left, but they still had to divvy the household, and Penn would have to find a job. And, and, and, she was going crazy...

Well, Mummy perked up, visibly. She ate her entire bowl of chowder instead of pushing it away with complaints. She even ordered and finished dessert; her appetite had surged. Penn grasped the reality of Mummy's elation; Mummy saw a benefit in the new situation—no husband would be competing for her daughter's attention.

After the meal Mummy wiped her mouth and folded her napkin. She brushed at Penn's minimal chest, where cracker crumbs clung to the grey angora sweater.

"Don't worry about your father's reaction, he'll get used to the idea," she said. Penn's shoulders relaxed, and she sank back into the chair. Then Mummy had just one piece of advice. "Go see my therapist, Penelope, how do you think I've coped all these years? The Admiral doesn't approve of shrinks. We have to pass muster on our own steam, so keep a tight lip, but don't you worry about the bill. I have my own little bank account."

Two psychiatry offices would play into Penn's future, one negating any therapeutic effects of the other, but in that moment, Mummy wore a halo.

95. LILY

In the months following the hushed-up trip, Lily hovered over Callie's homework; she took Callie to every attraction Dirk hadn't. But Lily recognized in Callie her own brand of silent suffering. The eight-year-old rarely spoke of *that creepy* golf camp. When she did, much to Lily's regret, the wounds inflicted by a domineering father and an absent mother were apparent.

During this time Lily's heroic attempt to salvage her marriage epitomized her moral fortitude. "We've entered the 'for worse stage' of our marriage," she explained to herself. "We'll weather it." To suppress recurrent angst, she brewed many cups of exotic black tea. Sometimes she listened attentively as Dirk lectured on her lack of finesse in budgeting, housework, and intercourse. She rationalized herself into a calm state. After all, she'd fallen in love with Dirk's creative spirit and his intelligence, hadn't she? Weren't both qualities still very much intact?

But when February 1980 rolled around, and the new administrative assistant at Antonio Caldo wisely suggested that a CPA be hired to prepare the taxes—bypassing Dirk—Lily was sufficiently riled at Dirk's intermittent dalliance with Darleen to agree.

Looking up at Lily through his round bifocals, the CPA calmly pointed out large cash withdrawals and missing deposits. Antonio Caldo's three-year climb up the sales ladder showed a healthy profit, but did not accurately reflect Lily's history of designing with originality and producing within budget. Embezzlement? Dirk? There was only one blatant answer.

That very evening, Lily, broom in hand, attacked the sandy tiles of the patio waiting for Dirk's return from golf. Wind kept blowing the sand back again; the task seemed futile, but felt cathartic. Hearing the Porsche enter the garage, Lily closed her eyes and braced herself. She gripped the broom as her husband approached.

"Aren't you a fright? What's up?"

"I forgive your affair only to find out you've been stealing?"

Arms extended in mock innocence, Dirk scoffed. "You can't call it stealing. It's my money too."

"Spending it on Darleen, I'll bet."

Dirk continued to smirk shamelessly.

Lily let loose, her tone quiet, but commanding. "How dare you. Get your ass out. I want a divorce."

"Sure that's what you want, Lily? I'll get Antonio Caldo. Hell, I'll even get your beloved beach house."

"Dirk, you wouldn't!"

96. CAT

The onset of Cat's "monthlies" in October and again in November brought a mixed bouquet of emotion to the San Carlo house. Pietro reacted as if there had been an actual loss. His sad brown eyes grew even sadder. Noni criticized Cat's infertility while she and her peers gossiped in the ladies room after Sunday morning Mass. Cat continued to take her birth control pills while affirming the opposite; she never had to actually *lie*. Pietro believed what he wanted to believe.

Maybe it was the thought of another son changing Pietro. Maybe, no certainly, she'd ripened sexually on Capri. Now Pietro found her tantalizing in the bedroom, more so than even in the early years. He appreciated the layers of Italian lingerie that teased his senses. He slowed down his approach to savor her flesh, flesh she revealed inch by inch; appropriately his kisses covered a broader range of pleasure zones.

Cat still held her goal of a career tightly, privately repeating the phrase, *I am woman*; she could and would have it all. Cat no longer fought Noni's control of Beppe's Cantina. *Let her do the work,* she reasoned, *I have contacts to develop.* She took long lunch hours and spent them at Quinton's studio trying to be helpful and learn the ropes.

Quinton's behavior puzzled her. Instead of paying her attention as he had on Capri, his answers to her questions were clipped. Once he admonished her rudely when she suggested a tiny but amazing correction for his lighting on a set. The client had actually liked her idea better. But the art director—what was it about art directors—told her to "butt out." Aside from that, Quinton never seemed to have a paying job for her; he allowed her to peruse his Rolodex of fellow photographers, but when she phoned and identified herself, none of those photographers had styling work to offer her either.

Cat called Lily repeatedly, but Lily had issues: contractor issues, Callie issues, Dirk issues. Or she claimed exhaustion. "Not right now, Cat, you've caught me at a bad moment." *Poor Lily*, Cat thought. *How I used to admire her. She sure can't handle stress.*

Cat hoped Grace could introduce her to clients in the glamour/cosmetic biz, ones that Grace modeled for. She followed Grace to jobs and was introduced; she showed her portfolio and left business cards. It should have been glamorous and productive. *If* any client had phoned her, which they hadn't, yet. *If* Grace had been herself. Grace clammed up when questioned about Marc. What a witchy face Grace wore under her makeup. Where was her fun-loving friend?

Penn never answered the phone anymore. Instead, she let it ring until the machine picked up. Only Amelia seemed herself. Amelia said she'd come by the Cantina and take Cat to lunch. Cat finally nailed down a date with Amelia.

Cat festered as Amelia took her sweet time answering any questions. She waited patiently as Amelia excavated the broth and bread from her French onion soup; waited less patiently as Amelia cut into the cooling cheese topper. Finally, Amelia delivered the update as if it were old news.

Cat gasped in disbelief, "You and Penn are separated with divorces pending?" No one had told her a word. Cat felt ill. She missed the sisterhood. Why was she overlooked now? Had they all gotten together over the holidays and left her out? She still had her Christmas gifts for each.

"No, hardly a festive season, sweetie," Amelia reassured her. "We all muddled through for the kids. That was about it. So don't take it personally. In fact, Deedee hasn't talked to any of us for months. She could be back on Capri with Bob, for all I know."

97. DEEDEE

Deedee breezed into the restaurant, pushed her huge tortoise-shell sunglasses up onto her head, and looked around for her lunch dates. Ah, there they were. Penn and Amelia sat in the far corner, a private booth. Well, as private as you could get at Bob's Big Boy. She took a breath in preparation for what she knew lay ahead; first, the scolding for not staying in touch, then catching up on their lives since their return from that wonderful vacation. Well, wonderful for her, at least.

After the classic hug-hug-kiss-cheeks greetings, Deedee scooted into the booth. "So how've all y'all been doin'?"

Penn arched an eyebrow. "You might already know that if you'd thought to pick up the phone once in awhile."

"Just a simple yes or no will do, Deedee. If Penn hadn't invited you to lunch today, would you ever have called us?" Amelia's frustration with Deedee's habitual lack of communication added an edge to her voice. "We've been back from Capri for months and barely a word from you."

"Oh, just hush up and take it easy. I've been awful busy since we got back," Deedee explained, not in the least offended by Amelia's tone. She plunged a straw into the tall glass of iced tea the waiter set before her and gave him a wink.

"Not as if any of us would know what you've been up to," Penn reiterated. "You haven't returned our calls."

Deedee studied the menu for a second, came to a decision about her meal. "Has it ever occurred to either of you that life is too short to be actin' like ol' ladies before your time? Goodness, you're both worse than Mama, an' she *is* an ol' lady! You two gotta learn to relax and enjoy life."

"Like you obviously have." Amelia gave up. There was no changing Deedee.

"Wish I could," Penn muttered under her breath. Only Amelia heard.

The waiter came to take their order and refill their glasses. Looking appreciatively at his backside as he walked away, Deedee opened up the next order of conversation.

"All right, now we got through the chewin' out part, let's get to the catchin' up part. I'll start. You already know I'm divorcin' Hugh."

"Yeah, we know. That's all you've told us—no explanation, no nothing. When did this all go down?" Amelia asked.

Deedee related what happened at the airport "after that long plane ride. So once we got to Aunt Bea's, I said to Hugh, 'Y'all just go on home by yourself an' pack your trash. I expect y'all to be out by tomorrow.' Bless his little heart," she sighed, "he was gone when I got back to the house next day with Mama an' Nanette."

She then told what her last months had been like. "It is *peaceful*. Like it hasn't been since I hooked up with Hugh. Heck, the divorce'll be final soon—we did one of those do-it-yourself things. Got the forms in a stationery store. We didn't have any property together, and he doesn't make enough to pay alimony. Worked out real good."

"Wait, are you saying your household is peaceful now that Hugh's out of the picture?" Amelia asked. "What about Mama? I suppose her physical condition is much improved once you removed the thorn from her paw."

Amelia, like the others, suspected Mama of playing to Deedee's tender side when it came to her health. Amelia doubted that Mama had any appreciation for the good care Deedee provided, but having Hugh out of the equation would be one less person for Mama to find fault with.

"Oh, Mama's not much better. She just gets more an' more demandin'. Don't know what I'd do without Nanette to help out. But let's not dwell on Mama. I wanted to tell you girls about my new man."

A swift look from Penn to Amelia accompanied the swift kick under the table. *A new man?* Did we hear correctly?

"I know what y'all are thinkin'. It's too soon."

Penn and Amelia nodded.

"Well, it's never too soon to fall in love with the right person. Like I been sayin', life is short." Deedee went on filling in details about meeting Terrence. The chance encounter at the dentist's office, both with a toothache. He was a fiddler in a zydeco band at night, an anesthesiologist during the day. He thought Nanette was a howl, and Mama the sweetest ol' lady.

"We make some music together, I can tell you."

"I hope you aren't contemplating marriage. Surely you've learned your lesson. The way you vaulted right into it with Hugh…your divorce from

Ryan was final on Tuesday and by Saturday, you were Mrs. Stone," Penn reminded Deedee.

"Well, this is different," Deedee sort of assured them. "I'm makin' no promises. Not to you and not to Terrence. Not yet anyway."

Their meal was served. Deedee liberally poured ketchup on her fries, added more sugar to her iced tea, bit into her hamburger. "All right, now it's all y'all's turn. I talked enough to put a puppy to sleep, an' I want to enjoy my burger."

"As it happens, we're both on our own now." Amelia carefully removed the slice of bun between the two meat patties of her burger.

Deedee dropped a french fry back onto the pile. "Hush up! *Both* of you? What in the world? I thought you two were good to go. You gettin' divorces?"

At the ensuing nods, Deedee pushed for more information.

"I may have turned a blind eye while Ken Jr. played around in someone else's compost pile, but there wasn't a chance in this life that I'd let him add another rose to the harem," Amelia said. "I planted his Virginia Creeper in Sarah Rosenberger's front yard. Good riddance. Oh, and my children now have a little half sister. Ken Jr. is hoping I'll soften up and want to see her. I won't and I don't."

Amelia felt sad and regretful, but knew she'd made the right decision for herself and her children. What kind of moral code did Ken Jr. live by? Certainly not one she wanted her kids to learn.

"Well, that man is deluded, I tell you." Deedee was appalled.

"Tell her the best part," Penn urged.

"I'm turning my passion into a business," Amelia stated proudly.

"You're turnin' your kids into a business? Shoot, how's that work?" Deedee asked. "I wish Nanette could get a job and help out with expenses. Course I did finally make manager at Nordstrom, and now I'm my own boss," Deedee digressed.

"Gardening! Don't you pay attention to anything?" Amelia wondered how it was that Deedee kept skipping through life unscathed. "I'm working on starting a business. Right now I'm consulting for Tiny Tom's Green Thumb Nursery. And I'm good at it. When I have more contacts, I'll strike out on my own. As it is, we have to sell the house, and I won't have a garden when the kids and I move into an apartment."

"Well, I'd hire you, if I had any spare cash. Or a yard. But I just know y'all will be a success. Now how about you, Penelope? How is it that you're footloose too? I had you figured for a lifer."

Penn slumped back. She picked at the ever-offending cuticle, then proceeded to bring Deedee up to date on the status of her soon-to-be former marriage.

"Ah shucks. I'm sorry it all went down like that, sugar. Well, at least you can collect a boodle in alimony and child support. That George always did okay in the paycheck department, didn't he?"

"I haven't seen a cent from him. Can you believe it? And it's not like I can tell him he can't see the kids unless he helps support them—he hasn't even asked to see them. My attorney tells me not to worry, eventually we'll get him into court, and he'll be ordered to pay up, but for now, I'm driving around the old VW bus and praying it keeps chugging along."

"Penn, you gotta get yourself a job."

"I already did, Deedee. I found a job managing an office for a group of wacky psychiatrists. They'll drive me crazy, if I don't get there on my own." She shook her head and continued, "I got their billing and payables and patient files organized in less than a week. Of course, they haven't moved out of the dark ages when it comes to equal pay, so I clip coupons. Hard to stay afloat."

"Those nut jobs are darn lucky to have you, Penelope." Deedee quickly switched gears. "I don't suppose either of you has talked to Lily? Or Grace? You got any idea what's goin' on with them?"

"I've talked to Cat a time or two." Amelia was reluctant to discuss their other friends. "I know she's trying to get into photo styling. It sounds like Lily isn't as cooperative as she could be. Nor is Quinton. I'd certainly think they could lend her a hand."

"Oh shoot. Lily's up to her knickers in gnats. Dirk's threatenin' to take her dad's house away from her, an' that nasty nitwit forced her to sell Antonio Caldo so he could cash out. She's stayin' on for a year as a consultant, but all her designs an' patterns belong to someone else. That Cat's got nothin' to bellyache about. 'Cept maybe Noni."

Deedee pulled out a mirror and applied a fresh layer of lipstick. When satisfied with the results, she turned to Penn.

"I'm sure y'all have heard about Grace an' Marc. Guess it's no surprise. She told me Marc moved in with his friend—on the hush-hush. But I don't s'pose you'll be blabbin' his secret." She tilted her head and gave Penn a meaningful look.

Deedee picked up the check. "I know you two are strugglin'. I am too, but not as much as you, so I'll treat today." She slid out of the booth with a, "Y'all keep in touch, ya hear?"

98. LILY

And then Lily became furious with herself—such a trusting, stupid patsy she'd been! Even Dirk's departure enraged her. Once while navigating stacks of his moving boxes, the putting machine caught her eye. Angered, she stuffed it into an already overstuffed box and cracked it.

"Don't beat yourself up," Grace pleaded, attempting to ease her pain. "If only we had both been more alert."

Lily's attorney, Miles Silverton, a British gentleman, had positive news. "Bad form, Dirk's threats, but you hold title to the house, and he knew it. Bob's your uncle, so keep your pecker up." Lily laughed at his lingo, startling both herself and Mr. Silverton.

Lily's Mediterranean Collection took off. The *H.I.S.* magazine spread garnered new retail opportunity. Sales hit the highest mark ever. Dirk, at this advantageous moment, demanded he be bought out. Quinton encouraged Lily to apply for a loan and keep Antonio Caldo. Worn down, she declined, and the company sold in a bidding war. The new owners required Lily be retained as consulting designer for the first year at least; she'd earn a sizeable retainer, but they would own her patterns. *Yes, financial security*, Lily thought, *but so much for the dream.*

And then Lily withdrew, losing heart and inspiration. Lily was not much of a communicator whilst in pain. Didn't she realize that talking about the divorce would help? Grace, Cat, and Deedee hardly saw their newly gaunt and unkempt friend. Amelia and Penn still kept to themselves.

Grace demanded Lily get herself together. "Enough of this malaise." In June, with Grace and Deedee's insistence, Callie went to spend a month with her cousin Nanette. Lily's inertia had become serious. She needed *something*. But what?

99. LILY

Lily drove the Pacific Coast Highway northbound while the sun sank, coral melting into metallic blue. A nude male mannequin occupied the passenger seat beside Lily. He sat upright, as did she; each seemed oblivious to the magnificent sky.

"Take a good look fella, this is all that's left of *my* Antonio Caldo. Two dummies and a bolt of fabric."

Framed by enormous Monterey pines, Cecilia de la Mar Convent welcomed her at dusk. An unsmiling monk led Lily to her quarters. He bowed as he left her alone. Lily allowed her duffle to drop to the polished stone floor, noting the austere interior with no regrets. She wilted onto the hard bed. Her appearance: rumpled linen, straggly ponytail, barefaced. She stared at the moon through the clerestory window until it slid past, trailing silver clouds. She discovered a swath of stars in the darkening ink of sky. And after sleep held her captive, the sun woke her. A tray of food appeared at her door each morning and evening. The cycle repeated for days on end.

Lily had entered the Montecito monastery as a guest seeking enforced solitude and silence. Although she tried to find comfort in the almighty outstretched hands that comforted the monks, no miracles occurred for her.

Slowly, deprivation from troubling stimuli heightened her imagination. Now when she looked out the clerestory window, or walked among the cypress trees under the haze of coastal sky, she saw visions: bold tropical prints paired with fluid woven solids, well-placed pleats, angled pockets, and buttons made of bamboo. Old desires returned. Lily traded numbness for pain. And she could finally weep, grieving the loss of family for Callie and herself.

One morning, after actually tasting the breakfast egg, hard roll, and orange, she wandered to a grove of pines that swayed in a slight breeze.

Beside the grove she encountered a garden of calla lilies circling the statue of St. Celia. The bronze plaque read: "St. Cecilia, A Martyr—The Lily of Heaven." Lily gasped with self-recognition. Martyrdom, how naturally it came to her. She'd been drowning in it. Lily kneeled. Strangely compelled, she looked up to face the open armed statue. St. Cecelia's eyes seemed to glow, emanating compassion. *Stand up!* she told herself.

The breeze freshened. Playful shadows began to flicker along the boundary wall, transforming into dancing images of menswear. Lily laughed, an honest hearty laugh, and followed running. Even the stern monk, cut flowers in hand, livened his step as he watched her.

100. QUINTON

Quinton had promised himself a few days on Pompeii, but his enthusiasm wavered after the events on Capri. Nevertheless, he convinced himself to proceed on his earlier desire. *After all, I am in Italy now with no plans for a return visit.* A weathered archeologist took a personal interest in Quinton's photography of the ruins and guided him to remote areas. Quinton returned home with exceptional additions to his portfolio. His tensions eased.

In retrospect, the *H.I.S.* job was a boon. Quinton thought the magazine spread was perfection. *Surely it will bring me more assignments, since Edwin and I have begun to brainstorm future locales, Pompeii among them.*

The *H.I.S* coverage also boosted Lily's growing business. *Rotten timing, though, for Dirk to get greedy and demand his share of the company,* Quinton bemoaned. But as painful as it was to witness Lily's despair, he knew she'd be ahead of the game *without* Dirk, once back on her feet.

Perplexed, Quinton observed the new distance between Lily and her friends. *Far be it from me to probe the mysterious dynamic of girlfriends.* With unexpected sadness he grasped the heavy toll the Capri sojourn had taken on this once-inseparable sixsome. First the loss of husbands; now the comfort of one other.

Camps had been set up, not-so-invisible boundaries drawn. Lily, loyal to Grace, cooled communication with Penn and Amelia—who seemed to not mind the arrangement. Deedee and Cat easily skated the borders with a foot on either side and provided tidbits of information to both factions.

Cat was languishing. After failing to explode into the world of advertising as a photo stylist, she blamed Quinton and Lily for not using their influence to get her work. Quinton wanted to set her straight: *Cat, you fail to recognize it takes years to build a career. And a hundred jobs to get your name out there. Not to mention talent and tact.* He held his tongue.

According to Cat, Amelia was flourishing; she surprised Quinton. Striking out on her own, designing gardens and beginning to make a name for herself. In Ken Jr.'s field—*oh, the irony of it!*

It sounded like Deedee's life was business as usual. Neither Grace nor Lily could detect any injury Deedee might have borne during her second divorce. Reading between the lines, Quinton guessed Deedee was getting ready to swallow Terrence whole. She was looking for a wedding ring. With a diamond!

Grace was bearing up. She and Quinton worked together frequently, kept each other updated on their lives. Socially, she was all but shut down. Occasionally she'd meet Quinton and Lily for drinks or dinner, but otherwise she was focused on two things: raising Jemima and being mindful that she was in her thirties and had to work harder at keeping her profession moving.

Quinton confided in Lily, "My assurance that the camera would love Grace well into old age was met with a laugh and the rolling of her eyes. 'Rose-colored lenses,' she joked."

Apparently, Penn was enduring. She continued to labor away for the shrinks, gathering impetus for her own neurosis. Cat pointed out Penn's unconsciously incongruous belief: the doctors are worse off than their patients. But Penn's pay had improved. Good thing. Her three boys were like locusts in the kitchen and growing out of their clothes at a light-speed pace. Hearing about Penn caused Quinton a twinge; he hoped they'd never cross paths again.

Quinton also had his doubts about returning to Capri. *I can't foresee any reason to. Beautiful as it was, none of us left that island unscathed.*

LOS ANGELES, CALIFORNIA

THE YEARS PASS

1979–1982

CAT AS CATALYST

101. LILY

Lily missed the days before Capri. Loneliness loomed with every flip of the calendar. If it wasn't a holiday, it was a birthday to be spent without the camaraderie and support of good friends. Twelve years of traditions were eclipsed: no more gourmet luncheons, beach picnics, or kids' parties.

Of course Lily saw Grace, but Grace had less free time, working more frequently after her divorce. They talked about the blinders they must have been wearing during their marriages. This led to conversation about being blindsided on Capri by Penn and Amelia, who obviously misrepresented whatever went down. Old anger stirred up.

Grace and Marc had developed an enviable amicability, one that she and Dirk had not. Oftentimes Dirk showed up with Darleen when he gathered Callie for a weekend. As much as Lily had forgiven the affair and the stealing, she simply detested the sight of her cocky ex. His new address was Darleen's condo in Port Hueneme. Callie didn't like sleeping there on the hide-a-bed. But she liked playing dress up in Darleen's high heels and jewelry.

Cat still checked in with Lily regularly, mostly to petition Lily for new/ more business introductions. She was taking a back seat at the cantina, with Pietro and Noni's blessing. Both were newly protective of her health because she might just be pregnant soon. It was true; she'd been short of breath lately and even fainted one hot afternoon.

"You want another child?" Lily asked. Cat laughed as if that were an answer.

Although Lily harbored dark thoughts about the way Amelia and Penn had acted on Capri, if either one would pick up the phone and say the simplest kind of "sorry," Lily could let go of it. But Amelia didn't call. Ditto, Penn. When Lily grew lax, her mind wandered back to the early years with Penn. One particular memory kept resurfacing. She and Penn were digging holes in the sand for their pregnant bellies while reading. What was it? *A Thousand Names For Your Baby.* Callie and Charles played so well together right from the start, bouncing in Jolly Jumpers, practically sharing pacifiers in the Porta Crib. Although Callie was always a better little surfer than Charles. *We used to think these two would end up marrying,* Lily mused.

Lily would shut the memories off. Memories hurt too much. But Callie forced Lily to reckon with the situation. "How come we never see Auntie Penn anymore? When's Charles coming to the beach? Why can't I invite everybody to my birthday party?"

Deedee's communication with Lily was sporadic, and although she flitted from friend to friend, she didn't make overtures about being a group again. With her gossip, Lily and Grace gleaned the reality of Amelia and Penn's homecomings.

To hear Deedee tell it, Amelia had been whistling Dixie thinking Ken Jr. would miss her and quit messing around. Well, Deedee had warned her. Anyway, how dare he be thinking Amelia wouldn't raise Cain about Sarah Rosenberger as a whatchamacallit?

"Another wife in the harem?" Lily asked. All three divorcees laughed at the image of Ken Jr. surrounded by exotic women and dozens of children.

"Seems Penn had a rude awakenin' too, hers right off the bat," Deedee said. "I swanee, how Penn was cryin' through lunch when she told me. It was somethin' pathetic. Between Mummy and her psycho job, Penn is more a nervous nellie than ever. At least she won out on the house. Not that she has time or energy for keepin' it spiffed up."

Lily felt thankful to have retained the beach house. She had plans to remodel the upstairs master bedroom into a studio. For starters, a long worktable and filing cabinets made the room newly functional. Best, the setup diffused memories of bedroom intimacies. She moved her sleeping quarters to the extra downstairs room, right next to Callie's.

Most evenings, side by side on her king-size bed, she and Callie played at being a tourist in Italy. Who? What? When? Where? They asked and answered in Italian, Lily dreaming of a visit to Italy with her daughter. Rome, Florence, Venice, Milan were must-sees. Perhaps even a return to Capri.

Lily's talent and diligence led to another, and then another, successful season for Antonio Caldo. But she wasn't content designing for owners who reaped the profits. She grew restless for the year on retainer to end, although she knew freelancing would bring financial anxiety. She'd probably scurry from one freelance project to the next, with no resting on the laurels of past success. New ideas cropped up. She sketched on her own time, created patterns, and kept an eye out for appropriate fabrics. The master bedroom/studio was practically wallpapered with inspiration.

▨　　▨　　▨

More time passed, and Lily's news about Penn and Amelia continued to be secondhand. Cat and Deedee lounged on the beach with Grace and Lily that August 1980, while the children built sand castles.

According to Cat, Amelia had obviously learned plenty from her tenure in Ken's landscape firm. As Deedee put it, "I'm blown away, seein' how many contracts for rose and vegetable gardens she has. Her business is blossomin'. Shows smug Mr. Ken Jr. a thing or two. Bet that just dills his pickle."

Cat ran into Penn occasionally, with Jason's schedule. Penn's boys were into sports, big-time. T-ball, soccer, and swimming. Cat didn't mind saying that Penn looked like hell, wearing men's flannel shirts with jeans while sitting on the sidelines or the bleachers.

"You mean wearin' a suit and heels nine to five is an excuse for bein' sloppy off the job?" Deedee asked incredulously. "She'll never be findin' a new husband this way."

"Does she want to?" Lily asked.

"C'mon now, sis, who doesn't?" Deedee shot back.

Lily didn't. Neither did Grace. "Marriage, *never again,* no way!"

"Terrence is the best thin' ever crossed my path. If he offered me somethin' big and sparkly enough, I wouldn't refuse it."

Lily had gone with Deedee several times to hear Terrence's gig. They'd shared drinks afterward. Terrence seemed every bit what Deedee claimed. Broad shouldered, good-hearted, intelligent, talented, modest, and could he dance. All that helped Deedee survive dispensing lingerie. These days she laid off complaining about Mama and Nanette.

Grace had renewed her relationship with Hope and Jimbo. Still active as TV personalities, with Marc as director, they thrived on Grace's success and happily babysat their cherub granddaughter, with assistance on the set or by themselves at home.

Grace had been able to find more lucrative modeling jobs than she had ever anticipated. Thanks to Quinton, Grace would say. Grace and Quinton were thrust together job by job, or recommended each other to an art director whenever the opportunity arose. They groused, complained, opined, and bragged to each other, went months without contact, and effortlessly picked up where they had left off. When Quinton had casual girlfriends, Grace knew the state of his heart. For his part, Quinton knew, and accepted, that Grace's broken heart had repaired itself with a steel casing.

■   ■   ■

Lily received Cat's call July 8 of 1981; she noted the date because 7/8 was her mother's birth date. She considered it a lucky pairing of numbers. Cat invited her to lunch. An important lunch—she needed Lily's input. Right now. Lily met Cat at the Cantina, greeting Pietro and Noni graciously, not suspecting that Cat would momentarily unfold a plan these wine merchants would hardly favor, even though it involved wine.

Cat dug into her shrimp cocktail, hungry, starving; she'd been dieting, could Lily tell? "I'm probably wearing your size now." She'd had a job offer, one she'd gotten *all by herself*, thank you very much. From a wine distributing company. The rep had invited her to a special lunch at the winery in Santa Ynez. She and the owner had hit it off. He'd been impressed with her knowledge of wines, of course. He offered her a job as a rep with an exciting Northern California territory. She'd be traveling: expense account, company car, commissions!

"Should I take it, Lily?"

"Would Pietro be happy about this?" Lily asked, her fork hovering over her Crab Louie.

"No! He'd expect me to be a sweet-strong-soldier-of-a-dear and keep trundling along following orders, his orders, Noni's orders." Cat dug into her cocktail viciously, finding only celery chunks at the bottom. "I leased the perfect condo in Chatsworth. The boys can stay with me when I'm in town. That way they can keep their bedrooms in the house and all. You think I should, don't you? You are the only one who gets my need to be, to be great, to contribute, to find out how high I can fly. You think I should, don't you?"

Lily sat silenced by the question. It sounded like an announcement and hardly begged an extraneous, perhaps negative answer.

Lily began tactfully. "You've made up your mind, so does this mean you're asking Pietro for a separation?"

Cat squared her shoulders; her green eyes shone. Her lips pursed, fighting off a proud smile.

"I'm in love," she said, "with the owner of the winery. Sebastian Cavilieri. And he with me."

"For how long?" asked Lily, dumbstruck.

"Long enough for me to know what I want. And it's not Pietro."

102. GRACE

Cat reclined on her Jacobean print sofa with tapestry pillows propped behind her back. Sheer curtains floated inward, propelled by the breeze of the open windows. Deedee sat beside Cat, painting her nails a deep red. Grace set a low bowl of floating camellias on the center of the table, while Lily folded napkins in the shape of a bishop's miter.

"Now my toes," Cat instructed Deedee once her fingernails were complete.

"Listen here, I was invited for lunch, not slave labor. I don't like paintin' my own toes, and I wouldn't consider paintin' anyone else's." Deedee brushed out imaginary creases from her clingy sheath dress as she stood. "When are we gonna eat?"

Oh Lord, Grace thought, *Cat lies around like a darned lazy Roman while the rest of us prep the meal for her party. How did we get roped into this anyway?* Turning to Lily, she asked quietly, "Do you think there's any chance Penn and Amelia might be no-shows?"

"Well, we answered the call. I believe they will too. This is the first lunch in how long? Cat was especially insistent."

Grace shrugged. She didn't want to think how long it'd been since she'd seen the others. She didn't feel ready to face them, to chitchat about inconsequential things. She wasn't ready to reveal herself. Not like she used to. Neither of them had reached out to her, and she'd certainly not made any overtures to them.

"Look at that. Ms. Persistent has managed to manipulate Deedee into a pedicure. There's no end to Cat's hubris. Wish I had her moxie." Grace shook her head, went to Cat's small kitchen, and began to slice grilled chicken breasts into strips.

Within moments, Lily joined her. "What can I do?"

Grace gestured to a huge pot on the stove and the pasta next to it. Lily obliged, swirling the pasta into the boiling water.

"Look at you!" Lily said. "So comfortable in the kitchen." She smiled at Grace. "I remember when you were a pro at making reservations, not meals."

Grace smiled back. Lily was right. She'd discovered that cooking could be satisfying, enjoyable, therapeutic. One good thing that came from the Capri trip.

"Where are Penn and Amelia? They promised to come," Cat hollered out, then succumbed to a coughing fit. Grace and Lily rushed from the kitchen.

"Goodness, Cat. You gonna be okay? You made me mess up your big toe. Now I have to start over. Can one of you girls get the polish off this toe? I don't want to smudge my own nails."

Lily saturated a cotton ball in polish remover and rubbed the crimson mess from Cat's toe. Deedee stood and walked to the window.

"Well, lookee there, Miz Cat. Those gals aren't missin' after all. They're sittin' in Amelia's car. Still holdin' grudges, I expect. We got us one itty-bitty prediction here," Deedee reported.

"*Predicament*, Deedee." Grace touched Deedee's arm. "I'm sorry." She knew she needed to break her habit of correcting Deedee's inaccurate vocabulary. Deedee just waved it off.

"They're probably feeling buttonholed. We've never patched things up. Grace, come with me—we can make the effort." Lily looked at Grace hopefully.

"Okay, I'll come, but don't think I've forgotten the whole Capri blowup."

▨   ▨   ▨

Grace looked around the table and assessed her friends. Everyone seemed shy. Gone was the easy banter they'd earned through years of friendship.

If it weren't for the lack of conversation, Grace could almost pretend that nothing had changed. Cat's table showed off her china, crystal, and sterling; and there were several empty wine bottles on the buffet.

"Goodness! I'm about bored to tears," Deedee exclaimed. "I could've stayed home with Mama if this is all the excitement all y'all got to offer. Somebody say somethin'!" She looked around the table, "Okay, I'll start." Deedee then proceeded to relate what had transpired the Wednesday before last.

"You eloped? To Las Vegas?" Cat sputtered.

"Yep. I had the day off. The night before, Terrence worked the four-to-midnight shift in the emergency room. He went home and instead of crawlin' into his bed, he called me and said the time had come. We drove to Vegas, and by six a.m. I was a newlywed. Now I see y'all lookin' for a ring, but I don't have it yet. Terrence is havin' his mama's ring sized for me. With all the rush…well, y'all understand. An' oh, it's a big one!"

Grace gushed along with the rest of them for appearance's sake. How could Deedee take the plunge again? Three times? Grace fervently hoped the old adage held true. Her ears perked up when Amelia bashfully talked about working toward getting a patent for a rose she was culturing. Penn was reticent, mostly remarking about George, and if he had been lacking as a husband, he was even worse as an ex.

Lily had wimped out and let Dirk get by with a pittance for child support and no alimony. It was with relief she divulged that she'd landed a contract with a leather goods manufacturer, designing jackets and vests for both men and women. The company had a profit-sharing plan and security—eliminating the financial worries of freelancing.

The friends all looked at Grace expectantly. If she didn't perform and the chasm between them widened, did she care? Uncertain that the friendship was even reparable, she decided to acknowledge the nightmares she used to have, the ones she never talked about.

"Before Marc left, I used to wake up at three thirty or four a.m., terrified. I'd wake Marc up, tell him I was scared, and he'd hold me till I fell asleep again. I didn't understand my fear—that is, until Marc was gone. When he left, so did my night terrors."

"Oh, Grace, you never told us," Lily said. "I guess once the worst that could happen happened, you were left in peace."

"More or less," Grace replied with a crooked smile.

A knowing look passed between Penn and Amelia. And then Cat made her big announcement.

103. CAT

"You guys, I spent last weekend in the hospital." A tear glistened as Cat looked from face to face. Amelia gasped, Lily's head cranked toward Cat, Grace's face had that *now what?* expression. Penn shouldered up to Amelia and whispered, "If she's faking just to get us back together..."

Amelia was the only friend with enough presence to reply. "What was wrong, sweetie? Are you getting better?"

Cat explained in some detail how she was driving to Cambria for a magnificent wine tasting she'd planned, two hundred guests invited, all important people, they'd know the names for sure, and she just couldn't breathe. Scariest thing ever, just couldn't breathe. She followed the *H* signs to the hospital and was rushed into emergency for tests.

"You have no idea how it feels to be all alone. I was all alone in that bed and they were telling me, 'you are very, very, very sick.'" Cat looked around dramatically. "It just struck me. Like a grand epiphany. How much we need each other. Don't you get it?"

"Where was Sebastian?" asked Deedee.

Cat gave Deedee the stink eye. Deedee had upstaged her by announcing that hasty elopement. Now Deedee was trying to dig for dirt too. "He *would* have been with me, *but I told you*, we had an elaborate event going on. He couldn't leave right then." No question Cat was riled.

"So you've got to be quittin' your job and gettin' surgery or something. Or is it determinal?"

Grace started to correct Deedee and stopped.

"I am not dying! It wouldn't be fair. I'm finally in love and have this fabulous job and a condo I've fixed up just like I want it, so how can you ask that?"

"They have prescriptions for these things, don't they, sweetie?" asked Amelia in her most soothing voice. "She's going to keep it under control, Deedee. Right, Cat?"

Penn started in on Cat. "What about Pietro? He's there for you, isn't he?"

Cat felt as if she were on trial, sitting there before judge and jury answering difficult questions. All she wanted was some sympathy from these prying women; they used to know how to comfort her. Maybe when they heard about Pietro and Noni, they'd understand how hard it was to be in her body.

"Pietro says I'm a coldhearted bitch, and I broke his heart, and if he never saw me again, the four of them would be better off." Cat gazed into each friend's eyes, looking for the flicker of compassion she needed.

"Well, excuse me for speaking out of turn, but George as much as said the same to me, so don't feel like the Lone Ranger, Cat," Penn said, redirecting the conversation to her own woes. "You're not the only one feeling alone. At least you have Silvestri whatever."

"Oh, Penn, I know how hopeless you feel, how much it hurts," Grace said, startling Cat with her newly acquired sympathy for Penn.

Penn attacked. "You have no idea how I feel. *I've* lost a husband. By your own admission, you and Marc were…" Penn didn't utter the ugly words Cat was imagining.

Penn looked away. Grace winced at the jab.

"You don't give a damn about my cardiopulmonary congenital defect, do you? My misplaced aorta, my defective valve? All you care about is yourselves!" Cat turned as florid as the moiré drapes behind her.

Lily spoke quietly, using her literary voice. "And so, the wives sharpen their guillotines, once more forgetting how much they need one another." Without hesitating she changed her tone. "I brought champagne. Let's toast to everyone's good health, and renewed friendship. Oh yes, and to the new wife in our midst, Deedee!"

"Yes, please, let's toast to my good health," Cat implored. Grace opened the champagne, launching the cork across the table and straight into Penn's chest. Penn yelped with pain. She broke down and her shoulders shook as she sobbed.

Cat wanted the last word. "Like I said, high time to make up."

104. AMELIA

Amelia checked her watch—2:05 p.m.—and picked up the pace. She had one hour to help Cat complete her shopping before the twins needed to be retrieved from school. Andy and Don had been kicked off the bus again—one more offense, and they wouldn't be able to ride for the rest of the school year. And here was Cat, hell-bent on examining every single Christmas ornament Nordstrom had on display. Yes, the carolers were especially charming to listen to, but tonight was the Christmas holiday program at Jennifer's middle school, and Amelia still had cupcakes to frost for the event.

"Cat, dear, let's get those gifts for the girls—Deedee is waiting for us in the lingerie department. She's put aside a few things for you to choose from. We'll get this done quickly; Deedee always makes suitable selections." Amelia put her arm under Cat's elbow in an attempt to hustle her along.

Amelia couldn't help but ask herself, *why isn't Grace doing this? She's the one with the most free time. Or Lily? She has more patience with Cat and her demands.* Amelia hadn't wanted to shop today and truly was laden with her own responsibilities. But Cat had been insistent. It had to be today. And Cat was sick and Amelia was healthy.

"Amelia, slow down. Can we grab a nice cup of tea and some pound cake? I've loads of time this afternoon. You promised we'd have a good old-fashioned shopping trip."

"Sweetie, we've been at this long enough today to qualify for a marathon. And we had lunch less than two hours ago. I don't have much time left."

"Oh, fine. You know, if I were comfortable shopping alone, I would. Dr. Hounkah as good as told me to not do anything strenuous on my own. So let's just get this over with, and you can go dig in your rose garden or whatever it is that's more important."

Amelia felt guilty and frustrated. Cat demanded attention, but rarely showed appreciation. Since Cat's kids were with Pietro ninety eight percent of the time, she had little consideration for a mother's obligations. Thankfully, Amelia spied Deedee close by, arranging silky nightgowns on a rack. Deedee would bring some much-needed cheer to Cat's sad-sack mood.

"Hey there, gals. What's cookin'? Don't ya love the holidays? They're just so merry. Now come on over to the counter. Here, Cat, you take a seat right there an' let me just show you all the goodies I pulled out for you to look at." Deedee was dressed in a drab black, which was the current staff uniform. But true to her defiant nature, she sported red and green Christmas tree earrings that caught the light and shimmered whenever she moved her head.

Spreading eight or ten colorful teddies and a few silk kimonos across the glass top, Deedee began to make her case for each item.

"Well, I'm not gonna lie. This here red one has my name all over it. Course you can make the final decision, but I thought this bright white one would be perfect for Lily. Glows, doesn't it?" Amelia and Cat oohed. "Now this here butter yellow would look perfect on you, Amelia. An' this cool jade, well, that's Penn. Don't agree? I'm thinkin' maybe the aqua or the coral for Grace."

"Deedee these are delightful, but you know I can't afford teddies *and* kimonos. I can't even get one for myself. Do you have anything a little less dear?"

"Ah, sugar. Y'all just go with the teddies. I was plannin' on givin' you my employee discount. Give me the cash an' I'll ring this up later and drop the whole bundle off when I finish my shift this evenin'. Terrence is workin' late an' we can have a little visit. I'll even help you wrap 'em up."

Amelia felt the weight of Cat lift from her shoulders. Bless Deedee. Now Cat wouldn't mind going home with something to look forward to. Amelia rejoiced when the carolers strolled by.

105. PENN

Lily's drive was full. Penn paralleled into the tiny parking space, happy to have found one along the beach lane. She should have carpooled, but she wanted the option of leaving early. Penn sat for a moment. Other times spent at this house flashed by. *How Dirk used to rule over Lily*, she thought. And yet Lily always had a unique style and strength, one she probably didn't even recognize.

Penn sighed. Oh, that moment on Capri when Lily acknowledged Dirk's deceit and lost herself, as if without him she was nothing. From that moment on, it seemed to Penn, Lily's heretofore-crisp white shirts grew limp on their antique wooden hangers. But look at Lily now. Lily was a reinvented flower, no longer relying on a white-shirt formula for identity. Lily had pulled herself together after the wounds of divorce.

"What about me, Lord?" Penn beseeched. "Why can't I pull myself together?" And then Penn shuddered. *No, I don't want the Almighty's answer.*

Penn knocked softly. Lily greeted her cordially enough. The beach house shimmered with Christmas décor. Not the country-craft Amelia set out, not the Hummel figurines Deedee collected, not even the religious decorations Penn favored. Lily's holiday setting reflected a modernism, startling Penn at first. The others were hanging up jackets and exclaiming over one another's outfits, shoes, or hair.

Lily offered a tour of the newly completed remodeling. First Callie's room, colors and fabrics picked out by the young lady herself, built-in shelves for a growing book and record collection, and a drafting table with a swivel stool. Jemima was anxious to look through Callie's supplies and start in on "secret" items. The girls remained behind, whispering and giggling as Lily led the five moms upstairs.

Penn twinged with envy. Lily could work from home. The well-lit studio clearly made sense—functional, yet uncluttered. A sleek metal table took up the length on one side. Bolts of fabric fit nicely in the reconfigured wardrobe. Displays of patterns and dressed mannequins shouted work in progress. An antique pecan table fit comfortably at the window with several matching chairs (modern and antique together?). Penn was surprised to see a girl-child mannequin and an array of pretty fabrics pinned on an adjacent panel.

"You're designing for little girls now?" she asked.

"Just on a whim," Lily answered. "I have a cheerleader, you know."

The six settled downstairs to enjoy Lily's sumptuous spread. Penn found the mood a touch somber. Everyone was so concerned with Cat's wheezing. Cat had given up her pack a day habit and only smoked occasionally when drinking. (Someone should shake Cat until her teeth rattle.)

Callie and Jemima, pleased with themselves, served platters of home-baked cookies. They wore construction paper hats and vests.

"We're Santa's elves, can't you tell?" Jemima asked.

"Look at our shoes," Callie instructed. Indeed, their party shoes were adorned with pointed-up toes and attached jingle bells.

Gifts were to be exchanged. "Excuse me, but let's go one by one," Penn requested. Simultaneous gift opening seemed so rude.

"Okay, if we're making rules, mine have to be opened last!" Cat said a bit loudly. When the time came, Cat handed Penn hers first.

Deedee, knowing full well what the box contained, coached Penn playfully. "Y'all be noticin' the first-class wrappin', pretty please, before ya see what Cat gotcha."

Penn opened the gift, acting silly as she complimented the wrapping. She dug into the tissue and held up the lingerie, a blood-red teddy. She forced a polite expression, inclining her face toward Cat.

Cat burst into song, her voice a whispery rasp, entreating Santa to hurry down the chimney.

Deedee couldn't contain herself. "Lordy, Penn! A fella'd heat up like a horny toad seein' you in that."

Penn wanted to defend herself. (She wasn't going to "heat up" a man, no horny monster ever, ever, again, she'd learned her lesson…)

Penn's eyelids fluttered. She convulsed. Nightmarish images swirled. *Jax, crazed, pulls her close. Rough, he's rough. Jax forces her to face him. Forces her. She struggles. His kisses wet, his long tongue pushing into her unwilling mouth. All the noise around them. Leave me alone!*

Penn staggered up, eyelids still fluttering, remembered haunting images. Intent on escaping, she tripped over gifts on the floor and fell to her knees.

106. LILY

The effect of the Capri melee had begun to flatten under the wheels of time, helped along by Cat's unrelenting role as the group's event planner.

"Grace balked, but I insisted!" Cat bragged to Lily. "She was so stubborn, though! She said, and I quote, 'It has to be an announcement event.

With no gifts. Or I'm not going along with it."' Obviously Cat was still peeved.

"Well, the others won't be informed of an agenda then," Lily said calmly.

"I hope they'll all come without a good reason then. Daulphine says there's still bad blood in our group."

And so, that bright Sunday, June 16, 1982, the six-some gathered for luncheon at the Inn of the Seventh Ray on Old Topanga Road. Passing under the ironwork arch with its hammered metal signage and entering the lush garden, they waited beside a marble cupid who held a cluster of roses. Amelia inspected the blossoms and commented on the varieties.

After a brief wait and some chitchat—Penn not having the right clothes for this place (the choice between jeans and a suit was no choice), Cat expounding proudly on the amenities, Deedee complaining, "I don't get this unimpaved walkinway, just like on Capri," and Grace holding her tongue, respecting certain niceties expected of a bride-to-be—the ladies were seated at a white-clothed table, creek side. A choice table it was, Cat informed them. A wedding was in progress just out of view. Lily felt a twinge. Life's bittersweet cocktail—the blend of past defeat and newfound hope—intoxicated her.

Cat, looking especially frail, held up Grace's left hand.

"Is this some rock, or what?" Cat asked, obviously posing a rhetorical question.

Deedee took the bait. "Grace! You went an' got yourself engaged?"

"Yes, I did, and the invitations are in the mail."

Penn, Amelia, and Deedee burst into squeals, taken completely by surprise.

"Where was I when all this was goin' down? You said there'd never be another man in your bed. An' now you're gettin' married?" Deedee halted her rapid-fire questions only momentarily. "Hey, you got a tadpole in lady town?"

Penn picked up the thread with sarcasm. "Excuse me, are you impugning our Lady of Virtue?"

"Of course not!" Deedee answered quickly, only to wonder at the alteration again. "Just that they've been good ol' buddies forever. What changed?"

"Yup, Grace and Quinton, good old buddies," Lily said. "Even though I watched all the evidence unfold, I stayed oblivious to the possibility of romance between them. It only makes sense, though. She's silk to his tweed." Lily grinned, pleased with the metaphor.

"So tell it like a story, Lily, we know you want to," Cat taunted.

Lily began in a literary voice. "Who can imagine the curious moment when love will spark? For Grace and her fiancée, it was one propitious day as Jemima shivered with fever. When the call came, there was Grace, stuck behind the camera for indeterminate hours, calf deep in a makeshift pool of water, turquoise lacquered hair interwoven with artificial seaweed, yards of sea-foam silk wrapped around her torso and held securely along her spine with innumerable alligator clips. Unable to leave the set, she directed the receptionist to call, first her parents, and then me. No success. Becoming a bit frantic, Grace thought of Quinton, who worked in the vicinity of the Ballet Academy.

"To say that the sight of eight-year-old Jemima, her face blowzy with flu, contentedly draped over Quinton's broad shoulder, her skinny legs unhumanly pink against his jeans, her narrow arms in their black leotard sleeves dangling from the folds of his tweed jacket, ignited Grace's heart, would be accurate."

Grace continued the story. "As corny as it sounds, it's true! Quinton laid Jemima on the couch, walked to me, his eyes so bright. He was smiling. I reached out, tripped, and fell into his arms. I'm telling you, the studio spun and melted into a blue paradise."

Deedee stood and lifted her glass. "Grace, I propose a toast to you."

As they each stood for the toast, glass in hand, Grace blushed. "I must admit I *am* floating."

Lily's heart surged, seeing Grace's face lit from within.

After the toast, Cat became somber. Wheezing as she spoke, she made a pronouncement. "You're floating now, but in the long run we only have each other."

Penn nodded in agreement and hugged Grace. At that very moment, a wasp circled Penn's head, buzzing angrily. Penn batted at it, jumped, screamed, and ran in circles. Amelia rushed to her aid, but not before the wasp found its target on Penn's cheek.

107. PENN

Deedee's Terrence wielded a fork and tongs cheerfully, just like George used to. As a single mom, Penn appreciated the invite for July BBQ; it was hard to plan and fix meals during the summer (every single meal *and* snacks) for three ravenous sons. Just now Charles was hollering a giggly "Polo" in response to Nanette's beguiling "Marco." Penn watched the bikini-clad teen glide underwater. Henry and Phillip burst into hilarious laughter as Nanette grabbed Charles's legs and upended him. Penn took a sip of her margarita and turned back to Deedee.

"Did ya hear what I was sayin'?" Deedee asked. "'Bout time for your cotillion. It's comin' on three years, sugar." Deedee held up three fingers, wiggling them for the wallflower to count.

Terrence sidestepped the friends' history. He simply charmed Penn with his easy manner. She must come see the gig he was having next weekend. Between sets, a DJ spun dancing music. Deedee always enjoyed herself immensely. Penn would too.

"I don't want to disappoint you, but I don't trust a sitter with my rambunctious boys." That sounded like a pretty good excuse.

Deedee scoffed. "If your boys could survive with George in charge, surely Nanette can rein them in for a few hours. Besides, she needs the spendin' money."

Penn agreed to join Deedee. She didn't know why.

And suddenly there she was at the club, trailing behind Deedee's wiggle of a walk. Her own severe ponytail contrasted with the glimmer of curls ahead. *If only she could have asked Grace to style her hair and makeup. But those days were over.* She wasn't going for glamorous, Lord knows. But did she look dowdy? Could everyone tell she was wearing the expensive push-up bra Deedee had foisted on her? Cat had hauled her into Nordstrom in an attempt to update her wardrobe. The new top was too tight, and her new pants were too baggy, no matter what Cat had said.

As long as she sat at the bar with her glass of wine, she'd be okay. Deedee was out there dancing. The music was good and loud. Too loud for conversation if anybody—like the fellow sitting beside her—tried to flirt.

But when a slow, quiet song began, that fellow, whose name was JJ, asked which wine she was drinking. He ordered another merlot for her and another Corona for himself.

"I've been muscled here by a bachelor pal," he stated. "Been divorced a while and this single scene feels awkward. I'm guessing you're in the same boat?"

"What makes you think that?" Penn retorted.

"Wearing your engagement ring on your right ring finger is kind of a giveaway." His tone was so matter-of-fact, his intelligent eyes so kind, Penn didn't take insult. Turned out JJ worked as a CPA, was a sports enthusiast, a swimming coach, *and* active in the PTA, with one son (just Charles's age). Penn volunteered some witty remarks about her job in the nutcase factory, about being a newly initiated sports enthusiast, mother of three swimmers, *and* active in the PTA. JJ chortled, appearing genuinely amused by her brand of humor. The music gained volume as a rock n' roll piece blasted.

"Dance?" JJ asked, sliding off the barstool and extending his hand to Penn.

Penn froze.

How she had gotten into that bathroom stall, she didn't remember. She sat with her panties down to her ankles, her bowel rudely eliminating its contents. She felt sick. Clammy. Her abdomen clenched. *She could hear the party raging on out there. People were taking drugs and dancing half naked like animals. She knew it. Why had Amelia dragged her here? Forced her to come. "We'll stay together." Well, that was a lie. Where was Amelia?* No, not Amelia. Who had dragged her here? *Who wanted to press his body into hers? She knew what was coming; he was getting wild.*

"I don't want to be here, I don't want to be here," she moaned, flushing the toilet so as to muffle the awful sounds coming from her body. She wound her arms around her middle, hunching in misery.

"Penn! Penelope? Are ya in here?"

"Deedee?" Penn croaked.

"Dang it, girl, what's up? That JJ fella is worried about ya. Cute, isn't he?"

"Tell him I'm sick. I'm sick. I have to go home now."

"Hey sugar, there's a big ol' comfy faintin' couch right out here. You just lay yourself on it and come on out when you get to feelin' better. Terrence an' the boys be startin' up soon. JJ is savin' your seat, and I'll be dancin' up front."

Thank goodness most gals just came into the *Ladies*, did their thing, and left quickly. Except the few who *just had to* ask, "Are you okay?" When Penn heard the live jazz begin, she got up, splashed her face with cold water, and leaned close to inspect the stranger in the mirror. *What had come over her? This wasn't that horrifying night on Capri.* Timidly she made her way into the dark club, where she leaned against the wall, hoping not to be noticed.

108. LILY

Lily slid a cameo on her wide gold necklace. She smoothed her sheath dress and slid into heels. She touched the pin fondly as she stared at her own peaceful face in the mirror. *No matter what trials she's been through, Grace has endured*, Lily thought. A June wedding. The summer will fly. July, August, and then another Fashion Week in Milan. Seeing the clock she hurried, not wanting to arrive late to this ceremony.

Grace had penned calligraphy on the envelopes for her wedding invitations, while Lily had designed and made Grace's wedding suit. Together they selected raw silk. Color? An amazing neutral, according to Lily, a color that evaded precise description but charted somewhere between oyster pearl, abalone cream, and muted lilac. The suit gently and surely enhanced Grace's minimal curves, affronting Cat—who, eager to upstage the bride in her expensive, tight, pink dress, felt compelled to compensate.

Glass in hand she plied her charms on each and every male in attendance. Several were photographers who had not taken her seriously as a stylist. Lily overheard Catherine San Carlo discussing "her" winery and her next project. Using her new skill, calligraphy, she would design the upcoming Chablis labels. Lily hoped this demanding job of Cat's provided the satisfaction portrayed so publicly.

When the words were spoken, "Ladies and gentlemen, I present Mr. and Mrs. Quinton Keller," Lily took hold of Cat's arm. Cat, not so newly divorced from Pietro, whispered through her tears, "That frigging Mr. Cavilieri went to Provence…with his ex."

109. DEEDEE

"Can you adjust the air conditioner a bit, Deedee? I was so hot when I came in, and now I'm getting a chill." Cat was curled up on Deedee's sofa. She'd kicked off her shoes and pulled a crocheted afghan over her legs. "Maybe a cup of tea?"

"Gimme just a sec, sweetie," Deedee called back from the kitchen. "I'm makin' Mama some tea, an' it's no trouble to get y'all some too." She wiped her hand across her damp forehead. What the heck was Cat talkin' about bein' cold? Had to be close to eighty degrees here in the kitchen. Cat and Mama seemed to be sharin' the same body temperature lately.

When Deedee got Mama settled with her evening medication and the TV remote handy, she closed Mama's door. Must be awful, goin' deaf, not bein' able to hear a thing. Mama had the TV so loud, it could blow up, and she would think it was part of the show. Minutes later Deedee, china cup in hand, stood in front of Cat, who snored softly on the sofa. *Girl's all worn out. That drivin' up and down the whole state tryin' to peddle wine must be plum exhaustin'.* She set the tea down on the side table, but the chink of cup scraping against saucer roused Cat.

"Oh, sorry, I must've dozed off. I've been doing that more lately. It's getting hard to stay awake in the car, especially on that Golden State Freeway. And I'm driving it every week. There's no interesting scenery, just blah."

"Seems like this job is gettin' to be too much for you. It's sappin' your starch. Maybe y'all should find somethin' that's close to home."

"What? And not work with Sebastian? Never." Cat was taken aback at Deedee's suggestion. "We have a five-year plan. And a winery of our own in the future."

"So how's that all workin' out with that guy? I thought you said he was diddlin' his ex-wife now and again," Deedee said with distaste.

"Oh, he hasn't seen her *that way* for weeks now. They have children together, so it's impossible not to come in contact with each other. Did you adjust the AC? Feels too cool."

Mama's bedroom door flew open and hit the wall. Mama toddled out on her walker, looking for someone to murder. Spying Cat, she sped up to one mile per hour, huffing till she arrived at the sofa.

"You the one usin' my blanket, huh?" Mama snatched the afghan from the legs of a startled Cat. "What're y'all doin' here again? Ever' time I turn around, y'all're sittin' on my sofa, with my favorite blanket. An' I'm real cold!"

Deedee jumped up, embarrassed. "Mama, watch yourself. Cat is our guest. Y'all don't talk to company like that. Let me help you back to your room and getcha settled again."

"Not movin' in, I hope. There's enough of us in this house already," Mama threw over her shoulder as Deedee escorted her back to the safety of her bedroom.

Deedee returned. "I don't know what gets into Mama. Never know what'll set her off next." She gave Cat an apologetic smile, then noticed Cat's quivering chin.

"Your mother makes me feel like excess baggage."

"Ah, sugar, don't take any notice of Mama. Y'all know you're welcome. But honey, I gotta turn the AC back on, I'm gonna cook. I'll fetch another blanket."

■   ■   ■

"But Mom, you promised I could have a sleepover. It's Saturday. Why is Auntie Cat here again? She's coming all the time now. And she's no fun anymore."

"Nanette, keep your voice down and y'all just cut out that whinin'. I can't just turn your Auntie Cat out. We're practically her only family these days." Deedee and Nanette were huddled in the bathroom. Cat had taken up her proprietary spot on the sofa and was relaxing with a soothing cup of tea.

This is the third weekend in a row I've had to go back on my word to let Nanette have her friends over for the night. Well, heck, just a minute now, Cat has shown up unexpected again. She was supposed to be in Napa this weekend. Poor Nanette has done all her chores as pledged.

"Know what? We're gonna have that sleepover anyway. I'll order the pizzas, then take Auntie Cat out to the movies. She'll have to sleep on the couch this weekend, if she's plannin' on stayin', an' y'all can have your room back."

Nanette squealed delightedly.

"Hush up, girl! Y'all're gonna have to keep an ear open for Mama, though. We'll probably get back around ten thirty or so. I expect the house to be spotless. No girlie messes layin' around, an' all y'all will be cozied up in your bedroom by then. Terrence'll be home at midnight, an' I don't want any screechin' or shriekin' goin' on. Got it?"

"Oh, thank you, thank you, thank you, Mom. You're the best mother in the world. I swear there won't be a mess, and I'll look after Gran, and we won't make any noise after you get home." Nanette rushed to telephone her friends. *How nice to see her happy an' excited*, Deedee thought. *I can hardly blame her for feelin' pushed out of shape at havin' to give up her plans again. Cat has practically taken up squatter's rights here, but what can I do? She needs a friend an' a little special attention. I think that boyfriend of hers is just usin' her when his ex-wife isn't available.*

▪　　▪　　▪

A few days later, Deedee was on her porch watering a hanging basket of colorful petunias when a familiar car pulled into the driveway.

"Terrence, sugar, throw on another pork chop. Cat just drove up an' she'll be hungry," Deedee called out toward the backyard where Terrence stood at the BBQ, poised to lay meat onto the grill. He shook his head and set the plate of chops down.

"Well, Miz Cat. How're y'all doin'? I thought you weren't due back in town till next Monday. Y'all look totally tuckered. Come on in an' sit down. I'll getcha some sweet tea, I just brewed it up." She met Terrence in the kitchen scrounging up more food to fill an extra plate. "Cat does love your cookin', darlin'."

"Deedee, I'm not the kind of man to complain, but this is my night off. I thought at least tonight we'd have some time to ourselves. We haven't been alone—well, we're never all alone—for weeks. Doesn't Cat understand that she's kind of pushing the envelope here?"

"Oh, T. I'm in such a pickle. An' I am sorrier than I can even say. I don't know what to do 'bout this situation. Cat's tired out an' never feelin' good. An' she doesn't much of any place to be. She's lonely."

"What about that nice condo she bought and fixed up when she left Pietro? That's where she should be. Not hunkered down on our sofa whenever she's in town." Terrence put his hands on Deedee's shoulders. "Did you work today?" At Deedee's nod he continued, "Blondie, you are on your feet for hours each day. Coming home to wait on Cat and your mama, and be a mother to a needy teenager is too hard on you. Physically and emotionally. Not to mention how much I miss our playtime."

Deedee felt the truth of his words. Big tears welled, and one slid down her cheek. "I'm simply worn out, T. But Cat doesn't have any family. I can't turn my back on her."

"I'm not asking you to do anything drastic. Maybe you should give your friends a call. Couldn't they help out here? I'm only saying this to protect you and your health," Terrence said kindly. "*And us,*" Terrence added sternly.

110. GRACE

"Thanks Deedee, see you there. I'll give the others a quick call now." Grace hung up the phone and stared at the new information she'd just written into her pink paisley address book. Data that had been burned into her brain and easily recalled whenever needed, was now unknown. She'd had to call Deedee to get Amelia's telephone number and address.

Luckily everyone else had been able to stay in her own home; Cat had moved of her own volition. Marc insisted Jemima feel the security of her own room. George didn't like it, but the judge ruled in favor of Penn and the boys maintaining their abode. And thankfully Lily's attorney had been tenacious about the beach house. *What are you doing, Grace? You need to get to the job at hand. You told Lily you'd take care of the calls, and now you're just dawdling.*

Grace dialed the number and listened to the ring. Little ripples of anxiety, ginger ale bubbles, popped in her stomach. How would Amelia receive the news? Deedee had refused to believe it, certain that "Cat was simply needin' a rest, some time to get her stuffin' back. Lily must be mistaken." But Lily was not.

Grace thought her apprehension about calling the girls was ridiculous. It wasn't as if they weren't speaking. Or was it? They'd all attended her small wedding, but which of them had even called her since? To be fair, there'd been no effort on her part either.

"Hello?" Amelia answered on the eighth ring, startling Grace so that she had to scramble to remember who she'd called. "Oh, Amelia, it's me. It's Grace. Have you got a minute?"

"Penn and I are heading out the door. Sale at JCPenney. What's up?" Amelia's tone was not *unfriendly*, but there were no amenities observed. No query as to how Grace might have been over the last bunch of months. And that was A-OK. She'd take care of business and let Amelia pass the word along to Penn.

"It's Cat. She's taken a bad turn. Lily and I thought we could all help out. We're going to meet at Cat's tomorrow evening to divvy up some chores. Can you and Penn be there?"

"Grace, dear, are you sure you and Lily aren't misinterpreting Cat's customary drama?" was Amelia's common-sense approach to the problem. "I've talked to Cat recently."

Grace clenched her jaw, then took a calming breath. Amelia wasn't being unreasonable. They'd all been subjected to what they'd believed to be Cat's hypochondria. Grace and Penn had snickered a bit between themselves about how Cat could malinger when the seasons changed. Cat had her autumnal flu, or her winter complaint, or it might be her spring syndrome. What Amelia didn't yet know was that as it turned out, Cat *was* sick. Had been sick. Seriously sick. And none of them realized it.

"Not this time. Cat's leave of absence expired, and she's been sacked at the winery. So much for Sebastian and their 'five-year plan.'"

111. PENN

As much as George used to berate her habit of "lists, lists, and more lists," this talent for organizing had its place. Master plan in hand, Penn passed assignment charts to Amelia, Lily, and Grace.

"Excuse me, but is Deedee making a show anytime soon?" Penn asked.

Cat, watching Penn unite her friends, perked up. "Promised she's gonna help me too," Cat wheezed in Deedee's defense.

"Cat, shouldn't you be using your oxygen?" Lily asked gently.

As Cat complied, Lily returned to washing and trimming the farmers' market produce. Grace sorted a basketful of laundry. Amelia popped meatloaf in the oven then set to washing dishes. Penn tacked a colorful Chore Wheel on Cat's bulletin board, pushing the existing cards and memos off to one side in a triple-layered cluster.

Deedee appeared, nimbus lit, fuchsia leather bag slung over a shoulder, a carrier of coffees thrust forward in her hands. "Thinkin' we might like an energy boost, workin' so hard for Miz Cat an' all. Flavored lattes all 'round!"

The three workers gladly left their efforts and savored the offering. "Mmm, caramel," Grace noted. Lily dried her hands and rested on a kitchen stool.

"Taste good to you, Cat?" she asked. Cat nodded happily, taking tiny sips of the hot sweet liquid. Amelia sat on the couch beside Cat to share the moment of relaxation.

Brickle, Cat's Persian, wound around Deedee with affectionate persistence. She stooped to pet the golden creature. "Think I got me a new best friend, this here Butter Brickle. Don't ya know? Mama would love on him somethin' fierce."

Cat's eyes glittered. "Don't go getting any ideas."

"Yes, but—"

"Back off! It's not like I can't take care of my own cat!"

"Do you mind? Come take a look over here." Penn might as well have blown a whistle. Four startled friends, lattes in hand, gathered obediently while Cat watched from the couch. Not one protest was raised as Penn outlined the division of labor. It seemed comprehensive, and split five ways as it was, not terribly burdensome.

When the workers set to new tasks, Cat tried Penn's approach. "Do you mind? Come sit with me. You're all so busy, I'm just alone here. I don't like being sick like this and needing all this help."

Grace consoled her. "Cat, you'll see, it won't be long."

"Dr. Hounka's going to call any day now," Lily joined in. "And once you've got your new heart—"

"We'll all go back to Capri. I wish we could go right now."

Penn nudged Amelia, her eyes suddenly wild. "Never again," she whispered, her heart pounding wildly. Pounding just like that nightmarish time: *Eerie fog. She's running terrified. Running, tripping on cobblestone, she's reeling backward as a high heel snaps off.* Penn, eyes closed, held on to Amelia.

"Breathe, try to calm yourself, sweetie," Amelia whispered.

Cat, eyes closed, took deep breaths. "I was never more alive than on Capri. Lily, wasn't I fabulous?"

112. LILY

Lily let herself in, after knocking quietly, only to be greeted by fumes. Brickle wound between her legs, mewing as if he were imparting serious news. Lily scratched the scrawny cat's forehead.

"I know, I know." She scooped the litter box mess into a bag and took it out to the garbage.

She had arrived early in hopes that Cat would be ready. These four o'clock coffee dates disrupted her schedule, all the more so when Cat overslept. Like today.

Thoughts of work grabbed her mind. The trouser patterns had been taking a back seat to the doctor's appointments, mini emergencies, and coffee outings. The trouser deadline, however, would not be extended. She promised herself some late nights to catch up. *Oh dear, had she invoiced the tweed blazer pattern?* Lily forced her mind back to Cat's needs.

In the kitchen, several bananas and apples, permanent residents of the fruit bowl this week, attracted flies. Lily checked the refrigerator. Amelia's casserole looked untouched; the coleslaw floated in its dressing, uncovered. A week's worth of aluminum-wrapped entrees shone expectantly when Lily opened the freezer. Obviously the farmers' market shopping and home cooking failed to engage Cat's lackluster appetite. Concerned, Lily inspected the trash. The evidence brought a twinge of anxiety; who the heck was Cat soliciting for Twinkies and Ding Dongs?

Lily headed for Cat's bedroom and the sounds of troubled breathing. Cat dozed, cheeks sunken, her lips tinged blue and her oxygen not in use. How tiny she looked in her jeans, now several sizes too large. Cat stirred as Lily picked up scattered clothing.

"Finally," Cat whispered, her enormous eyes tearing. "You have no idea."

Lily despaired. "I'm taking you home with me, the whole kit and caboodle here." Before her words were uttered, she felt a head rush. Pure dread.

■　　■　　■

Had Cat been ensconced in her bedroom for weeks? Or months? she wondered as she watched the ambulance depart, sirens and rotating lights in emergency mode. The nightmare of Cat's decline left her weak-kneed, unfocused. Was Callie at Grace's or the Suttons this week? Or was Callie at home now? Lily turned toward the bedroom, expecting to see an answer. No, no, Callie was with the neighbors. Her mom instincts had seen to that. The trial of Cat's illness was mercilessly stealing the patient's civility while it gouged Lily's own healthy heart. Nothing for a child to witness.

Jittery, Lily dialed the phone, knowing she'd wake Grace. Grace first. Then plunging ahead, she woke Penn and Amelia with the news: Cat's "episode," the panic, the aspirin, the call to 911. Deedee was at Terrence's gig, according to an annoyed Mama. Lily left an abbreviated message.

"We're meeting at the hospital, it looks serious." She phoned the Suttons, still lively, playing poker; yes, Callie was welcome to stay as long as needed.

Now, where were her keys? Fog thickened her brain. Fear twisted her gut. *This couldn't be happening!*

113. CAT

Tucked in like a baby. Warmed cotton blanket up to her chin. Her fingers at the edge. Look how still she could lie. Cat practiced lying as still as a stone with her eyes closed. As still as a stone. The IV pinched. The oxygen thing hurt her nose. *What was all that machine noise? How could she lie still and think?* Nurse Boyett fiddled with the machines. Nurse Boyett fed her ice chips from a spoon. Very slowly. Nurse smoothed her tickly hair off her face. A soft hand. A hand like a flower. And she the stone. She still, like water. She the flower. Like the poem. *Lily reads it to me. Again. I want it again. About the flower, in a jar of water…how it steadies itself, by remembering itself. Another time. Time. I want time.* "Tell Lily—"

A coughing fit interrupted Cat's whisper. The whooping-like cough overtook her frail body; her chest caved and arched in obedience. Exhaustion forced her deep into the pillow.

"To bring the poems," Cat whispered. But Nurse Boyett had snuck out.

She must have dozed off. Dreams seem so real. Her dreams seemed so real. Leo, a baby again. Tuck him in. Warm blankets. His warm cheek against her hand. His damp curls. All real. Just like the visitors. Talking. Asking questions. Seemed so real. Why would she want a priest?

"No." She wasn't Catholic. And the blue-eyed doctor. He had nice eyes. Like Quinton's. He was older, though. Crinkly lines around his kind eyes. What had he said? About passing? "Serious." Did she know it was serious? Like school. Getting it right. Getting a good grade. Was she ready to pass? She hadn't studied. Was she bad? *Am I good enough? Who knows I'm stuck here with this test? Where is Lily? I want Grace. Amelia? Penn knows. Penn is smart. What was the crinkly doctor saying? If I lie as still, as still, as still. It will pass. Please God.*

114. AMELIA

Amelia organized the magazines. Five tables, twenty-five messy magazines. She assigned one type per table. Each got a sports magazine, a *National Geographic*, a *Good Housekeeping*, a *Readers' Digest,* and a *Cosmopolitan*. Wasn't *Cosmo* a little racy for a hospital? She watched Penn picking at her cuticles, face pinched. *None of us look any better*, Amelia thought. Deedee sat sniffling into Amelia's hanky; Lily was beyond pale, with dark circles under her eyes; and Grace? Head resting on Lily's shoulder, chewing on her lip. Frightened.

"This is it. We're here to say good-bye." Amelia was surprised by the sound of her voice. She hadn't meant to speak aloud.

"Hush, Amelia! Don't say it," Deedee choked out, still denying that the worst could be true. "We know she's gonna pull through. She's too young."

"Deedee, the doctor told me there's nothing more that can be done for Cat," Lily said, her emotions raw. "Amelia's right. When the nurse calls us in to see her, we've got to be strong and show her we care."

Grace stood, stretched her long back. "Who's for coffee? I'll go—" She stopped short as she spotted the CCU nurse at the double-door entrance, motioning to the friends.

Everyone gathered round, huddled close to Nurse Boyett. "You may visit Catherine. I must caution you to keep calm. No hysterics. It's hard for her now. Normally we'd only allow two at a time, but I understand you're all family. And"—the nurse dropped her voice—"having you close can't hurt."

Amelia felt her body sag in distress. She told herself to buck up for Cat. How easy it was now to see that Cat had always needed the girls, but until she became so ill, each of them had withheld a little. Cat's expectations were unrealistic. She required a lot from her friends. If you weren't careful, she could suck you dry. You'd end up feeling used and manipulated and aggravated at yourself. It all seemed petty.

Amelia put her arm around Penn, who stared at her bloody cuticle. They followed Lily, Grace, and Deedee into Cat's cubicle. The medical equipment beeped and clicked, the noise of it pounding in Amelia's ears.

Cat opened her eyes, blinked, and reached out for Lily's hand before closing them again. A moment later she struggled to speak. "Villa Jovis. The spirits. I'm going there to be with them."

It was shocking to hear Cat voice her fate. *She seems at peace, without fear*, Amelia thought as she looked around at her friends, their heads nodding in empathy. But more shocking was the glaze that covered Cat's eyes. As if she were already dead.

"You all have to be there, together. To celebrate my life." Cat gasped for more air.

"Of course we will," Lily assured Cat. The others nodded agreement.

Penn pulled Amelia aside. "We *all* have to go *back* to Capri?" Her voice shook. Amelia wasn't crazy about the idea either, but could Penn's fragility stand a return trip?

Cat continued to struggle, her voice dropped to a whisper. Lily bent close to better hear the labored words. Cat coughed, and continued, and when finished, she panted for air.

"Okay, she wants us to cooperate. To write the story of our time on Capri and how we almost let our friendship go." Lily relayed the information, looking into each of her friends' eyes, stressing the importance of the request.

Cat took a breath, tugged at Lily's hand. Lily leaned close to listen.

"She said, 'Remember, it was *me* who brought us back together. I was unwilling to throw our history away,'" Lily repeated.

Cat wasn't quite done. "Promise me, each of you. Now," she croaked out.

"Promise," each member of the group pledged. Cat slipped into a doze.

Once back in the waiting room, Penn slumped into the closest chair. She put her head between her knees. Amelia kneeled beside her and rubbed her back.

"Take some deep breaths, dear. Slow and deep. That's it." Amelia knew the core of Penn's fear. As bereaved as she might be, it wasn't due to Cat's impending passing.

115. PENN

The wait seemed intolerable to Penn. Lily had said perhaps they should stay a bit longer, just in case. Just in case they could assure Cat once more that they would all return to Capri. No one spoke up with another bright idea. And so they were waiting. *Must they return?*

There sat Lily now, in the opposite row of chairs, her eyes closed. Suddenly she was speaking. "Listen. Our circle of friendship is all Cat has. You realize we have to keep our promise."

Grace chimed in. "So we write the dramedy of our muddled vacation, read it aloud under the statue, then dance upon the ruins with the departed?"

Penn held her breath, hoping someone would dissent.

But Grace continued like a traitor, "I can do that."

Lily gave Grace one of those goo-goo-eyed looks of hers.

"Ah, come on! Is there no end? Now we've gotta be writers?" Deedee expressed what Penn wanted to scream out.

Grace, in such a tiny voice, said she'd get coffees downstairs and headed out. Deedee, her arms crossed over her chest, rocked and rocked. Amelia blew her nose for the third, fourth, and fifth time. Why was Amelia so loud blowing her nose?

Penn's head throbbed. If only she could pray, if only, if only. Penn crumpled, her forehead on her knees. All the while she shuddered, violently, as if receiving a series of electric shocks. Her heart pounded. Pounding just like that nightmarish time: *Eerie fog. Dark shops passing in a blur. Where is she? Her bare feet slapping the cobblestone. Her new heels ruined. Is her dress bloody? Blood there on the skirt. Everyone will know. What she has done? What has she done?*

Startled, Penn gasped and jerked as Grace patted her shoulder again. *Oh, it was Grace handing her a coffee.* As Penn took calming breaths, the shuddering slowed. She reached out a shaking hand and accepted the coffee gratefully.

"Thank you." Penn could think of nothing else to say. She looked around to see the others in downcast concentration.

The group continued their silent vigil until suddenly Nurse Boyett glided thorough the double doors. She seemed at once an angel of mercy and an executioner. Penn's trepidation filled her head with cotton. But she stood with the others in a team-like huddle as the nurse approached.

"Cat has passed. Would any of you like a parting visit? I can let you have a moment now."

No! NO! Pleasssse… Penn slipped to the floor in a lifeless faint.

116. LILY

"You know what Aunt Maude used to say: 'Things work out,'" Lily told herself, trying to find conviction for this platitude. As evidence, Callie wore no visible scars from the ordeal they had just weathered. Further, Deedee adopted Butter Brickle; Pietro and sons attended the funeral, displaying the utmost reverence; Amelia deftly handled the flowers; and Grace hosted the potluck with, well, grace.

On the other hand, the five estranged friends had not truly reconnected as Cat believed. Sure, they made a show of cooperating. But, like a fine seam, with no backstitching, they had already pulled apart.

"Just how will we keep our promise to Cat?" Lily asked Grace. "Penn's become a neurotic—the mere mention of Capri, well, you've seen. With Amelia protecting her, there's no getting through. Deedee applied the brakes straightaway. Besides that, they'll all cry poor. Which, might sadly, be the truth."

"Simple, dearie," Grace answered quickly. "We're going to have to spearhead it. You and me. And make ourselves really popular, again."

■　　■　　■

Perhaps the Antonio Caldo mannequins dressed in brandywine vests had whispered. Or maybe the leather itself had sighed. Because the words *Villa Bianco* hovered in Lily's workroom unbidden. In response Lily seized upon an idea. Several attempts to reach Angelo Bianco failed. But one Sunday afternoon after dialing, Lily found herself responding to Angelo's, "Pronto!"

Their conversation had the air of fantasy and left Lily giddy. Villa Bianco was booked through December. After that Angelo would no longer be renting the property. Instead, he would set up his own household there. No, wait. Lily listened to the transcontinental static while Angelo checked his book. When his voice resumed, Lily's heart sped up. He'd found a vacancy in the fourth week of August due to a recent cancellation. And then, with condolences for their loss of Cat, Angelo offered the group a week's stay, gratis. How could Lily refuse?

Before calling Grace, her touchstone of reality, Lily walked across the dunes toward the Suttons. Seagulls mewed above her, wings spread against the updraft. Beyond the surf line, Callie and Jimmy sat astride their boards with no great waves on the horizon. The tide had left opal scallops of foam on the wet sand. Lily walked there, enjoying the sensation as her feet sank and left momentary prints. Was it only three years ago that the six of them had gathered on this beach making such optimistic plans?

117. AMELIA

"Andy! Don! Stop spinning the roundabout. You're going too fast—Kenny is turning green!" Amelia did not want to clean up puke. Not today, not any day. The twin devils she'd spawned were taking the opportunity to heckle their older brother. Again. No doubt they'd calculated that with enough other kids in the park, their mom wouldn't notice. But Amelia did.

"Oh crap!" she screamed as Ken III lost his lunch. "You two go directly to the washroom and get a bunch of wet paper towels and hurry. Are you pleased with yourselves?" The brats snickered and moseyed on over to the washroom without a thought of speed.

"Kenny, we'll get you cleaned up, don't worry about a little PB&J on your shirt. You're going to be fine and so will your clothes," Amelia assured her middle child, who'd been humiliated by the little monsters. "I'll impose a stiff consequence for each of them."

Amelia was embarrassed by the boys' naughty behavior. But Penn's children were no better—her three boys were murdering one another on the monkey bars while Penn tuned in to her own misery. Perched in a kiddy swing, she half swung, half pushed herself with her feet. Amelia took the swing next to Penn with the intent of arguing Penn into doing what Cat had asked.

"Penn. We *will* do this."

"Uh-uh! Not me. You go. I'll even watch your kids. But I won't go." Penn began pumping in earnest, swinging higher, tucking her legs close under her.

"Penelope, you promised Cat. We have an obligation."

"Amelia, I doubt Cat even heard me promise. Deathbed promises don't have to be kept."

"I guarantee she heard you. She heard us all. It was our promise that allowed her to pass on. She was waiting for us to give our word. And *all* promises must be kept." Amelia began to swing, keeping time with Penn. "Besides, Lily has made the arrangements."

"And that's another thing. Who appointed Lily in charge? Where'd she come up with the date? She made a decision and told us what to do. Maybe August isn't a good time for me." Penn continued to be disagreeable.

"Lily didn't unilaterally come up with the date. That week in August is the only time the Villa is available. Lily clearly explained it." *Just how exasperating could Penn get*, Amelia wondered.

"But it's almost August, and of course Miss Perky Grace takes it all in stride. Her little act at the hospital about 'returning to Capri to write the dramedy of friendship'…no sweat, she can do that! Of course she can. She isn't the one who…" Penn's voice, initially strident, became shaky.

"Penn, sweetie, I promise if you go, we will never talk about it."

"I'm afraid. Grace is married to Quinton."

CAPRI

AUGUST

1982

KEEPING A PROMISE

118. LILY

Two convertible taxis traveled up the winding road, with the ocean slipping farther and farther below. In one, Lily, Penn, Amelia, and Deedee shared silence. In the other, Grace and Quinton talked animatedly.

Arriving at Villa Bianco, Lily's eyes welled with unbidden tears. She stood apart from the others, unspeaking, as the luggage and camera equipment were unloaded. Airport tags from Los Angeles, Zurich, and Rome fluttered in the afternoon breeze; the scent of lemon floated. *What is this emotional response?* she asked herself.

Their advancing shadows merged with the motionless geometry of the iron gates. Lily watched the fleeting patterns on the tile walkway. The entourage followed Lily through the formal rows of hydrangeas. Then, choosing a diverting path, she led the silent women and Quinton to the marble benches. She stopped at the Pan fountain, as did they.

It was Quinton who broke the silence. "Ladies, I promise to stay out of your way. Get that saga written." He kissed Grace meaningfully, Lily noted. No doubt he was hoping that the writing wouldn't eat up all of Grace's time while here. Mario met the group and offered greetings. He pointed them back to the main walkway and began to gather their luggage.

Across the gardens, Angelo came into view. He waved as he approached from the arbor, his whistling traveling to them faster than he.

Lily, leaving her luggage and her friends, headed toward Angelo. Her heart beat quickly as they neared each other. Lily held her hands out; Angelo clasped them.

When he greeted her, this time in person, his voice had the rich timbre she remembered. "Once again, you are a guest at Villa Bianco, and I am the handyman. It must be August."

They wandered side by side as Angelo showed off the grape arbor ready for harvest and the fruit trees heavy with fruit.

Later, a silly smile on her face, Lily ascended the Villa's rounded stairway approaching the shaded terrace. She turned around and lingered for a moment, reluctant to dismiss the panoramic view. Cypress, palmetto, and lemon trees punctuated the horizon to the east, and to the west, beyond the vine-covered arbor, the earth dropped away to meet the Blue Curacao-infused sea.

Once inside, she climbed the arc of stairway slowly. "Mario brought your luggage up," Grace called down to her. Lily stopped on the landing, rested against the massive banister, and looked down across the salon. She was struck by the brilliance of the library's tall glass doors as they ensnared the orange sky.

■　　■　　■

Penn spit it out. "Forgive me. But for all I know, Cat never asked us to do anything of the kind. You just made it up because, because—"

"Because you think you're some kind of writing whiz." Amelia finished Penn's accusation, looking both nervous and proud. "And you think this will be a best seller if you can force us to give you some dirt. Of which you and Grace have obviously concocted plenty."

Lily turned away and closed their door. She could not stand the sight of them one second longer. Her heart squeezed into a fiery lump and then froze. What had she done but inquire as to their comfort with the accommodations here at Villa Bianco? Suggest they begin on Cat's request tomorrow after a leisurely brunch and perhaps a stroll. Tears stung her eyes. She hurried past the blue-tiled bathroom and into the bedroom she and Grace had shared. She threw herself face down on the bed. And wept. Wept for herself. And for Cat, whose presence she felt like a shadow at your back when the sun is low.

119. LILY

Angelo would disapprove, if he knew. She, a guest of his, heading out alone despite serious cautions against this very action. But she had tiptoed out anyway, leaving behind a sleeping household. Lily imagined Quinton and Grace would rise early to enjoy caffé on the Villa Bianco terrace. The others, jet lagged of course, might sleep all morning out of spite. It seemed as if Penn and Amelia's attack cast her in the role of an evil stepmother. And Grace the wicked witch.

Lily turned around, looking up the hill. Fear tugged her back as fiercely as intention drew her forward. If wind accompanied the changing tide, she'd be trapped in the grotto. Trapped, with no escape for hours, or days. But Lily discounted the possibility as she descended the ancient stairway. Morning bathed the twisted pines with stickiness and smothered the twittering of birds. The scent of juniper teased. She hurried, although straggly shrubs reached out to scratch. Her caftan billowed, delineating her torso and legs—one might imagine she could fly at any moment and join the gulls. She passed multi-limbed cacti, as tall as dancing partners. Turning neither right nor left, she merged with the hillside's burst of green.

At the lowest viewpoint, Lily turned around once more. But her proximity to the water accentuated the slap of waves and reawakened the urgency of her mission. *I've got to pull myself out of this funk.* She removed the broad-brimmed hat, pulled the embroidered linen over her head, and wrestled off boots. Scrutinizing the terrain, she was satisfied—no hikers in view. Her possessions would be safely out of sight, anchored between two boulders. Now, as if trying to recall a conversation, she took one last look at a creased square of paper. A Polaroid image.

Funny how this photo hustled her backward. Past the days when Divorce wrapped itself around their still-girlish waists and whirled them away, one by one, into strange rhythms of single parenthood. Back to those days when their children played together, glistened with Coppertone, and grinned with missing teeth. She ran a finger across the six eager faces—her own, and those of her friends, as they share that pivotal beach day. Three sit in sunshine, three sit in shadow; each smiles broadly with unmistakable triumph. The horizon angles down to the right, and Penn seems to be sliding off the edge. The photo was taken by a child. Her Callie.

Lily tucked the photo away with a sigh. Eastern cliffs blocked the early sun as shadow united her body with the adjacent Roman ruins. She faced the sea. And dove.

The shock of cold, the stifled breath. "Holy bells!" Sting on her index finger as salt water found a wound—this morning's mishap with a pearl-handled grapefruit knife. The grotto beckoned, disguised as a triangle of darkness carved into the cliffs at sea level. She swam for it, rising on the swells, paddling through the troughs, forgetting to keep her mouth closed, choking, spitting.

Lily was gasping by the time she finally grabbed the entrance chain. The slick of rust and slime coated her palms as she pulled herself hand over hand into the opening. Rocks grazed her thigh as the current washed her legs forward. Darkness blinded. Seconds passed as she dogpaddled for a handhold, although the Tyrrhenian salt water buoyed her with indifference, just as it would a feather, a timber, or a corpse.

The Blue Grotto commanded awe. Turquoise waters lit from beneath fluoresced while shadow obscured knowledge of dimension. Science explained the effect. But magic held reign. Several feet within the grotto, Lily was unable to see her hands, even held in front of her face. Working her way around the perimeter, she found an underwater ledge. Seated there, she immersed her arms, elbow deep. She stirred the electric blue; bubbles clung to her neon lit fingers.

And then she dove, challenging herself underwater. Going down, straight down, kicking and stroking to the source of the light. The grotto's floor was far below, she could not possibly reach it; the pressure built in her ears, her lungs burned. Still she propelled herself down. Almost out of breath, she gathered the light to herself like a bouquet of energy.

Accelerated thrashing of limbs, sugar-hot rush of adrenaline. She rose into the darkness and gasped, greedy for the heavy air. Cautiously she found the underwater ledge again, where she sat to catch her breath. Breathing heavily she collected her thoughts. She might have an hour of privacy left. If the sea remained calm, boats would arrive outside the grotto to begin the day's business. Before then, she should swim back to the stairs, dress, and catch a bus homeward. *I have time. I don't need to rush.*

Calming herself, Lily pushed away from the ledge, rolled onto her back, and floated, arms crossed over her chest. Buoyant in the salt water, her hair fanned, forming a turquoise corolla. Cool water dripped from the arched ceiling. Drops struck her face intermittently and ran down her cheeks like tears from sacrificed virgins. Lily did not brush them away. *I found it once, why can't I find it again?* she whispered. Silence answered. Breeze and tide stirred, water sloshed against the walls hypnotically, images fused with the glistening ripples. She allowed the memories to rush in. Memories of humiliation, forgiveness, and courage.

Lily felt water break over her chest and splash on her face. Her daydream broke. There in the near darkness, she was forced to paddle as aggressive waves pounded. Instinctively, she looked for the opening, for the way out. It was covered with waves. *Don't panic!*

■　　■　　■

Lily's caftan fluttered in the breeze; the scent of lemon floated as sunlight sifted through the weave of her hat. She watched the sparkles within shadow flicker on the tile path.

"You should have checked the tides. Scheduling a boat ride would have been smart. I would have gone too." And still Grace ranted on, just like a mother. Lily wished she hadn't divulged today's foolhardy behavior.

Lily walked a bit more quickly, stubborn about the correctness of her intention. It was true; her reappearance at Villa Bianco before lunchtime required the assistance of one attentive fisherman. It was true; she was shivering, exhausted, and battered by the time he pulled her into his rowboat, navigated the waves, and deposited her at the rock stairs.

Grace stopped at marble benches flanking the fountain. She circled around the familiar Pan, that mischief silenced in bronze. *Hush, hush,* the streaming water whispered in a hopscotch of bubbles.

Lulled by the sounds, Lily tried to explain again. "Their behavior feels like a slap in the face. Like disrespect to Cat. How can I write objectively while we're all still bearing grudges?"

"We were, sadly, witness to their *lapse*. And I'm being generous. That wolf whistle fast track wasn't exactly…wasn't remotely the straight and narrow we wives vowed to follow. They resent our knowing."

"I was trying to find forgiveness, the best way I know how. I thought if I could be the first to let it go…"

"What, they'd turn around and forgive *us*?"

"Something like that."

"So, have you? Forgiven?" Grace asked, curiosity twisting her face.

"I'm ashamed to say, no. I guess I need for them to make even the tiniest shift."

120. DEEDEE

"Lookee, y'all. Here we are again. It's like no time at all has passed. You two sleeping in the same room, the same beds even." Deedee was chipper as she snapped up the roll-down shades in Amelia and Penn's room. "Nothin's hardly changed here at Villa Bianco, did y'all notice?"

"Deedee, get out of here! What time is it? We only just got to sleep." Penn groaned.

"Now, that is not actually factual. Ya see, I peeped in your room at eight, nine, and ten. The two of you were sawin' Zs. It's ten thirty now, an' I'm ready to see Capri. An' you two are comin' with me, so get your lazy-dog bodies outta bed and let's get goin'," Deedee commanded. She plunked down at the edge of Penn's bed and folded her arms. "I'm waitin' an' I'm not gonna move till you do."

"Can you die from jet lag?" Penn asked as she stepped into slippers and pulled a robe on.

"Yeah sure, maybe when you're real old. An' that does not include us. So move it. Slap on some lipstick, you'll feel brand new. We'll get some lunch out."

"Come on, Penn. It'll be fun. We can catch some of the sights we missed on our last trip." An unlucky choice of words by Amelia; Penn's eyes squeezed shut, her mouth pinched with distress.

■   ■   ■

"Sorry to mention it, but how amazing that the bus drivers haven't improved," Penn commented. The ride to Anacapri was as harrowing as Penn recalled.

"Ah, shoot, Penn. Quit complainin' 'bout ever'thin'. We're gonna have a darn good time sightseein'." This from Deedee, who took the bus's swaying in stride. "An' frankly, I'm not feelin' up to sittin' around writin' some story when there's lots of other good stuff to do."

"I agree with Deedee, Penn. Let Grace and Lily get the job done, since they're so darned gung ho. Nothing we can add anyway."

"I told y'all they wouldn't even notice we'd slipped out. Bet they're shut up in the library workin' away. Probably still don't know we're gone." Deedee chuckled at their cleverness.

Once their feet felt the firm ground, the three wandered Via Monticello till they found a little café, where they ordered pasta and wine.

"After lunch, let's rent Vespas down at Marina Grande. We can scooter around the water an' look at the yachts," Deedee suggested. "The longer we're gone the better, far as I'm concerned." Deedee couldn't think of a single reason they should hurry back to the drudgery of writing.

Amelia nodded enthusiastically. Penn smiled wanly. A young waiter flirted. Deedee flirted back. Amelia laughed. Penn looked away.

Heading back to catch a bus down the mountain, Penn was drawn to San Michele, the white baroque church near the center of town. "I want to go in, now. It was on my list. I missed it before."

"Lordy, no churches, Penn, sugar. I had a bellyful of churches when I was a kid, an' I got no hankerin' to hang around another one." Deedee was adamant.

Penn was just as adamant. "I'm going in. You two can wait. I'll only be a moment." She tugged on the enormous wooden door. She struggled with the weight of it, managing only to open it enough to slip through before it closed tightly again.

Amelia and Deedee rested on a sun-dappled bench and basked in the tranquility of their surroundings. "What the heck is Penn up to, visitin' a church? An' a Catholic one at that? Isn't she some kind of protestor-type?"

"Sheesh, where's Grace when I need a translator?" Amelia rolled her eyes. "Deedee, do you mean Protestant?"

"Whatever. I know for sure she's not Catholic. Tell me, how's your little business goin', sweetie?"

"Kind of okay," Amelia said with pride. "Taking the time off to come here was tough, but my client seemed to be fine about starting her garden a week later. And even if I can't afford those expensive tennis shoes everyone's wearing, my kids haven't had to do without any of the important stuff."

"I just knew you'd make it work, sugar. All those years with Ken Jr., why, you were bound to pick up landscapin' tips—even if you weren't lookin' for 'em." Deedee had always had faith in Amelia's ability to succeed with her business venture.

"I meant to ask, how'd Terrence take the news you were coming back here?"

"Well, he wasn't too thrilled with me bein' gone, but he said it was important to give Cat a swell send-off since we'd been friends for a full third of our lives. Mama was another matter. There was no reasonin' with her. She whined and complained somethin' fierce, but Terrence and Nanette promised to take good care of her—told her they'd let her have sweet tea, like I never do, 'cause we gotta watch her sugar diabetes. She calmed down, told me to bring her somethin' from the Vatican. I told her sure, sure, Mama, I'll do that."

"Deedee, we aren't going remotely near the Vatican. How are you going to accomplish that?" Amelia asked, perplexed.

"Ah, Mama doesn't know that. I can pick up any little touristy thing, an' she'll believe it came from there." Heck, didn't take a brain surgeon to figure out how to trick Mama.

"Penn's been in there awhile. I think I'll go check on her."

"She's about as skitterish as a mare on ice. Hope she can settle herself down, or she's not gonna get any kind of enjoyment out of this trip."

Amelia tugged at the church door. The thing was astonishingly heavy. Using all her strength, she pulled it open. Penn fairly staggered out, wild-eyed.

"I couldn't get the door open. I've been pushing and pushing on it. There was no one to help me." She fell into Amelia's arms and began to sob.

Before the door slammed shut, Deedee caught a glimpse of an extraordinary Garden of Eden scene on the tile floor. *Hmm, this might be one church she'd actually like to go into.* But not now. There was a Vespa with her name on it waiting at Marina Grande.

121. PENN

Amelia and Deedee granted Penn's request to be alone, as flimsy as her excuse was. Let them race off to Marina Grande if they wanted adventure. She didn't. *How pleasant to sit and do nothing*, she thought. Sunshine heated her breasts right though her freshly ironed shirt, and yet the tile bench felt cool to her thighs. Feeling hot and cold in the same instant, a paradox. Paradoxical too, this being apart from her friends and liking it, all the while feeling alienated. Working for shrinks had twisted her brain like a dish towel, she reasoned.

Anyway, her excuse was the truth; Vespa riding didn't rank on her to-do list. But the word *truth* caught in her chest. *Seek ye first the Truth and all these things will be granted to you. Was that how the scripture went?*

Somehow friendship had become a heavy cross to bear; she felt the weightiness of expectations and disappointments. Ever since she'd laid eyes on Capri, she'd been gaining and losing ground with her friends. Round and round the wheel went while she struggled, even sliding backward, like Phillip's hamster on his wheel. She scoffed at the comparison and looked around self-consciously. Sometimes Amelia seemed snappy with her for no good reason. Deedee hardly paid her attention. And yet life would be unbearable without her friends. The precious few she had left.

She fought away memories of Grace. Was it so long ago they could chat for hours in the evening? She ironing, boys in bed. Both of them, lonely wives waiting for husbands to come home. Shopping with Lily overtook her mind. How Lily found bargains, pulled together outfits, and accessorized them for her. Snip, snap, so effortless. Penn realized she had taken Lily's help for granted. Cat's gourmet offerings too. Maybe that's how friendship was supposed to be, simple. Penn sighed. What was once simple had become complex and troubling.

Penn turned her mind away from smiling images of Cat and Grace and Lily. Now the images that affronted her in the church bothered her once again. At first she'd been astonished by the majolica floor depicting a garden with strange creatures. Then Adam and Eve shown in shame ruined any enjoyment. "The Expulsion of Adam and Eve from the Garden from Eden," the little sign read. She had intended to pray. Who could pray with that in sight?

She'd intended to pray for answers. She'd come this far in honoring her promise to Cat. Now she was stuck. *What can I tell Lily and Grace, God? Answer me that. Not the Truth! The truth, the whole truth, and nothing but the truth. Is that how it would go in court?*

122. GRACE

Grace and Lily were comfy on the soft, cushioned recliners on the terrace. Taking a break from their writing, Grace had been glad when Deedee wandered out. She and Lily had been struggling to craft Cat's chronicles. Now was a perfect time to quiz Deedee on some details for their task. The task that seemed to have fallen exclusively upon them.

"Join us, Deedee. We thought we could huddle and make a plan for the story, but you three disappeared on us." Grace again felt the prick of betrayal she'd suffered that morning upon discovering the others had jumped ship.

Deedee tipped her head to the side. "Can you just remind me again why, out of all the years we've known each other, y'all picked this week to record?"

"It wasn't our choice. It's what Cat requested. You can't have forgotten what she said." Grace was disbelieving. She looked to Lily for backup.

"Cat was specific about the window of time," Lily agreed. "Her experience on Capri was the very best in her too-short life."

Grace smiled to herself at Lily's unintentional use of guilt. Whatever it took, Grace was fine with it. But she sobered instantly. It was true, Cat's life had been all too short.

"I just don't know why Cat wanted to air the dirty laundry. Don't you gals get that it's been scrubbed and folded? None of us mind y'all writin' a story about our friendship, but let's use an itty-bitty lick of common sense," Deedee cautioned. "An' I'm pretty sure Penn and Amelia aren't thrilled havin' to recount this particular time."

"Chicken hearts," Grace said. "Why should they be so resistant? The dynamic of the previous trip could *never* be repeated."

"Never! For heaven's sake, we'd been let loose like starved mice in a kitchen," Lily said. "It was important to Cat that we not forget that critical time in our friendship."

"Critical? If I had an ugly stick, I'd use it on you two." Deedee's frown formed lines between her eyebrows. "Truth is, I'm embarrassed. I don't wanna wreck what I got with Terrence. He's gooder than gold with Mama, and takes Nanette and her teenage junk seriously. Not to mention what we got once the lights go out, if you get my drift. If he got ahold of this story and learned about me and my flyboy…he'd think I had grits for brains."

"I think you need to have more faith in Terrence," Lily said. "He knew you liked to party when you met. And he still fell in love with his 'lady in red.'"

"True, Deedee. And just a wild guess here, probably you weren't the first girl in his life. No doubt he's had his own lapses in judgment," Grace added, convinced few men were saints before they settled down.

"I s'pose it's much easier bein'y'all," Deedee paused. "Since you two got no regrets about the last visit. Oh, go ahead, write it, but don't ya dare be makin' me out the floozy of the group!" She flounced off with her signature toss of hair.

123. GRACE

Grace and Lily plugged away, intent on fulfillng their vow. Emotions waxed between nostalgia, confusion, amusement. "Lily, I'm loathe to admit it, but I'm sort of enjoying the process here. We've shared such a giant slice of each others' lives, haven't we?"

"An understatement. Aside from the teeth pulling for information, and the effort of the storytelling, I'm grateful to be back at Villa Bianco."

"Oh, yes indeed." Grace chuckled, reading into Lily's remark. She relaxed her secretarial posture, slid her pencil into her thick ponytail, and sprawled on the sofa.

Amelia limped into the library, heat radiating from her rosy-hued skin. "Hey gals, any sunburn relief around here? I overdid on the Vespa today." She held her white linen shift away from her chest.

"Ouch!" Grace winced. "I'll ask Marie Elena."

"Sit tight, Grace. I know where she keeps aloe vera. Be back in a flash." Lily hopped up and dashed off. She returned, waving the bottle that promised a respite for Amelia's lack of sense about the Caprese sun.

While Lily smoothed the green gel onto Amelia's shoulders and back, Grace began her interrogation. "We really need your input here, Amelia."

"I know I haven't been much help, but honestly, I cringe at the thought. What do you want to know, honey?"

"We've hit a hump. We're at the part where you and Penn…"

Amelia stiffened. Whether from unpleasant memories or Lily's ministrations, Grace wasn't sure.

"Sweetie, it's nothing I want to admit, but I was seduced. What can I say? Mick seemed worldly, exciting, he appreciated me. Imagine Richard Harris telling me how enchanting I was. He paid attention to my butt and boobs. Not that Ken Jr. had been ignoring them, but his appreciation had slipped over the years. And if Penn says I forced her, well, you were there, what did you see?"

"I saw her say 'Oh crap,' when the three of us walked into the restaurant," said Grace. "She sure wasn't looking for girlfriends right about then."

"It was all in the moment, we were caught up in the moment," Amelia defended.

"That's it? *That's all?* You and Penn just ate dinner and hung out in the bar all night drinking and nuzzling?" Grace sensed only a kernel of truth in Amelia's story and continued to drill for facts. "The bars close about two or three."

"Use what I've just told you. Say we came home around three. Why can't you use it?" Amelia wheedled. Grace slanted her eyes toward Lily and raised her eyebrows questioningly.

"You said…" Lily's voice was encouraging.

"Oh, just shoot me!" Amelia took a big breath. "You asked for this. After a little innocent smooching, Mick was all over me to, you know, so we all headed back to their hotel, San Michele." Amelia relayed the story about her and Penn in the bathroom, dithering about staying a teeny bit longer, and vowing to call the other's room whenever one of them wanted to leave. "Then we made up a story to tell you two, especially *you,* Grace, about a party on the far side of the island and seeing the sunrise, in case we got home late."

Grace felt unease take hold of her insides. "What happened?"

"It was horrible. You'll have to ask Penn. I've said too much; she's going to kill me." Amelia snatched the bottle of aloe vera from Lily's slippery fingers and scurried off like a panicked teenager.

124. LILY

Familiar whistling lifted from the garden; it flowed across the balcony's red ornamental rails and swirled through the shutters. Lily awakened with a start as Angelo's tune lilted into her bedroom. From the hallway she overheard Quinton with Grace as they headed downstairs. Lily freshened and dressed. She hadn't seen much of Angelo or Quinton these past days. Perhaps they could share the continental breakfast Marie Elena had prepared by now. *The current guests with their unpredictable eating habits must give the conscientious domestic a fit*, Lily thought.

Angelo hadn't come inside, Marie Elena reported. Lily hid her disappointment as she spooned pears and yoghurt into her bowl. Quinton had just left with a brown bag meal, Grace explained. His project? Capturing views from Arch Rock this cloudy morning. No surprise, Quinton kept disappearing these hot stressful days while she and Grace exhumed the past.

Lily felt like disappearing today too; why shouldn't she and Grace?

■   ■   ■

"I'm excited to take a boat ride around the island again," said Grace as they entered Piazza Umberto, where they gave in to the temptation of lemon gelato.

"It may not be the perfect day, but I hope if we back off for a spell, they'll ease up too. And hang around." Lily dug into the pale treat with her tiny plastic spoon.

Joining tourists and locals, Lily and Grace descended to Marina Grande via the cable railway. Wooden fishing boats crayoned the postcard-perfect beach with reds, yellows, blues, and greens. Lily easily located

Giovanni farther along in the harbor, where boats bobbled in their slips. The two stepped into his fishing rig made passenger friendly for summer months with the addition of large terry-covered foam cushions.

Clouds obscured the sun as the boat headed east around the island. Grace shivered, pulling the sleeves of her chenille sweater over her hands. She tucked the corners of a flapping towel under her heels as her attention switched from the choppy waves to the rugged rocks, then back to Lily, who sat cross-legged, camera in hand, sharing snips of conversation with Giovanni. Their skipper spoke so little English that Grace depended on Lily for occasional bursts of translation. Wisps of hair rose from Lily's head like lightning bolts defying her tight braids, Grace's patient handiwork.

Lily found it impossible to relax. "Let's review what we've already written, edited, and typed," she suggested.

"Okay." Grace sat a bit straighter. "'The Beginning,' the wives declare unity of desire and intention for a getaway. 'The Rakes,' the wives tarry with pilots and feelings are stirred. 'The Flurry of Preparation,' wives undertake beautification for dinner with the wolves and our own dubious participation."

Lily pulled a photo from her duffle. "Cat gave me this, lest we forget."

"How can we forget? And remember how Marie Elena kept herself busy organizing the linen closet while observing us?" Grace asked. "She told me yesterday, she thought we must all be movie stars."

"Mm-hmm," Lily responded thoughtfully. "Do you still like the title 'Fork in the Road,' for this next chapter?"

Grace nodded and started in. "The embarrassing dinner flirtations. Our dear friends blinded *to our very presence* by the allure of male flattery. Us, stunned. The unthinkable happening."

As the boat picked up speed, Grace wrapped an extra towel around herself. The clouds, low-slung, steel gray and dense, threatened to produce a drizzle, if not a dramatic storm.

Lily's imagination, prompted by the dark sky, jumped again to the chapter they had last written. The danger posed by similar weather and beguiling pilots back then suddenly seemed like a metaphor for the distressing episode. Lily enjoyed the comparison and began eagerly.

"Remember the cloudburst after our venture to Mount Solaro?" Lily asked without waiting for an answer. "It was like the prelude to an opera.

Bells sound, lights dim. Let the show begin. At first you and I were merely the audience, captivated by the opening solo, where Penn got the results of her 'tryout.' You played the hysterical narrarator while I rested with a cool washcloth on my forehead. Next Amelia and Penn performed a screeching duet as the 'chosen ones.' In a cameo appearance, Deedee twirled onto the stage with an earthquake of a bare-chested shimmy, slid out of her panties, and kicked them into the wings. Yeah-yes!" Lily mimicked Deedee's whoop.

Grace smirked in spite of herself. "As hard as I tried to stay neutral, my conservative engine shifted into gear. What the hell were Deedee and Penn cooking up? Was Amelia just going along for the ride? Something about Bob; I didn't like the guy. Mick and Jax weren't exactly prize catches either. That's when I decided not to go to dinner with them! But you said, 'We've got to stick together, Grace. Besides, I invited Quinton.'"

Lily resumed the storytelling. "And so, keeping quiet their skeptical opinions about the unfolding scenario, Grace and Lily got sucked into the drama by Cat's clever use of champagne and smooth talk."

Lily studied the photo again. "Indeed, who knew that Amelia's pouting lips were so full, or that Penn's enormous eyes sparkled like black diamonds, or that Cat's feline face could be so seductive? But Deedee's glamour was, well, simply Deedee, whose strapless, red dress was sure to attract attention."

Lily broke from the story with a disconcerting insight. "What were we *thinking*? Helping them gussy up like lambs for the slaughter? Why didn't we just tell them we thought it so very ill-advised?"

"Even harder questions coming up about the next turn of events," Grace said, continuing to shiver. "Amelia wasn't much help on the subject yesterday."

"I imagine Amelia had a little powwow with Penn after she left us. What about Penn? She seems such a wreck lately. I hate to ruffle her further." Lily paused and smoothed her hair. "Cat may have intended to underscore our friendship with her dying request, but I think it's actually undermining the strained bond we have left."

Both sat mesmerized as the water roiled, divided behind the stern, and shimmied away. Puffy foam grew thin and partnered with bruised purple shadows.

125. GRACE

"Lily, I suppose you'd think it too forward of me to march into their bedroom and demand some info. That Amelia was like an oyster peeping out of her shell, spitting out a tainted pearl, then slamming back into it when she realized she'd said too much. We don't have the luxury of years to get Cat's story written." Grace was feeling the pressure of a nearing deadline. "My expectation of this week was that the five of us would work together in the morning and then enjoy the island."

Lily shrugged and gave Grace an I-know-what-you-mean look.

"We're in paradise, and except for our little boat trip, you and I haven't left the villa," Lily said. "Meanwhile, Penn, Amelia, and Deedee are playing tourist. How peculiar that sightseeing has taken on such importance."

"The stars are brilliant tonight," Lily said as she gazed out the library window.

"This is where Penn would break into song—appropriate song—given a random topic sentence about stars," Grace said.

Lily laughed. "Suddenly I have this image of Penn in August of seventy-nine, arriving on Capri, guidebook in hand, her sons' photos in her passport pouch, travel binoculars around her neck, queasy with speed and height."

"Are you talking about me?" Penn surprised them both. "Amelia said you're playing Sherlock Holmes, and you had some questions for me. I want to make sure…"

Knowing that Penn could shy like a deer on the trail, Grace began to speak slowly, and looked to Lily for support. "We're trying to piece together that night that you and Amelia will never discuss. We *could* fabricate something if you don't want to talk about it…"

"Good guess. *I don't!* You think I haven't tried to forget that night? I never wanted to go out with him in the first place."

Grace scrunched her face like yesterday's Wonder Bread and discreetly mouthed, "*What?*" at Lily.

"That's not how I remember it." Grace had a quick memory of discovering that Penn, Amelia, and Deedee had sneaked out and her own resulting disappointment at their duplicity.

"Jeezo! Jump right down my throat, why don't you? It wasn't my idea. Amelia egged me on, saying she couldn't go alone. Amelia, the little wallflower, embarrassed by her own nude reflection, I should have known better, I *did* know better. Deedee's what's-his-name pilot acted suspicious from that very first night in the Tavern, and Mick and Jax—all pal-sie, wal-sie, like birds of a feather, but Amelia had the hots for Mick, he reminded her of Richard Harris. She begged me…"

"We did try to give you an out, planning that sunrise hike to Villa Jovis. You brushed us off, Penn." Lily reminded her friend of the facts. Grace heard an uncommon note of harshness in Lily's voice.

"I'll bet you wonder how I could ever forgive myself." Penn's voice shook with emotion. "Pastor Barnes used to say the Lord will forgive us as we forgive one another. The truth is I still haven't forgiven myself. *Or* Amelia. And don't tell her I said so."

"Forgive yourself for what?" Grace prodded Penn on.

"Forgive Amelia for what?" Lily dug a little further.

"She promised me…"

"Promised you *what?*" Grace and Lily asked, their curiosity spiked.

"Wait a minute, what has Amelia told you?"

"Nothing," said Lily, "nothing."

"Nothing, *yet.*" Grace felt the ground they'd gained slip away. She'd thought Penn was on the brink of finally talking about that damned night they were so stuck on. But that wasn't going to happen. Penn disappeared as quickly as she'd come.

"I wouldn't want to be Amelia right now." Grace was almost sympathetic.

Lily nodded her agreement. "You know Penn's cross-examining her."

126. PENN

Grace awakened to find Lily, watering can in hand, hovering over the geraniums on the terrace. Morning had spread itself like pastel butter over the horizon.

"Lily, there was a note from Penn under our door when I got up." The calm of Grace's voice deceived Lily for one second only. Water overflowed the indigo blue pot and splattered the chaise as Lily twirled around.

Grace read Penn's short note aloud.

"Read it again," Lily commanded. "This is bizarre."

Grace read:

"Dear Lily and Grace,

First off I want to apologize for taking so long to talk about anything. Not my favorite subject. Forgive me, but here's what happened best as I can remember. Phrase it however you want for the book. Now I'll just list events in order:

1. Amelia and Penn making out at the bar with Mick and Jax after dinner

2. Both couples taking a taxi across the island to join locals for dancing

3. Both couples smooching in one of the bedrooms until the pilots (now high on coke) try going all the way

4. Penn kneeing Jax in the crotch, dragging Amelia away from Mick (now hobbled by his dropped trousers)

5. Amelia and Penn barely escaping

6. Penn falling on the road, hurting her hand and her knees

7. Penn and Amelia finally making it back to the center of town

8. Catching their breath, hearts beating out of their chests

9. Watching a sunrise (grateful for something beautiful)

10. Getting a ride back to the villa in the back of a pickup truck

11. Getting chewed out by their friends at the villa

12. Penn and Amelia retiring in shock to the safety of their room

The rest is history, and now you know. Please don't think less of me. I would probably never have gone to the party if Amelia hadn't wanted to so badly. She was having a good time (better than I was, anyway). Will you let me know what parts of this you are going to use? Please?"

"No signature?" asked Lily. Grace shook her head. "Well, finally we have Penn's shorthand version of the mystery night minus a signature."

"It bears a curious resemblance to the yarn Amelia referred to as 'the saving face for Grace' story!" Grace smirked. "Is the truth worse than this, you suppose?"

"I'm intrigued with Penn's third-person format, utilizing gerunds so effectively! It softens the sordid tale a mite," said Lily shaking her head.

Marie Elena interrupted, entering from the kitchen to present espresso and steamed milk while sharing morning pleasantries. Once Marie Elena returned to the kitchen, Lily continued, "Not to be unsympathetic, but was this horrific enough to cause Penn's three-year trauma?"

Grace thought for a while. "Maybe Amelia did twist Penn's arm somehow, and then Penn regretted it. But what fantasy scenario were they expecting?"

Grace peeled a banana and offered half to Lily. "It's as if Penn wants to reveal something, but can't quite bring herself to."

127. AMELIA

Amelia zipped up her lightweight khaki Dockers and reached for her tennis shoes.

"Hurry, Penn. Unless you want to spend the morning getting the old third degree." How she dreaded Grace's probing query and Lily's soul-searching eyes.

"Not again in this lifetime." Penn put her sunglasses and a tube of ChapStick in a fanny pack. The two headed out for their long-delayed hike to Villa Jovis.

"I left the note for Lily and Grace."

"It was a good note, Penn," Amelia comforted. "Comprehensive—even for their questioning minds."

"I pray they can continue their crusade now without further conversation about *that night*."

"I invited Deedee to join us. She looked at me like I had a pox. She was going to do more Christmas shopping. I asked her how much she had left. She has bags of booty stashed in her room." Amelia was all for getting the holiday shopping done early, but if Deedee wasn't careful, she'd be paying a premium for duty at customs.

"Christmas shopping!" Penn burst out laughing. "Amelia, she's at the Beauty Farm. Getting spa treatments. Facials, massages, pedicures. Those bags are filled with special ointments and oils and creams. You don't really think Deedee's going to give griping Mama grapefruit scrubbing salts? What would she do with them?"

"I guess Deedee's been Christmas shopping for Deedee." Amelia wished she could be more like her self-indulgent friend, who always found a way to treat and gift herself.

It wasn't long before the sheen of perspiration appeared on their faces and drops gathered on their necks. "We should've left earlier, but I couldn't pass up a good sleep-in," Amelia commented. "Never get to at home."

"And we won't in the near future either." Penn stopped and leaned against a garden wall. She poked about in her fanny pack, pulled out a map of Capri. "Wish we'd left when it was still dark. We've a ways to go." The two trekked on, huffing as they went.

They reached the highest point on the eastern side of the island, the Church of Santa Maria del Soccorso atop Villa Jovis. Any other tourists had already departed, probably taking refuge from the morning's heat. Amelia and Penn were left alone in the eerie shadows of crumbling glory.

"Do you smell that?" asked Penn, "Geraniums or lemons or—"

"Or Yves San Laurent," said Amelia. "Cat used to wear that scent." She felt the hair on her arms rise. Taking advantage of a low wall, she plopped herself upon it. "Hard as I try now, I can't remember what I liked about Cat."

"You mean her highness, Catherine San Carlo," said Penn, imitating Lily's author voice. "Or, foolishly fearless Cat. Coaching each of us to push the envelope, be it glamour, wine, or our budgets."

"Setting the perfect example of fearlessness herself. How she wanted to be fabulous at sports, at photography, singing…"

"At *something*, anything."

"Always claimed she thought more like a man than a woman. Remember how she'd stick up for *our* husbands. But never for Pietro, her own sweet husband." Amelia thought, not without a hint of bitterness, how Cat used to flirt with the husbands. Oh sure, it was harmless, just one more thing she needed to be remarkable at—having the husbands think she "got" them, understood their trials of life.

Amelia was suddenly struck with compassion. "Penn, Cat died alone. Her folks were gone, her siblings had severed ties—too busy with their own lives to deal with her drama. Even Pietro took a harsh line against her. No doubt at Noni's behest, but how awful to die like that. I guess I can understand her need to be remembered as someone exceptional."

"No disputing that it's tragic, but Cat could drain you if you let your guard down," Penn declared. "Terrence came to Deedee's rescue. He put a stop to it. Cat would've moved right in and let Deedee nurse her *and* Mama." Penn shook her head. "And even though we all pitched in, brought food, it wasn't enough. Look at how she took advantage of Lily, had her cleaning the cat box, doing all her errands. Like she didn't have a business to build and Callie to see to. Once Lily brought Cat to her house, it got worse. She ran Lily ragged."

Amelia recalled Lily's gaunt appearance, the way her formerly fitted clothes hung on her too-slender frame. It had taken a few months for Lily to reclaim her previous healthy self. "You're right, of course. I'm just saying that I don't want to die like that—" Amelia stopped abruptly.

Penn grabbed her arm and both stared at the apparition. Cat hovered midair beside the statue of the Virgin and Infant Jesus.

"Why can't you remember my *virtues*?" Cat stomped her delicate white foot on Mary's shoulder.

"She's wearing that pink jacket dress," Penn whispered. "The one she wore to Grace's wedding. Pushed you out of the way and caught the bridal bouquet. Then flirted shamelessly with Grace's dad."

Cat straddled Mary's shoulders, posing dramatically with the wind ruffling her hair.

"She's casting a shadow on the Infant Jesus. How can that be?" Amelia said under her breath.

"I can hear you, so quit whispering! Why can't you remember anything *good* about me? I was witty, a natural entertainer. Amelia, it should have been *my* house, not yours, that was photographed for the magazine. I chose beautiful birthday gifts for each of you, even when I didn't have the money. I wrapped each package with a flower, my special touch. Why can't you remember any of this?"

"Cat, honey," Amelia began, but wondered if she'd lost her mind talking to a spirit.

"Shut up, Amelia, just shut up! No one wanted to help me. Oh, Deedee tried, but Terrance scotched that. And you two? You think all I needed was casseroles and fresh vegetables? How about Quinton! That turncoat didn't help do a thing to promote me. Just married Grace right out from under us. And sweetie-sweetie Grace was too absorbed being a wife and lover to pay me any attention. Lily should have gotten me some jobs as a stylist, but she was selfish—wouldn't make contacts or give me a reference."

"That's not true, Cat. *We all tried.* Lily took you in." Amelia resented Cat's unfair tirade. "She'd lost her business because of Dirk. She was trying to take care of herself and Callie."

"Well, I used my skills, thanks to no one, and got a wine rep position. I set the record for wine sales in my territory. Memory coming back?"

"You excelled, Cat," Amelia said firmly, intent on placating the specter.

"But then, when I was at my very weakest, you gave me the cold shoulder. My best, best friends slowly backed away." Cat began to scream, "It's not fair that I had a congenital birth defect. It's not my fault!"

Amelia and Penn began to cry.

"What are *you* crying about?" Cat was composed. "I made one small request. Asked only one favor. And?"

"And what? What request?" the two sniveled together.

"For you all to collaborate on the story—about me, how our friendship was almost destroyed and how I brought us back together. I heard each one of you promise. *Instead*, you take the time to tour the island because you didn't see enough before? Not to mention, you're leaving the job to Lily and Grace. That's not fair." Although clearly living among the spirits, Cat had not gotten off her "fair" soapbox.

Amelia and Penn continued to weep.

"Not to malign the sainted Lily or beatified Grace, but if I were you, I'd want to tell my side of the story."

Penn looked up, horrified.

"Obviously no one takes deathbed requests seriously. Even God let me down. I prayed, 'Please, God, don't let me die alone.'"

Amelia got up and tried to hug the frail ghost of a friend, but Cat disappeared.

"We were all there, moments before she died. Didn't she hear us trying to comfort her?" Penn sniffed.

Amelia felt somehow put out. "Wait a second. What just happened? No. It didn't happen. And we don't have *anything* to feel guilty for. You left that note. That's our contribution. No. No reason for guilt."

"You may not, Amelia. But what about me?" Penn whimpered.

"Mercy, Penn. For three years you've been bawling about that night. I've told you a hundred times to forget it."

Penn sobbed, "I can't. I've tried."

Amelia envisioned reassuring Penn for the next fifty years of her life. She didn't think she could do it. "Penn, if you won't listen to me, then talk to Quinton."

128. GRACE

Distant thunder rumbled in the dark sky. Grace, Lily, and Deedee were tossed around the inside of a taxi as it raced down the rough, twisty road.

"Don't y'all think I don't know this shoppin' trip to buy fish is just an excuse to put the screws to me for information." Deedee peered tentatively out the window, catching glimpses of the whitecapped ocean.

"We weren't trying to trick you, Deedee," Lily assured her.

"Of course not," added Grace. "But you've got eyes. Surely you can see that we're coming up short in the story department here. We've been left to tread water on our own."

"So much has happened since that trip, it's all foggy now, but I do remember thinkin' I'd been sent love on the wings of a *rich* flyboy. Dang, was I stupid. Bob spent money on me and I stayed high. I was blissed with fabulous sex. Didn't give a thought to protection. Venerable disease never crossed my mind."

"*Venereal disease*, Deedee." Grace had automatically corrected, then regretted. "Sorry."

Lily nodded encouragement for Deedee to continue.

"As for Penn and Amelia, it's not rightly mine to tattle, but I reckon Cat would approve."

The taxi's brakes squealed, the driver honked twice and stopped abruptly, then pitched ahead continuing the journey.

Deedee settled herself and continued, not without a bit of drama, "Here's what Amelia told me about the night of silence and guilt. The four of them left the bar. Went to a party and got themselves all hot and loaded, then tramped off to the guys' hotel."

The girls lurched in their seats as the driver sped up past a stalled car.

"Now, Amelia was gettin' it on with Mick. Quite happily too. Payback to Ken Jr., I'd say. Y'all probably agree. Penn had cold feet at the start, but she got laid, and *liked it*."

Lily nodded knowingly.

Grace was surprised by her own lack of revulsion at her friends' actions.

Deedee lowered her voice. "And then, something horrificatin' happened. Scared 'em near to death."

Lily, Grace, and Deedee all screamed as a careening bus headed straight at the taxi, veering at the last possible moment.

"Oh my God!" Grace and Lily breathed in unison.

"Oh my God! We could've died!" Deedee screeched. "Hey y'all! Watch it, will ya?" she hollered at the driver, who was still calm and unaffected by the near misses.

"What happened then?" Grace asked, now fearing what might come next.

"After that, Amelia clammed up." Deedee sat back in the seat and tried to relax.

"That was a big help," Lily remarked.

"Who can blame them for not tellin' *y'all*, you little prudes? Amelia not wantin' to say she loved every second of illicit sex, Penn too ashamed to discuss the wages sin wrought on her."

The taxi driver blasted the horn at a passing car, once again interrupting Deedee's dissertation.

"Look, Amelia got madder than hell for the first time in her life about what that jerk did to Penn. And found out how dang fine it felt to be powerful. Penn vowed she'd never take shit from a man again. And you two *have* mellowed in the self-righteous department."

Lily, Grace, and Deedee slid together as the taxi took a sharp turn on two wheels.

"It's all good in the outcome," Deedee waxed philosophical. "What if this had never happened?"

"*What if this had never happened?*" Lily repeated.

129. GRACE & LILY

"Finished brushing your teeth and stuff?" Grace inquired as she entered Lily's room.

Lily stood on the balcony, hands gripping the rail as the breeze sighed in the cypress trees. "Come here, Grace!"

Grace looked below, and off to the west, following Lily's gesture. The two watched as sheets, hanging out to dry on the clothesline, flapped and twisted. "Wait a minute," Lily whispered. Suddenly the shifting sheets revealed Penn and Quinton standing together. And just as suddenly, the unlikely pair was hidden from view of the Villa again.

"What the…" Grace had no explanation to offer.

▪   ▪   ▪

By the time Lily and Grace came back downstairs, Marie Elena had cleared the brunch remains from the dining room table and replaced the casual bowl of fruit with a more formal centerpiece, a silver basket of grapes, fresh from the arbor. She had removed melted stubs from the glazed candlesticks and replaced them with tall, fat candles. Wiped to perfection the goldframed mirror and placed fresh flowers on the breakfront. Within seconds she noiselessly disappeared into the kitchen.

"Signore Bianco runs a beautiful ship here," Grace said. Lily nodded in complete accord. They walked through the tall glass doors into the library, still befuddled by the sight of Quinton and Penn.

Lily plumped up the turquoise and chartreuse pillows on the chocolate-leather sofa but felt too uneasy to settle. Grace sat at the typewriter but twirled in the chair instead of attacking the keys.

"There's an elephant in the library," said Lily. "Do you see him? Right about now he's sitting on the typewriter!"

Grace burst out laughing. "Too true. I have no idea what to write next given everyone's caginess. Let's just review what we have? And then go somewhere?"

Lily placed the notes and manuscript on the marble coffee table and got comfortable on the sofa. She began: "Okay, after the Blue Grotto, the three divulge they've planned another *un-date* with those jerks. Hearing the news, didn't Cat say something like, '…and what would your mothers think of you now?'"

"Her strange brew of piety and envy cut close to the bone," Grace scoffed.

"And then they snuck out!" Lily flipped a few pages.

"You and I? Not invited to tag along, and definitely not interested," Grace said, turning her chair around and around. "Quinton had sure made himself scarce. Probably kept his distance after getting stuck with Cat the night before. No encores on his agenda."

"We found them at the restaurant down there at Punto Faro Carena. Tried to coax them away. Reminding them about the sunrise hike to Villa Jovis."

"Punto Faro, sounds like the Point of No Return," said Grace, remembering the night that Amelia and Penn decisively steered their course in a new direction.

"I'm tired of stewing over the writing," Lily whined.

"Let's make up something and be done with it," Grace offered, being flip.

Lily stepped to the dictionary lectern and began to speak, sounding like an erudite author. "At the restaurant Penn finds some aspect of Jax and Mick's behavior disconcerting, alarming even. She passes the info to Amelia. Amelia, quite smitten with Mick, pooh-poohs Penn's suspicions.

But you, Cat, and I arrive, and—without being judgmental—we steer our friends away from perceived trouble. We return to Villa Bianco all together and watch something like *Three Coins in the Fountain.*"

Grace chimed in using a singsong voice. "Influenced by all that innocence and romance, we talk about trying to appreciate our husbands more."

"We say to one another how lucky we are to be married to great guys! Then it's just like *Enchanted April.* Our husbands join us and the island blooms with love." Lily couldn't contain herself, waxing romantic.

"Charming, simply charming!" Grace chorused as they burst into unrestrained laughter.

"If only it were true," Lily lamented and then shifted gears. "It's wishful thinking; we can't change history by writing this fairy tale." She collapsed onto the couch, arms crisscrossed over her face, and remained motionless.

"Alora," Marie Elena exclaimed as she passed by the library, dusting feather in hand. Grace's look of consternation was enough in itself to elicit the response.

An hour passed, and then half of another. Grace sat quietly rereading the manuscript.

Marie Elena passed by again. This time she hurried in and knelt by Lily's side. *"Lily, con permesso, che cosa è errato con voi? Che cosa posso fare?"* And then addressing Grace, "What the problem is with Lily? What something I can do?"

"Unfortunately, we're stymied writing our book, Marie Elena. You know our subject, I'm sure."

Marie Elena smiled without any self-consciousness. "I hear your talk of all the *signore bellisima* here in Villa Bianco. Years go by, but still I remember. Much of the laughing, much of the crying."

Lily slowly righted herself. "Marie Elena, what *do* you remember?"

"Quello non mia riguardia, ho detto a nessuno circa questo. Has not been for me to talk of; I tell no one about all of this."

A rapid-fire exchange in Italian ensued between Marie Elena and Lily. Grace listened attentively. Although unable to comprehend the words, she grasped the weightiness of Marie Elena's disclosure.

▪   ▪   ▪

Afterward Marie Elena seemed agitated, although Lily reassured her repeatedly that no harm would come from the information divulged; for several long moments, they hugged. After Marie Elena retreated, Lily translated for the impatient Grace.

"Murder! I can't believe Marie Elena understood properly!" Grace buried her face in her hands. "She's mistaken. Flat-out wrong. She must be! The language issue distorted the facts. Her misunderstanding is a peculiar translation of the actual truth. Whatever the *truth* is."

"But if she *did* get it right..." Lily's somber tone gave them both goose bumps.

"Could we in good conscience tread there?" Grace asked.

Perplexity glued Lily and Grace to their seats, like models posing for portraits. They stared at each other, eyeballs round with confusion and fear.

130. MARIE ELENA – 1979

Marie Elena placed fresh flowers on the bureau of Penn and Amelia's room. She was grateful that both the *signore* had returned safely to the Villa. There'd been some tension between *signore* Lily and Grace and the two who'd returned later than prudent. Now the latecomers were having a serious discussion of their own behind the bathroom's closed door. Marie Elena lingered to pick up scattered clothing. She hadn't intended to eavesdrop, not exactly.

Amelia's voice carried through the bathroom door.

"Where *were* you? You left the room, didn't you? I knocked again and again. There was no answer! I got the night manager to open the door. It was six o'clock, and I was out of my mind with concern." Amelia nagged like a worried parent. "Where did you go? Do you have any idea how difficult it's been for me not to tell the others and ask for help?"

Penn sounded exhausted. "I wanted to come back, really. We went to Jax's room, and we, and well, after we..."

Marie Elena stepped in closer to the door. She had a good idea about what Penn had done, but had not admitted aloud.

"He was going for another hit, but I knocked the vial off the night-stand, and the rest of his gram vaporized into the rug," Penn continued. "He was pissed, asked if I had cash on me. Then he dragged me off to some party where he knew there'd be coke. I didn't want to go, but we went anyway. After all, it was my fault."

Marie Elena had heard enough—for the moment. Alarmed, she left the room and returned quickly with fresh sheets and towels. She set about making up the room. *Signore* Penn and Amelia were speaking more loudly now. Even the sound of water filling the bathtub did not disguise the voices of the two friends. Marie Elena was privy to every word.

"It started out to be such an adventure. I'd never been with anyone but George…Oh, Amelia, that party was shocking. There were mirrors and razor blades and white piles everywhere. People were lying around having sex—not caring who could see what—and there was plenty to see, believe me! I told Jax I wanted to leave and finally we did, but by that time he was so weird. I don't know what he took. He was hanging all over me. He kept kissing me…all wet and slobbery. It wasn't like earlier, when I wanted to do it too. I tried to push him off, but he had a death grip."

"Oh, sweetheart, how awful for you," Amelia said, sounding sympathetic, Marie Elena thought. Had these two been *her* sisters, she would have knocked their heads together for their naïve and impulsive behavior. Then told their mama.

"He was trying to make me do it in this little alcove right in the lane. He must have been drugged out of his mind…I couldn't peel him off me." Penn's voice cracked.

"It's okay, dear, it's okay. You're safe from him now."

"I was terrified!"

"He didn't force you, did he?"

"I pushed him away, and he said I was a tease. I screwed him before, but now I was too good for it. I begged him to let me go. I told him I wanted to go home, I had to get back to you, and he said you were a slut and needed a good screw too. That whores like us love the game."

"That prick!" Amelia sputtered. "He doesn't know the first thing about us."

Penn began to cry. "He unzipped his pants and tore my dress, then he ripped my panties. I think I elbowed him in the stomach and started to run, but he pushed me down to my hands and knees. He was on me, on my backside, with his hand covering my mouth. I thought I'd suffocate or choke to death."

"Oh, Penn, everything went so wrong last night. You shouldn't have—"

"Amelia, you don't know the worst of it! I tried to fight, and when he finally went limp, I turned him over and socked him. Under his chin. I think I knocked him out. He wasn't moving."

Marie Elena held her breath and pushed her ear closer to the door.

"Penn, dear, here, your bath is ready."

"Then I ran as fast as I could."

"To get help, of course," Amelia deduced.

"Quit interrupting me! I was trying to *get away*. I needed to find the San Michele and get back to you. I fell on the street and broke my heel, and when I got to the Phoenician Steps, I saw Quinton."

Marie Elena could hear the water splashing in the tub.

"Quinton took me to his hotel. There were no taxis, so we rode in a vegetable truck. He gave me a shot of whiskey. He tried to bring me back to the Villa but I wouldn't go without you. He promised to look for Jax and find out where you were."

"I got home around six thirty or so. I couldn't wait any longer for you. Mick had an early flight and had to check out. What was I supposed to do? Sit around the hotel lobby? I prayed you'd be here," Amelia said, filling in the blanks for Penn as well as Marie Elena.

"Yeah. Thanks for sticking to the plan," Penn said accusingly.

"Dear, that's not fair. So what happened to Jax?"

"Quinton couldn't find him. He assured me he wasn't lying in any lane. But what if someone else found him? I think maybe he's *dead*!" Penn cried harder.

"Don't talk crazy."

"You didn't see him!" Penn howled. "You don't know what else I did to him. I kicked his ribs and shoulders. And his head. Again and again. I didn't stop till I saw the blood all over the street."

"I won't hear another word about it, Penn. It's positively ludicrous to imagine that you killed him. Everyone knows *you can't kill cockroaches!*"

Marie Elena jumped, hearing their laughter. Shrill, nervous, and loud.

131. GRACE

"Marie Elena's story kept me awake," said Grace as she kicked at leaves strewn across the garden path.

"My heart aches for Penn. What she's—" Lily was interrupted by the appearance of Penn, who held out a letter. Lily reached out to give Penn a hug.

"Not now! Here, read this and we'll talk later." Penn strode up the path with confidence. Deedee and Amelia waited for her some yards away.

"We're goin' shoppin'," Deedee shouted out and waved cheerily. "See y'all later."

Penn could be heard singing as she disappeared down the path.

Grace turned to Lily, confused. "What the heck? She's singing again?"

Lily looked at the letter. "It's addressed to you and me." They walked to the Pan fountain, where Grace perched on the edge. Lily paced, in a quandary.

Angelo joined them. "A beautiful day, such long faces." He set his rake aside and began to fish stray leaves from the fountain's basin.

"Cat set us on an impossible task. We're on a quest for the truth." Lily flapped the unopened envelope. "And this will only make it worse."

"*Alora.* The truth will find you. And you'll know what to do." Angelo picked up his rake, wandered a little ways to a patch of garden, and gave it his full attention.

Lily's interest was captured by his whistling. She gazed at him, seeming to forget the important missive she held.

"Lily, we might want to think about opening that," Grace prompted.

Lily, bemused, gave a little chuckle, then slipped her thumb under the glued flap. Grace peered over her shoulder, and the two read through Penn's schooled cursive.

"She begins with a sweet apology for misleading us," Lily said sincerely. "She wants us to use this—maybe some reckless girls will benefit."

"To what can we attribute the change of heart? This confession." Grace wondered.

"The past is still changing us," Lily replied thoughtfully. Lily and Grace continued to read Penn's letter silently.

Grace cocked her head. "Wait. Penn's story *almost* matches Marie Elena's. She had to fight for her life. *But* she doesn't mention running into Quinton."

"*Or* that one little detail. You know, leaving Jax for dead," Lily reminded.

"What *did* happen to Jax? And was Quinton helping Penn that morning, or was he at the Villa like Cat told us?" Grace was perplexed.

132. QUINTON

The three stood at the balustrade and watched clouds transform, Grace and Lily with lemon water, Quinton with amber bottle in hand. They exchanged banter about Quinton's photographic adventures today. And then about the taxi ride to the fish market that resulted in seafood for tonight's cioppino.

Finally, Lily, hands on her hips, changed the tone. "Look, our nosing around for the story has brought a serious and perhaps unsolved mystery to the fore."

"Nice. A dramatic hook for your story." Quinton's eyes twinkled, and he planted a kiss on Grace's cheek. "I have missed you, young lady!"

Lily wouldn't be put off. "With consequences of its own, and to say the very least, we're concerned!" Lily's voice sounded a teeny bit sharp, even to herself.

Marie Elena, unobserved, leaned on her broom and listened from the balcony.

Grace picked up Lily's agenda. "By any chance did Penn strong-arm you into a conversation? Let's say, recently. Perhaps at the clothesline?"

Quinton's discomfort was obvious as he nodded. "So where is everyone?" he asked.

"Shopping." Grace's quick, flat answer was followed up cleverly, Lily thought, by her next question. "Was it anything to do with your coming to her rescue on a particularly bad morning?"

Quinton concentrated on pinging his beer bottle.

Lily's desire for answers escalated as Quinton seemed to retreat. "Penn wrote us a letter. She confessed something shocking."

"Why *did* Penn corral you?" Grace asked, eyeball to eyeball with Quinton.

Quinton flushed slightly and began, "Look, your good friend Penelope was having her concerns about your examination of the past. *She's so uptight.* She wondered if I had ever revealed anything to either of you."

"You've never said a word on the subject," Grace whispered. "To me, anyway."

Lily felt sick as the weight of what Penn had imposed on Quinton became clearer.

"You know?" Now Quinton was acutely curious. "What do you know?"

Grace tried to explain. "Penn has been a holdout, evading our questions. She invented a plausible story, after crosschecking with Amelia, we think. But then poof! An about-face. She wrote us a letter laying out the whole wretched experience. Blow by blow."

Quinton relaxed. "I'm glad she told you. Not that I've given it any thought for eons. Honestly, I thought Penn had forgotten or moved on long ago. *Man, was I wrong.* Secrets take their toll on our psyche, don't you think?"

"Tell us your version," Grace said, not quite yet convinced that Penn and Quinton had the same tale to retell. "This should be interesting."

After a little hesitation, his words spilled out in a mad rush. "I found her bloody and hysterical just after that pervert had attacked her. Close to the steps, under the Sphinx. At the time, what she had gone through, well, she acted like it would be the end of the world if the rest of you found out. Alcohol, cocaine, sex, more cocaine, with a virtual stranger, she a married woman. Penn can be neurotic anyway, but you have no idea! Nothing would do, I had to find out if Amelia had retuned to the Villa. Penn was hyper about some promise she couldn't break about returning without Amelia. I tried to convince her to let me take her back to the villa, right then. But oh, no. What if Amelia hadn't returned? *Dang!* I took her to my hotel, calmed her a little—"

Lily halted his flow. "Now wait. She said she sent you back to the lane to check on Jax first. She thought he might be dead, that she might have killed him. You know, by kicking him in the head!" Her words seemed to be spoken in slow motion.

Quinton's body went rigid.

Grace began again. "The possibility of Jax lying there dead has obviously been huge for her."

"Right." Quinton's one word answer left Grace and Lily hanging.

"So you did go back to look for him?" Lily asked impatiently.

"Anyway, how did you know for sure where to go?" Grace sounded like a detective.

"Hey, you two, I figured it out. Okay? So mainly she wanted to question me again about Jax, still imagining the worst. You know Penn."

"How did you placate her guilt?" Lily questioned. "Because you must have. Here she was, honestly relieved, for—well, think about it—for the first time in three years, if you look at her behavior. Attacking, withdrawing, evading, fabricating. And now presumably coming clean because of something you said to her."

"Good, I'm glad." Quinton pinged the empty glass bottle repeatedly by cocking his index finger with his thumb. He attended the dull clicks, head tilted right. His eyes closed.

"Help yourself to another beer, if you like, Quinton," Lily said, playing hostess.

Quinton nodded; he gave Grace's shoulder a squeeze.

133. QUINTON

Heading indoors, Quinton's face hardened into resolve while unwanted images jostled for attention. It's 1979 once again, and he's back on the desperate errand for Penn:

Locals cluster in an alley, their gates open to atriums with green rambling gardens, twisted trees, and cracked tile walkways. He hears the tone of their hushed conversation, the universal language of shock. Several words he understands literally, however. Americano. Emergenza. Ospedale.

I presumed Jax was in good hands, better than he deserved, Quinton thought to himself as he entered the kitchen. *Penn needed calming, not more details to fuel her anxiety. I told her Jax was not a corpse on the sidewalk. That wasn't deceit, was it?*

Quinton opened the refrigerator and retrieved a chilled amber bottle. Still another image washed up. An encounter with Cat at Villa Bianco while on his next errand of mercy for Penn.

Cat is coquettish as usual, annoyingly so as his day slips away. Cat reports that Amelia has indeed returned. Issuing a request not to be disturbed, she is now locked in her bedroom. "Amelia looks like hell from partying till dawn, if anyone wants to know," Cat says as she leans back against the counter, braced on her flattened hands. Smiling, Cat offers more: since Penn and Deedee are still out, and the prudes have gone hiking to Villa Jovis, would he like to fool around for a while?

Diplomatically dodging Cat, chasing from Anacapri to Capri and back, coaxing the frenzied Penn to steadiness, this is stuff a guy could forget. Were it not fused with another image. The blue light from the refrigerator heightened Quinton's pallor.

When Quinton returned to the terrace, his bottle of beer was unopened, but he seemed not to notice as he gripped it.

"So tell us, *how* did you calm her any better this time than you did before?" Grace would not let up. Grace and Lily turned away from the view and faced him expectantly.

Quinton pulled himself tall. He spoke like an orator, newly calm and precise, his eyes seemingly focused on pages of a script.

"I told her *exactly* what I told her before. Jax was gone when I got to the lane. And, if I *had* found the creep with one shallow breath of life left in him, I'd have told that SOB to get the hell out of Dodge. I'd have taken him back to his hotel room, watched while he packed his bags, and then I'd have made sure he got on the jet boat to Naples. And *this* time I bolstered Penn by stating another truth: she never knew what hit her!

"Look, she'd hardly been farther than the grocery store or the pediatrician's for years. Having a smooth guy make over her, pay some special attention...It didn't take much to turn her head. I gave her some advice, 'Forget the whole friggin' event, and get on with your life.'"

134. GRACE & LILY

Grace and Lily stared at each other, stunned. Words evaded them. They turned again to watch the clouds shape shifting from ribbons into wisps.

Grace broke the silence. "Finally, I can understand what Penn and Amelia were hiding. And why."

"We let it separate us…" Lily's voice trailed off.

"But their laughter, Lily. I should be better than this, but it still rankles."

Lily drew her brows together. "Had to be nerves. What with the fear, the danger. They were giddy with the relief of escaping."

Grace reflected about the amount of time she'd wasted, time when she'd made no overtures to repair the ripped friendship, and felt the cramp of pain. "I've been so wrong. Practically ruined the friendship with my arrogant conclusions."

Lily put an arm around Grace. "We were in it together. I carried the torch right along with you. But I believe we can make amends. The door isn't closed. Penn and Amelia *did* come back to Capri, after all."

"Isn't it great for everybody to be at a place in their lives where the secrets no longer matter," said Quinton, taking a deep breath of the fragrant air.

Marie Elena left her post at the balcony with a sigh of apparent relief.

135. LILY

Lily looked around furtively as she and Grace hurried to the library. They closed the tall glass doors for privacy. Lily led Grace to the desk below the Bianco family photos and opened it. Lily pointed to the contents within.

"I saw these in the display table during our last visit. I've already asked Angelo if we could utilize them. He said they belonged to his mother and she would have been proud to assist our cause. So Angelo transferred everything into the desk to make us a convenient working space."

The two whispered with a new sense of direction. Lily sketched out her idea, and Grace nodded appreciatively as the idea became tangible.

"This puts a positive spin on something that's had a perpetual downward spiral," Grace said, gesturing dramatically.

"I hear Angelo. I'll thank him again." Lily departed purposefully.

In the kitchen Lily saw Angelo turning the wobbly stools upside down, one by one. He looked up as she entered with tablet and pen. Seeing Angelo, she felt unexpectedly giddy.

"*Buongiorno,* Lily, you wear a smile. Things are better?"

"*Grazie,* Angelo, yes, much better."

Angelo's enthralled smile matched Lily's. "I am needing my measure, I'll be right back," he said. "You will be here?"

Lily nodded. Angelo gave a comic bow and exited the back door. Lily prepared to wait. Setting her tablet and pen on the counter, she spied Angelo's pencil. She picked it up with a wink at Marie Elena and stepped out of the kitchen.

Angelo returned through the back door carrying a toolbox, a tape measure, and glue. He looked surprised, not seeing Lily as expected. With a shrug he searched the counter for his pencil, certain where he had left it. But the pencil had gone missing as well.

"Marie Elena, have you seen my pencil?"

Marie Elena ignored Angelo, smirking up her sleeve. Angelo found Lily's pen instead. He set to measuring the stool legs and writing numbers as Lily walked in.

"Marie Elena, have you seen my pen?" Lily asked, all the while keeping an eye on Angelo.

Marie Elena watched, amused, as Angelo looked at the pen in his hand and then at Lily, who held out his carpenter's pencil.

Angelo and Lily burst into laughter as Cupid struck; two arrows flew, unrestrained this time, and hit their mark.

"It seems we have both found what we are looking for," Angelo said, wiping his eyes where tears from laughter collected.

"It seems so," said Lily, stepping close and exchanging his pencil for her pen. The couple—Angelo finding Lily so close, Lily feeling Angelo so close—did nothing to resist the embrace.

Angelo took Lily by the hand and led her to the salon. Grace, who had finished selecting items in the library, was witness to Lily and Angelo's first kiss.

136. GRACE

Grace pushed back the desk chair. "Any chance of a back and neck rub?" she asked Quinton, who was well settled into one of the library's overstuffed leather armchairs. "Even the torture rack sounds good to me now. My kingdom for a good stretch."

"Happy to oblige, ma'am." Quinton stood and tossed the *New York Times* aside. It was last week's anyway, but Angelo always kept up with what was going on in the States. Parking himself behind Grace's chair, he used his thumbs to loosen her tight deltoid muscles.

"Hey, Angelo tells me that come September, he's going to reside full time here at the Villa. No more renting to tourists. I'd thought that maybe we'd come next summer, bring your folks and Jemima, but I guess it's out of the question now."

"That's what Lily said. We're fortunate to be guests this time. It'll be like saying good-bye to two friends, Angelo *and* Villa Bianco, when we leave."

"It's mind-boggling to think you and Lily cracked your story out in this amount of time. I'm impressed by your tenacity." Quinton continued kneading her neck, shoulders, and back while Grace moved appreciatively under his ministrations. "Now, are you almost done with your extra credit, sweetheart?"

"Couple more lines, and I'll be getting my gold star. I made great progress last night. I couldn't sleep, so I put a few hours in on it. Didn't you even miss me?"

Grace didn't wait for an answer. Quinton did many things well, but his knack for sleep was one of the most enviable to Grace. "I've put so many hours into this. Lily and I *know* it'll be a perfect solution."

Lily's idea to have Grace write their story in calligraphy was inspired. But daunting. Grace quickly agreed to take it on, with a caveat.

"I'm good and I'm fast, but without a team of monks, it'll take years to complete." The two of them laughed hard and long at the image of Grace overseeing a group of God's chosen laboring away at sheets of parchment, quills in hand, tonsures glistening in the candlelit monastery.

"If you agree to an edit, a *big* one, I think it's doable." Grace had been exhilarated by the prospect.

"I've already thought of that." Lily motioned Grace to join her at the dining room table. She spread out the fruits of their effort, chapter by chapter. "Let's take a look at every event, then we'll select a highlight from each for you to transfer."

Lily had taken Grace to the library, pulled on an elaborately carved handle of the desk. A pungent woodsy smell had wafted up from the little used drawer. "Ooooohhhh." Grace's eyes had widened as she spied the beautiful handcrafted paper, the pens organized so tidily, a box of nibs in every size, all awaiting her expertise. And now she was at the finish line.

"Are you feeling any less knotted, Gracie? I'm going to the kitchen, see if I can sweet-talk a sandwich out of Marie Elena."

"Thanks, much better. I'm ready to resume. Just need Lily's stamp of approval."

▨　　▨　　▨

Lily sighed. "Well done, Grace. The summary of our imprudence looks positively poetic in calligraphy." She set down Grace's handiwork, the newly crafted version of their story, and picked up the typed manuscript.

Quinton knelt before the fireplace and crumpled up newspaper, then broke a few sticks of kindling and placed them strategically amongst a small bundle of logs. He struck a long fireplace match and set fire to the little pile. The walls of the library took on a warm hue.

"Here you go, girls."

Lily handed half the pages to Grace, who had squeezed her eyes shut to prevent tears from falling. "Ready?"

Grace nodded, overwhelmed, couldn't speak just yet. They'd come full circle.

Together the two friends tossed the typed pages of what they'd always think of as *Cat's Chronicles* into the fire.

"Lily, I didn't realize it before, but she gave us a gift," Grace said as the fire's glow reflected on their satisfied faces.

Lily smiled and nodded. Grace had come to the same conclusion as she. "Let's go tell the girls. It's time for the release party."

137. QUINTON

"Our promise to Cat is all but complete," Lily said. "Only the celebration is required now." She left the library to rally the others.

Grace gave Quinton a quick kiss and left to check Marie Elena's progress on the picnic preparations.

Quinton paced in front of the fireplace, watching the final ashes flutter above the sparks. And his conscience kicked in. *It was my damnable curiosity that led me to the bowels of the island—and to the answer to a question I prayed never to be asked again.*

It felt like a nightmare, this memory of August 1979: *He's opening the hospital entry door. Locating the information desk is easy enough. Inquiring about a patient is too. The nun shakes her head and points to the stairs just beyond the single door marked "Ufficio del Coroner." He takes the stairs, continues through double doors, and is dazed by a seemingly endless white-tiled corridor. At the far end, the coroner beckons to him. Trepidation grips his gut. The sheet is inevitably pulled away, exposing Jax's pale face. An unthreatening mask of a face. Quinton feels his heart lurch. He turns away from the corpse.*

"Do you know this man?" the coroner asks in heavily accented English.

"This man is not my friend. How did this guy die?"

The coroner eyes him suspiciously and opens the file. "Drugs, alcohol, and lethal trauma to the head. Identity? Pending valid ID."

Quinton remembered leaving the hospital, distressed by his knowledge. What he cannot remember are the gardens with cypress trees and statues designed to offer tranquility.

And then it was so much later. Too late for changing my mind. Too late for revealing the worst. With Penn safely in the comfort of girlfriends. With those six headed from the island toward the hazy silhouette of Vesuvius on the mainland.

To have reopened the wound now? Quinton turned away from the fireplace and the burnt-out fire.

138. ANGELO

Angelo stopped under the wrought-iron gate, enveloped by the sunburst's spoke-like shadow; he shaded his eyes as he watched the group head out. The ladies looked younger today, he thought, and more lighthearted. He could see Lily holding hands with the one named Penn. The nervous one. Somehow her time at Villa Bianco had taught her to smile again.

For Angelo thought and prayer intertwined.

"Oh capricious Isle," he intoned, "you dangle promise to aching hearts, and then withdraw it. How harshly you punish the lustful. And then, as if on a whim, you grant love to strangers. For that, I thank you. *Grazie mille.*"

From far below, two bells resounded, barely discernable.

139. QUINTON

Gnarled trees swayed in the afternoon breeze as Quinton wandered the ruins of Villa Jovis. He stopped to photograph a cluster of wildflowers in the rocky terrain. *Look at these tenacious beauties.*

From below he heard the voices of Grace and the others. Up the path they walked, chatting, colorful in billowing dresses. They waved to him, and he waved back. Gone was the cold war he'd been witness to. Quinton took several quick photos; *they'll want to remember today.*

He tested his balance walking along the *tepidarium* walls, from which he could see the girlfriends. They chose a grassy spot on the bluff to stop. Amelia, Deedee, and Penn anchored the corners of the colorful spread, and Grace positioned Marie Elena's basket of picnic.

Lily pulled a bottle and glasses from the basket she had carried. Champagne spurted as she released the cork. Following Lily's lead, the group raised their glasses.

"A toast to Cat, with love," Lily said.

"For putting us through hell," Penn continued, then paused for a second. "And for making us realize what we have." The five gals, sharing smiles and nods of agreement, raised their glasses once again.

Grace and Penn faced one another. "I've missed you," Penn said quietly.

Grace reached out to Penn, and they shared a hug.

Amelia turned to face Lily and Grace. "I've behaved badly toward you, and I'm not proud of that," Amelia whispered earnestly. "I said some mean, wretched things, and I've been stonewalling. I want to apologize, before we read the horrible truth of it all."

A back-of-the neck prickle announced the *unexpected* and Quinton looked upward. The statue of Maria del Soccorso atop the chapel clasped more tightly her wayward infant. With her head tilted, she looked benevolently upon the women below. *How seemingly lifelike.*

Deedee's question broke Quinton's fascination. "So, when do we read this thing we've slaved over?"

The breeze ruffled Lily's hair as she answered with a strength Quinton knew was borne of hard choices. "We've done as Cat asked. We've remembered, we've written. The past is history; we've each chosen to let it go. It's time for a *release* party."

Penn, Amelia, and Deedee seemed not to get the significance of this at first. But Quinton observed their "aha moment" when Grace pulled papers from her satchel. She passed several sheets to each. All three took time to admire the calligraphy text on handmade paper. Their mistakes and antagonism were now tangible, forced by Cat's desire for purpose.

Quinton's heart raced. *To have opened the wound offering new information? I would not. A blow to any one would resound upon each. How like a chain-link fence these women have become over the years. Bound together, with curious spaces in between.*

The rejoined friends released the pages over the cliff's edge high above the sea. Caught by gusts of wind, the pages flew off against the blue of sky, transforming into a flock of birds.

ACKNOWLEDGEMENTS

Genie: *INVENTED AUGUST* owes its presence to the encouragement and unending patience of my husband, Rick Higbee. I appreciate his insight and fact gathering, not to mention his domestic skills, invaluable when the writing monopolized my attention. And to Melissa, what a gift you've given me, sharing the day-to-day realization of fictional personas who've taught us a thing or two.

Melissa: Thank you to my spouse, Tom Otero, who coaxed me to leave my dearly loved/dearly dreaded job to do something creative; and who gifted Genie and me with a trip to Italy, thus inspiring our story's locale and once again providing us that paradise to research, Capri. I'm also compelled to extend thanks to Genie Frisbee Higbee, my longtime friend, who challenged me to put words on paper, instigating our first collaboration, *Six Silver Bracelets* (soon to be published).

As Co-Authors: Thank you to our friends of forty-plus years, for allowing us to swirl their unique personalities in a blender and create six fictional characters who dashed off to invent their own escapades as we wrote.

Gratitude to:
Our "sisters," irreplaceable female relatives and friends who share life's passage as mothers, daughters, and wives.

Recognition of:
Our book groups, for lively conversation.
Our writers' critique groups, for reading, listening, and asking questions.
Our focus groups, for offering opinions.

Appreciation of:
All the authors whose books we have savored, currently enjoy, and those works yet to be read. The inspiration keeps us writing.

ABOUT THE AUTHORS

Melissa Farnsworth & Genie Frisbee

Genie Frisbee Higbee, resident of Coeur d'Alene, Idaho, a freelance writer/ designer, concentrates on women's fiction, poetry, and oil painting.

Melissa Farnsworth, from Hollywood, California, writes inspired by the common-sense influence of her father, Oscar-nominated actor Richard Farnsworth.

When our characters lead you into the unexpected, gift you with the unpredictable, and leave behind something to ponder…then we are rewarded.

Our infatuation with the Isle of Capri, coupled with on-site research, informs the luscious backdrop for *INVENTED AUGUST*.

CONNECT WITH US

Visit our web page for bonus material: frisbee-farnsworth.com.

Follow our blog at: Blog.frisbee-farnsworth.com.

Your comments and questions are welcomed. We look forward to hearing from you.

Made in the USA
Charleston, SC
09 November 2013